A Flute in the Willows

The Spies of World War II

Carole Brown

Story and Logic Media Group
Printed in the USA
...For the discriminating reader
...because we believe story *needs*
logic.

A Flute in the Willows : © 2017 by Carole Brown
The Spies of World War II, Book 2

 **Published by STORY AND LOGIC Media Group**
New Carlisle, OH 45344
... For the discriminating reader ... Because we believe story *needs* logic.

Cover Design by SAL media
Printed in the USA

ISBN 13: 978-1-941622-46-9
ISBN 10: 1941622461

Library of Congress Cataloging-in-Publication Data
Brown, Carole
Title: /Carole Brown
ISBN   (pbk)

1. World War Fiction 2. Military Spy Fiction 3. Historical Romance 4. Romantic Suspense 5. Inspirational Romance 6. War and Women.7. Woman Patriots Fiction I. Title.

I. Title. Library of Congress Control Number: 2017958779

A Flute In The Willows
Praise for The Spies of World War II

American WWII spy Jerry Patterson was terribly injured behind enemy lines in Germany. On the Home front, his wife Josie is closest to him imagining he's there figure skating with her, as she's winning competitions. Then he comes home broken. Unbeknownst to them, his enemy has followed from Germany bent on revenge. This story captures the emotional horrors returning soldiers suffer and their loving wives endure. Relevant and realistic, it strikes the perfect balance between despair and hope. ~

Nike N. Chillemi, multi-published detective story author, *The Veronica "Ronnie" Ingels/Dawson Hughes Trilogy, That Special One*

This is a wonderful romantic suspense novel written in the WW2 era, which always intrigues me. Jerry and Josie could never have imagined anything that could threaten their love. Then came the war. Confident and capable, Jerry becomes a spy in Germany. Then everything goes wrong. He returns a different man. But the war isn't finished with him. Enemies within and without follow him home. Josie, a free-spirited newlywed, must grow up quickly to deal with the heart-breaking and dangerous world her husband brings back from Germany.

I loved the array of characters author Carole Brown brought to this story - each so vivid and individual. Filled with family affection as well as danger and romance, this sweet story kept calling me away from my chores. Nicely done! ~

Cheryl Colwell, author of *The Proof* and other suspense novels.

The time of loss and growth and learning for both Josie and Jerry carry a timeless message. Not just for young couples or for military marriages, but for everyone whose dreams have been impacted by their own bad choices, guilt, true accidents, and the damages wrought on them by the choices and actions of others. Whether in wartime or in the increasing chaos of modern times, some things are unchanging.

Through this novel, the author speaks to the ages, and offers examples and explanations that can speak to the wounded, seeking heart and mind.~

Michelle Levigne, award-winning, multi-published author and editor;
http://www.mlevigne.com/

How far would you go to serve your country? In Flute in the Willows, a WW2 romantic suspense, Carole Brown weaves intrigue and espionage throughout this story of a man who struggles, when serving his country as a spy, and feels he's betrayed his wife's trust. Meanwhile, his wife, Josie, has her own dark night of the soul on the home front...where things aren't as they seem.~

Tamera Lynn Kraft, author of Alice's Notions and Resurrection of Hope

WWII Expressions and Words

Alreet: jive slang for all right

Babe: affectionate term for male or female
Battery acid: coffee
Bender: drinking spree
Bobby soxer: teenage girl who wore white socks pushed down around the top of the shoe.
Bonkers: over the top; wild
Bowler: hard hats made of felt, very short brims.
Brainchild: an idea
Buy the farm: croak; die
Buzz: excitement

Call girl: prostitute
Carrying a torch: to ardently admire/have a crush on someone
Cat's Meow: the best
Chew out: berate, scold
Chicken: coward
Cock-eyed: backward/crazy/illogical
Cookie: cute girl

Dish: good looking female
Dope: scoop/information

Eager-beaver: Ready and likeable person

Fat head: stupid or foolish person
Fink: a loser
Fuddy-duddy: an old fashioned/not mainstream person
Folding Lettuce: paper money

G-man: special agent of the government
Gobbledy-gook: nonsense

Hard-boiled: jaded or tough man
Holy mackerel: an expression of surprise
Horsefeathers: an expletive

Jerk: less than desirable person

Joint: jail

Knuckle sandwich: a punch in the mouth

Lulu: Something beyond the pale; excellent or outstanding.

Mellow man: attractive young man; hunk of heartbreak, twangle boy, heaven sent

Pally: friend, chum, sometimes used sarcastically
Pork Pie: Similar to a Fedora hat, but with a flat top. Brim is shorter and turned up.

Run out of gas: disinterest

Shot: giving something a try or a go
Souse: Become inebriated
Spook: either means to frighten or a spy
Swell: excellent/positive/wonderful

Two cents worth: opinion
Take a powder: leave

Victory garden: vegetable, fruit or herb garden planted at a private residence or occasionally in a public place. These small gardens helped in the war effort by freeing up farmland for major crops such as wheat.

Wacky: out of sorts or wild

Zoot suit: men's outfit with a knee length jacket, high shoulder pads and exaggerated lapels and baggy pants tapered at the ankle

German Words:
Ach: oh, expressing surprise, wonder, amazement, or awe, preceding an offhand or annoyed remark

Du Bist Ein Dummkopf: You're a fool

Sehr gut: very good

Acknowledgments:

In writing a novel, especially an historical one, there
are so many items to research.
Finding those who are knowledgeable about what
you need to know is a true blessing.

Just recently, I was able to learn a bit more about
WWII that brought that era alive for me again.
Thank you, Shirley, for that timely post.
Thank you to those who shared their knowledge
about the language of that day.
To those who write about Germany, the war, the
styles of clothes and so many other necessary items
that are valuable to me, my gratitude is great.

Thank you to those who take the time to critique for
me, to those who endorse, review and share pages
about my book.

Thank you to those who brainstorm with me,
ACFWOhio group.

Jamin and hubby, you both never cease to amaze
me with your ideas and suggestions.

Most of all, once again, I thank God for his help and
encouragement.

Dedication:

To the women in my world who, like Josie, has had to understand and pray for a hurting and troubled man. They are the strong ones, determined to overcome, to conquer, to make it, with heads held high.

I salute you!

Foreword

We hanged our harps upon the willows in the midst thereof. —Psalm 137:2

...for the joy of the Lord is your strength. Nehemiah 8:10b

Willows were very plentiful in Babylon. There was such a great quantity of them on the banks of the Euphrates that Isaiah called it the brook of willows.

We wonder perhaps, if the Israelites, after resting from toil, and maybe wishing to spend their time religiously, took their harps and prepared to sing one of the songs of Zion.

In a foreign country now, with thoughts of their far off land troubling them, they could not bring themselves to sing. Their harps were available, yet they hung them up on the branches of the trees around them to give way to their grief.

Every man has a harp that makes sweet and delightful music.
We have joy and gladness. Every sight and sound, every scene and action, all things fair and good, and bright and godly, are but fingers of Nature's skillful hand which touches the strings on the harp of our being.

In **A Flute in the Willows**, **Josie**, physically hung her flute (harp) on a willow by putting it aside from her life. Coming from a loving, devoted family, Josie needed to learn to appreciate the love, loyalty and devotion, her father and sisters gave to her. Her interests in gaining her desires, her self-centeredness, her lack of discernment, all led to a period of spiritual drought in her life.

Jerry, on the other hand, had no real guidance to what

his "harp" was. With a father who was both distant and demanding, he cut himself off from anyone who might attempt a "too-close" relationship and held himself aloof from friendly intimacy. Even in the warm and family oriented Rayner Boarding House (in book one), he sometimes appeared as uncaring.

Just like Josie and Jerry Patterson experience in **A Flute in the Willows**, there are times of sickness or calamity, sadness and heartache, deep discouragement and despondency. The music has silenced, and it is then we hang our harps on the willow trees.

Do not cast your harp away, but wait. The weather will clear, the sun will come, and the music will surge in our beings once more. It is then we can again pick up our harps. Peace and joy, and music will reign.

For Jerry and Josie, underneath those powering actions and emotions, lay hearts that could be touched and nourished by the right circumstances and pain that was ahead for both.

Enjoy their journey toward *life*!

Carole Brown

A Flute in the Willows

An angry spy
nearly destroyed their lives.
Can the music heal them?

The Spies of World War II

Chapter One

1943

Jerry Patterson stared out the yawning black hole in the side of the plane. Seconds to go before he dropped. Night time parachuting was always a risky thing, but the pilot was one of the best who'd keep this baby right on target, lessening the chances he'd have to hit water. Trees were another matter, but with any kind of luck, the landing would go smooth.

Then to meet his contact and move into the German military high life. His pulse revved up. It was a dangerous game he was about to play.

Josie's face flashed in his mind, and Jerry felt his heart soften. How he loved his tomboy wife. She was a beautiful butterfly dancing on ice, but put her in a social setting, and she was like a wild creature let loose in a maiden aunt's prim parlor.

Three weeks of marital bliss. It'd been heaven on earth for him. One rapturous day—and night—after another. She'd cried the night before he'd left, but had been strength personified when he'd boarded the train the next morning.

If—no, when—he got home, he'd wrap his arms around her and not let her out of his sight.

Jerry stepped into the hole and dropped rapidly, counting. One thousand...One thousand one...One thousand two... With a jerk he pulled, the parachute opened above him, and he drifted earthward toward his assignment.

Chapter Two

Jerry Patterson checked his image one last time in the mirror, brushed at a piece of lint on his dark coat, and tucked a handkerchief in his pocket. Flawless. He looked good, if he said so himself. A suave—if a bit aloof— foreign gentleman. Smooth and well educated, with just the right touch of intrigue.

The perfect spy.

That's what the general had assured him.

He was careful to lock his door, but he wasn't fool enough to believe that would keep them out if someone wanted in. But then he had nothing incriminating. Nothing but what he held in his head.

Descending the stairs, he heard the usual pre-dinner noises which whisked him back to Cincinnati, to the Rayner House, to Josie. The safety and fun. The evenings of music and laughter. Here there was music and danger. Maybe excitement, but definitely no fun. Not for him.

His highly polished boots clattered as he entered the drawing room, and a vision of loveliness stepped up beside him and clutched his arm. "Major Bhaer. I wasn't sure you'd be back in time for dinner tonight."

He smiled down at the beautiful woman, well aware of her attraction to him. "How could I not hurry back when such beauty waits for me to behold?"

She dimpled, pleased at his gallantry, but there was more to her than mere beauty, and he knew it. Intelligent and well attuned to the military life—with both a father and a brother serving in the Germany service—she was an instrument of knowledge to be played with dexterity and care.

"You flatter me, but I like it. Come, my brother is here tonight, and he has with him a man he wishes you to know."

Jerry darted a glance toward the fireplace where Herr

Winfried Rhoderick stood with the man, but he had no chance for an in-depth study. Vanda Rhoderick called out as they approached.

"Did I not tell you Jerry would be back tonight?"

"Ach. I see you were right, as you have a fondness of being." Rhoderick's affection for his sister radiated from his indulging smile. "Bhaer, you surprise me. I understood your business would keep you away for at least a month. Not that I'm complaining. If for no other reason, my sister would have been forlorn without your presence for such a long time."

"You exaggerate." Vanda patted her brother's arm but glanced at Jerry from under her dark lashes.

Rhoderick nodded at someone passing, then returned his gaze to his immediate friends. "Let me introduce you to a colleague and college friend. Harry Marshall, from the states who studied with me at our country's finest school. Harry, Jerry P. Bhaer. He is the one I've been telling you about. A possible collaborator to our plans."

Rhoderick and his friend exchanged a long glance. Jerry tried to read the look but found nothing alarming in either set of eyes. He thickened his German accent, not that he was worried. If the Rhodericks had accepted him for face value, then an American would have no suspicions.

"It is good to meet a friend of Winfried's." He tipped his head just like he'd seen his German maternal great grandfather do a hundred times. "I hear you studied at Yale."

"That is true. And why would you be interested in helping Germany's cause?"

Rhoderick turned to his sister. "Will you get us some drinks? We'll be in my office."

"Don't be long. Dinner's served in thirty minutes." She placed both hands on Jerry's forearm and gazed up at him even though she continued to speak to her brother. "Jerry's just returned. I want to hear how much he's missed me."

"No. No. We won't be long. Go for the drinks, dear, then you can visit with Herr Bhaer the rest of the evening."

Jerry had to admit that Vanda's pout was a lovely

thing. He allowed his lips to tilt upward and placed a hand on the ones laying lightly on his arm. "I'll see you shortly."

Strolling along behind the other two men, Jerry studied them. His captain had informed him that Herr Rhoderick was one of the smartest and most dangerous men in Germany. Taller than his twin sister by only a half foot, he was as handsome as she was beautiful. But the hardness—or was it shrewdness?—that shone from his eyes detracted from his good looks.

Herr Rhoderick shoved open the door and ushered the other two men inside the room. He lifted a cigar box and offered it to them, but Jerry shook his head and watched as Harry Marshall accepted and went through the ritual of lighting it. Only then did they settle back in the late nineteenth century high-backed chairs.

Rhoderick drew on his cigar, savored the smoke, then studied it as it circled above his head. "Bhaer comes highly recommended to me. I believe he is the man to do the job for us."

The look Marshall shot at him was full of suspicion, no doubt from Jerry's failure to answer his previous question. He spoke to Rhoderick but kept his gaze on Jerry. "You checked his references? You have no questions? Why is he so willing—"

The question again. Must be determined to gain an answer. Not from him, he wouldn't.

"Exactly what I was wondering about you." Jerry flipped the statement straight back at Marshall.

The American's face reddened, lips curled into disgust as he retorted. "That's none—"

Rhoderick guffawed. "He's quite quick witted, wouldn't you say, Marshall? I wouldn't try to interrogate him. Besides, he has already done two small, but delicate, important jobs for me that has proven his worth."

Marshall crossed his legs and gazed at his polished shoe. "Hmmm."

"Herr Bhaer was sent to the states for preparation to serve our country. His grandmother came from one of the most respected families in our country. Even today, his uncle serves as one of Hitler's most trusted men."

Yeah, Uncle Fitzgerald, the black sheep of his mother's

family, the rebellious, do-less, scoundrel man who'd done nothing but the wrong thing.

At least, so he'd heard. He'd only met the man once, and that'd been when he was a child. But he'd never forgotten the stir and upset Uncle Fitz had caused everyone. Dangling Jerry, a six year old child, over a third story porch ledge had sent such terror in himself, he'd never forgiven or forgotten the man, let alone like him.

"That all sounds good." Marshall nodded.

But his eyes—some emotion—still lurked in them. For one second, Jerry felt a stirring of disturbance. Did the man know something he was hiding? If so, for what reason?

"You have brought the names?" Rhoderick leaned forward, the fat cigar dangling from his fingers.

"Of course. Would I be here otherwise?"

"Come. Give them to me." Rhoderick's face lit with a fiery fanaticism.

Jerry held his breath. The names. What he'd risked everything to find.

A low chuckle emanated from the Marshall's throat. "All in good time. Here is your lovely sister and just in time. I am thirsty."

Their host's nose flared. Would Rhoderick allow such a slight pass without a rebuke?

Jerry accepted the glass Vanda offered and held it to his lips, but didn't sip. He needed all his senses about him. Tonight especially. Who knew when he'd have to make his move?

Rhoderick hadn't liked being put off. The American had better watch his back. He'd pay for that arrogant snub. Who was he anyhow? A senator, no doubt, or the son. Perhaps a close employee of one.

The hostile look Rhoderick shot Marshall didn't bode well for their working relationship. The German's lips thinned. His fingers clenched and unclenched as if he'd love to wrap them around the disrespectful man's neck.

When Rhoderick rose, Jerry followed the man's lead.

Their host stood staring down at the American. His voice held daggers of ice when he spoke again. "I will see you at one tonight. Don't be late."

Marshall puffed on his cigar and allowed the smoke that came from his mouth to drift toward Rhoderick, the amusement in his voice taunting. "By all means. One suits me fine."

Violent anger flared in Rhoderick eyes, and his mouth pressed into a tight-lipped frown, but he jerked away.

Jerry went with him and didn't look back. He knew now he'd have to make his move tonight and time it just right. If Rhoderick got hold of the list before him—well, it would be virtually impossible to retrieve it.

Vanda claimed him as soon as they reentered the front room, and when Rhoderick led the company of people toward the dining room, she made sure Jerry sat on her right hand. Her dark-eyed gaze rested on him more than he liked during the course of the meal.

Halfway through the meal, she chided, "I don't believe you heard a word I've spoken for the last ten minutes."

Alarm rampaged its way through him. He couldn't afford to gain unwanted interest. He dragged his attention from the quiet conversation two couples were sharing and riveted it on the lovely creature sitting beside him. She was too well bred to blatantly speak of her affection for him, but Jerry could read it in her actions, see it in her eyes. He shut off the clanging bells inside him.

You reap what you sow.

His dad's favorite words. The ones he raised his two sons on whenever they crossed the rigid line he'd drawn for them. Look where they'd gotten his older brother. Look where he'd gotten. As far from Mr. Patterson, the perfect lawyer, as he could get.

Robert Patterson was the reason he'd volunteered as soon as he could. His old man had nearly had an apoplectic fit. Jerry had been delighted that he'd disappointed the old man.

And, yet, he needed to trod easy around this gorgeous woman. Sweet, gentle, and smart, Vanda would be a trophy as a wife. She was in her element at a social sitting. Vanda Rhoderick wasn't anything at all like Josie.

But his wife was in *her* element at simple, specific gatherings. Josie's features could only be described as more interesting than beautiful, but she was intelligent and knew her own mind. Dress her up, let her enter this room, and every man would itch to speak with her, and would know when they did, they'd get more than flirtatious words and coy smiles. Josie could hold her own in most debates.

Yes, Vanda was indeed everything Josie wasn't in so many ways. But only one woman resided in his heart.

He allowed one side of his mouth to lift. "If I'm not mistaken, I believe you were giving me several reasons why I needed to attend with you the invitation-only concert being held this weekend."

Her dimples played hide and seek with her rosy cheeks. "You were listening."

"Of course."

"Then you will go—as my escort?"

"I'd be honored." It was a lie, but a little one. He would be honored to go. He just doubted he'd be here to do so.

When she stood to lead the guests to the sitting room, she leaned close to him. "Let's get a breath of air."

The night was quiet, and Jerry's heart lurched at the thought of the same sky looking down on a certain home back in Cincinnati.

Vanda strolled down one of the garden paths, her long skirt brushing against the late spring blossoms, scents rising like an invisible ground fog. She stopped in front of a gigantic fountain, a stone woman holding a jug with water pouring from it. "I've always loved this fountain. She's been my confidant for years."

He scorned her words lightly. "As if you'd have secrets to hide."

Her lips lifted in wry amusement. "Not so much now that I'm older. But she's lots of company when my brother and father are gone."

"You have no desire to serve?"

"A desire perhaps, but orders forbid it."

"Your father?"

"And brother."

Josie wouldn't have asked.

"I know what you're thinking. I should think and do what I want."

"Your father and brother are only protecting your

future."

"Perhaps."

"I'm sure you do your part with all the entertaining."

"Yes. I do that very well." She looked down at her hands. With a sudden move, she pressed closer. "Jerry."

It shouldn't have happened. One minute he was looking down at her lovely distressed face, and the next she was in his arms, her lips trembling and begging to be kissed.

"What's wrong, Vanda?"

"I want—want—"

She didn't finish, but she didn't have to. Jerry knew what she wanted.

Him.

She was a true blooded, well-mannered lady. Elegant and classy. Her lack of words told him far more than if she'd proclaimed aloud her desires. Denied serving as many of her fellow countrywomen were bidden to do, a yearning for usefulness welled up that occasionally demanded freedom.

The temptation was there to comfort her. Her lips, full and pink, beckoned. Her skin, soft and tender, invited caresses. Lashes, dark and thick, lay against her cheekbones, then swept up, imploring him to—what?

He couldn't blame her. She had no idea he was married. He was to blame if there was any fault here. Slowly, the heat dissipated. Josie's dark eyes stared at him from his mind; her mouth twitched upward in a full-blown laugh.

Sucking in a deep breath, he patted Vanda's arms. "I know you might want to do more for your country, Vanda, but your brother and father are right."

She faced the fountain again, in slow motion, as if reluctant to leave his arms. "It's not so much that. I'd just like a change of pace. I get so bored with society life. Is that all I'm meant to do with my life? Will I live to be eighty and not have known anything but teas and dancing and smiling at boring people?" Her dark hair swirled around her face when she shook her head. "Sometimes I think I'd rather die at twenty and have had done one thing worthwhile."

Feeling as if he'd been granted a reprieve, Jerry

followed Vanda as she walked toward the house. Vanda slipped inside, but Jerry paused at the french doors. He stepped off the patio and edged toward the corner of the house.

Was that Marshall hissing out some protest? One more step, and the words wafted clearly through the night air.

"I've seen him somewhere."

Talking about *him?*

"Quiet, you fool." Rhoderick lapsed into German for several sentences then snapped back into English indicating his mood was less than happy. His long legs straightened into perfect rods as he goose-stepped an even four paces to the left, then to the right. Smoke from his cigar trailed him like a smoke stack from a speeding train. "Then you should be able to remember that fact."

Jerry leaned forward, straining to hear the next words coming from Marshall, but try as he might, they were muffled. Watching them mosey closer as if heading toward the French doors, Jerry moved lightly away from the corner and re-entered the house.

When he tried to retire at ten-thirty with an excuse of needing an early night, the reproach in Vanda's eyes almost—but not quite—caused his resolve to waver.

"I've had a busy week. Surely you can forgive me if I neglect to pay any more attention to you tonight." The conversation between Rhoderick and Marshall nagged at him. Would intelligence from home provide Marshall the information, if he inquired about him, Jerry Bhaer? Timing was everything, and if he stayed too long...

It was time to get away from this German society.

"I can but I don't want to." She smiled. "If you must then. Will I see you tomorrow? Can you spend the day driving me?"

If she only realized, he could very well be gone. "Let's see what the morning brings."

"If I didn't know differently, I would almost suspect you of avoiding me." She stood on tiptoe, kissed his cheek, and walked off. She tossed a saucy glance in his direction, hesitated. "Good night. Dream of me, will you?"

It was the closest she'd ever come to expressing her feelings in words.

He watched her mingle among the other guests, then he headed toward Rhoderick. Now to make his excuses with him. Hopefully, he'd get in Marshall's room and be out and in his own before any of the other guests headed upstairs.

But it was not to be. As he stepped into the hallway, Marshall emerged from a shadowed corner and stepped in front of him. "Early night?"

Jerry debated shoving past the man but decided against it. No need to rile tempers unless he had to. "Been a long hard week. I'm calling it a night."

"Hmmm." Marshall rooted in the inside breast pocket of his jacket, his attention fixed on Jerry, a hint of sardonic disbelief edging the pupils of his eyes. "Seems strange."

Jerry watched as the man pulled out a cigar, studied it, then replaced it within his coat. "What do you mean?"

He'd rather have ignored the man. Nothing good would come out of standing in the hall playing some kind of cat and mouse game with a man Jerry had to assume was a spy too. For some reason—and Jerry couldn't pinpoint the reason why he felt this way—below the society level the Rhodericks enjoyed. Yet Marshall must have an "in" with Rhoderick and his house, if he'd been here enough to be working with Rhoderick. As if he was privileged to information that Rhoderick didn't know about or, for which the German officer held a healthy respect.

"You. How did you get into Rhoderick's favor so quickly? He's not known to be a trusting soul."

"My good looks? Intelligence?" Jerry shrugged. "What do you want me to say?"

"I hear you." But his expression said he was far from convinced. "I'm going to be watching you."

Jerry had no more time for palaver if he wanted to accomplish his mission tonight. "There are a lot of strange things in the world today."

Hopefully, the man would forget about him and return to the festivities still going strong in the drawing room.

The sounds receded as he climbed the handsome stairs, and his mind kicked into high gear. He wasn't sure which room was the American's, but suspected he'd been given the rear left one.

He leaned against the door, listened, checked the hallway again, then slipped the pick into the lock. In seconds, he swung open the door, stepped inside, and locked it behind him.

He stood silent, adjusting to the surroundings, and allowed his vision to absorb the darkness, as he planned his strategy. The man wouldn't be so foolish as to store the list of names in a pocket. His briefcase would be the obvious place, so Jerry turned away from that. On the nightstand lay a book as if Marshall anticipated reading tonight.

The book beckoned, and Jerry answered. Picking it up, he admired the hard cover then skimmed over the first page. The sound of footsteps penetrated through the heavy oak door, and for a moment Jerry hesitated, listening. Then he flipped rapidly through the pages and sighed in relief as a sheet of paper fluttered to the floor.

Pulling out a folded sheet of blank paper he'd brought along, he inserted it into the book, then replaced the book on the stand. He bent over to snatch the fallen one and heard the key being inserted into the lock. Jerry knew he didn't have time to escape through a window, so clutching the paper, he dropped to the floor and rolled under the high bed just as Marshall stepped into the room.

Jerry measured his breathing, forcing himself to take slow, quiet breaths. He grimaced as the man sat on the bed.

"Ah, my beauty. Tonight you will make me enough to escape from the constant money worries." The soft sounds of the man lighting a smoke, the scent of the expensive tobacco floated around the room.

Who was the man talking to?

A loud slap as the book he'd obviously picked up, landed back on the nightstand. The bed squeaked when Marshall stretched out upon it. "Now for a catnap to prepare for the evening ahead."

Obviously, the traitorous spy hadn't checked the list or he'd be roaring like a wild beast instead of napping. Jerry's heart settled back into a steady, even beat instead of the racing steam engine it'd been seconds ago.

Jerry wasn't sure if the man would ever go to sleep by

the way he tossed and turned. But when he'd listened to the gentle snores for at least fifteen minutes, he edged out from under the bed. He hesitated again, rolled to his knees, and peered at the man in the dark. He could hear voices in the hallway outside, so the window would have to serve as his route to freedom. He tiptoed across the floor and touched the frame, getting a feel for the strength needed to raise it. Then drawing in a deep breath he lifted the window.

Marshall stirred, rolled onto his side, and Jerry froze. Was he awake, watching? He waited then thrust a leg through.

"Stop. What are you doing in my room?"

No time to wait around to answer the question. He barely skimmed the man—now sitting up—with a glance. He started to scoot out onto the balcony when pain shot through his whole body, and he wanted to scream. He pulled himself from the window ledge and staggered forward two steps before falling on his face.

What had happened? Marshall's bellow echoed outside his head, but the world had faded to mental darkness. His left leg had gone numb. He shook his head. He couldn't lose consciousness. To do so might mean death. He hung over the rail and surveyed the climb he'd have to make. His stomach churned with nausea.

Throwing his good leg over the rail and dragging the useless one after him, he gripped the holds he needed to descend to the ground.

Hands tore at his jacket in a deathlike grip, and a rough voice demanded, "Who are you? Why are you in my room?"

For one minute, Jerry nearly panicked as he felt his weak body yielding to the strength of the other man pulling him back over the rail, toward trouble and death. Then drawing his arm forward, he rammed his elbow as hard as he could into the man's face and heard bones crunch.

Marshall's grip loosened, and Jerry pulled free. Hand over hand he hobbled along the banister until he reached one of the posts that held up the balcony. Sweat stung his eyes, but he blinked it away. With his whole body shaking, he wrapped his arms around the post and slid to the ground. As his feet touched, he nearly passed out again. Then strong hands lifted him bodily over a shoulder, and Vanda's voice—now firm and resolute— instructed the other person which way to go.

He let himself slip into blackness, even as the gun- thunder exploded once again in his ears.

Chapter Three

Soft hands brushed at his hair, and as light as the touch was, it brought him back from the dark world. Firm hands smoothed the blanket covering him. The crooning voice brought thoughts of Josie to mind. Her straight nose and daring eyes. The wild, curly, auburn hair. Her firm, strong body. Her . . .

"Jerry?"

That voice wasn't Josie's. Who was it?

Where was he?

He slid open his eyes. Vanda's anxious face hovered over his.

"Wh-ere am I?"

Her lips tilted, but the frown that marred her smooth brow stayed. "You're in one of our guest houses."

"What happened?"

Her gaze flicked to the bottom of the bed, then back. "You were shot."

The memory of that night swarmed in. "How long—"

"Must you talk? You're still pretty weak."

"How long?"

She sighed. "Two weeks. You almost died."

He allowed his eyes to question her.

"You want the whole story? Can you eat first? I smug—have some chicken soup—"

"No. Tell me."

"After you retired that night, I mingled with our guests for awhile, then stepped outside to get a breath of air. I don't know how long I wandered around in the gardens. It was then I heard the gunshots—"

"Gun*shots*?"

"One at first. Screaming. I looked up, and there you were climbing down from that balcony. You fell the last five feet. By the time I got to you, you'd passed out."

"You couldn't have carried me."'

"No. A distant cousin of mine had followed me out and

26

helped me get you here."

"So I take it no one knows—"

"No one knows you're here, Jerry." But her beautiful eyes reproached him.

"And this distant cousin, won't he talk?"

"No. His devotion to me is overwhelming. He will do anything I ask. He carried you here. I made him promise his silence."

"I see." Jerry studied her downcast face. "Why did you do this?"

"Must you ask?"

She swiveled away from him, but he caught the sudden flame in her cheeks.

"Because I-I care about you."

He wanted to evade that soft questioning he knew lurked inside her mind, but he owed her. No doubt she'd saved his life. "You risked your life."

"Perhaps. Winfried doesn't know you're here and is furious at your disappearance. No one knows but my cousin." She stood, crossed to the window and stared out.

Something bothered her. He felt a jolt of regret. He'd used her to gain what he wanted and never been entirely honest with her. He should have prevented this. Yet even now, he knew he couldn't let her know who he really was or what he was doing. She might have suspicions, but she didn't know, and he would do his best to keep it that way. He owed her that much.

"I suspect you're not who you say you are. Perhaps you're not even the great-grandson of one of Germany's best generals." She whirled to face him. "I don't really care. All I want is for things to be like they were before."

Answer a question with a question. "Why do you think that?"

Her eyebrow lifted. "Marshall shooting at you? Winfried going around like a permanent thundercloud? You talking while unconscious?"

"I talked?"

"Yes. A lot about someone named Jo and plans."

Josie.

"She's why you wouldn't kiss me that night, isn't she?"

Her words were accusatory. Her eyes begged him to

deny it.

When he didn't speak, she shrugged, reached into her pocket and pulled out a paper. "And this. I wondered if it could be the reason my brother and Herr Marshall tore the house upside down. I found it in *your* pocket."

"I see." The crackling paper in her slim fingers drew his attention.

"I'm not sure why everyone—and I'm assuming that includes you—is frantic to obtain it." She studied the paper. "Names. Just names. They must be important. Is it dangerous? Something to do with Germany's safety?"

Best to ignore that one. "And you're going to return it to your brother." No need to ask. It was a foregone conclusion.

Vanda smiled, amusement and warmth in the action. "No, Jerry, I'm going to place it back into your pocket. I love my brother, but I am not stupid. I know he does things I don't approve of. I wish..."

Jerry threw back the covers and eased his legs to the side of the bed. A sharp pain shot from the back of his knee up his leg. He winced and fell onto the pillow.

"Jerry. Lie still. You're too weak to get up."

Squeezing his eyes shut, he gritted from between his teeth. "I have to. It's too dangerous for you to be coming here."

"I don't mind."

"I do. Help me, and I'll try it again."

"I wasn't able to get a doctor. Our family doctor is not to be trusted. You almost died. Medwin—my cousin—has a bit of medical training, and he thinks a bone or bones was shattered in your leg. He did what he could but your leg still became dangerously infected. I thought—"

"What?"

Vanda bit her lip. "I thought we'd lose your leg if not your life."

"The infection's gone?"

"Yes-s. But it still looks bad." Her brow lined with another worried frown. Her gaze flicked to his legs and back. "I-I'm not sure you'll ever completely recover from that wound."

"I'm tough." He stretched out a hand. "Please?"

Her lips firmed, but she took his hand and slipped an

arm about his shoulders. "Are you ready?"

No, but he had no other choice. With muscles tense, leg throbbing, and mind on the virtual edge of blackness, Jerry willed his body to move. He rested and used all the strength he had to keep from panting like a pursued deer. Then slowly he scooted to the edge of the bed and touched the floor with his feet. He leaned on Vanda's arm and allowed his body weight to rest on his legs.

The pain soared as his left leg buckled, and his mind blanked into the dark void he'd been in for the last two weeks.

~*~

Jerry was alone when he woke the next time. For a few minutes he lay still, orienting himself. Then he tentatively stretched his muscles. He grimaced at the pain still in his leg, but it wasn't as bad as before, and at least, he didn't black out. Convinced he could handle it, he pulled himself into a sitting position. He held his breath as he positioned his body to stand and saw the crutches leaning against the nightstand. Someone had anticipated his attempt. Probably Vanda.

This time he was smart enough to stand only on his right leg and gradually lowered his left foot until it rested lightly on the floor. Using the crutches he hopped forward a step. Stopped and rested. So far so good. Two more steps, and he swiveled and limped back to the bed.

Sweat beaded his forehead, and his body shook, but he felt like he'd won a race. He gave himself a half-hour then rose again. This time, with the aid of the crutches, he limped five steps away and five back. When he sat down, his trembling body warned him he was close to exhaustion. He needed food and more rest.

The sun was setting when he heard the door opening and tensed. A man entered the room, a basket dangling from his hand. He stopped at the sight of Jerry sitting up.

"I hope you're Vanda's cousin." Jerry smiled and gripped the crutches he'd slipped beneath the sheet.

"I am her cousin, Medwin Arlo." He lifted the basket. "Vanda sent some soup. She couldn't get away. Rhoderick is paying particular attention to her today."

"Too bad. The soup sounds delicious." Jerry's stomach

growled. "I must be recovering; I'm hungry."

Arlo arranged the soup and tea on an antique tray from a cupboard, placed the napkin beside the bowl, and laid a spoon beside it. He looked at Jerry. "Do you want butter and jam on your bread?"

"Yes. Thanks." Jerry studied the man. Tall and too thin, the man was anything but handsome, yet if he hadn't looked so grim, Jerry thought there would have been something pleasing to the female eye. His military attire fit him well, his boots were highly polished, his hair trim and neat. "You really love her."

The butter knife clattered to the table and Arlo looked up. He turned and strode to the window. "Yes."

Jerry picked up his spoon. "You're not going to feed the wounded?"

"You're a man, I suppose." Arlo tossed him a scornful look. "Buck up and fend for yourself."

"Vanda would delight in feeding me."

"Vanda's not here." He whirled and marched to the door. "And *I* would not be here if it wasn't for Vanda. Do you need anything else before I leave?"

"Ah, the promise." Jerry couldn't help himself. He shouldn't bait the man, but the injured air angered him. "I would take her rejection like a man, if I were you."

The man's back stiffened but he hesitated only a second before striding away.

"I'm fine. Don't worry about me," Jerry called after him and chuckled.

The soup was good, the bread homemade, and the tea freshly brewed. When he'd finished Jerry sat back satisfied. That had been the best meal he'd had in a long time.

He walked four more times before the evening was over, and by the time he was ready for sleep, he'd progressed to the window, still limping, still hurting, but stronger and more balanced with the crutches' help.

Sometime in the night he wakened to the sounds of hurrying footsteps and strident whispers. Before he could reach for a crutch, two figures burst into the room and hurried toward him.

"Jerry, wake up."

Vanda.

The other figure grabbed for and tossed back his covers.

"What's going on?" he demanded.

"Shh! There's no time to explain. Winfried is coming."

Jerry wasted no more time on questions. "My clothes. Help me, Arlo."

The man bent, picked Jerry up and situated him over his shoulder. "Vanda, grab some clothes and one of the crutches. Let's go."

He would have protested that he could walk, but he knew differently. Arlo was right, and Jerry concentrated on being the best burden he could be. By the time they descended the stairs, Vanda was behind them.

She slipped past them at the bottom and whispered, "This way."

At a side door, Vanda cracked it open and listened. "I don't hear anything. Are you all right, Medwin?"

"I'm strong, Vanda, and ready."

She turned and touched her cousin's arm. "Thank you. I'll never forget this."

Then they were out the door and trotting through the woods, putting as much distance as they could from the oncoming searchers. Once Jerry thought he heard distant shouting, the soft thudding of footsteps, and the snarl of some beast.

"Do you need to stop?" Vanda's voice was warm with concern.

"Go on."

She didn't answer, but took off with a steady pace. They hadn't gone twenty feet, when the sounds grew louder and intruded into their temporary feeling of safety.

Vanda stopped so abruptly that Medwin bumped into her. Her voice held fear, but no panic when she voiced the word. "Winfried."

"Yes, and he's smart. We didn't have time to clean up the room. He'll find the clues fast enough and be on our trail in minutes. We have to keep going."

"You're right."

"How much farther?"

"Twenty minutes. Maybe thirty. There's a wall at the edge of the Rhoderick property, but Winfried and I scaled it many times when children."

"We're not children now, and we've got—"

Him. Their weight. Their burden. In fact, they wouldn't be in this predicament if it weren't for him.

Vanda stepped up the pace, and Arlo kept up. The man began to pant, but he didn't slow down. Jerry's admiration for him jumped a notch.

He wanted to shift to ease the uncomfortable pressure on his stomach, but worse, with every bounce, Medwin's trot was an agonizing jolt to his leg.

He could hear the pounding of footsteps and the occasional shouts, and estimated Rhoderick only seconds behind them. He hoped Vanda knew what she was doing. Rhoderick might spare his sister's life, but for Medwin, treason wouldn't sit well with a high ranking German official like Rhoderick. Other than a deep desire for all the torture Rhoderick could pour out, he couldn't imagine anything but instant death for himself.

"There. Up ahead." Vanda's whisper floated to them just as she halted in her trot.

Arlo eased up beside her. "Up you go. When you reach the other side, I'll follow you and hand him down."

Vanda shook her head, and in the moonlight, her dark hair reflected the light. "No. Go Medwin, there's a rope at the top. I won't be able to pull him up. You can do that. On the other side, I'll be strong enough to steady him as you guide him down."

"Absolutely not. You first."

"Listen to me. It's the best way." She gripped his arm with both hands and shook it.

"Catch them before they get over the wall." Rhoderick and his men were almost there. The words were clear in the night.

"Winfried. Please, Medwin." Vanda's plea would have touched a miser's heart.

Arlo didn't argue any longer. He turned to the wall and began to climb. Jerry could hear his grunts. The man had to be worn out, but he ascended the wall with the skill of a mountain climber.

At the top, Arlo tossed down the anchored rope. With Vanda's help, Jerry wrapped it around his waist but before he could finish, Arlo was pulling him up and barely had him positioned when a light flashed across the wall.

Arlo called out. "Vanda, hurry!"

Jerry could see her climbing, almost running up the stone wall, and when she reached the top, she didn't hesitate. "Go, Medwin."

The man jumped lightly to the ground on the opposite side.

"Down you go. Careful, Jerry."

"Jump, Jerry, I'll soften your fall. You, too, Vanda."

Shots rang out. Some of them hit the wall and zinged off, carrying chips of rock. Much too close. Jerry jumped and both men landed on the ground. But Arlo shoved Jerry off him and scrambled up. "Vanda. Quickly. Jump."

Jerry clamored to his one good foot and stared up where Vanda gripped the top of the wall.

She half-stood as if in preparation to obey Arlo's command.

The gunfire hadn't ceased, and of a sudden, Vanda jerked. Blood spread across the front of her white blouse like a spider slowly unfolding it's multiple legs.

Vanda stared down at them, her body swaying as lightly as a delicate hummingbird. The moonlight reflected the softness of her gown as she held Jerry's gaze. Then her gaze swiveled to Arlo's, and her lips formed his name. But she didn't speak. She didn't tumble to the ground either, but almost seemed to be floating, and Arlo caught her.

His voice held panic and love and disbelief as he whispered her name over and over while he cradled her limp body in his arms.

Jerry could hear some of the men as they began their climb up the wall, their shouts loud, Rhoderick's furious as he urged his men on to the capture. No doubt a few were looking for the only gate as an easier access. Jerry laid a hand on the man's arm. "We have to go."

Blankness radiated over Arlo's face when he looked at Jerry. For a long moment he couldn't seem to focus. Realization of the acute danger they were in finally registered, and resignation spread across his thin features. Kneeling he laid Vanda's body on the ground

and touched her hand, then stood, and without ceremony threw Jerry over his shoulder again. In seconds he was in the forest, the pursuers on their heels.

Vanda's wish from the night when they walked in the garden weeks ago, echoed in Jerry's mind. *Sometimes I think I'd rather die at twenty and have had done one thing worthwhile.*

Someone had granted Vanda her desire.

Chapter Four

"**I** want to be kept in the loop on this, Phil."

"You know I'll do what I can. Some things are classified." Captain Philip Bosworth rearranged the already neatly organized utensils on his desk.

"Hogwash. I know you can share with whomever you want. I happen to be the one who saved your life—not once, but twice. Or have you forgotten?" Captain Ossie huffed his rebuke from between angry lips.

"How could I forget when you keep reminding me?" Captain Ossie's long time buddy from WWI laughed long and loud. "How many times must I repay this debt I owe you?"

"Till I say." Captain Ossie's quick reply was taut but the grin on his handsome mustached-lips belied the sharp retort.

"Just what I figured. Never." His exaggerated sigh was drawn out.

"If you hear any dope about Patterson, be sure to let me know." Ossie Rayner encouraged the other man. "You've sent my son-in-law on a dangerous mission, and I do *not* want anything to happen to the man."

"He was the best choice for this work. Quite possibly the best we had."

Captain Ossie nodded. "Of course. I can believe that. I've always sensed the advanced capability and intelligence in Jerry."

"He's one smart, but hard-boiled spy, I give you that." Captain Phil smirked, then sobered. "Maybe too much so."

"Overly confident, you mean."

"Yeah."

"Let's pray he isn't."

Regardless of the thoughts running through his buddy's mind, Captain Ossie's bordered on worry over his second daughter's husband. Phil had only given him as much detail as he claimed he was allowed, but it was enough to know Jerry Patterson was in dangerous fields. Whether the boy came home or not was in God's hands.

Whether Josie could handle it if God saw fit to—

Captain Ossie couldn't finish the thought.

Strong willed and fierce in her loyalties, only a few people realized how tender and easily hurt Josie was inside. It would devastate her to lose the man she'd high-handedly accepted as her husband.

"I suggest utilizing Mason's talents. I know him, and he's a sharp young man." Captain Ossie squinted a look at the window.

"Is that right? Heard of him, but he hasn't crossed my radar yet. I'll have him checked out."

"Good." Captain Ossie stood. "Seems like old times when we used to serve together. Stop by anytime."

"Love to, but not sure that's wise with the circumstances like they are."

"Understood. Perhaps when this interminable war is over."

Chapter Five

Josie Rayner Patterson slammed into the Rayner Boarding House and screamed. "I've got a letter."

Doors opened first, then footsteps clicked on the stone hallway floor as her father and sister hurried to her. Emma Jaine, with her well-rounded, pregnant stomach, panted at her. "You almost gave me a heart attack. Do you have to screech like a banshee?"

"I've got a letter." Josie waved the object in the air then peered at her sister. "I like to scream. It releases some of the tension I feel. You ought to try it sometime."

Emma Jaine frowned at her, but Josie could see her lips twitching.

"Don't you want to read it by yourself?" Papa lifted a white eyebrow and accepted the kiss she laid on his cheek.

"I will. I was just so excited I couldn't wait to tell you." Josie tucked a strand of hair behind her ear. "Give me a minute, then I'll read you some."

"Go ahead. I'll finish with Harriet and be right back. Don't read without me." Emma Jaine waddled from the room.

"I won't." Josie settled on one of the love seats in front of the fireplace and opened the flap carefully. She might be what Emma Jaine insisted she was—the world's clumsiest female—but when it came to the letters from Jerry, they were treated with reverence and all the daintiness she could muster. The missives were much too dear to tear into.

Mrs. Jerry Patterson

How she loved that name. She whispered it softly just to form the words on her lips.

501 West Mulberry Street
Cincinnati, Ohio
Dear Mrs. Patterson:

Josie frowned at the formal wording. She'd thought it

37

was from Jerry. He wouldn't address her as Mrs. Patterson, although she'd dearly love him to.

She skimmed the words. What? Unbelievable. She reread the letter again. Her mind whirled in dizzying circles as she read and reread the words.

Missing in action. Missing in action. Missing in...

She looked up, stretched out a shaking hand to her father and felt the blackness envelop her. "Papa, no. No."

She thought she screamed—again, but it might have been her mind.

From a distance her father called out, and Emma Jaine ran into the room, her face anxious as she knelt beside her. Josie wanted to tell them to let her die, not to bother with reviving her. She didn't want to live.

But the words wouldn't come. Only the words from the letter—*missing in action, missing in action*—spun in her brain, until she couldn't hold on to the consciousness any longer.

She released her hold on her father's hand and allowed the darkness to pull her away from the pain in her heart.

Chapter Six

The temptation to gnash his teeth in vexation was overwhelmingly strong, but Winfried Rhoderick's face muscles never so much as rippled. He stared down at his sister's body lying in the elaborately ornate casket.

He wanted to kill.

No. He wanted to find the fiend who'd done this to his sister and torture, maim, *then* kill. He'd set his best agents on finding this person—the real name of him. And they would with his wrath behind their frantic search.

He heard the sniffling, the quiet sobs around him, but no tears flowed down his cheeks although his heart felt as if it was drowning in sorrow. He had no time for useless emotion. All his focus remained on getting even.

After he'd killed Herr Bhaer—only then could he mourn.

His arm rose as he repeated, "Heil, Hitler." The mourners around him followed his example with downcast faces, but he ignored them.

God willing, Herr Bhaer would die.

Chapter Seven

Josie executed a hydroplane, then rising, spun in a circle faster and faster. With the wind whistling past her ears, she did a series of the butterfly spins, until she reached the point of conscious slowing, her head drooping, her arms lifted straight up.

The single burst of enthusiastic clapping brought her out of the dream. She straightened and looked at the tall woman in ice skates ten feet away. Josie beamed.

"Sehr gut." The woman skated toward the shore and motioned for Josie to follow.

Josie stared after the always-articulate woman—so much so, that she routinely irritated Josie with her overly proper words. Why was she murmuring now? "What did you say? I couldn't understand you."

"Never mind. I want to talk with you while you remove your skates."

Josie skated after her but protested. "I was going to practice another hour." She bit her lip when the only answer came as a skeptical look.

Diana DeNapp sat on the bench and bent over to unlace her skates.

Josie settled on the seat beside her but ignored her action.

The instructor looked pointedly at Josie. "Well? Do you not obey the instructions of your long-suffering mentor?" she asked in an injured tone.

Her instructor's accent was stiffer than usual. "Of course, I do. You know that. But I've only practiced four hours today. I want to get in at least—"

"Another hour?" Diana interrupted. "Ach, Josie, I know you. You would not stop until at least two hours were gone."

When Josie refused again to speak, Diana raised her hands as if beseeching heaven for help. "Look at you.

Have you looked into the mirror lately?"

Josie knew her face flamed. "No-o. What's wrong with me?"

"Circles under your eyes. You've lost weight. You're unkempt." Disgust as thick as the molasses Papa loved laced the woman's voice. "No one wants to watch a messy skeleton skate across a pond."

"Surely I'm not that bad."

"Oh, but you are." A nod of insistence bounced her instructor's well-coiffed head. "Now. Here's what I insist upon. You are to go home. No more practicing for one week. Rest and get some full nights of sleep. Eat. You need to build up the stamina or you will find your muscles uncooperative when you least expect it. Relax. Enjoy your family. *Then* we will resume, and you will feel like a new woman. Your practice will be much better because of the break."

Jerry's dark, handsome face flashed in front of her eyes, and Josie blinked to get rid of the image. Now was no time to brood. Yet she knew rest was not what she needed. To rest meant to think, and she couldn't bear life thinking about her missing husband.

"All right. I guess I can do that." She waved the woman away. "Go ahead. I'm going to sit here and think for a bit."

Another of Diana's disbelieving glances scorched her, but her instructor made no more reproaches. Josie ignored her departure. She appreciated the woman although she could be brutal with her demands. But she'd taken Josie to another level. If this war would ever end, who knew where Josie could go with her skating? Meanwhile she had to content herself with contests and skating events that were getting her name noticed.

The sound of angry voices disturbed her sorry-for-myself musing. Josie swiveled and stared at the man and woman arguing, and she knew one of them. Their gestures and raised voices were quality clues. Diana, and who? She didn't know the man.

When Diana suddenly slapped the man and stomped away, never looking back, Josie raised her brows. Yeah, she knew her instructor had a temper, but she'd never seen her lose control like this.

The man stood gazing after Diana, rubbing his face, his shoulders slumped. Should she go to him and assure him she'd get over it soon enough?

No, that was a wacky idea. This time, she'd better mind her own business and let Diana tend to her own.

With Diana gone, the pond seemed to lure her to it, but Josie gripped her will and dragged the longing glance from her favorite place. If she showed up in two weeks' time, clumsy and uncoordinated, Diana would have no one to blame but herself.

She was good. Maybe more than good. At least Diana thought so. Not that the woman said so in words. But Josie could tell.

The sun reflected off the pond, turning it into a glittering frozen land. She'd love to get in a few more hours of practice, but sighed. Diana might just double back to check up on her. She bent and unlaced her skates, replaced them with her sturdy walking shoes, and stood. Slinging her skates over her shoulder, she headed home.

At least back to her father's home. Where she'd lived ever since she'd received that horrid notice from the military about Jerry.

It couldn't be true. Not for her Jerry. There was no way Jerry could be...dead. Her heart would have known. It might beat with fear and uncertainty because of his absence, but there was no despair there. She knew if—no, when—he could, he'd write again.

Of course, the letter hadn't said he was—gone. Just that he was missing. Missing. Almost, but not quite as bad. The unknown looming forever in her future. This not knowing was killing her. Every day she wanted to bash in something to vent some of the frustration building inside her.

Emma Jaine was forever telling her to not give up hope.

As if she would.

To trust God.

As if she could.

As much as Josie loved her older sister, Emma Jaine had it easy. A handsome husband and a baby on the way. No problems.

Papa patted her back, worry in his eyes at her distress, and mouthed platitudes that did nothing for her. She half suspected he didn't really realize how worried she was. He and Shirley—no, that wasn't fair. Though what she was going through was far from fair.

She wanted someone to make all this go away, to assure her Jerry would be home tomorrow. Josie wanted Jerry. And she didn't think she could bear it if she had to go the rest of her life without him.

It was beyond thinking about.

Josie blinked away the tears. She wouldn't think about all that. She couldn't. She'd concentrate on her skating, to be the best in the country, and when this war finally ended, maybe she'd get the chance to show what she could do.

And when Jerry came home, they could travel together when she competed. One thing for sure, she'd never leave his side again.

~*~

"I don't want anything to eat." Josie flew about her room four weeks later, gathering her outfit.

"You haven't eaten all day. Just a bite of something." Emma Jaine patted her own well-swollen stomach and frowned at her. "Jonah's waiting with the car. Are you sure you don't want me to go along with you?"

"Stop worrying. I'm fine. I'll see you at the competition." Josie left the room. She definitely didn't want Emma Jaine smothering over her. She needed some breathing room. Ever since she'd fainted four weeks ago, her sister had been like a mother hen, worrying and fretting over her from morning till night. You'd think she'd contracted a fatal disease.

She needed a drink.

Jonah pulled straight up to the building, and before he could jump to help, Josie hopped out, her outfit and skates clutched in her arms. "Thanks, Jonah."

Inside, she headed for her room, glad tonight's competition was on her own turf.

Diana turned as she entered. "You're running late."

"Give me a drink before I change."

"You should cut that out."

"Just a sip to steady my nerves." Josie smirked at her

ever-patient mentor. "You do want me to do my best, don't you?"

"I wouldn't waste my time on you otherwise, but you'd better have more ambitions than my desires if you want to succeed." Diana reached for a glass. "I take it you do?"

The thimbleful drink slid down her throat in one gulp, and Josie closed her eyes. "That was good. Yeah, I want to succeed. More than anything in the world. I haven't let you down yet, have I?"

"You've done well, but some of your toughest competitions are coming up. Don't get too confident."

"A piece of cake."

"We shall see. Now, get changed. You've had your drink. No more. Concentrate on the evening ahead and put all thoughts of everything else out of your mind."

Josie stripped out of her street clothes and pulled on her skating outfit. The red one tonight. Diana said with Josie's chestnut red hair, it set her aflame. Josie checked the mirror, smoothed her tresses back, then headed for the outdoor rink. She hesitated at the edge and smiled when the girl fumbled an execution. Only a bit, and she recovered nicely, but Josie couldn't hold back the triumph that sprang to life.

This one wouldn't be hard to beat.

When the skater finished, and Josie was announced, she stepped onto the ice and glided to the center. Her gaze searched for and found her family, their beaming faces proof that she had loving support from the stands. She waved and the crowd erupted into an enthusiastic roar. They'd seen her perform before and loved her.

Confidence and excitement surged through her. She hoped when the war was over to qualify for the Olympics, but for now she had to be satisfied with as many competitions as would further her dreams and hopes.

Her musical cue played and she skated backward, loosening her muscles, cleansing her mind of all but the skating, and prepared to launch into the best performance she'd ever given.

She glided. Danced to the music, focused on the feelings building inside her. Her memory tumbled backwards...

Jerry, skating beside her, his hands on her waist,

lifting her into the air, then allowing her to slide to the ice again. His strong, agile hands never missing the timing needed, following her cues and twirls as if born to it. In sync and totally in harmony with her every move. His anticipation for her routine was a miracle...

They slowed in her imaginary mind world, hands outstretched, fingertips touching.

And then the space between them widened, breaking the flow...

The stomping and screaming of her name over and over brought her back from the world where she tucked herself when she needed to give it her best. She looked up, dazed for an instant, and then she smiled, waved and acknowledged her fans' adoration. Gliding to the edge of the ice to stand beside Diana, it took a several deep breaths to calm the raging emotions rolling through her.

"How did I do?" Was that her voice, breathless and dampened-down enthusiasm edging her tone?

Diana motioned with her hand. "What does it sound like?"

Josie studied the people surrounding the ice. She cocked her head. "Will I win?"

Before her trainer could reply, Josie's name came through the loud speakers, and Diana was pushing her gently back toward the rink. "Congratulations."

Another win. Another step toward her goal.

~*~

Josie sat at her table in the temporary room she inhabited after moving into the Rayner Boarding house. An action taken because of the "missing in action" letter from the department of defense. She hadn't wanted to, but pressure from her family prevailed against her usual rebellious stance.

Emma Jaine had wanted to fix up a room for her, but Josie had drawn the line at that, and had absolutely and loudly declined. She would not, could not accept it. After all, when Jerry returned home... She didn't want to have her roots firmly planted in her previous home again.

Josie clenched the pen she held, wanting to squeeze it into a flat glob of nothing. Today was not the day to dwell on whens and ifs.

The outside view of the street drew her attention, and Josie stared at the drab scene, wishing the sun would shine. Anything to ease the ache inside her chest that she feared would never feel warm again.

Two men, in long overcoats walked slowly past, both of their faces turned toward the house. They paused briefly as if reading the house number, then moved on, and seemed to be discussing something.

Josie shrugged. As far as she knew, she'd never seen them before and couldn't care less who they were or what they were doing.

A knock on the door interrupted her disinterested musings, and Shirley opened the door at Josie's bidding.

"Are you busy, my dear?"

Busy? Her? Josie gazed down at the letter she was trying to write to Jerry. No matter what the state department said, she cradled the hope that somewhere Jerry was waiting for another letter from her.

"Come on in. I'm just scribbling."

Shirley's wise eyes studied her, but she made no response to Josie's comment. "I wondered if you'd be interested in attending a local concert downtown tonight."

"Uh..."

"I wish you would. Some of my librarian cohorts and a few of the higher intellect in the university are sponsoring this, and I really would like to go. Emma Jaine is not up to it being so close to her delivery time, and your father had to back out at the last minute because of business with his cronies." Shirley gave a small chuckle. "Really not interested in crossing town on my own."

What could she say? "Tonight? I don't have any competitions until Saturday."

"Right. We haven't forgotten that. So you'll go with me?"

Horsefeathers. How did she get herself in these fixes? She'd just about run out of gas with these affairs—including church—that her family shoved at her. Couldn't they see she wanted to be left alone?

"I'll go. What do I need to wear?" Too bad her tone wasn't quite as gracious as it should be with someone as sweet as the librarian. She hated being roped into events with which she held no interest.

Seven hours later, Josie sat in front of her mirror, Claire's capable hands performing magic. The warm rust color of her evening gown gave Josie confidence even though a knot of nervousness lodged in her stomach. Claire, with her adept fingers had swept Josie's hair off her neck and pinned and tucked her curly strands, allowing more than a few to escape freely. Then the youngest Rayner sister stepped back and sighed.

"I cannot forgive you for looking so elegant."

Josie gazed at Claire, the real beauty in the family. She'd tormented and teased her sister all her life, and to imagine that Claire—for any reason—would envy *her* was beyond thinking about. "Can't imagine why. You're the beautiful one."

"I know that." Claire smirked. "But what I wouldn't give for your nose. And that long neck of yours?"

If anyone could bring off a sarcastic sniff elegantly, Claire did at that moment.

She frowned at her own image in the mirror. She detested her long, pointy nose, and her neck. Who wanted a giraffe neck? Josie frowned harder. Her gaze swiveled to Claire. Obviously, she did.

"Well, thanks for helping me out. Doesn't look half bad. I think."

"If you'd only quit your tomboyish ways, you'd be a sensation in looks. You don't know when you've got it good."

Standing, and before Claire could swivel out of the way, Josie tweaked her sister's nose. "Gotta take a powder. I think that's Shirley calling."

"You really should cut out the slang, Josie." Claire exited Josie's room and headed to her own. "Makes you sound low class."

"Me? Who cares?" Josie shrugged her disdain at society's conventions.

"It's all right for the guys, but you?" Claire paused. "Have fun and behave, will you?"

Shrugging into the wrap Claire had loaned her— reluctantly, Josie hurried on to the front door where Shirley stood. "Am I making us late?"

"You're fine, dear. And that gown is superb with your coloring. Brings out the warm color in your cheeks. You look lovely."

Her cheeks grew red. She could feel the heat in them, and she eyed her father's friend. She'd never had that much to do with the librarian living at the Rayner House. Her father and Emma Jaine seemed to think the world of her, but she'd projected the image of a school marm too much to lure Josie into friendship. Still, it was swell of her to give her two cents worth.

"Thanks." Josie jerked at the door handle just as Jonah, the Rayner House's live-in, man-of-all trades employee, opened the door and stepped inside.

Staggering back, Josie laughed and caught Jonah's grin before the man sobered to direct his attention to the librarian.

"Ready, ladies?"

Twenty minutes later, Jonah deposited them at a downtown hall lit up like a Christmas tree. Cab drivers rushed up to the street curbs and emptied their vehicles of concert-attending people. Harried couples congregated in the lines beginning to form at the door as the overcrowded foyer spilled out onto the sidewalk.

Shirley stood eyeing the crowd as she pulled on her gloves. "Come, Josie. Let's enter through the side door."

Josie snickered. "You don't mind going in a *side* door?"

"Of course not." Shirley tossed her head and gave Josie a mischievous glance. "Who wants to tangle with that motley group?"

"Well..." Josie giggled. "...might be fun."

"Maybe for you. I have too many years to my name to wait in that long line. Besides, you should always take advantage of privileges when you have them, Josie Patterson." She gave a quick knock, and the door opened.

"Miss Largett, come in please."

"Mr. Thomas, why are you answering the side door?"

The worried lines on the man's forehead seemed to go along with his personality as he fidgeted and hem-hawed his response. "I sent our regular man out front to help with the overflow of attendees. If we'd only known how popular the concert would be, we wouldn't have opened it to the public."

"You couldn't have known, Thomas. This should drive up the price for our next event."

"Perhaps. Depends on who we schedule, I would think." He shifted as a loud argument at the front door penetrated down the hall to where they stood.

Shirley hesitated and stared toward the foyer. "What's going on?"

But Thomas had hurried off. Shirley cocked her head, one brow lifted. "Shall we mingle a little closer? My curiosity is getting the best of me."

"Let's go." Josie chuckled and led the way to within twenty feet or so of the general confusion. "What's going on?"

The man beside her acknowledged her question with a tilt of his head, but his attention remained fixed on the arguing figures just inside the door. "Seems the guy thinks he can attend the concert without a proper ticket. That grubby-looking paper is hardly impressive enough to gain his attendance."

His tone was condescending, and Josie got the feeling he didn't much care who heard his sentiment.

The man beside her held a gray-suede homburg in his hand, his non-descript, long gray coat folded over his arm. In spite of his ordinary dress, there was something striking about him.

The gray-clad man moved forward and spoke to the greeter in an undertone, far too low for Josie to hear what he said. Something passed between them— money?—and the greeter stepped back, allowing the argumentative man to enter.

The man with the homburg patted the other man's back, his head lowered to catch the whispered words being said in a frantic manner. The Homburg man snapped an answer, gave the man another look and walked away.

As he passed Josie, he glanced at her, touched his forehead, but kept moving. When Josie looked back toward the entrance, the other man had disappeared.

A hand touched her elbow, and Josie turned.

Shirley.

"Sorry, Josie. I got waylaid by a friend. Are you all right?"

"Of course, I'm fine."

"Did you see what was happening at the door?"

"Some guy trying to enter without an invitation or ticket, I guess."

"That's strange. It was properly announced open to the public but pre-concert tickets must be obtained first. None would be handed out at the door." Shirley's features were twisted in puzzlement. "Let's move to our seats, study the program, and watch the attendees entering, shall we?"

Josie grinned and nodded. By all means, she loved watching people.

Minutes before the concert was to start, Shirley leaned close to Josie and whispered. "There's Guy. I wonder—"

"Who's Guy? Wonder what?"

"Guy Delaney.

"Who's Guy Delaney?"

"That's right. You haven't met him, have you?"

"Guess not."

"He's Emma Jaine's newest boarding house tenant. Came about a month or a little less ago. He's quiet and keeps to himself. Seems to enjoy our evening gatherings though he doesn't do much socializing. Just sits in a corner and watches everyone else."

"He's here?"

"Yes. Across the room to the right. The short, thin, rather non-descript boy. And one that, strangely, seems to pull at my heart strings whenever I'm around him."

Josie swiveled to find the person Shirley Largett was talking about and located him. It was the man at the door without a ticket who'd hardly seemed dressed to attend a concert.

He leaned against a mustard yellow wall-papered wall, as if trying to make the impression he was a casual by-stander. Instead, he came across as a nervous employee—or attendee, perhaps—who definitely felt out of place.

Although dressed well enough, his clothes were not quite as elaborate as they should be, his hair a shade too shaggy to fit in with the fashionable crowd, and his overall bearing uncomfortable.

Her heart melted at his obvious discomfort. She'd been there and knew exactly the strain he was in. And because of that, she grinned, knowing the action was as much for her own social awkwardness as it was for the boy standing across the room.

His gaze swept the room and stopped abruptly on her. Was that a hint of a blush? His head barely tipped, then his gaze moved on.

Josie turned back around and gave the librarian a look. "You think he's watching *us*?"

"My imagination running rampant, I'm sure." Shirley's eyes danced with sudden mischief.

"You've been hanging around me too much, I think." Josie settled back in her seat, but before the lights dimmed, she glanced to the right again.

He was gone.

The concert turned out to be interesting and entertaining. Josie surreptitiously wiped away a few tears when the flutist rendered a solo so sad that Josie's heart ached with longing for Jerry. When the concert drew to a close, the audience stood to their feet, clapping and generally showing their appreciation of the talent displayed.

The foyer and hallway were packed so Josie and Shirley hurried out the side door where Jonah waited. As Josie climbed into the car after Shirley, she glanced back at the hall. No sign of Guy Delaney, but the Homburg man stood at the entrance. Watching them.

~*~

"You have the toughest competition you've ever faced tonight." Diana faced Josie and ran her gaze over the outfit Josie had donned.

"I've got it covered." Josie whirled away from Diana's critical eyes and frowned at herself in the tall mirror. The silver and blue outfit wasn't her favorite and she hated the way Emma Jaine had done her hair. She should have let Claire do it tonight.

"Don't be over confident—"

"I know. I know. Pride goeth before a fall, but I know what I'm doing. I'm ready for tonight. You even said so."

Her instructor stared at her, then the grim look faded

and her lips tilted. "You are that. Just stay focused. You'll be fine."

Josie nodded. "I need a couple minutes by myself."

Diana headed for the door, but tossed back. "No drinks."

She didn't want a drink. Not tonight. She'd heard—by the grapevine—that some skating officials would be here evaluating, searching for a possible candidate for the future Olympics. If the war ever ended. Diana knew, but she wouldn't have wanted to tell her. Too much pressure, she'd think.

Well, she did know, but she wouldn't let it faze her. She was determined to win tonight.

The time ticked slowly by. When at last Josie entered the skating arena, minutes before her routine would begin, she couldn't stop thinking of Jerry and the horrible emptiness inside her.

Diana had chosen a slow piece written especially for Josie's performance tonight, and Josie was well aware of where her thoughts would rush. She'd schooled herself to be on guard, afraid the emotion she felt about Jerry's absence would overwhelm her.

But immediately—just seconds into her routine—Jerry's presence was there, as if he was physically skating beside her, and Josie felt the magnetism of his personality pulling her deep within her imaginary vision of him.

Sulky eyes roved over her face. Lips tipped up in a crooked smile, defying her to deny her love for him. Muscular arms spun her away, then drew her back, close to his chest.

His sinewy arms lifted and tossed her like a light-weight, fuzzy dandelion seed, into the air, floating, floating, floating higher and higher until, as she began drifting back to the ice floor, he caught her, setting her on her skates, guiding her to yet another magical dance move...

The music poured over her, spread through her until she was sure she'd scream in delight—or at the worst, in pain—at the agony of his beloved self. The intensity built to such a dizzying height, that at last when Josie slowed the spin she'd been in and allowing her head to fall to her chest, she slid delicately to the floor in a graceful swan-like position. Tears poured down her cheeks. Her chest rose and fell, every bone in her body felt as mush. She had no idea, no sense of whether it'd been her worst performance ever or her best.

There was a silence that seemed an hour long. Then, from a distance the roar drew her back from the world she'd been submerged in for the last four minutes. She lifted her head and realized the crowd was going wild, and her lips spread slowly at first, tentatively, wanting to be sure it was all for her.

Rising, she beamed at her adoring fans, delighted at their enthusiasm. Her gaze searched the front row for her family and found them. She lifted a hand, kissed her fingertips, and flung her hand in their direction. The exhilaration of knowing she'd performed well evened out the melancholy that had guided her through her routine.

Claire bounced on her seat, face flushed. Emma Jaine leaned on Tyrell's arm, a maternal glow radiating from her happy face. Papa's big hands clapped enthusiastically.

The roar ebbed, and Josie skated toward her family. In spite of their annoying habits, she dearly loved every one of them. How could she not? Even when she'd disobeyed and run from the house time after time, missing church and meals, Papa had forgiven her over and over. Emma Jaine had covered and intervened for her time and again. Claire had tearfully endured her ongoing teasings.

Now, Papa enveloped her in a huge bear hug, tears of pride and happiness streaming down his worn cheeks. "Beautiful job, my Josie. You touched this old heart of mine."

The babbling voices around her faded, and the loneliness engulfed her again. What she wouldn't give to have Jerry here, rejoicing in her victory, sharing in her triumph. He wouldn't say much, not right now in front of her family, but at home, tonight...

Josie shivered at the thought of Jerry's arms surrounding her, his dark head resting on top of hers.

"Come back with us, Josie, and we'll have a late night celebration. Most of the house people will still be up and anxious to hear how you did." Papa's normal loud voice was even louder, demanding the attention he wanted from the family he loved.

The laughter came easily. "All right, Papa. You go ahead and send Jonah back after me. I need a few minutes to calm down and change, then I'll be right home."

The others nodded, knowing how Josie loved her privacy, and walked away, some of them glancing back at her, radiating their joy in her success and love for her with their smiles and admiring glances.

The rink was emptying quickly. Only a few stragglers still lingered, and the janitors who would do the majority of their cleaning up tonight, readying the place for whatever activity was scheduled for tomorrow.

Josie hummed, skated and swirled in circles, then gazed around the rink where her emotions had risen to such a height. Her body relaxed, her mind drifted, remembering. Her lips tipped upward, and she half turned, almost ready to go to her room to change.

Josie's gaze caught on the figure who hovered against a back wall, in the shadows, and a shiver ran up her spine.

She was alone. Not frightened exactly, but the figure— he was so still. Josie paused, studying him back as he seemed to be doing her.

She tilted her head a little, but he held still. Then he stepped forward—only a foot or so—but enough that she could see his face.

The faintest of smiles edged sarcastic lips. A gaze, coming from dark and haunted eyes, rested on her. For a long minute, Josie didn't move.

A thin face.

Strange.

Familiar.

A face she loved.

And then Josie knew, and she moved. Flinging herself forward, she skated toward the most beloved person in her world.

Jerry didn't take his gaze from her; only watched her come. When she landed against the rail and whispered his name, he straightened and almost as if unwinding, unfolded his crossed legs and arms. Slowly—almost reluctantly—he stepped forward until he stood in front of her.

Josie searched his gaunt figure, lifted a hand and ran her fingers over cheekbones that seemed barely covered with skin. What on earth had happened to him? "Jerry?"

He wrapped his arms around her then. His shudder shook her, seeming to last forever, and she swayed with him, unable to stop it. And just when she thought he'd never let go, that life was perfect again, his arms dropped.

"Where have you been?" Josie smoothed a hand over his thin jawline again. "You're limping. What happened to your leg? They said you were missing in action. I've been so worried. Did you write? Why didn't you let me know you were coming? Are you home for good? Are you hungry? Will you go with me to Papa's? Jerry, I'm so-o-o glad you're home."

"Stop." Jerry took a step away. "I—I can't—"

Then, just as suddenly, he clasped her to his body again and groaned. "Oh, Josie, you won't ever know how I've missed you. How I've longed to hold you in my arms again." He pulled back enough to gaze into her face, his fingers in her hair, his eyes eagerly devouring her.

As if someone had pulled a black, black curtain over his face, a dark shadow crept into his eyes and over his face, like a mask, turning him into a someone she didn't know. What was happening? Where had her Jerry gone?

He stepped back, his hands unclutching her, his arms dropping to his side.

She didn't want to let him go, didn't want him to let *her* go and let her eyes plead with him. "Jerry, I need to get out of these things."

His glance was as cold and impenetrable as if he'd magically commanded an invisible wall to appear. It stopped her quicker than any words would have done. "Don't bother. Go to your family and celebrate your victory. I'll see you at home."

Josie clutched at his suit sleeve, but he shook off her grasp, and without another word, left.

Her heart froze in terror as if a tidal wave slammed into her. Something was wrong with Jerry. He didn't love her anymore or he'd never have turned away from her like he had. She stretched out a hand, her heart yearning after his retreating figure, and felt a strong, rugged hand clasp hers.

"Let him go, my Josie. He's hurting." Josie dragged her reluctant gaze from her husband's retreating back to her father's face. He didn't look at her, only stared after Jerry, unfocused as if seeing something beyond human visibility.

"But Papa..."

"What is it?"

"I thought—I thought when he returned it would be different." The trembling in her voice scared her, and that made her angry. She didn't want to be confused by Jerry's actions.

Papa pulled her into his arms for a bear hug, refusing to let go for long seconds. When he did, he gripped her upper arms. "Josie, I've seen men like this returning from the horrors of war. Men who've suffered unspeakable agonies. Men who've been driven half-crazy with the memories that dwell forever in their minds. You're going to have to be strong to get through the next few months. You're not going to understand Jerry's actions, or even like them. But if ever you need to grow up and be the wife he needs, it's now. Can you do that, Josie?" He shook her gently. "Listen to me. Can you?"

Josie stared back at her father, the fear in her rising at this unknown thing in her life. The desire to scream her defiance like she'd done when a child and bidden to do an unwanted task, begged for release. "I think so, Papa."

"Child, I'm afraid you're going to have no choice in the matter." He sighed. "God help you."

Chapter Eight

She was good, and a beautiful sight on the ice. The passion she portrayed, the natural adeptness that went far beyond any learned or practiced ability, gave her an unusual grace that delighted and impressed the viewer. She'd go far—if she had the time.

Once he'd accepted that Patterson had stolen the paper from Marshall—the paper that would have given Germany the names of some of the biggest U.S. spies working in his country—and that Patterson was a spy, he'd done the research. Contacts in the states' congress had been the help, along with a few of his close Germany government friends, to find the information he'd needed on *Major Bhaer.*

The cynical chuckle that spilled between his lips only deepened his determination to destroy the man.

It'd been a cinch from there to learn about Patterson's family and friends. He'd not exactly planned on meeting the wife first, but...

Why not? She'd be useful in gaining what he *did* want and maybe even more effective in creating the hurt he wanted to bestow. Much more effective.

He smoothed his handsome mustache.

Indeed, Josie Rayner Patterson would fit into his plans perfectly.

Chapter Nine

Josie knew instinctively Jerry hadn't headed for her father's house.

Before he'd left for military duty, he'd insisted on buying the property next door—for her sake and to give them some privacy away from her family. He'd grinned his devastatingly handsome smile when he'd said that last, and she'd taken no offense at his words or meaning. Sometimes her family was too much for her too. Besides, next door? She'd still see plenty of them, probably too much so.

Papa sat beside her now with Jonah at the wheel of their car. He still held tight to her hand, and Josie realized she was glad he was here. "How did you know I'd need you tonight?"

"Papas know these things. You don't raise children—especially daughters who are all beautiful, but so different—without knowing there comes a time in each of their lives when they need their father the most." He patted the hand he held. "I'm thinking this might be that time for you."

"I'm scared, Papa."

"I know you are, my dear, and you have a right to be." Papa Ossie was silent for a minute. "I've seen that look with many a man scarred by war. He probably won't want to talk about it. You may have to deal with heavy silence. Perhaps even brooding. Love him, care for him, be there for him, but try to refrain from too many questions."

"But I thought everything would be like it was before. I wouldn't ever have guessed he could change so much. I want him back. Happy, Fun. Wild and crazy."

"It's not fun and games anymore, Josie. Whatever Jerry went through overseas, has changed him. Perhaps not permanently, but you won't know for sure. Is your love strong enough to battle through this?" He peered at her in the darkness.

Heat warmed her cheeks. She was crazy over Jerry, adored him. But like this? She'd never been known as the patient daughter of the family. "I still love him, but you know me, Papa."

"Yes, I do. But I also know you've always been quick to defend the underdog, you're generous to a fault, and you see deeper than probably either one of your other sisters."

"Really? I always figured I was the least favorite..."

"Nonsense. Maybe the least obedient and the hardest to handle." He choked out a wry chuckle. "You're too much like me, I'm afraid."

Josie laughed. "That's what Emma Jaine always says."

Jonah pulled up in front of Josie's house and stopped.

"Sure you don't want to come on over for awhile?" Papa's intent gaze searched her face.

She shook her head. "No, I need to see Jerry."

"Then take care, my Josie. Shirley and I'll be praying a little extra for you. Come to me any time you need me."

Josie didn't answer, but hugged her papa's neck, flung open the door and stepped out. As the car pulled away, she watched until the Rayner house family car deposited her father in front of the boarding house, and returned his wave as he headed to his own front door.

Her front door clicked open, squeaking, and she hesitated. At what she didn't know. She wasn't afraid of Jerry, was she? He was the same man she'd married months ago, wasn't he? She thought the words, but her heart denied them. He'd changed, and that brief encounter earlier had convinced her the devilish, carefree man she'd fallen madly in love with had vanished, and in his place stood a person she didn't know, and worse, didn't know how to deal with.

The lump inside her throat grew as she quietly shut the door and leaned back against it, wondering what to do next. Confront him, demand an explanation? Ignore him? Run to him and soothe him with platitudes? Josie grimaced and shoved herself away from the door.

Dragging unwilling feet, she moved to the sitting room and paused at the doorway. It was dark in the room, but she could see his silhouette against the window. So he'd watched her falter her way to the porch. What now? Speak? Sit and wait till he did? Turn on a light or leave them off so they could brood in the darkness together?

That thought made her angry, and she cleared her throat.

He didn't turn toward her. "Come in, Josie. I suppose you think I need to unburden my soul to you. Give you all the gory details of my overseas life, huh?"

"Of course not. I know—"

"You know nothing."

His clipped tone sent her rising spirits into a nosedive.

"Don't expect me to sit around telling you tales in the evening. Don't ask me to attend your family's social gatherings because I'm not interested. I'm not your sugar-daddy. The best thing for you to do is leave me alone."

He drew in a breath, and Josie's anger eased when she heard the shakiness in it. What had the man been through?

"You go your way, do your skating competitions. Looks like you're popular. Just leave me alone."

The desperation in his voice broke her heart, scared her, and it was all she could do to remain rooted where she stood.

Clenching her fingers together, she asked in as steady a voice as she could muster, "I'm going to fix me a sandwich. Want one?"

She thought he'd refuse, but after a heartbeat, he answered, "Sounds good. And battery acid. I've missed yours."

Her heart bounded. Not much, but even in this early stage of reunion, it was better than minutes before. She'd take it gladly.

She didn't call him to the kitchen when it was ready. Instead, sensing his desire to avoid bright lights, she carried a tray to the sitting room, switched on a dim light and set the tray on the coffee table. She poured him a steaming cup of coffee, and without asking, added the one lump of sugar he'd always favored.

Not speaking, she settled back with her own snack and began eating, ignoring him and allowing him to make his own move to eat.

Thirty seconds later he took the chair across from her and reached for his coffee. He sipped and the moan was one of pleasure. "You always did know how to make a man's coffee, Josie. Best battery acid I've had since I left."

It was a begrudging compliment, but Josie grasped hold of it as if it were her first drink of water after being in a desert for a week. She took another bite of her sandwich and forced it past the lump that refused to be swallowed.

The rest of her sandwich ended up on her napkin. She sat back and sipped her coffee, plenty of cream.

The silence thickened as he drank the last of his brew and stood. "I'm going to take a walk. Night."

Nothing more. On this first night which should have been heaven. No loving touches. No endearing looks. No tender words. Josie watched the man she loved and thought she knew as he limped his way out the door.

~*~

The night wasn't any blacker than the darkness inside him. Jerry despised what he'd become. Who he had to be now. But he had no choice. Not if he wanted to foil the man he was sure would be coming.

They'd been so careful—he and Medwin Arlo—but the day he'd returned to their hiding spot, the spot where they waited on the boat sailing him to safety, he'd found his rescuer and Vanda's admirer and cousin, not twenty feet from the shack, shot in the back. Winfried would view his cousin as a coward and traitor to their beloved Germany, and a shot in the back would be exactly what he deserved.

Clutched in his hand was a paper—the paper he'd been sent to Germany to obtain. In the scurry of leaving the cabin where Vanda and Arlo had hidden him, he'd forgotten it, but Arlo—or was it Vanda?—had snatched it up, knowing it was important to him for whatever reason. Jerry took the time to grab and shove it into his pants' pocket.

He hadn't dared collect his meager belongings. Whether Vanda's brother figured Arlo was on his own or Jerry had already fled the country, he didn't know. He couldn't take the chance and had fled as fast as he could hobble away from the shack.

Jerry limped inside the corner all-night café and slid onto one of the counter seats. He nodded at the waitress who raised the coffeepot, and when she poured it, wrapped his always-cold fingers around it, soaking in the warmth. Waiting.

Till Josie went to sleep. She was a night owl, but if she'd kept to her old routine, she'd be exhausted after the competition and adrenaline boost. By midnight she'd be zonked.

Hopefully.

He paid no attention to the cute little number who tried to catch his attention, and stared into the dark brew as if seeking answers with only an occasional glance up at the clock on the wall.

When the hand finally swept up to midnight, Jerry slid off his stool, tossed a dollar on the counter, and left.

~*~

The creaking front door woke Josie. She shifted so she could see him when he entered their bedroom. He tried to be quiet. Josie could tell, but his left leg injury prevented the possibility. The scuffling sound added to the occasional bump increased her husband's agitation.

The gruffness in his mumbles said it all.

Jerry cracked the door, peeked in, and went straight to the closet and pulled down a blanket. But instead of leaving, he stopped by her side of the bed. Josie could feel his stare and wondered if he knew she was awake.

Then softly—almost as if a feather tickled her—he kissed her cheek and left the room, the blanket tucked under an arm.

Josie lifted her head, watched him go then settled back on the damp pillow, one hand covering the kiss he'd left behind.

Chapter Ten

Jerry made a point of being up and gone before his wife woke the next morning. He had to meet his captain this morning, early. Besides, Josie needed to rest after such a strenuous competition. And she hated mornings.

Liar. He stared out the cab window, the self-loathing rolling through his stomach. All he wanted was to forget. He didn't want to face her. He wanted to avoid the questions she'd want answered. Ignore the need to know what had happened whirling in her brain. He couldn't acknowledge her desire to hold him up as her hero. She didn't know, wouldn't understand what he'd done, what he'd been involved in.

Anyhow why would she want a cripple? He'd seen her last night, seen most of her competition. Her lithe body, her confidence and loveliness. The crowd had gone mad with enthusiasm.

"Sure you want out here, pal?" The cabbie's skeptical gaze met his in the rear view mirror.

Why did the men over these undercover jobs insist on the poorest part of town for their clandestine meetings? Jerry fumbled in his pocket and tossed the bill he pulled out over the seat. Without speaking he exited the car and eyed the rundown dingy building in front of him. Captain had said go to the green side door which would be in the alley. He'd have to step past all the trash cluttered there to gain access to it, and he disliked filth and trash.

The door opened before he could knock. The private who ushered him, gave him a broad smile. "Captain ordered a watch for you, sir. Follow me." The boy knocked once, listened, then flung open the door and motioned Jerry inside.

His captain stood as he entered and extended a hand. "Good to see you, Patterson. You're looking better than the last time."

Right. Captain was a good man but a liar and too

political. He wasn't about to let Jerry know he looked like death ready to happen.

"You wanted to see me?"

His captain's eyes raked over him, his brows drew together as if displeased, his lips pursed. "Yes. You did an excellent job overseas, Major. That list saved the lives of several of our men. I'm well aware you were sent home to recuperate and gain your strength back. The military appreciates your efforts."

The man's bushy brows drew together as he pierced the blind front Jerry used to keep people at bay.

Jerry felt his insides twisting, twisting, threatening to crumble into pieces. He clamped teeth together and willed his hand not to shake when he lifted and rubbed it across the side of his head.

"In fact, we value your service so much we believe you can serve us now."

"I don't understand, sir."

"You can serve your country. If you will."

A good play on his loyalties. They must be desperate to want a lame man's help.

"You need to be aware of what we've caught wind of. There's a two-fold threat."

"Sir?"

Fingers steepled, the man opposite him leaned forward. "Our sources reported suspicious people entering our country."

"People? And I need to know this because...?"

"Why do you think—in the time of war—an elite, valuable military German would suddenly leave his service for his country and evacuate to the U.S.?"

Rhoderick?

Was the captain saying Rhoderick had come to America? Nonsense. He'd never give up his place, all he'd worked for—the advancements, the prestige, the possibilities—for what?

Only one possibility. Revenge. Pay back for the death of his sister. Pay back for the loss of his so-called honor. Payback for losing out on the biggest piece of espionage he'd probably done.

"You think it's Rhoderick."

"We suspect, yes." Captain Philip leaned forward,

propping his elbows on his desk, lacing his fingers together.

"Or someone he sent." Jerry infected his voice with casualness and disinterest. Did the man really think he, a cripple, could stop someone like Rhoderick?

"Possibly. We think he's been sent here to find viable spots to drop a bomb."

"Anyway that's possible?"

"If they can befriend the right people they can get access to the information."

"But that would only be a very few people. Right?"

"Yes...and a lot of background checks has been done on those few. Still, something may have missed our guys' research."

"Hard to believe he would agree to do such a thing. He might be involved in a lot of things behind the scenes but actually committing the dirty work is a whole lot different."

"Not so hard when you take account he has his sights on you—" His captain's eyes narrowed. "My sources say he's here and has been asking questions."

"Is that right? What proof do you have that it's him, and how on earth could he gain entrance during war? "

Captain slammed both hands on the desktop and cursed. With a dangerous look in his eyes, he stood. "So it doesn't matter that all the questions were concerning your wife?"

"Josie?" Shock, terror and deadly calm swarmed over him in rapid succession. Jerry shoved his chair backward. He watched it fall in slow motion and made no move to stop it.

"Someone is definitely bonkers and sending out false information." He couldn't have stopped the sarcasm spewing from his mouth if he'd been facing the firing squad. "Coming off a bender, I'd say."

But it wasn't.

Who was he kidding? He'd known deep inside, Rhoderick would never let the theft slide. And the death of his sister? Vanda?

The icy shiver that crawled up his back was answer enough.

Captain Philip Bosworth might be a rough man, but

he had a kind heart. Obviously, he'd decided to overlook Jerry's rudeness.

"Why would he be interested in Josie? He doesn't even know she exists..."

His captain lifted a brow. "Easy enough to find out if you're determined and have a motive. And he does have, doesn't he?"

Somehow the man had made enough inquiries to find out. What was more reasonable than to go after a murderer's wife for revenge? And he was to blame for Vanda Rhoderick's death more than the unknown man who'd shot the bullet into her back. He'd used her to get close to Rhoderick. He'd encouraged her attention to cover his tracks. He'd lied and lied and lied to get what he wanted, what his country had requested of him. If it hadn't been for him, Vanda would be alive and living a good life with her cousin.

Yeah, he was to blame.

And it was something he couldn't escape.

That was fine, but asking Josie—or worse, not asking her but forcing it on her from his own actions—no, he couldn't, wouldn't do that. Josie didn't deserve to suffer because of his mistakes.

"What can I do?"

~*~

Had a week passed already? It felt like a month—no, a year—had gone by.

Jerry could feel Josie's glances. Studied. Curious. A little bit timid. He could have smiled at the suggestion. He didn't believe Josie had ever felt timidity. From the moment of her birth, he suspected she'd grasped hold and wrung life for every vestige of excitement she could get. That was his Josie.

No, not his. Not now. He wouldn't hold her to a marriage agreement he'd tainted.

She cleared her throat.

Jerry sat his cup down hard. "What is it? Just spit it out."

A touch of anger flashed across her features but not enough to allow her to use it. Mostly hurt filled her big eyes, and Jerry's heart almost softened. Instead he held his stolid gaze and waited.

"I-I thought, I mean, Tyrell wants us to dine with them tonight. Afterwards they're having a special service at the church to pray for our country and to talk about what we can do to help. We'll walk there to enjoy the weather, then return home."

"Since when have you started loving church so much?" He hated himself for the derogatory tone. Hated his crassness when the almost undetectable flinch registered in her body.

"I don't. It's just—"

"Just what? Don't expect me to toddy to your family's wishes anymore."

"I didn't know we ever had."

Her words were low, her eyes downcast, and the one glance she threw him showed only a spark of defiance. It was gone before he could pinpoint it. Her shoulders slumped forward. "I don't expect anything from you, Jerry. Stay home. I'll go tonight by myself and slip out early if I get bored."

No. Jerry bit back the objection. He had no right to tell her what she could or could not do. Yet the fear of Rhoderick getting his hands on her instilled such a horror in him, he'd be willing to suffer a church service, even two or three or—he desperately hoped not—for the rest of his life to protect her.

Willing or not, his evening was now planned. The half-formed plan of wandering the city for a hint of the whereabouts of his enemy was not to be carried out tonight. Protecting Josie was priority.

~*~

She'd skipped the dinner at her family's home, and should have backed out of the church service too. She'd only indicated to Jerry she was going to coax him to go, to be with him. But, obviously, her presence at any event wouldn't make a difference to her husband.

Josie fastened the wide belt around her waist and eyed her boyish figure in the mirror. Too skinny. Too dull. Certainly not a figure to attract a man's attention, even her husband's.

If only Jerry would show some interest in something. Anything.

Preferably her.

That wasn't going to happen.

Whatever Jerry had gone through while serving in this awful war, it'd been enough to change him. Always sullen in an attractive way, it hadn't affected their relationship before. She'd loved his sexy voice, his sultry handsome face.

Now?

Now they seemed to have nothing.

Josie unbuckled the belt and tossed it aside, then savagely tightened the new, flashy one around her waist. Claire had given it to her last Christmas but she'd never worn it. But tonight, flashy or not, she'd wear it. She shrugged the shoulder and neckline down lower, showing more of her skin.

If Jerry didn't like it, too bad.

There was no sign of her husband when she approached the front door, and Josie sighed. She'd hoped—

Had she not learned anything since his return? Hoping was useless.

She flung open the door and stopped. Jerry leaned against a porch post, a cigarette dangling from one side of his mouth. He seemed to be studying the neighborhood, and when he at last rested his gaze on her, Josie thought she detected a slight tilt of the lips.

"Finally ready? Since when do you dawdle over your looks?"

Not the best greeting in the world, but one he would have made jokingly before he left for the service. A tossed-back comment from her, and they'd both been engulfed in gales of laughter.

Before the words could be voiced, he turned away. "Let's go."

Josie flung her wrap over her shoulders and hurried to follow her husband.

Jerry didn't speak as they started down the sidewalk. But at the street he laid a hand on her arm and stopped her.

Her gaze flicked to his hand then to his face.

His stance was stiff and guarded, his gaze darting from house to house. Only after a minute did he relax. "All right."

"Jerry? What's wrong?"

"Don't badger me. It's nothing for you to worry about."

"But—"

He shook off her clutch at his coat sleeve and opened the gate. "Let's just get this over with." He nodded toward the Rayner house. "Here they come. Did you let them know we were going?"

"No."

"Josie, you decided to come. I'm so glad." Josie's older sister and her husband, Tyrell Walker, hurried down the sidewalk. Emma Jaine slipped her arms around Josie and gave her a hug. "We missed you at dinner tonight. Really hoped you'd make it."

Best to ignore that comment. She didn't want to have the discussion again of why she needed to attend church regularly or visit more often at her home, or any of the million items her sister thought she should be or do.

Tyrell nodded at Jerry. "Glad you came along."

"Sweetheart, we need to go." Emma Jaine, the ever-eternal time puncher, smiled at her husband. "It won't do for the pastor to be late."

"Sure. Jerry, walk with me. We haven't had a chance to talk since you've been home."

A slight hesitation, a look cast at Josie, then he walked off with his brother-in-law.

Josie watched them go, but when Emma Jaine linked her arm in Josie's, she let her lead her down the street.

"How are you and Jerry doing?" Emma Jaine's voice was low.

Emma Jaine had always been the sister Josie looked up to. Smart, vivacious and lovely, she was the image of a young wife in love and a mother who couldn't wait for the birth of her child. Emma Jaine and Tyrell were a well-adjusted family. Stuffy and normal.

Nothing at all like Josie saw herself and Jerry, and certainly not the image she wanted to attain.

"He's still not talking. Goes on a lot of walks late at night."

"That's too bad. Tyrell and I have been praying for him."

Her lip trembled, and she bit down hard on it. "I don't think he's coming back."

"Don't, dear. He will. It takes time after experiencing the horrors of war. Don't lose hope."

Easy enough to say when you didn't have to live with a stranger.

"When's your next competition?"

"Two weeks. Diana says it's a tough one."

"Are you worried?" Emma Jaine smiled at her.

"No. Not really. I know I'm good."

"You are. Still, don't get over confident. An attitude like that could be your downfall."

Sisterly advice unwanted and unneeded. Diana, her trainer, passed out more than Josie wanted after every practice.

"Where's Papa? Isn't he coming?"

"I think he's coming down with a cold, and I ordered him to stay home. He grumped about it, but Shirley backed me up so he had no choice but to acquiesce."

"Poor Papa. What's he to do when surrounded by a lot of women who thinks the sun rises and sets for him?"

Emma Jaine's beautiful hazel eyes laughed at her. "He loves it, and you know it."

"I do. But I'm afraid I've given him more heartache than laughter."

"I won't deny you've been a handful, but I think Papa's always admired his tomboy daughter. His love's not conditional on our behavior."

"Taken straight from Pastor Tyrell Walker's mouth."

"Silly girl. Why shouldn't I quote the dearest man in the world?"

"You love him a lot, don't you?"

"More than life itself." Emma Jaine drew in a long breath. "Don't you, with Jerry?"

The pain that clutched at her heart forced her to catch her breath. "I wanted to die when he was missing in action. I thought he was dead. But when he came home—the way he is now—it's worse than death. I think I'm going out of my mind half the time, and the other half, I want to scream and stomp and force him to be like he was before."

She hated the catch in her voice.

"Poor Josie. All the demonstrative reenactments from childhood won't bring the results you crave. You know it, and that's what's so frustrating, isn't it?"

Her sister's words were true, and it hurt even worse. Emma Jaine's understanding. Papa's advice. Her own savage wishes. There was absolutely nothing she could do.

Emma Jaine stared at her, the pity so obvious Josie wanted to protest.

Josie looked away. She didn't want pity. She wanted Jerry.

~*~

His brother-in-law was a good chap in his own way. A little too involved in other people's lives, but Jerry supposed Tyrell was only doing his duty as a minister, at least as far as he could see.

Jerry had never understood why Tyrell hadn't joined the service. He'd not talked about it, but then Jerry gave him no opportunity. What with his and Josie's whirlwind courtship and eloping, then joining the service right after, he'd been much too busy to worry about someone else. The fiasco in Germany had driven the desire to meddle in someone else's life right out of him. It was all he could do to cope with his own.

Tyrell talked in an animated tone about a couple of new projects, the community and the coming of his child.

Jerry stiffened. He'd never thought about having children of his own. His father had not been an object of admiration in spite of his wealth. Jerry had worked long and hard to become anything but like his paternal parent. He wasn't after his father's money and wasn't about to bend to his wishes to get it.

He'd make it on his own, or he would have if it hadn't been for—

His bum leg took that moment to throb, and Jerry rubbed a hand down his aching thigh.

Tyrell immediately noticed. "You all right? Shall we slow down?"

Pity? Jerry could stand anything but pity.

"Don't worry about it. I'm fine. You don't want to be late."

"Sure?"

Not trusting himself to speak, Jerry nodded. His good looking brother-in-law, the epitome of strength and health, the family man everyone looked up to as if he was God himself—he couldn't endure sympathy from him.

Almost, Jerry opened his mouth to scald the man beside him with curses, but stopped himself. Tyrell had always been friendly and understanding, and there wasn't an ounce of pity to be seen anywhere in him.

The grimace Jerry tossed Tyrell's way would have to suffice for a smile.

~*~

The service hadn't been as bad as Jerry thought it would be. In fact, quite nice as far as church services went. Tyrell was a born speaker, and if his heart wasn't warmed, it wasn't from Tyrell's efforts.

He stepped to the doors of the church and peered out. The dark had claimed the early evening. No street lights were on, but the moon was bright and lit up the area quite well. The worshipers exited the building and scattered in groups about the church yard, lingering, talking, wanting the brief moments of fellowship to blot out any war thoughts. Some drifted toward the street. A few hurried toward home away from the chilly late winter air.

Jerry studied the people, searching for the one figure he didn't want to find. No blond hair stood out, but it wouldn't as most of the men wore hats. But three men caught his attention. One on the southeast corner, and the other two, smoking, and laughing hilariously, almost as if they'd had too much to drink. Their occasional glances at the church attenders leaving the sanctuary didn't bother him so much. But the loner seemed to be staring soberly and steadily toward the stone church, examining each departee. Had the man stared a fraction too long at him?

Surely Rhoderick wouldn't be so blatant as to stand in the open inviting recognition.

Wouldn't he?

Defying Jerry. Taunting him. Daring him to approach.

Rhoderick's grief over the loss of his beloved sister could have made him mad with revenge.

Jerry glanced back into the church. Josie was behind him, but talking with Emma Jaine and a couple other ladies. He caught her eye and mouthed the words, "Let's go."

His admiration for his wife rose as he watched her. No hesitation, no questions asked, just an immediate move to follow his lead. Good girl.

When she reached him, he clasped her arm and repeated the words. "Let's go now."

He tucked her hand in the crook of his arm and whispered. "Stay close."

His mind registered her silent obedience, but his gaze swept the street again before stepping outside the church yard. No sign of the one lone guy standing at the corner leaning against the lamp post. A third guy had joined the two drunk men and they stood smoking, backs to the church.

The single man had vanished. Or was hiding. Waiting?

Which was all the more worrisome. He much preferred having his enemies where he could see them.

By the time they'd walked half way home, Jerry relaxed enough to let loose of her arm.

"What is it?"

"I told you. It's nothing for—"

They turned the corner onto the street where they lived, and Jerry glanced back.

Halfway down the block, a man followed them in a long gray coat and a Homburg hat. Just like the ones Rhoderick favored back in Germany.

Chapter Eleven

It was going to rain. From last week's cold, but sunny days when he and Josie had attended the Wednesday night special service, the weather had gone ballistic.

Jerry studied the dark gray clouds rolling across the sky. He clenched his frozen fingers and averted his eyes from the depressing scene. Too much like the Germany skies in winter. How he longed for the sunshine—even better, summer. Perhaps he and Josie could move to Florida.

No. That wouldn't work. He'd already decided Josie should not be forced to put up with a cripple the rest of her life, and he was pretty sure that was what the doctors had hinted at two months ago. Go easy. Rest. Look for—his body tensed.

He'd kill himself before he'd take a desk job.

But what else could he do? Josie deserved a man. A man who could look after her the way she needed. He hadn't missed the looks her family had cast each other when they thought he wasn't paying attention.

Her father was the worst. Not that he'd said a word, and that's what bothered him the most. The old man held his tongue, but his eyes gave him away. Concern must be eating away at him.

Not that he blamed him. If he had a daughter like Josie... He'd grab her and run as far as he could from a man like himself. The commendations and praise for his work in Germany did nothing for the blackness inside him.

Still it was too late to change things now. Even if he let Josie go—gave her her freedom—it was his responsibility to support her. To give her enough to live on so she'd always have a good time. And he definitely was responsible for her safety. If the whispers were true, then she was already on Rhoderick's radar.

So that brought him back around to: what was he going to do? Take the job offer from his father? The demand. The order.

The letter he'd received from his father right after he'd arrived back in the states still blazed a trail of hate across his mind.

I hope you've come to your senses! If you would have only listened to me in the first place you'd not be in the almost worthless state you're in. You wouldn't be whittled down to such uselessness as the doctors informed me. But maybe it was all for the best.

I'm willing to forgive. Come back and claim what you should have done years ago. You'll have to work hard to prove yourself, and to be frank, for me to know you have the loyalty and strength I strove to instill within you as a child, but if you do as you're told, soon enough you'll rise in the company...

He hadn't read the rest. Crumpling it, he'd tossed it and the words out of his mind. Until now. Not even for Josie would he ever work for his father.

The fence shook when he pounded it, and he heard the crack as the rusted iron rail let out a shrieking moan in protest. He shot an alarmed glance at the house, afraid he'd awaken Josie and she'd run out to check on him. He'd always loved her concern. No matter what he was doing, if she hadn't spoken to him in awhile, he'd hear her pattering footsteps running—never walking—to see what he was up to. She'd stand on tiptoe to kiss...

The hand that clamped onto his shoulder sent him inches in the air. He whirled, his fists raised and ready, and almost slugged his father-in-law.

Captain Ossie's voice broke the quiet evening as he ducked the punch he must have suspected was coming. "Hang it up, Jerry. Sorry, didn't mean to—thought you'd hear me clomping down the sidewalk."

He would have too if he hadn't been so self-absorbed in his own miseries. He bit back the curse that almost slid from his tongue. It wasn't Captain Ossie's fault he was a walking mass of nerves.

He turned away and thrust his bone-cold hand into his coat pocket. If he hadn't been shaking so much, he'd try to light one of the cigarettes he seldom smoked.

The Captain was talking, and Jerry forced himself to listen.

"Thought I saw someone out here, and since I couldn't get my head around financial statements tonight, I decided to take a walk around the block, meet Tyrell and walk back with him. And check on the loitering gentleman too."

His voice was calm and soothing with a touch of laughter in it, and Jerry's tense body relaxed.

"Wanna walk with me?"

Jerry hesitated then nodded. Might as well. He wasn't ready to return to the house yet.

Captain Ossie randomly talked of the boarding house, of his daughters, the boarders' latest antics, and Jerry only half listened to the calm voice. He'd always admired the captain—the way his girls adored him, his forceful, yet not overpowering way he had with keeping order in the boarding house, and his intelligence. He suspected the man knew more than he let on in most situations.

"Wondered if you'd do me a favor?"

Jerry tensed again and shot a glance at his father-in-law.

"Emma Jaine's rented one of the smaller rooms to an injured soldier who's really down in the dumps. Thought if you and Josie could come over a few nights a week, you might cheer him up."

Meaning the soldier and himself had a lot in common: injuries.

"Josie's always a lot of fun and good for laughter too. Think you could talk her into it?"

Right. As if he would have to. "I don't know. I'm awful busy right now."

Feeble excuse.

"I realize that, but it wouldn't take much time to spend two, three evening hours. Emma Jaine's just about to worry herself to death over him, and I've run out of encouraging things to say to him."

He seriously doubted that.

The pause stretched long. Jerry tried to wait it out, but his own guilty conscience warred against his determination not to get caught up in this family mine trap.

From the time he and Josie had initiated their elopement to the present day, he'd heard no declamations from the old man or any of the family. As much as Jerry hated to admit it, he owed the man. Ossie Rayner's support and the down payment on their house was a god-send, and a gift that made it possible for Jerry to leave for the service much more at ease.

So yeah, he guessed he owed him a little.

"Can't promise anything, but I'll see what we've got planned. Might be able to join you an evening or so." His lips curled as he heard his grudging concession.

"Swell. Sure you'll do the trick with Guy."

"Guy?"

"Yeah. The soldier. Doesn't talk much, but when he does, he speaks slowly as if uneducated and afraid of showing it. But he's a good sort, and all the residents like him."

"Where's he seen action?"

Captain Ossie shrugged. "Didn't say, and I didn't want to pry into his business too much. I know from my own past experience it's not a favorite topic of discussion."

An ugly fearful thought shook him. Surely it wouldn't—couldn't—be Winfried Rhoderick. He wouldn't be that bold, and Jerry knew he wasn't stupid enough to place himself in a position to get caught.

The sudden tenseness oozed from his body like melting chocolate.

"There's another thing I'd like to talk with you about while we're alone."

What now?

"Emma Jaine, Tyrell and I have talked about it and would like for you and Josie to be the baby's godparents."

Jerry stared at his father-in-law. Had the man lost his senses or was Jerry losing his hearing? Tyrell and Emma Jaine couldn't have made a worse choice. In fact, if Jerry took after his paternal parent, he'd be the lowest sort of person to choose to fulfill the role. Besides, what did he know about kids? The only thing he knew, they were into everything, noisy and always in the way.

Just the way his father had constantly described him.

"I don't know about that. Can't you get someone else

to do it? Surely there's someone in your church..."

Captain Ossie was shaking his head. "No, they insist it should be you and Josie, and I agree. They want you and Josie to do it."

"I'm no good with kids, and Josie's had no experience with them."

The man laughed and clapped Jerry on the shoulder. "Quit trying to get out of it. I'm afraid they've both quite set their minds on it and won't change them."

Jerry felt himself weakening, and he'd never felt weak in his life, not even when injured in Germany and depending on Vanda's cousin to get him out of the country. Not even when facing Josie, knowing he had to let her go, that he was a rope around her slender neck.

"Well...I'll talk to Josie—"

"Knew we could count on you."

Tyrell's church was just ahead, the gray-white stone almost a glow in the dark with the pale orb street lights reflecting off the sides. It was a strong building, the exact kind of place where a family like the Rayners would attend. It exuded an aura of assurance and strength.

It was almost blackout time. Past time to slip away from Captain Ossie to the corner café for a cup of coffee. If he dawdled long enough, Josie would have gone to bed, and hopefully, be asleep when he returned.

As they approached the church something moved in the enclaved shadow of the church doors. Jerry strained to see if it was a cat—or a person.

Rhoderick?

He grabbed his father-in-law's arm. "Someone's waiting at the church door. Better hang back till I see who it is."

He could sense the man beside him shaking his head, but he paid no mind. He hobbled as quickly as he could toward the doorway—aware that the captain was right behind him—at the same time as the person moved from the shadows. Instantly he realized it couldn't be Rhoderick.

His breath shushed from between his lips, and he slowed abruptly.

It was a kid, maybe twelve or fourteen. He trotted toward the two men and thrust out a folded sheet of paper at them. "Which of you is Patterson?"

"I am. What is this?" Jerry held out a hand. "What's your name, kid?"

The boy backed away, almost stumbling, then turned and shot off before Jerry could stop him. He stared after the lad wishing he'd had the sense to hold onto him.

At the same time, the pastor, Tyrell Walker stepped out of the church and walked toward them. "What's happening?"

Captain Ossie was talking, explaining what had just happened. Jerry heard but ignored them. He glanced down at the paper. Dove gray with distinct raised impressions, the paper reminded him of something...but what? He'd seen it before. He knew he had, but couldn't remember where. .

Too dark to see. He hustled over to the dim street light and held the paper closer.

How's Josephine doing ALONE tonight? Or is she alone?

That was it. No more information. No signature. Jerry frowned down at the scrolled lettering in fancy script. What on earth? Jerry's grip on the paper tightened ripping it half way down the page.

A friend feeling sorry for Josie at home alone? Emma Jaine or no one he knew would use such a sinister method of pointing out his mistakes.

Someone alerting him to the fact Josie was with another man? His heart seemed to quit pounding. Never.

The streetlight flickered and went out the same instant it hit him.

That paper. The color, the impressions—the very same his enemy had used in Germany. Winfried Rhoderick had Josie.

"What is it?" Captain Ossie demanded.

"Josie's in danger. Gotta get back to the house now."

Tyrell asked no questions. "Then let's go."

The pastor kept pace beside him, Captain Ossie following behind, as Jerry hurried as fast as he could, limping at a speed that seemed as slow as a turtle when his beloved needed him.

He was still two blocks away when his leg gave out. Jerry stumbled and grabbed onto the wooden fence to steady himself. He waved at Tyrell. "Go, man. I've got to rest a minute."

Tyrell took off, and Jerry watched him go, the bitterness in his heart leaving a bad taste in his mouth. The love of his life perhaps suffering at the hands of his enemy, and he had to leave her rescue up to his brother-in-law.

"Never mind, my lad." Captain Ossie laid a hand on Jerry's shoulder.

Perversely, he wanted to shake it off, but he wouldn't do that to the old man regardless of his own savage feelings.

Jerry took off again, but at a slower pace. The pain in his leg was unbearable the last hundred feet, but no worse than the terror in his heart. He limped up to the open door and started inside just as Tyrell stepped out.

"She's not here, Jerry."

His worst nightmare had come true. Rhoderick had her. Jerry slumped against the wall and ran a hand over his face. The groan building inside him finally exploded from between his lips in roaring words. "What have I done?"

"Maybe she's with Emma Jaine." Captain Ossie wasn't as nonchalant as he was letting on if his sweat-covered face was any indication. "I'll run home and see."

"Let me go." Tyrell insisted, and at Captain Ossie's nod, sped across the lawn.

Jerry watched him running. "He has her."

"Who has her? You're not making sense."

Shaking his head, Jerry straightened and drew in a long breath.

"Then come inside and let me make you a cup of tea. Or do you prefer coffee?" Captain Ossie didn't wait for Jerry's assent. "We can figure out what to do."

Jerry jerked his head in reluctant agreement and limped to the kitchen. He had to think. What to do?

Josie's father set about making coffee and ignored Jerry's mutterings. Thankfully, the man had the decency to refrain from small talk. He poured the steaming brew in two cups and pushed one toward Jerry.

"I can't sit here." Jerry jumped to his feet, but the older man motioned for him to sit again.

"There's absolutely no sense in going off half-cocked and edgy. Take a few sips of your coffee, then we'll plan our offense."

"That sounds ominous." Jerry started to chuckle, then stopped himself. How could he when a mad man might very well be hurting Josie? He moaned and rubbed his forehead.

"I'd like to help." Captain Ossie blew on then sipped his coffee. "Care to tell me why you think someone has Josie?"

The information his general had shared with him burned a hole in his mind, but it wasn't something he could share with his father-in-law. Or was it? With plenty of editing? "It's nothing. Military situation I'm dealing with from my last assignment. I'm being paranoid, as usual. Nothing for you to worry about."

The white-haired man lowered his head and studied Jerry. Carefully setting his cup on the table top, he folded his hands together and stared down at them for several minutes. When he looked up, he nodded.

Why did he want to squirm like a child?

"Son, did I ever tell you about my time serving during WWI? And the trouble I was in?"

"You?"

The captain nodded. "I wasn't actually signed up but was asked to "help out" occasionally with carrying supplies and ammunitions on my boats and ships when needed. To make a long story short, a new man came along, and to my defense, he was highly recommended by certain ones. He won my trust, and we became very good friends. I rewarded him with advancement in my business, ousting a guy who'd worked for me for years, who was loyal and a hard worker. I gave the new guy his job, and demoted my faithful employee."

The older man rubbed a hand over his head. "Trouble was, my wife couldn't warm up to this guy who dined in our home many a time. When I asked her why she felt the way she did, she could never explain except to say there was something wrong about him."

The agony that still showed in his father-in-law only echoed Jerry's own feelings.

"By the time I realized he was a spook, he'd already

passed on several details to which he had access. Fortunately, I was able to expose him before too much damage was done, but I still blame myself for what happened. How could I have been so blind? I not only allowed a spy to steal information but lost a good man's friendship and loyalty."

"Why are you telling me this?" Jerry asked. "I know you have a reason."

"Of course." The man's eyes twinkled. "Because I'm sure you saw or experienced some things overseas that trouble you. Don't let whatever it was destroy you. We've all been there, and if anyone can sympathize, I can."

"But you don't know—" Jerry despised the tremble in his voice.

"That's right, and I don't need to know unless you want to share. The thing is, I believe you've beat yourself up for happenings in Germany. But I also believe you love Josie and are a good man. Your cap—" Captain Ossie broke off, then went on. "Focus on finding Josie. Let me help. In the meantime, Tyrell's checking at the house to make sure Josie didn't run over there for some late evening hot chocolate with Claire or Shirley. I'll contact a couple people I know to see if they have heard anything by way of the grapevine. And, Jerry, think about what I said."

Jerry sat with downcast eyes as Josie's father left, disturbed at how close his father-in-law had come to the truth.

By the time Tyrell reported back that no one at the Rayner house had seen or talked with Josie today, Jerry had poured the rest of his coffee into the sink drain. Where could she be? He knew what her normal routine was, but Josie didn't always keep to the normal. She'd skipped out of many meals and functions at the Rayner boarding house and been the trial of Emma Jaine's life with her unorthodox habits.

But tonight? When he thought he had her safely tucked in their own home, away from vengeful and handsome German men?

He couldn't sit here and do nothing.

Jerry didn't know anything about Josie's present day haunts but he could venture a guess. The pond would no doubt still rank high on her list of favorite places, and it would be as good a place to start as any.

No lights lit the night, but Jerry didn't care. Other than his inability to use his sight as a protective measure, his other senses were kicking in. This uncanny ability to hear what others didn't, to feel what others ignored, had served him well in the military and helped him to progress higher in military rank than those who didn't or couldn't do the same.

Now, as he limped his way down Mulberry street, bound for the pond, he sensed before he heard the rapid tapping of shoes, the presence of another person heading toward him.

Jerry edged toward a tall oak, pressed against it, blending, and still as a stone, waited.

The faint panting, as if the person had been running, lifted his brows, but the slowed-down walking pace, as if to catch their breath, kept him quiet. There was a mutter but much too low to understand the words.

But he caught the voice and knew it.

Josie.

He stepped away from the tree and spoke her name softly, hoping to not startle her. He didn't succeed.

With a shriek, short and soft as it was, Josie was in his arms, babbling.

"Sorry. I didn't mean to startle you like that."

"No, *I'm* sorry. I know you didn't mean to."

She was rattled a bit, or she would have never rambled like this. Jerry felt his lips stretching into a smile. Josie could always do that to him. Make him laugh at the most inopportune moments.

Then he remembered.

He drew back and took hold of her shoulders. "What are you doing out this time of the night? Don't you realize how dangerous it is?"

"Silly..."

He could feel her staring at him, grinning up him, teasing him—like she used to do. Before he—

"...The night doesn't frighten me. Not normally."

His senses jumped straight up in the air. "What do you mean?"

She hesitated, and that in itself alerted Jerry

something was wrong. Josie, never, ever hesitated. She jumped in with both feet, always with something to say. At least, to him.

"I don't know. I couldn't sleep, so maybe that was the problem. I decided I would go to the pond and work off some energy for awhile. But..."

"Tell me now." Jerry shook her, just a bit, his voice too tense, and he regretted it immediately and softened his voice. "I need to know, Jo."

"After I got there, I began feeling like I was being watched."

"You didn't see anyone?"

"No. But it was so strong, it almost felt overpowering. Isn't that silly? I've never felt overpowered in my life."

She was rambling again, but the terror leaped on him, tried to strangle him, and tied his body as tight as a bound mummy. Josie was no dummy. If she felt a presence, then someone was there. She didn't cry wolf when dogs lapped her fingers.

With a jerk, Jerry pulled her tight against his body, his arms wrapped around her. He could feel the tension leaving her body, felt the moment she leaned into him, and tears choked his throat. How he loved this woman.

Her wild mop of hair tickled his chin as she rubbed her head against his chest, and he almost picked her up to gallop home with her.

And once again, his acute memory sprang to life. He couldn't. He couldn't gallop anywhere. And he'd already made that unspoken promise to her to let her go. Give her, her freedom.

He spread his arms and stepped back, but then gripped her arm. "We need to get home now."

She didn't utter a word, only turned and kept pace with him as he moved.

"Promise me you will never do this again. I don't want you to go out by yourself again. Promise me now."

"Jerry—" she was laughing.

"Now, Josie! It's too dangerous, and I can't protect you if I don't know where you are." His voice had sharpened, and he regretted it, but he was too scared for her to back down.

There was a second—or two—of silence, and then she

agreed. "I promise, Jerry. I don't understand, but I promise."

She would too. That was his Josie.

Chapter Twelve

He'd been brought in to keep an eye on Josie Patterson and be prepared to carry out further action if and when it was necessary. For now, reporting on her activities was the bulk of his work.

He'd scared her last night. He hadn't meant to, but he'd clumsily stumbled over a branch, and that had alerted her of someone's presence. After that, her often and suspicious glances told him she was uneasy.

He'd not met the woman, but he'd heard enough from the others in the boarding house to know she was a smart, talented person.

There was only one problem with the whole scenario. The more he learned about her, the more he learned about the whole family, the worse he felt about this job of his.

Chapter Thirteen

Jerry could hear his wife laughing even though he was in the next room—the next room being a spare bedroom. What was making her so happy this morning?

The sky beyond the window was as gloomy as the previous day's with no hope for some sunny weather. Jerry wanted to roll over and go back to sleep, but the sense of urgency to *do* something dug at him. He didn't have time to lounge around and play as if he was a mellow man.

That thought wasn't any more cheering, but he ignored it and pushed himself to rise. He groaned at the sudden aching in his bum leg. Useless thing. Anger like an enraged beast swept through him, but he gritted his teeth and held back the words he wanted to spew out at the world. Wouldn't do any good. He'd already tried that, and it had no effect on his leg.

Twenty minutes later, he limped his way down the stairs, the aroma of coffee filling his nostrils. That was one bright spot. Josie's spot-on battery acid.

He headed down the hall when a blur of chestnut red hair, rumpled clothes and a slim body tore from a side room and slammed into him.

It almost knocked him off balance, but he recovered and held out a hand. "You gone bonkers this morning, Jo?" He couldn't help it. Josie brought the teasing out of him like a farm hand squeezed the milk from a moody cow.

She waved a piece of paper at him before tossing it onto the table and heading into the kitchen to pour him a cup of coffee. "I'm in a buzz."

"Drinking this early?" Jerry's brows shot up at her exclamation.

"Sweetie, I had a brainchild, and it was the cat's meow."

"And what would that idea be?" Jerry took his first sip

of coffee. Had he died and gone to heaven?

"My dear brother-in-law wants us to be godparents of their baby."

"Yeah, your father told me."

Josie cocked her head and eyed him. "What'd you tell him?"

"Whadda you think?"

She placed her hands flat on the table and leaned in, her hair flopping into her face. "I say we agree...but only if we get to name the little darling."

"Josie, you are..." He didn't finish the thought. That was a place he had no intention of going. Allowing himself to get altogether too cozy with his wife. How could he ever let her go after that? He couldn't. "And your name choices would be?"

She laughed. "I thought Hank would be a perfect boy's name—"

Jerry burst out laughing.

"—and for the girl, why not Bette? I kind of remember Emma Jaine had a thing for that name."

"I dare you." He'd not laughed so hard since...Germany. Vanda.

Jerry stood up so abruptly, the chair flew backward and hit the floor with a bang. The hallway never looked so long, but he grabbed his coat as he opened the door, Josie's troubled voice behind him.

He didn't look back. He didn't want to see her distressed face.

~*~

Josie wanted to cry, but she didn't. She wanted to hurl angry words at the man she loved who was hurting and disturbed, but she knew better. Papa's words still rang in her ears. *You're going to have to be stronger than you've ever been in your life.*

She'd not cried herself to sleep, not last night, for the first time since Jerry had returned to her life. It was because of that terrifying hug he'd given her when they'd met on the street.

Why he'd been so afraid, she had no idea, but if it calmed him, she'd promise anything. Even to staying home at night, although she had no intention of doing so. Night time was her favorite practicing time. The best time to work, and she couldn't give it up. As long as she returned before that stroke of midnight, the time he'd returned home every night...Well, Jerry would never need to know.

The note from Emma Jaine beckoned, and Josie picked it up again and smiled. She loved it that Tyrell and her sister wanted them—she and Jerry—to be the godparents. Those two weren't making a great choice, but if that's what they wanted, well, she would give it a shot.

Of course, she was teasing with Jerry. Never would she mention the names, Hank and Bette, to Emma Jaine. It would break her sister's heart, even if Josie did it in fun. She loved her overbearing sister too much to want to hurt her.

The kitchen was a mess. Jerry hadn't eaten a bite of the overcooked, scrambled eggs—a product from and thanks to the Rayner house housekeeper who raised the chickens along with the Victory garden she was so proud of—and Josie had no appetite. She hated to waste them, but...

With a guilty glance around, she scraped them into the waste bin, and ran through the chores as quickly as she could, sweeping errant crumbs in the corner, straightening the least she could to make everything cozy and tidy.

The only place she took the time to do right, was their bedroom. She pulled out the wrinkles in the sheets, smoothed the quilt until, if it shone, would have looked like glass, and plumped Jerry's pillow till it was light and fluffy, although it was as fluffy as it'd been last night.

No dear, dark head had indented it. No musky smell from his cologne scented it even when Josie pressed it to her nose. Her imagination was as strong as she needed, though, and she breathed in deeply, remembering.

Enough of this. She did a hasty dressing for the day, grabbed her skates and headed out the door. First stop: the Rayner House, next door.

Jonah Mason, the house's chauffeur and all-around employee, greeted Josie when she burst into the hallway. "Good morning, Miss Josephine. I see you're up early and ready for the day."

His affectionate smile warmed her heart. She'd not had much warmth lately, not with Jerry...

Josie hastily shut the door on that thought.

"Is everyone up and about, Jonah?"

"Most. I drove Claire to her day of music study downtown. Your father's in his study, Mr. Walker's at the church, and Mrs. Emma Jaine's going over the week's menus with Harriet."

"Thanks, Jonah." Josie scurried down the hallway straight to the kitchen—one of her favorite rooms in this big, ancient house. Funny how every time she set foot in it, a kinda nostalgic feeling swept over her, in spite of loving her own home. Hers was too big for just Jerry and herself. When she thought about it, the image of kids—lots of them—sprang to her mind.

But that was ridiculous. She was way too busy, too focused on getting what she wanted, and well, she wasn't sure she ever wanted kids.

She was sure as anything Jerry didn't.

Shaking off another unwanted thought, she burst into the kitchen. "Harriet, I hope you have some hot chocolate simmering on that back burner."

Harriet snorted and rose. "Now when have you ever wanted chocolate, and I've not had it? Kind of thin nowadays what with the rations." She shook her head, gave Josie a sly look and poured a cup, then scooted it over to her. "I figured this rationing was coming and made sure to keep back a goodly supply. That's why you can have your occasional cup, Josie, and you better be plenty thankful for it."

Josie sipped and insisted, "Still the best in Cincinnati, thin or not."

"How's Jerry?" Emma Jaine's hazel eyes were big with concern.

The shrug Josie affected was anything but what she wanted to show. "About the same. Once in awhile I see a glimpse of the Jerry I fell in love with, but most times he's morose and sullen."

"Tyrell and I are still praying, Josie."

What good did that do? Josie wanted to voice the question, but wouldn't. Hurting her older sister wasn't in her plans this morning. "Stopped by to let you know Jerry and I accept—reluctantly—the honor of being godparents to the baby."

"Josie, I'm thrilled. We can rest easy now, knowing he or she will always have someone to love and look after them."

Really? Did they really think they were making a good choice in their selection? And surely they weren't planning on their deaths any time soon.

"Anyhow, I've got to go. Want to get in some practice this morning. The pond always gets crowded in the afternoons." She grinned at her sister in a sudden twist of jesting. "I'd ask you to go—sure it would do you good—but I'm not prepared to deliver my niece or nephew if you happen to fall."

Emma Jaine laughed. "Go on with you. I think you will never grow up, Josephine Rayner Patterson."

Josie waved a hand at the two women and hurried out. She longed to have a quiet talk with Papa Ossie, but knew mornings were his time to spend talking on the phone with business cronies. A chat with Papa would have to wait.

The gate to the property stood partially open. She must not have latched it properly when she'd entered. Near it, standing with one gloved hand resting on the iron fence, stood a tall handsome man in a long, dark gray overcoat, a light gray Homburg on his head, and a manner that said he was lost and needed help.

Josie studied him as she approached. She didn't think she'd ever seen him before, but that meant nothing. Strangers were a dime a dozen in these times.

Jerry's fear blazed in her mind, but it was broad daylight, in front of her family's home. What was there to fear?

She might have passed him by, if he hadn't looked at her as she passed through the gate—and made sure she shut the latch securely. Stray dogs after Harriet's beloved chickens wouldn't set well with the housekeeper.

"May I help you?" Josie glanced at the man as she pulled on her gloves. "Are you lost?"

The man stared, his dark, almost black pupils dilated

with...what?

And then, he smiled, and his irises expanded. "How did you know?"

His subtle accent was adorable. Josie loved it and dimpled up at him. "You had the look of a lost puppy. I've been known to rescue a few in my day. It's a very recognizable expression."

"I see. Then I suppose you could tell me where the West Street Grace Community Church is located. I seem to have gotten turned around." He flapped a piece of paper.

Josie eyed the light gray paper and smiled. "Of course, I can. I'm passing it on my way. Would you like to walk with me?"

"Thank you. That's very gracious of you. But I don't want to be a bother."

"No bother. Come along. I'm headed to the pond."

"To skate?" He tilted his head toward the skates flung over her shoulder.

"Yes. To skate. I practice every day."

"Ah, you are a young lady who likes to stay in good health."

"That." Josie shifted her skates higher onto her shoulder. "But I practice mainly to qualify for the Skating Olympics when they open again."

The man drew in a breath. "And you are that good?"

He was very good looking, not quite as striking as Jerry, but well enough. He was distinguished though, and had a worldly air about him that was quite attractive. "I think so. My trainer says I am. I win most competitions I enter. If I work hard, I see no reason why I can't get where I want. That's what Diana says. And Tyrell too."

"Tyrell, you said? Being your trainer?"

"No, he's my brother-in-law, but the best listener in the world." Josie smiled, remembering all the times Tyrell had sat patiently listening to Josie's ramblings and crazy talk. "Diana is my trainer, and a hard taskmaster."

"Ach. You are a—what do they call it?— free spirit? You do not care much for the taskmaster trainer?"

"Diana's all right. She's a bit hard boiled, but a good pally in spite of it."

The church was up ahead, and Josie pointed it out. "Right up there on the right. See the large stone building? That's the church you're looking for. Are you wanting to speak with Tyrell? He's the minister, you know."

"The church is very attractive. Thank you so much, Miss...?"

"Josie. Josie Patterson. And it's Mrs. not Miss."

"Ach, Jer—your husband—is a very fortunate man. I wonder if he appreciates your...talent and beauty?"

What was there to say? Before, she would have hastened to assure this man, that indeed, Jerry appreciated her. Now? She wasn't so sure.

The man turned away and walked several steps before turning back. "Perhaps I will have a talk with this Mr. Tyrell. This minister."

"You'll enjoy talking with him. Tell him Josie said hello." Josie gave a quick wave and hurried on toward the pond, smiling at the man's funny accent.

But when she came to the corner, she looked back. He still stood in the same spot, and Josie could swear there was a smile on *his* face.

~*~

"Why do you not listen to me?"

Diana's face was as angry as Josie had ever seen it. But then, Josie hadn't expected to get caught drinking again. At least to the limit she had tonight.

It'd been two weeks since her last skating exhibition, and she'd not had one drink in all that time. Why was her trainer ragging on her now? What was different than all the other times she'd downed a few—or more—sips?

Time to smooth her trainer's ruffled feathers a bit. She opened her mouth, but Diana beat her to it.

"Don't speak." Her trainer held up a hand. "I'm sick of your lies and your excuses. I'm very angry with you right now, and I'm leaving. You're soused. You have an hour to get yourself sober. If you haven't satisfied me that you've done so by the time I return, I will be canceling your participation tonight." She flung open the door.

"You can't do that. I've trained hard for this competition. You want this as much as me."

"Correction, Josie. I wanted this before. Now? I think I'm wasting my time. Prove to me I'm not." Then the door slammed.

Josie giggled but sobered quickly. She'd made Diana angry numerous times. She'd pushed her patience and stubbornly ignored her suggestions, but Diana had always been a Lulu and come around when Josie had performed far beyond the trainer's expectation. She'd been a sure thing.

Until now. Was Diana serious? No, she couldn't be. Not after all the work she'd put into training Josie, her protégé. Still, it wouldn't hurt to do as she asked, this time.

Josie went to the sink and splashed her face, slugged down a cup of bad tasting, hot coffee and then topped off the sobering with a half glass of Harriet's tomato juice.

Josie swayed with the liquid swirling in her stomach. Ugh. She felt as though she might...

She ran for the bathroom.

She was as sick as she could ever remember being, but it didn't last long. Stomach emptied, but weak as a newborn kitten, Josie sat on the floor with her head against the wall. Glad no one would see her like this, Josie thanked whatever god was upstairs for that.

No one would bother her—Diana had said she wouldn't be back for an hour, and the marvelous Diana had always made sure—she had never figured out how and quit worrying about it—that Josie had a private room and usually a restroom to herself for the time before a performance or competition.

Stumbling to her feet, she knew she needed something to give her some strength, but she'd refused Diana's earlier suggestion to eat lightly. There were some crackers and cheese, so she could nibble on those. For sure, they wouldn't upset her body like the alcohol she needed more and more to keep up with the demands on her life.

She'd thought preparing for the Olympics was hard. But Jerry re-entering her life as anything but supportive and loving and fun like he'd been before, was dragging her down. Josie sighed and crunched on a half-stale cracker. Not very satisfying taste-wise, but perhaps nourishing enough.

Two hours later, the crowd was larger than usual. Josie stood in her dressing room doorway, listening to the muted sounds of enthusiasm swirling with the growing excitement mounting inside her.

The excitement she always felt right before the calm. The calm that settled through and over her once she began her skating routine. Fortunately she'd always been able to blank out everything but doing what she loved while skating. She wouldn't have cared if President Roosevelt had suddenly stepped into the front row of spectators. Nothing mattered but giving her best.

And giving her best tonight was vital. Diana had hinted some very important people might again be in the audience tonight. She hadn't asked what that meant— she already knew. Scouts giving her a second glance. People interested in her skating ability. People looking to the future. The ones who mattered who wanted her in it—maybe. If.

If she accomplished what she planned tonight.

When Diana tapped lightly on the door minutes later, Josie was dressed and ready to go. Yeah, her body still felt weaker than it should, but she'd recovered her spirits and was eager to go.

Diana strode straight toward her and tilted Josie's head toward herself. Her dark eyes studied her trainee. "You still have black circles under your eyes, but they're clear. And you're wearing the yellow outfit. Good. Did you eat something?"

"Yes. A few crackers and a bite or two of cheese. I'm okay." Josie spoke as humbly as she could. No need to be a pain in the neck. Diana had the ability to stop tonight's performance, although it was questionable whether she'd really carry through.

The dark-haired woman spied the cracker crumbs and wrinkled her nose. "Ugh, but better than nothing. Are you sure you're up to this tonight? It will be strenuous, and there's a lot of pressure on you tonight, with that new maneuver."

"I'm good to go. I've practiced until I could do this blindfolded. See, no shakes." Josie held out one hand

and frowned when it trembled ever so slightly. Her gaze shot to Diana's face, but she'd turned away.

"Then let's go. You have five minutes before your program, and it won't hurt for your fans to see you."

Josie followed her trainer out the door. Two minutes later, Josie glided onto the ice and poised, listening to the music, her gaze searching for Jerry's face.

Her family's smiling faces and waving hands warmed her heart and sent a smile to her lips, but Jerry wasn't there. He hadn't promised, and she shouldn't have let herself hope. For a minute, all time slowed as if funneling into a tornado-like tunnel, and then...

She'd never be able to describe it—what drew her attention to the man. But the gray-coated man she'd met days ago, stood off, by himself, watching her. His eyes were shaded by his gray Homburg, but the mustached, half-smile was plain as anything.

And Josie saw it.

It at once both strengthened her and frightened her.

Strengthened because someone she didn't know had taken the time to come and watch her skate. Someone who'd had enough interest—not like Jerry, who knew her biggest performance was tonight, but failed to appear and support her.

Yet it shot a streak of fear in her too. How could she feel the encouragement she needed from a *stranger*? Why was she clutching at it when she should have been standing here relaxing, preparing, focusing?

Stunned, she missed the note for her first move, and had to—as graciously as she could—scramble to catch up.

And then she was caught up in her routine. But in the back of her mind she was very much aware that a distinguished man stood watching—admiring?—her. Worse, her mind struggled with Jerry's rejection.

Josie dipped and twirled, spun and swayed. And all the while, she knew she wasn't giving one hundred percent.

She was headed into the last third of her exhibit when a motion from the stands caught her attention. Normally, she paid no attention to the people surrounding the rink, staying focused and lost in her routine. But conscious of the smiling stranger, hurt from Jerry's lack of interest and weak from too much of everything, she was distracted and far from her normality.

Too late, she saw it, and stumbled, tried to correct her stance, and felt herself falling, her left foot twisted beneath her body as she crashed onto the cold ice.

There was no sound as Josie's mind screamed, dimmed and went dark.

Chapter Fourteen

She was beautiful, graceful as one of the swans back in—

Unconscious of it just made her that much more attractive. She had something about her that even his sister...as much as he'd loved her, as beautiful a woman as she'd been...had not had. Josephine Rayner Patterson had an air of simplicity and unconcern that lent an undisciplined grace about her. He'd dearly love to make her acquaintance in sincerity, but that wasn't possible.

Not with his goals. Not with his plans. Or was it? Could he lure her away from her husband? His sources insisted that Patterson, since returning from Germany, was morose and grim. Surely that played on both husband and wife. Could he use those emotions to create an even greater payback for the man?

It'd not been hard with U.S. connections to subtlety find what he needed about Patterson. Digging in the proper departments had given him everything he needed to do as he planned.

And that plan—well, suffice it to say—would be rendered shortly.

And quickly.

Chapter Fifteen

The first thing Josie saw when she opened her eyes was Papa Ossie's serious expression, and Josie stretched out a hand to clasp her father's. Claire's eyes were tear-filled and warmed her heart, but she didn't have the strength to pull her baby sister into her arms. Emma Jaine's worried expression scared her, and Tyrell's confident gaze assured her she was in good hands, whatever that meant.

Where was she?

Josie gazed at the ugly walls, then at the white-coated nurse at the foot of her bed.

Great. What had happened?

And she remembered. The conflict roaring inside her. The confusion over Jerry's absence and the stranger's encouraging smile. And the stick.

Josie groaned, and her favorite people surrounding her bed, tightened the circle. The next moment the nurse was shooing everyone from the room, and she did what she'd been trained to do.

Somewhere in the midst of that shot, Josie floated off to sleep.

~*~

Jerry had known when Captain had talked with him earlier, there was a possibility Winfried Rhoderick *wasn't* in the United States, even though evidence and tips had indicated he was.

But his heart knew. He hadn't lived in the man's house for weeks on end without discovering his personality. His ability and talents. His moods. His rage and contempt at those he considered traitors to his beloved Germany.

If Rhoderick had found a way into the states, without discovery, he was here. He would have built up an intense hatred, and he'd risk all to destroy Jerry. But, if that was the case, how had he discovered Jerry's real name? What all did he know?

One thing Jerry knew for certain, the man would never inhabit places of seedy or lowdown businesses. Not unless, of course, it furthered his plan. No, he would have the gall and the ability to fit into the classiest places. The presence to fit right in with the glitterati. The ability to sway others to befriend him.

That's why Jerry was checking out all the hotels in town. There might be a war going on, but the rich didn't cease to crave the attention or the pampering they thought they deserved.

And, of course, it took time to check out each temporary resident of said hotels. This was his fifth one today, and he'd seen nothing more suspicious than a man—whom he was sure was married—sneaking in with a decked out call girl. He was about ready to give it up for the day.

Nearly falling out of his chair in excitement, Jerry slouched lower. Was that *Harry Marshall*, the one from whom Jerry had stolen the list of names that night in Germany in Rhoderick's home?

It was. The same white-blond, wavy hair. The same lazy, arrogant stride. That look that said he was a bit better than the one unfortunate enough to be near him. Who was that dish hanging onto his arm? She looked familiar, but Jerry knew very well, he'd never circulated in Marshall's social life so there was no way he'd ever known this babe.

She was tall and lithe, as blond as Marshall, her hair piled in a stylish manner, but a cold fish who looked both fit and haughty. No one to tangle with, for sure.

Jerry was so absorbed in the woman, trying to figure out who she was, that he almost missed Marshall's abrupt turn, as if a sixth sense warned him of someone's study. Jerry froze and didn't move. He'd learned enough in the military to know that a sudden, frantic move to hide would capture more attention than a quiet blending in.

As the couple headed to the front desk, Jerry limped his way outdoors and hailed a cab. Climbing awkwardly in, he sat back. "Hold it, I'll tell you when to go."

Just as he thought, Marshall and his babe exited the

doors and, with a chauffeur opening the car door, entered the vehicle that sat idling two cars in front. When they pulled out, Jerry spoke again. "Follow that car, and don't lose it. An extra buck for you if you manage to keep them from realizing they're being tailed."

The cabbie nodded and slipped two cars behind the sleek black car.

"You some kind of g-man?" His dark-eyed gaze rested on Jerry from the interior mirror.

"Nope." That wasn't exactly what he'd call his clumsy attempts of searching for his nemesis.

"Musta been in the service." The guy gave him a knowing look. "Seeing that bum leg you got. Real hero, were you?"

The anger inside Jerry reared its head, demanding release. Blood pounded in his suddenly throbbing head, and he had to deliberately unclench stiff fingers before he spoke again. "What makes you think that? Got it in a car wreck. Yeah. Last week."

That ought to shut the man up.

It didn't.

"Thinking I'm a pushover, are you?"

Jerry switched his gaze out a side window, ready to crack up and hating the smothered feeling surrounding him. "Drive, man. Don't lose that car."

"Just thought you ought to know, there's another vehicle behind us that's been on our tail for the last block. Not sure if it means—"

Jerry slid lower in his seat and peered out the back glass. "Which one, man? Why didn't you say something earlier?"

The cabbie's shoulder lifted. "Wanted to make sure. But since you're so-o-o, so—"

"So what?" The explosive question was out of his mouth before he could stop it. "You think I'm a cripple? A misfit cause of a bum leg? A chicken? What?"

The alarm in the cabbie's eyes told Jerry he'd lost control. He dug in his pocket for twice what he knew he owed the man, and tossed it over the seat. "Let me out now."

With an abrupt squeal of tires, the cabbie pulled to

the curb, and Jerry exited, slamming the door none too easy. A second loud squeal, and the car pulled away. Jerry felt his lips tilting in a sarcastic twist. Guy was probably in a buzz that he'd escaped with his life. Jerry would be the talk of cabbie-ville for the rest of the evening.

Pulling his collar high, Jerry shoved his hands deep into his coat pockets and began walking. There was no sign of anyone following him, and that was good. Because of his temper, he'd lost the chance to find Marshall's target destination tonight. What good that would do, he had no idea. What had he thought? He'd go barging in on the dinner or show or wherever the man was headed?

Could be it hadn't been Marshall. It'd been months since he'd seen him. He could have a twin running around Cincinnati.

Jerry turned a corner and stopped dead. Parked fifty feet away was the black car Marshall and the woman had entered, the same chauffeur leaning, alone, against the vehicle. There was no sign of the two, but the house was lit up like a Christmas tree and the music blaring from it gave good evidence that a party or gathering was going on.

There were a couple chauffeurs flapping their lips across the street, but he couldn't see anyone paying him the least mind. He studied the house, the lights in each window. Could he? Just to take a gander around and see what was what.

Winding his way through a path of bushes and low-to-the ground trees, he made his way to within feet of the house. Closer to the huge place, Jerry gave it a more cursory study. He wasn't dressed well enough to blend in as a guest, and neither did he want to attempt that foolhardy act. Marshall, if it was him, would recognize him for sure. No. Better to sneak in as a waiter or kitchen help or some such thing.

Jerry headed toward the back of the house, and nearly fell over backtracking when he spotted Marshall, another gentlemen and a woman—the same woman he'd seen earlier—with their backs to him, standing in a gazebo. The men smoked cigars while the woman held a cigarette in a long holder.

Sweat beaded his forehead. That'd been a close one.

The gazebo sat in an open part of the back lawn so there was no way he could get close. He'd have to be content with studying them from afar or tossing in the towel with this stupid idea. Hightailing it out of here would be the best solution, but Jerry never was enthusiastic about the easy way. Too convenient and not worth half the price.

It took ten more minutes before the three decided they'd had enough smoke, and probably the cold, to walk toward the house again.

Marshall, on the far side, had his face turned toward him. Easy to recognize, if he hadn't already known it was him. But the other man wasn't as easy to see. Talking and gazing toward Marshall, his features were averted just enough, it wasn't possible to spot anything defining about him.

Except...

The second man wore a Homburg. Gray and worn at the right tilt, the hat projected a confident attitude. Just like Rhoderick's self-esteem.

Yet, was it him? He wasn't the only man in Cincinnati to sport a gray hat for dressy affairs. Jerry realized he could make a number of observations that could— might—point to Rhoderick, and still be wrong.

He needed to know. It was too serious to guess. Josie's life could be at stake. His? Didn't matter about him, damaged goods as he was.

Time to move.

~*~

"The doctor says you can go home today."

The trim, capable nurse bustled around the room, her words and tone spoken in an overly enthusiastic manner meant to bring some kind of good thoughts to the patient.

Unfortunately, it didn't work for Josie, but she gave her a lame smile, hoping the woman would leave her alone until Papa Ossie could pick her up.

Giving her a questioning glance, the nurse patted her arm and left the room to get a wheelchair. Probably glad to be rid of such a disagreeable person.

She had a right to be disagreeable, or at least, Josie figured so. After all, she was the one with a different, difficult husband, a damaged beyond repair ankle, and questions that persisted in plaguing her.

For instance, why had the gray-clothed stranger shown up to watch her perform? And if that wasn't crazy enough, she was almost positive that stick had come from his direction. But why? Why?

The nurse helped Josie into the wheelchair, talking and reminding Josie of the restrainments the doctor had issued.

Josie tuned out the patient, boring voice as the nurse wheeled her down a hallway.

She tried to remember when she'd first met gray-coated man—coming out of her papa's home. He'd been so pleasant. A handsome man who'd seemed to be a bit diffident to bother her. And he'd taken an interest in her, asking questions that showed a keen mind and intuitive thought. He'd assumed she wasn't married—

Josie frowned. Something was wrong with that image. She couldn't quite pinpoint the problem, but it was there.

"You ready to head for home, Josie? Jerry wasn't home, and Papa Ossie had unexpected guests, so I'm filling in."

And it hit her. The stranger had corrected himself when he'd almost spoken Jerry's name. Why hadn't she realized it then? How had the man even known Jerry's name if he was the stranger he seemed to be playing?

Josie looked up into the dark green eyes of her brother-in-law, Tyrell Walker. His teasing voice was meant to cheer her, but, unfortunately, all it did was reinforce the knowledge that Jerry wasn't here. Not one time since she'd been admitted, and not today when she was going home.

Too busy no doubt. For her, anyway. At what, she had no idea.

She nodded. "Yes. I just want to go home."

"You've got it, Josie. Home it is."

That's what she liked about Tyrell. No arguments. No droopy looks of sadness.

104

Diana had stopped by once. But the indifference in her attitude when she'd left, wasn't much encouragement to Josie that she'd see her again soon.

Her family—and particularly Emma Jaine—had hovered over her the first few days. She would have stayed all night that first night except Tyrell had put his foot down and insisted Emma Jaine go home to rest. He'd gently coaxed Papa to go with his daughter, and that left Tyrell to sit slouched in the only armchair in the room, snoozing when he could, but alert when she'd tossed from side to side, moaning.

"How's your ankle? Sure you're okay?" Tyrell crouched in front of her.

"It's okay. I'm ready to go."

"Good." He rose and glanced at the nurse standing behind the wheelchair just inside the entrance doors. "My car's parked right outside."

The nurse nodded and pushed Josie through the doors and up to Tyrell's Ford sedan. After he opened the door and they had her seated in the front seat, Tyrell strode to the driver's side and climbed in. He reached for the ignition key, then paused.

"If you want to talk, Josie, I'm here. I can tell you're in the dumps."

Josie stared at this man who'd entered their lives, wooed her sister, and been a real friend to her. From the first, he'd been easy to talk with and someone who could be trusted with the darkest secrets. She'd had experience, she should know.

It was a quiet ride, the music from the radio soft and low and soothing. Tyrell made a comment or two, but nothing that needed answered or her attention. She was free to sit here and brood in her own sour way.

Josie was quiet, and she definitely didn't want to tell Tyrell how she really felt. Screaming and stomping—if she'd been able to—wouldn't impress him, not that she cared about that. But neither would those actions bring Jerry back into her life.

And they certainly wouldn't do anything to miraculously heal her crushed ankle bone. A bone so severely damaged, the doctor had sadly shaken his head when she'd questioned him on her future skating.

Nope. She was done for.

~*~

Jerry entered the kitchen area and nodded at the workers who glanced at him as he strode through with as much confidence as he could. Once into the hallway, he followed the noise and music and thought perhaps he'd make it up to the balcony where he hoped he could gaze over it to get a look at the attendees at this shindig.

Halfway up the stairs, a huge giant of a man started to pass by, then halted. "What are you doing in here?"

Jerry paused only long enough to dig out an old badge of questionable authority he'd been given months ago for espionage use, and which he'd carried on his person for whatever reason. He flashed it at the man and began climbing again, hoping that was the end of it.

"Hey, you. Hold up."

Wanting to groan, Jerry turned and put every bit of haughtiness he'd used in Germany into his sentence. "Are you speaking to me?"

It wasn't much, but Jerry caught the faint and fleeting glimpse of surprise in the other man's eyes. He opened his mouth to speak, but Jerry ran over top of his attempt.

"I'm late getting here. Marshall's expecting me. Do I have to send for him and let him know *you're* the reason I'm later than ever?"

Obviously not. The flash of fear didn't fade as the man—Jerry supposed a guard or valet or something—nearly fell over his own feet stumbling on down the stairway.

Turning and straightening to his almost-six-foot height, Jerry marched as steadily as his bum leg would let him to the top. He wanted to chuckle but knew he couldn't afford it. He was too near an open fire to rejoice now. Getting burned—caught—wouldn't be pleasant.

Except for a man servant standing near a closed door, the landing was empty, and Jerry pulled in a breath of relief.

He was being foolhardy, he knew. What purpose would it serve if Marshall caught him hanging around here?

But he had to know. Was Rhoderick here, in this house or close by?

Scanning the landing quickly, he chose a dark corner, with a view over the railing, that afforded a good look at the mingling guests below. When the servant's attention was focused in a different direction, Jerry headed there.

By the looks of the brightly colored evening dresses and the suave suits and military uniforms, no one would have guessed a horrendous war was raging across the seas. But was it not just as dangerous here on the home soil? Who knew what Marshall was up to? Just because his first attempt in Germany at sabotaging good, loyal men, had gone wrong—because of Jerry's work—didn't mean the man had quit his treason-ish acts. In fact, why hadn't the man been arrested while re-entering the states?

He was about to give up on recognizing anyone on the floor below, and hightail it out of here, when the door across the landing opened, and same trio he'd seen in the gazebo exited.

Waves of cigar smoke rolled across the space and tickled Jerry's nose as he observed the servant inserting a key into the door and locking it, then returning to his stance as if guarding a treasure of gold. Jerry lifted a hand cautiously, rubbed his itching nose and stared at the servant. What was in that room that it needed to be locked?

The threesome's voices were low, and he caught few of the words, but their tones indicated serious business was afoot. From the corner of his eyes, a form drew his gaze. A huge form. The man who'd accosted him earlier on the stairs, running *up* the stairs now, as if he was late for a date.

Jerry hugged the wall.

"Sir, I'm sorry to intrude."

"What is it, Samson?" Irritation and coldness edged Marshall's voice.

"I've got strong suspicions there's someone mingling among the guests who shouldn't be here."

"What are you talking about?"

It would take a brave soul to argue with Marshall.

In brief detail, the man—Samson—laid out the details. "The kitchen help informed me minutes ago of a strange man with a limp who came through the kitchen rooms. I stopped a man climbing the stairs, but after flashing a badge and speaking of you, Sir, as if he knew you, I assumed he was a late guest and let him pass."

The blond woman turned and spoke in a low voice, her tone crisp and sharp, but still too low for Jerry to make out the words. She'd shed her dark coat and hat, but her pile of elegantly-styled hair and glittering gown set her apart. She had an air about her that drew attention, that brooked no fools.

The other man was quiet and never turned in the right angle to identify him, but the hair was styled in a different way than Rhoderick had favored in Germany. If it was him, Jerry couldn't be sure.

Even from Jerry's dark corner, he could see the sudden shift in Marshall's stance, the alertness in his body. He stroked his chin. "Hmmm. I wonder. Seems impossible, but..."

"Wonder what, Sir?"

"Never mind." As if he had awakened, Marshall flapped a hand at the man. "Have you seen him since? Talked to the housekeeper to see if he was assigned a room?"

The man shook his head. "Not a glimpse, and yes. There's no one unaccounted for in any of the rooms. Everyone of your guests was either on time or has been seen and recognized."

"Marshall, you and your men had better find this intruder." The woman's voice clanged with anger and danger. Clearly, she wasn't happy with the circumstances. "We can't afford any carelessness. You should have warned your staff to be on guard."

Marshall nodded at his servant, and Samson ran from the landing, back down the stairs, motioning to someone Jerry couldn't see. Then shrugging at the woman, Marshall glanced at the other man still standing quietly across from him. "I'll have to ask you to excuse me. Go and enjoy yourself, and I'll see you later. I have a feeling we may discover someone you'll be interested in after this search for our intruder. Babe, take care of him till I return, will you?"

The other two laughed as if Marshall had told the joke of the year.

Somehow, Jerry didn't think it was so funny.

The woman and man started down the stairs, but Marshall headed the other direction, and Jerry raised a brow. Where was he going? Or were there two stairwells?

And how on earth was he suppose to sneak out of here, now that he was being searched for?

He studied the milling guests downstairs again, but there was no way he'd blend in with that overdressed bunch. A glance at the servant who still stood by the door, and who seemed to be staring right back at him, startled him. Was the man smirking? Probably anxious to see how he would get out of this fix.

No way around it. He could either skulk here and hope the servant would keep mum or try to bluster his way out.

Jerry stepped out of the shadows, and the servant glanced first one way and another, then beckoned frantically at him. What?

No time to wonder. Jerry moved, and as he drew closer, the servant pulled the dangling keys from his side, chose one and inserted it into the door's keyhole. When it clicked, he hastily opened it and motioned Jerry inside.

It was a large room, and looked like an office. A long desk sat on one side and behind it, covering the wall, were bookshelves with, what Jerry supposed, would be, any kind of book you desired to read. There were two nice pictures that looked expensive, and one that looked to be a distant relative of Marshall's.

But he had no further time to linger. The servant was speaking.

"There's no way out. They'll have every other door covered, and I'm sure they're searching all the rooms." The servant strode to the double exterior doors across the room. "Go down these stairs and turn right. Straight across the yard, along the tree line, and you'll reach an alley. You should be all right if you hurry."

"Why are you doing this, man? You don't know me."

There was only a dim light from the fireplace, but Jerry could see another smirk lifting the corners of the man's mouth.

"But I do. I know you very well, Major Patterson."

If the man had hit him, he wouldn't have been any more floored. The man gave him no more time for questions, but shoved him out the door.

Jerry tossed back a whispered, "Thanks." and then the door was shutting quietly behind him.

Pulling in a breath of the crisp air, Jerry started down the stairs, when he heard voices coming from the room behind him. He paused and leaned close, listening.

"What are you doing in here...?"

The words faded, and to Jerry's irritation, he couldn't make out the name.

"I'm sorry, Sir, but I thought you were done for the night, and was just checking the fire in the fireplace and making sure the exterior door was locked before reporting to you."

"And was it?"

"Sir?"

"Was the exterior door locked?"

"Yes, Sir. It was."

A grunt. "I figured. You can go. I've got a bit of work to do before seeing the guests off. Report back in an hour or so."

It was time to make his escape. But before he could move, footsteps crossed the room, and a curtain moved.

Jerry could almost feel the eyes searching the dark, straining to make out his huddled form hugging the side of the house. Only when the curtain fell back into place, did he continue his descent.

And never looked back.

Chapter Sixteen

It'd been two whole weeks since Josie had seen her husband. Of course, she'd been in the hospital for two of those nights, and then sent home to recuperate, relax and let nature take its course. As if she could ever do that. She missed Jerry so much her heart hurt, and she wondered if it was anything like having a heart attack. If so, she never wanted to experience it. This was excruciating, and made the pain in her ankle seem like nothing.

Where could the man be? Ribbons of jealousy surged through her mind. Another woman? Someone at least who knew how to tame her hair. Who knew how to dress without having to have a sister choose an outfit for her. A woman who could cook and prepare all the foods Jerry loved.

Not like her. Who knew how to do none of those things. And didn't care.

Josie picked up the hand mirror and gazed at her mirror image. Disgusting. The scissors laying on her bureau across the room beckoned, but she was too disinterested to even make the attempt on crutches to reach them. If she did, she'd whack off every last strand of her wild curls and tangles till she was shorn like a sheep.

Yeah, a lot of good that'd do, and certainly wouldn't help woo Jerry back.

Gazing into the mirror again, she studied her face. Nose too long. Mouth too wide, Neck too long. She looked like a goose, and Josie laughed at her description.

But she had nice eyes. Everyone said so even if you couldn't believe Emma Jaine. She was prejudiced toward her sisters. Now, Claire. There was one who spoke her mind and did it in such a gentle, lady-like way you didn't know you were being insulted until after the fact.

Josie sighed and tossed the mirror to the side and

heard the faint crack. If only...

If only she hadn't drunk so much that night.

If only that stick hadn't been on the ice.

If only she hadn't been distracted.

If only Jerry had showed up then.

If only Jerry would come home now.

Josie reached for the crutches. She wasn't suppose to walk without someone with her, but what would it hurt? She'd only take a few steps...

Planting her good foot onto the floor, she eased the crutches under her arms and stood. Walking slowly, carefully, she hobbled around the bed to the window.

The day was gloomy and suited her downcast mood. She turned away to avoid looking at the outdoors.

"Josie, my dear..." Shirley stood in the doorway, the worry coming through loud and clear even though she tried to keep her tone mild and uncondemning.

"You scared me. What are you doing sneaking up on me like that?" Josie bit her lip and adjusted her crutch.

"I'm so sorry, dear." Shirley set down the tray she carried and hurried over to her. "Here let me walk with you."

"I can do it myself."

"I know that." She gave Josie a sideways glance. "But I've been given orders to not allow you to walk by yourself and to keep a tight rein on your—uh, high spirits. You don't want me fired from my job the first day, do you?"

"Your job?"

"I volunteered to help you get back on your feet, so to speak." Shirley helped Josie ease herself into the flowered wing chair. "Emma Jaine needs to stop worrying about you, your father has his hands full with business right now, Claire has her music and Tyrell, of course, the church. That leaves me, and I was only too happy to keep you company off and on for a few days."

What was she suppose to say? Thanks?

She was bored stiff at the inactivity, cranky with her family, and sick of her own self. The only thing she really wanted was to have a good session of skating...and Jerry. Neither of those were going to happen.

"You seemed...sad...when I entered. Are you okay?"

Shirley's usually smooth forehead wrinkled with concern.

"I suppose. I was thinking of the night I broke my ankle." Josie allowed a sigh of regret to escape. "I don't understand how or why that stick was on the ice. I'm pretty sure it wasn't before I started."

Shirley shook her head. "Your father was very upset over it. He's had the cops interviewing different ones trying to get to the bottom of it. Perhaps a child flung it over the rail."

She doubted it.

"I heard at the library this morning that the flutist we heard at the concert downtown—remember?—she's volunteered to give an hour of her time to the wounded soldiers in the hospital. They're going to air it at two this afternoon. Would you like to listen?"

Unexpectantly, Josie's heart leaped. Master flutist Sarah Maria Handleson certainly knew how to bring out the delicacy, yet vibrancy of the instrument.

As a child, she used to love the flute and had driven her family mad with her constant practice—until skating had taken over. She'd had to choose one or the other. Diana's accidental sight of her one night practicing had made the choice easy, what with her enthusiasm and promises of fame and opportunity. And now, look at her...

She clamped the lid tight against that thought.

"I'd love to. Thanks, Shirley."

The woman smiled and nodded. "Wonderful. I'll be back later then to bring you a snack and a fresh drink while you listen."

"I can get those by myself."

"I'm sure you could, but let me do it. You'll be back in your own home soon, with plenty of chores to do."

Josie shrugged, not caring one way or the other.

Hours later, Shirley returned with the promised items. She adjusted the radio dial and slipped out of the room.

Josie laid her head on the back of the chair. Heaven was about to begin.

~*~

He'd been gone too long. He hadn't meant to stay away that long, but after his getaway from the Marshall house, he'd reported to his captain, who'd sent him to investigate another rumor. Took longer than he'd wanted, and by the time he got to the bottom of it and a couple other leads—which proved to be useless—two weeks had passed.

He hadn't called Josie, and why? Afraid she'd beg him to come home? His own lousy desire to distance himself?

Be honest, he chided himself, then allowed himself a grimace. Yeah, right.

Walking up the sidewalk to his front door, he unlocked it and slipped inside. Silence greeted him, but he hesitated, almost hearing his and Josie's past laughter, their shrieks of teasing when one or the other played a joke. Was that a whiff of Josie's favorite perfume, although she seldom took the time to actually use it?

A chuckle escaped him, but he disciplined himself. Quiet. As late as it was, she was more than likely asleep. He headed to the kitchen hoping to find some left over morning coffee, but the pot stood rinsed and empty. Alreet, he'd settle for a glass of water.

Finished, he rinsed the glass and turned it upside down in the sink, then headed upstairs. He tiptoed to their room and touched the door which swung open with no squeaks. It was dark with the curtains pulled, so he edged closer to the bed and bent a little.

It looked...It didn't look slept in. Suddenly, frantic at the crazy thought that raced through his mind, Jerry felt the coverlet and realized the truth.

Josie was not in bed. Had she heard him come in and ignored it? Or was she gone?

For good?

~*~

Josie woke, her heart pounding. What was it? She tilted her head. It almost sounded like... Pulling herself up in bed, she listened, and there it was again. A rattling sound coming from...

Josie edged her legs to the floor and stood, reaching for her crutch to help her hobble to the window, and peered out. Someone stood on the lawn below, but she couldn't tell who it was. Jerry?

Balancing herself, she lifted the window and leaned

out. "Jerry?"

"It's me. Wills. I'm coming in to talk with you, but didn't want to startle you or disturb the others."

Josie motioned for him to come on and headed for the two side chairs at the other end of the room. What on earth was he doing here at this time of the night? And why not head on down to his parents quarters?

From the first floor, came a quiet click as her friend unlocked the door, then hurried footsteps ascended the stairs. Will's beloved face peeked through the doorway, and Josie laughed at the expression of delight playing across his features. Same ole pal.

"You up to taking a slide down the stairs?" His grin was positively tempting. He smacked his forehead. "Wait. Is Claire here?"

"Of course. Where else would she be? And since when do we care what Claire thinks?"

"Thought she might be out and about."

"At this time of the night?" Had Wills lost his mind? Papa would have called in every policeman in the city. "What's with the midnight subterfuge?"

Wills' face sobered quicker than a frog catching his supper. So something more important than an escapade was up. Whatever it was, she was eager to hear it.

"I don't know how much Jerry's shared with you."

"Are you kidding?" Her face grew warm at her involuntary words. As much as she loved Wills as a best friend, he didn't need to know the trouble her marriage was in.

"Jerry is...he's..."

"What?" Josie sat forward. "Is he in trouble?"

"No... Well, I don't think so. At least, not yet."

"Then tell me. Now, Wills. Now."

"Your husband is involved in some seriously dangerous, uh, let's call it, work."

"What kind of work?"

The plaintive expression crossing Wills' face gave her a clue. Jerry was doing something, not only dangerous, but illegal. Could her heart break anymore?

"What can I do to help?"

"I need you to keep tabs on him. If you see anyone

lurking around, give me a call."

"Why not tell Jerry?"

"He's too independent and right now, far too easily offended. Even if it was for his good. If he thought too many were keeping tabs on him, he'd be angry and insist we back off."

"But—"

Wills head shook before she could finish. "Josie, promise you won't say anything to him. Promise?"

"Of course."

The look of appreciation he sent her soothed her troubled heart.

"I could always trust you. There's a lot going on in the world today, and Jerry's part of it. He's one of the best, but even the best needs backup at times. And this is one of those times. I'm his backup, and you can help me. Will you do it?"

"Doesn't sound like much."

"But it is. If you can help me keep Jerry from trouble, you'll be helping your country."

"And Jerry too?" She knew her voice sounded like a scared little girl but didn't care. Her heart was breaking anew. What was her husband into?

"And Jerry too."

~*~

He was almost positive Rhoderick hadn't stolen his wife away. After searching the house over thoroughly and seeing no signs of either a struggle or her suitcases gone, he knew she'd taken off by herself. Wherever that was. For what? A fling with girlfriends? A new night time job? An overnight at her father's because she couldn't stand his absence any longer?

Or another man?

Could he blame her?

The sun was pretending to rise when he took his pride by the bootstraps and hobbled down the sidewalk to the house next door. The Rayner's Boarding House. Josie's family. He was ashamed to go asking for her, to find out if she was there or gone. But the terror inside him was far more predominate than any shame he felt.

Just as he turned onto the sidewalk that led to their front door, the door opened, and Ossie Rayner stepped out, wrapping a scarf around his neck. The man had stepped off the porch before he caught sight of Jerry.

"Jerry. Where have you been?"

He studied Josie's father but saw no signs of anger or rudeness. An honest question, maybe puzzled or perplexed.

"Have you seen Josie? I finally got home last night, and she wasn't there. I've been a little worried—"

"You haven't heard?"

Surely only a second had passed since his heart had hit the sidewalk. "What's happened to her? Tell me. Now." He grabbed hold of the Captain Ossie's arm and shook it.

"Come with me. I'm headed down to the corner cafe for a spot of coffee if they have any left. But don't tell Harriet. She'd have my hide." He winked and kept walking so Jerry was forced to follow or go on to the house.

The man cast him a glance. "What do you think's happened to her?"

Frustration like a speeding train raced through him. "How should I know? I left home one day, and when I return, she's not there with no indication of where she's gone. What am I suppose to think?"

They walked another twenty or so feet before Captain Ossie spoke again. "At Josie's last competition, something went wrong."

Wrong? Jerry frowned. "What do you mean?"

"I knew when I first saw her that night something was not right. Her actions were jerky, her face stressed. She didn't look like my usual confident Josie."

"And?" If only the man would get on with it.

"Josie missed her first musical cue to begin, then she stumbled and broke her ankle." Captain Ossie swiped a large, well-worn hand across his face. "The problem with that scenario is, why did she stumble? I thought I saw something lying on the ice, but wasn't sure."

Josie, hurt?

~*~

Jerry stopped at the bedroom door. The thinner-than-usual figure standing at the window drew his attention.

A crutch leaned against the wall nearby, but she stood with her weight on her right foot, the left one barely touching. She'd laid her head against the pane, her chestnut hair, the wild strands that always wooed his fingers to tangle in them, hiding her face. But once in a while he could see her shoulders heave with the heavy breaths she drew in, and his heart ached for her hurt.

It was his fault she'd hurt herself. The way Captain Ossie had described her actions and face—he knew. She'd been upset over his absence, the way he'd left.

Groaning over his stupidity wouldn't help.

He strode silently across the room and slipped his arms around her. How could he do less?

Her reaction was instant. She whirled in a half-hobble, clutching at him to aid her. Her head buried in his chest, her fingers gripped his shirt and her lips mumbled his name over and over.

A minute later, her damp tears had soaked through his shirt onto his chest. He didn't want the lump in his throat to prevent his usual nonchalant voice to speak or the muscle called his heart to soften at her sudden neediness. But they did, and he couldn't do a thing about it.

He patted her back soothingly, his arms wrapped around her protectively. Before he could manage to swallow that embarrassingly gigantic lump, she raised her head, her eyes a dewy plea for understanding. And something else.

"Jerry, you're here. I'm on the verge of insanity. I cannot stand this incentive boredom." Her head plowed into his chest again.

His lips twitched at her habit of using the wrong words, and he whispered ever so softly, "Incessant, Josie."

But she paid no attention to his correction and gave his chest a sound wallop. "Where have you been? You could have told me. I thought—I thought—"

"Let's sit. I'll see if Harriet has some tea."

"I'm sick of tea. I want to go home."

Her plaintive wail had him smiling again, but he sobered quick enough. Shouldn't he refuse? Ignore her plea and let her stay here where she might have a modicum of safety. She wouldn't like it, but keeping her safe was his best option right now. The thought of Rhoderick getting his hands on her was unbearable.

She must have guessed his thoughts because she glared at him. "Jerry, even if you don't help me, I'm going home. Today. I need some time alone, and I'm constantly being battered by someone wanting to wait on me."

Badgered, but he didn't say it aloud. Sometimes he wondered if she did it on purpose.

"I see she's talked you into going back to her own home." Shirley spoke from the doorway. "I wish you'd give it another week, Josie."

Stiffening, Jerry settled Josie in her chair, then turned to the librarian. "She's quite determined."

"In that case, let me help you pack, Josie. Jerry, if you could get her coat from the closet and gather up all the miscellaneous stuff. Do you want the flowers, Josie?"

Josie shook her head. "No, give them to one of the hospitals."

Shirley latched the suitcase. "There you go, my dear. If you don't mind, I'd like to stop over every day and make sure you're doing all right. It will ease my mind, but more important, will ease your father's mind. He's been quite worried."

"About me?"

"Yes, about you. He adores all his daughters, but you are his favorite middle one." Shirley coughed trying to hide the smile.

"Since I'm his only middle daughter, that makes it quite easy on him, doesn't it?" Josie's words were a bit dry, but she was pleased.

Jerry watched the interaction between the two women, appreciating Shirley's tact and insight in talking with his wife. With both of her sisters more socially adaptable, Josie felt like the odd-man-out, as if she didn't fit, and Jerry certainly understood where she was coming from.

His wife's laughter was spontaneous and loud, but oh, so good to hear. He hadn't heard much of it the last few weeks. Not that it was her fault.

~*~

Josie stood across the hallway from the study and

stared into her husband's personal room. He'd made sure she was settled securely in her room upstairs earlier today, then disappeared. After two hours had passed and there'd been no indication he was returning, she'd had enough. Grabbing her crutch and muttering to herself, she headed out of her room, down the hallway to the stairs.

She knew she could conquer them by herself. She'd always been strong and lithe, the tomboy of the family, quite capable of climbing any tree in the neighborhood faster than her friends and unafraid to accept the most dangerous dare they'd enjoyed throwing at her.

So, no, the stairs weren't the problem. But Jerry finding her downstairs, having accomplished the feat all by herself just might present a problem. Especially when he'd said to her, "Josie, stay put and relax, or I'll regret having brought you home. I'll be back later on to check on you."

Regardless, she was going to see this brainchild through. He wasn't here now and wouldn't find out.

She was only a third of the way down, when the front door slammed open, and an angry Jerry stomped into his study. He was slapping an envelope into his other hand—over and over. He never looked her way, only finally tore open the envelope and glanced at it. With an angry oath, he crushed it and tossed it toward the waste can. Standing with one hand on his desk, he stared down—at nothing, she assumed—for minutes.

Wills had asked her to keep track of Jerry, insisted he was doing dangerous work, and he needed to know of any strange people hanging around. So whatever that paper was, it'd distressed him, and it was up to her to find out why. A solid reason to continue descending these stairs. Not that she'd tell Jerry any of that if he happened to look up and see her.

Josie wanted to run to him, but the savageness crossing and re-crossing his face stopped her. But what really scared her—and Josie was no chicken—was the hand gun lying only inches from that hand on his desk.

~*~

As soon as Jerry slammed his way outside again, Josie hurried as fast as her bum foot would let her, the rest of the way downstairs and straight to the study. She took the time to make sure he wasn't loitering on the porch, and reassured, bent to retrieve the envelope and the message he'd tossed away earlier. For moments, she stared at the gun, wondering if she should hide it. But Jerry was anything but a fool, and would know it'd been her doings. Besides, he'd always been responsible—at least in the past.

Sighing, and without another act, she re-climbed the stairs and went straight to her room.

She was almost out of breath from the hurrying so when she collapsed into her favorite loveseat, she took a minute to rest her head on the back of it and to prop her leg upon a stool.

Then, unable to put it off any longer, Josie drew the envelope from her pocket and stared at it. The return address had no name—only an address. Slowly, tentatively, she withdrew the single sheet of paper and unfolded it. Her gaze dropped to the bottom of the sheet, and she gasped.

~*~

Jerry strode as fast as his bum leg would let him, straight to the corner cafe. Anywhere but in his home where the letter lay crumpled. As if coming home from war damaged, wasn't enough, as if worrying about Josie wasn't enough, now he had to get letters like he'd just received. He'd never been so angry. Or felt so helpless.

Well, the old man might as well not waste his paper. He had no use for him or his propositions. He'd not read the whole letter, only parts, and that much had driven him insane. Did his father think he could change his mind, beckon, and Jerry would come running?

He hoped the man wouldn't hold his breath for it to happen.

~*~

Son, you've ignored my previous letters, but I hope and pray you'll see fit to read this one through and respond. Recent events have changed my life, including a diagnosis from the doctor that isn't the best news I've ever had. I feel I must talk with you in person to set things right. This may seem like an impossibility to you as our past has

been, for want of a better word, tempestuous, but I assure
you, I'm sincere.

Trusting I will hear from you soon.

Robert Patterson

Josie let the letter drop to her lap, stunned at the words. Was Jerry's father apologizing? Or was it another scheme worded in shaded meaning to capture his son's attention and lure him back to his company?

It would never work.

Still, what did the man really want?

Josie reached for her crutch and walked to her desk. Sitting, she pulled out paper and pen and began writing.

~*~

Jerry headed downtown two days later. He'd never finished his search of the hotels and was pretty sure it was pointless. He'd found Marshall's residence and figured if it had been Rhoderick there that night, he'd spy on him. If it hadn't been him, then he'd be at the best hotel in the city.

Rhoderick wouldn't stay in a sleazy place, so he'd ruled out any hotel that wasn't top notch. Three more to go, and he'd have checked them all.

Inside River's Edge, the grandest of all the hotels, Jerry glanced around, then chose a seat in a far corner, half hidden by the tall potted plants. He picked up a newspaper from a nearby stand and sat, but he wasn't reading.

Hours later, he'd seen no sign of Rhoderick and was about to leave for the day, when in walked Marshall and the man who'd guarded Marshall's study that night when Jerry had invaded the party. He ignored Marshall and focused his attention on the guard. He'd seemed genuine enough then, helping him escape, and hadn't given him away or tricked him, but why would he be working for a fink like Marshall? He'd give a lot of folding lettuce to know that answer.

He watched both of them as they moved toward the elevator, the guard a step or so behind Marshal. Just as the elevator door opened, and Marshall stepped inside of it, the guard turned, only a bit, but enough to catch Jerry's eyes.

And he winked. Then two seconds later he'd stepped

into the elevator to join the other man, and Jerry was left wondering what that wink had been about and how he'd realized Jerry was sitting in the corner of the lobby.

Chapter Seventeen

"Look who came with me today." Shirley peeked into Josie's sitting room.

Tyrell Walker peeked in as well, his handsome face wreathed in a big smile. "Am I welcome?"

"Of course, Silly. You're always welcome." Josie laughed in sheer happiness at having some company. Contrarily different than days before, where she yearned for her own privacy—if Jerry continued his usual habit of leaving early in the day and not returning till late at night—well, she was about to do something crazy.

"Harriet sent supper over for you and Jerry. I'm going to do a few chores while you and Tyrell visit. Anything I can get you?"

"I'm fine. You want some water or something, Tyrell?"

"I'm good." Tyrell settled into a chair close to her. "Have you been outside? It's warming up. Probably have an early spring."

"I haven't been anywhere. Everyone's forsaken me, even Jerry." Josie bit her lip—hard. She sounded like a whiny child, and that, she usually wasn't. A rebellious one, quite often, but never whiny.

"Sorry about that. Emma Jaine's had to rest more with the baby due next week, and we haven't seen much from Captain Ossie. It seems he's keeping hours similar to Jerry's." Tyrell picked up a book Shirley had loaned Josie then laid it down again.

"Have you and Emma Jaine decided on a name for the baby?"

"Yes, we have. A boy will be named Peter Oswald, after your father and my grandfather and, if we have a daughter, Jaine Marie, after Emma Jaine and your mother."

"I love both of them. I cannot wait to meet my niece or nephew, although I have to confess to being a little timid facing such a formidable person."

"I'm not afraid to admit the same. Emma Jaine seems as calm as a cucumber—have you ever seen a calm cucumber?—and laughs at my fears."

"She would." Josie chuckled. "She's a lot like our mother, from what I can remember, and as capable in all womanly arts. I never understood why I was the ugly duckling in the family."

"You?" Tyrell scoffed. "Don't be silly. Being different doesn't mean ugly. You're far from that, and I happen to know for a fact that Claire would die for your nose and neck and Emma Jaine says you have the loveliest hair in town. So easy to arrange, I think she put it."

"This mop?" Josie sputtered in disbelief, her laughter nearly choking off her words. "You're making that up."

Tyrell raised his hands. "I'm not. I promise. Every word is what I happened to overhear them saying one night when they thought I was busy studying in the next room. I figured I could use that knowledge someway, someday."

"Really? And why are you using it today, with me? I wonder what the preacher has up his godly sleeves." He was, after all, her favorite brother-in-law, even if he was her *only* brother-in-law.

"You've got me." Tyrell looked a bit shame-faced. "Our special for this Sunday at church cancelled, and I wondered if you'd consider giving us a selection from your flute?"

"You mean play my flute in church?" Would lightning strike her at even thinking such a thing?

"That's what I'm asking."

"But I'm not a member and don't profess to be, Tyrell. I wouldn't feel right."

"I understand and don't want you to be uncomfortable, so here's the deal. There's a tiny platform off to the right of the main one. We could set you up there where you'd be less conspicuous and wouldn't offend your feelings either by having to perform on the main platform."

"I don't know. Can I think about it?" Josie grimaced. "Though I've played a little here and there for my own amusement, I haven't seriously practiced forever. Might not be able to get a squeak out of it, let alone music."

"Josephine Rayner Patterson, as your sister and my wonderful wife would say, I would bet, if I was a betting man, that you could play that instrument with your eyes closed.

Her brother-in-law exuded confidence in her ability. Too bad she wasn't as sure she could do it, or even wanted to.

~*~

Josie pulled her flute case from the closet and set it on the stand after Tyrell left, clicking open the locks, and staring down at the instrument. She'd been only a child—six years old—when she and her sisters and Papa had settled into the music room to listen over the radio air waves to the famous flutist sharing a concert with the world.

She'd fallen in love then. From that day forward, she'd not looked back, but had coaxed and begged and nagged for a flute of her own, until—finally—for her seventh birthday, she'd unwrapped the long package and gazed upon the most gorgeous gift she'd ever received. It had been her prized and beloved treasure.

Now, she lifted it, took the cloth she used to clean it and gave it a thorough going-over, polishing until the wood gleamed with beauty. Then, slowly she lifted it to her lips and sat silent a moment. Her gaze drifted to the tall willow tree outside her window. Wouldn't be as good as sitting beneath it, playing for the birds in the branches...or Jerry sitting close by, as they'd done several times before he left, but close enough.

She tucked her flute beneath her arm and hobbled to the window.

The first notes became second ones, and then the song was pouring from her flute. When the last note ended, she allowed her arms to lower and smiled at her image reflecting from the glass window.

She'd not forgotten.

~*~

Josie sat on a side seat, half hidden from the rest of the West Street Community Church congregation, fingers shaking, a lump the size of an apple stuck in her throat. Unlike the minutes before a skating competition, where she always felt excited and on edge to begin, faint traces of nervousness spread through her body, which was crazy. She'd coaxed music from her flute for years, and not once, even at the recitals her teachers had required, had it bothered her.

She'd practiced all week. That wasn't the problem. Being in church, *performing* in church was. From the time Jerry and she had eloped, she'd not set foot in her family's church more than three times. What if the people disapproved of her being here, or worse, hated her music?

Whatever. Tyrell had asked, and she'd finally given in and agreed. Wouldn't kill her this one time, and one time was all it would be. Being in church made her itchy. Too many goody-goodys. *She'd* certainly never been described as such.

When the worship leader introduced her, Josie stepped to the microphone and began the song. Nearly a third of the way through, Josie sensed the music was taking hold of her. The sweet, clear notes encircled her and reached down into her very being and touched something private and hidden.

Tears pricked at the back of her eyelids, and she closed them, pouring herself into the music even as it tugged at feelings she'd kept buried for years, deep in her heart. Almost, as if a loving spirit was beckoning—wooing—her to yield, to come closer, to experience something she'd never discovered before, a powerful drawing tugged at her heart.

She reached out—mentally, tentatively—for that illusive unknown and felt as if she'd clasped hands with God himself.

When at last, the final note ended, Josie stood quietly, her flute still close to her lips. What had happened? The sunshine seemed brighter. The color-tinted window scenes seemed more alive.

The church was filled, and faces were lifted toward her.

But what stunned her were their expressions, the tears on scattered cheeks, the raptured, quiet look of worship on dozens of faces.

And then they were clapping and standing to their feet in a gracious move of appreciation. Josie stared, awed at their approval. Strangely, for the first time in her life, and she had no idea what it was unless...was it humbleness sweeping over her? She'd never felt such a thing so how was she to know?

She barely heard a word of Tyrell's sermon, but when it was over, and she was moving toward Papa and the rest of the family, she found herself swamped by people wanting to relay how touched they'd been at her *anointed* music.

Anointed? Her? She doubted that, but it was nice of them to say so.

By the time she got to Papa Ossie, her head was spinning. She clutched at his outstretched hands.

He studied her face. "Everyone go ahead. Shirley, do you mind? Josie's walking home with me," he ordered, and as if by magic the rest headed for the doors, leaving father and daughter alone.

"Here, let me carry your flute case. Anything else? Got your jacket?" At her nod, he placed her hand on his arm and led her outside. "Glad to see the sun shining and warmer weather. I'll have to confess the cold gets to me anymore."

At the bottom of the steps stood a tall man, looking quite dapper in his pin-striped gray suit—no make-overs in his clothes. Even Josie could tell a good suit from a hand-me-down.

The man watched them walk toward him, a faint smile touching his lips. When they drew close, he nodded and touched his Homburg. "Good morning."

Papa nodded, touched his own PorkPie and made as if to move past.

"I want to compliment you on the inspiring and touching music this morning. It was powerful, wasn't it? Very moving. Not sure I've heard anything that quite matches your talent."

Josie stopped dead in her tracks, halting her father in his stride to move past the man. It'd been several weeks since she'd seen him. It was the man on the street who'd needed directions. "I know you. You asked for directions here."

"You remembered." The man beamed at her. "I didn't want to be presumptuous in approaching you, being new in town, but felt I could not fail to express how impressed I was with your rendition this morning."

"Thank you." What a nice person he was. And handsome to boot. Josie felt the ever-so-soft nudge from Papa.

"Oh, I'm sorry. Papa, this is a friend I met a few weeks back." Josie smiled up into the man's dark eyes. "I don't know your name…"

"Walter Greye, and you are Josephine Patterson, correct? I'm assuming this is Captain Ossie Rayner, your father?"

"Yes, but how did you know that?" And how did you know my husband's name weeks ago? As sure as anything, Josie knew she'd never mentioned it to him.

"I'm here on business. I plan to host a dinner event where I will give the proposal speech for the business I'm representing. I've been searching for entertainment, but so far—although quite good—not exactly what I'm looking for." He stared intently at Josie as if trying to judge her response. "Then fate was kind to me. I heard about a young lady who was not only talented but lovely. It was easy enough to get your name and address."

"So you came here today to meet my daughter?" Papa's normal gruff voice held more than it's normal gruffness. Being his usual protective self.

"That was my primary purpose—" Walter Greye nodded at Josie. "—and why I was looking for this church, to speak to the pastor about you."

"I see."

With all the reserve of a doting father, Papa Ossie studied the man opposite them, and Josie was sure he was deciding whether to trust him or not.

"Then I suppose I must invite you to dinner to learn for myself whether this is something Josie would be interested in."

"Papa. I can decide for myself."

"I know that, my dear, but it will ease my heart to know I can trust our new friend to keep you safe in these dangerous days."

"I understand, Papa." Josie grasped her father's arm again. "You're welcome to join the family dinner, Mr. Walter Greye."

"Then I accept."

~*~

"Papa, I have *never* ever experienced what I did this morning. It was almost as if *God* was reaching down to touch me. I thought I was going to rise up in the air from the emotions flowing inside me. It was crazy, but wonderful too. What was wrong with me?" Shame tugged at her breathing such personal feelings. Not even to Jerry, and certainly, not to anyone else, had she ever spoken like this.

But Papa Ossie's face held no condemnation, no ridicule and no loftiness at her confession. Instead, there was a look of amazement and happiness radiating from his very being. "Josie, my fearless daughter. Your mama wrung her hands many a time trying to control your tantrums. It was only when she turned over your discipline to me, that we made a little progress."

"Poor Mama."

"It wasn't an impossible task, just a matter of finding what worked for you as punishment. Denying you outings with your sisters and mother didn't work. You just stuck that nose in the air and pretended you didn't care."

"So, what did you do?"

"Took away your books, your skates or your flute. Worked like a charm."

"Oh, dear, what a horrible child I must have been."

"Never that." Papa Ossie sighed. "I saw too much of myself in you to despise you, Child."

"So what happened to me this morning? Was it a mood? Worry over Jerry? The music?" Josie leaned her head against Papa Ossie's shoulder.

"I think God was speaking to you. He was drawing you close to him, wanting you to accept him as your Savior."

"I can't believe that. I mean, look at me. He wouldn't want the likes of me. I'm much too—too—I'm not good enough."

"None of us are."

"What about Tyrell and Emma Jaine?"

"They, too, had to accept Christ as their Savior."

Was Papa right? Had God, uh, tried to communicate with her? Seemed crazy. She, of all persons had never given a thought to God and that he might be interested in her. Her main objective in life had been to go straight on toward what *she* wanted.

She didn't understand it, but it had felt pretty good. Almost other-worldly. Josie felt a grin tugging her lips. "Why did those people act the way they did? I thought people in church were stuffy and quiet and boring."

Papa Ossie chuckled. "Some could be described as all that, Josie, but not all. I haven't been the best example in the past. I let work and life, and anger at God for your mother's death, keep me from doing all I should. It's only been Tyrell and Shirley's encouragement and prodding that set me seeking the right way again."

She studied her father, trying to understand what he was saying. "But why did they act that way? I'm not that good although I suppose I do a decent enough job. And I do love my flute even if I've neglected it."

"That's exactly why they loved your music. You may not be perfect, as you claim, but when you play, you have a passion inside you that comes through your music. It was the same with your skating. This passion speaks to the heart and draws one closer to God."

"Well said, Captain." Tyrell walked into the room. "Sorry to interrupt, but Jonah says dinner is served."

"Good." Papa waved a hand at her, motioning her to go ahead. "Tyrell, a word. We'll be right there, Josie."

Josie exited the room but hesitated. She was glad she did when she heard Papa ask Tyrell in a low voice, "Did you get a chance to ask your sources about Jerry?"

She couldn't hear what Tyrell answered, but as she walked on to the dining room, she wondered why Papa had wanted Tyrell to check up on Jerry. Did they know something she didn't?

~*~

Emma Jaine had placed Walter Greye beside Josie. He held her chair for her as she sat, then settled into his own. Leaning a few inches closer, he spoke in a low voice after Papa asked the blessing. "This is quite a gathering."

"Emma Jaine runs the boarding house, so we always have a diverse bunch for Sunday dinner. It's a lot of fun, but I haven't eaten here much since I have my own home now."

"Is that right? And is your husband serving in the military?"

"Not now. He was injured in the war and is recovering now. He's, uh, pretty busy, which keeps him gone quite a bit."

"That's too bad. Where does he work now?" Mr. Greye scooped a spoonful of potatoes onto his plate.

For a second, Josie had no idea what to say. She didn't know where Jerry worked or even if he did. She'd just assumed that he did. Maybe he stayed away because of her.

Appetite gone, she wanted to bolt. The thought that Jerry didn't love her, had lost the passion they'd once shared, strangled her.

"Is something wrong?" the man's voice lowered even more. Anyone listening would never have heard a word.

"No. Yes. I'm sorry, nothing of concern. I'm not very hungry."

"I see. You must keep up your strength to heal from such a serious skating accident."

Was he looking into her soul? For a moment, Josie forgot about her dinner, appetite or anyone sitting at the table.

"How did you know I injured my foot? Were you there that night? I thought I saw you." She frowned. How could he have known that, and if he did, did he also know she'd never skate professionally again? Did he know her plans for the Olympics were gone?

His question troubled her, yet she had no idea why.

"I suppose I must have picked it up from someone. Or I could have seen you limping. Does it matter?" His hand touched hers but immediately pulled away. Hardly noticeable. "You fascinate me. You're an extremely unique blend of mystery and ingénue that pulls one in then pushes them away when that one gets too close."

His eyes were brilliant, skimming her face, with a shade more—was it enthusiasm?—than Josie felt comfortable with. She wasn't use to being scrutinized by a stranger.

Why didn't he want to admit he was there that night? What was he trying to hide? But then maybe he was being subtle about admitting it, thinking she'd make more out of it then there was.

Time to change the subject. "What exactly were you interested in if I consent to playing for your dinner affair?"

Lips tilting in a knowing half-smile, he studied her face again, only this time, boldly—too much so.

Josie realized he recognized her move for what it was.

"Simply attend the dinner. It's a dressy affair. You'd have, oh, maybe forty-five minutes of performance, and, of course, will be generously paid."

"Any preference of songs?"

"Ja—um, Yes, and, if you agree, I'd like you to play a classical piece perhaps by Hans Henze? Are you acquainted with his works?"

What had he been about to say? The name of a song? A person's name? "The German composer. Not much. I'll see if I can find one not too hard or do some adapting."

"Good. Maybe some swing? 'Lili Marlene'?"

"I know that one." Josie nodded and smiled. "And I love 'We'll Meet Again'." No need to tell him she'd sung it in her mind day after day waiting on Jerry to return.

"Then I'll leave it with you. If you can get me a list beforehand?"

"Sure. I'd also like to invite an escort to go with me."

"Your husband? Perhaps he will be too busy to attend?"

"Perhaps. But I have others I can ask." Were they in a battle?—a genteel one, and it excited her. She loved a good fight, whether a word contest or an arm wrestle.

"By all means, feel free to." He touched his lips with his napkin and slanted another glance her way. "I did think perhaps you might consider going as my escort."

"Yours?" Was he serious? She barely knew the man. "I think I prefer my own escort, thank you. That's even if I decide to do this."

No need to give in too quickly.

His head tilted. "As you wish."

Josie never felt flustered, yet she did now. No one in their right mind had ever singled her out—except for Jerry, of course—with her sisters around. Given that Emma Jaine was happily married, pregnant and ready to deliver her baby, she could understand that a male might hesitate to make a move on her, but Claire?

Her gaze shifted to her younger sister. As usual, the strawberry blond held the attention of both men on either side of her. She was a mixture of daring—definitely not the tomboyish type—and flirtiness, and more than one man had walked away from Claire Rayner with a broken heart.

Though Josie had teased her sister to tears while they were growing up, Josie would never confess to being a little in awe of her. She'd never seen Claire at a loss for words whether to cut down someone for size or to flatter the other person to get what she wanted. She seemed totally confident in whatever she attempted or did.

So what was with Walter Greye's seeming interest in *her*?

Chapter Eighteen

Jerry shut the door. It was early, too early to be home, but he'd needed to change clothes. If Josie was here, well, he'd have to leave again. He walked quietly into the kitchen and sniffed. Ah, coffee. Even though she'd had to water it down because of the war rations, she always managed to have coffee for him since he'd been home. Probably robbed some of it from Harriet Mason's cabinets. Jerry chuckled. Whatever, it was far better than the corner cafe served. He poured a cup and sipped. Good. Just what he needed after another fruitless day.

He started up the stairs and heard her off-key voice singing from the bedroom. It brought a smile to his lips, and he shook his head. There wasn't a thing that woman did but what it made him happy.

Stepping to the doorway, he peeked in.

~*~

Josie flung back her wet hair, and her gaze flicked to her husband standing at the door of their bedroom. His gaze slid away, but the glimpse of the fire in his eyes was better than any sip of the fortifying drinks she'd sneaked throughout the last year of his absence.

He obviously hadn't forgotten her in the most intimate sense. But did he still love her? The heat roaring through her body clued her in: she had no doubts about her affection for him. But his? If the way he'd acted the last month was any indication the prospect for a warm and fuzzy ending didn't look promising.

Still, a little wifely flirting never hurt anything.

But what did she know?

And why was he home so early anyhow? She could count on one hand the times he'd been home earlier than midnight. Tonight of all nights, when she was headed to Walter Greye's dinner event. But then, there was always time when a wife was fighting for her husband's love.

She twisted her long, curly hair into a knot and

secured it with a glittering silver comb then studied her image in the mirror and frowned at the length of her long neck. Her heart lightened when she once again saw Jerry staring at her, his smoldering dark eyes alight with a flame she loved. Whirling away she shuffled her outfits from one side to the other.

"I always loved you in blue." His voice was low and a bit on the gravelly side.

Josie reached for the dusty blue and rose flowered taffeta, not caring that Claire had suggested the yellow. Nothing mattered except what Jerry wanted, desired. "Did you? And now?"

She allowed her gaze to meet his then jerked her gaze away. Careful with the teasing. He wasn't quite ready. Give him time. Let him make his own move.

She jumped when his image appeared behind her and his hands touched her shoulders. Fingers searched for and found the pins in her hair and removed them, one by one, his gaze riveted on her face. When her curls tumbled to her shoulders again, he stroked her neck, her cheek, then lifted first one strand and another of her hair before letting them drift against her skin again. For a second his shuttered eyes blazed hot and wild, his lips touched her neck, and she wanted to moan with delight.

Her eyes closed, and she allowed her head to bend giving him access to her body.

But his hands gripped her upper arms, and Josie opened her eyes at the pressure.

"You should never have married me."

"What?" The one word came out as a whispered question. Shock and terror played for dominion inside her body.

For what seemed an eternity, his tormented gaze rested on her face, and then it was over. He flung away, cursing, slamming out of the room, his dark mutters echoing along the hallway, bouncing against the walls, sliding into their bedroom. Taunting. Tempting. Final.

She rubbed angrily at the sudden moisture on her cheeks. Her heart pounded, and with each aching sound within her, she cried his name.

Jerry.

Jerry.

Jerry.

Useless begging.

No matter what had happened to him overseas, he didn't love her now. It was gone, and she was very much afraid, he had no desire to reclaim it.

~*~

What was the matter with him? Couldn't he be strong enough *for* Josie when he knew in his heart it was for *her* best interests? She might not realize it, but he knew. Jerry loved her too much to allow her to sacrifice a good life with the likes of him.

He'd already be gone, if it wasn't for his fear of her safety. He wouldn't walk away when it was his responsibility to care for her. Just because he could barely be in the same room and not wrap his arms around her—it wasn't a legitimate excuse.

The sooner he finished finding Rhoderick, if it was really him here in the U.S., the sooner he could let Josie get on with her life. Regardless of her injury and her surety she'd never skate again, he knew how strong and determined she was. She could do it if she wanted to.

His captain was insistent the man was stateside and was equally convinced Jerry would find him. But other than the vague, could-be sighting at Marshall's house that one night, Jerry had not gotten a hint of the whereabouts of him. What was he doing wrong? Or was it just the luck of the draw?

He needed to ante-up his search. Why not try to question some of Marshall's employees? That guard seemed a good possibility. Might as well start with him.

Streetlights lit up the evening. Houses were warm with subdued lamps, preparatory to the black out. Everyone on board and supportive of war efforts. Few were out and about yet, although later, couples would be strolling or heading to important functions. Singles would be looking for luck or love or opportunity.

Unlike him.

Or Josie.

Josie? Jerry stopped in his tracks.

Why was she dressing up as if going out? And in that seductive dress. Josie had always had a tendency to dress *down.* Did she realize how dangerous it was to go out alone at night?

But maybe she was headed over to the Rayner's Boarding House for an evening of socializing.

Jerry relaxed. That was it. She probably planned to encourage that young soldier Captain Ossie had told him about.

Yeah, that was it. Jerry resumed his limping-walk and heard the footsteps behind him.

~*~

Josie hadn't really wanted to ask Papa to go with her to Walter Greye's event, but she'd had no other option. Jerry had given her no choice, and she didn't want to take Tyrell away from Emma Jaine as close as she was to her delivery date. She could have asked Guy Delaney, but doubted he'd accept.

That left Papa. When she'd asked if he'd go, he'd swiveled his chair to stare out his window, then swung back to her with only one question. "Are you sure about this?"

"Do you see a problem I'm not seeing?" That question might encourage more papa-worry than she'd bargained for, but if he had a legitimate reason, then she wanted to know it before jumping into this event.

"Nothing more than my gut feeling about the man."

"I see no harm in it. I have to do something, Papa. With Jerry gone so much, I'm bored out of my mind. If I can help the man raise money for whatever his project is, then I'll do it. Will you go?"

Papa had agreed, and now she waited downstairs for him. When Jonah pulled up out front of her home, she hurried out, making sure to lock the door, not waiting on Papa or Jonah to escort her to the car.

"You look very beautiful, my dear." Papa reached for her hand to help her into the car. "That dress is an excellent choice for you."

"It's Jerry's favorite." Josie settled her skirt and shrugged her light shawl onto her shoulders a little more comfortably.

"Perhaps he thinks it brings out your feminine side?"

Papa's teasing grin coaxed a smile to her lips.

"Have you seen Jerry today?"

"Hmmm. A few minutes. In and out." Her heart still hurt from her husband's rejection. "I don't understand what I did to Jerry to make him...make him hate me like he does."

"Nonsense. Jerry doesn't hate you."

"Then—"

"What?"

Josie lowered her head and whispered the admittance. "He wishes he'd never married me."

"I can't believe that. He adores you." Papa Ossie patted Josie's hand. "He's suffering, child. Besides his injury—and for a strong man like him, that alone was devastating—there's something serious bothering him. Whatever he faced or endured while overseas, it has taken its toll on his mind and heart. You'll have to give him more time."

Her father didn't scare easily, so the troubled note in his voice, scared her. "What if he doesn't want to come back to me? I'm not sure I can go on..."

"Remember what I told you at your last skating competition?"

"Yes, I'd have to be stronger than I'd ever been in my life."

"That's right, Josie. You've always been strong. You inherited that fighting streak in you where you don't give up under pressure. If my guess is right, I'd say, you'd fight tooth and nail to get what you wanted, and right now, that is Jerry."

The chuckle was impromptu, but welcome all the same. For some reason, her spirits lifted, and though the worry and heartache still resided inside her, now she could go on. For how long, didn't need resolved tonight, and she wouldn't attempt it. Tonight, she'd concentrate on playing as well as she could. "Thank you, Papa. What would we do without you?"

"I ask myself that question quite often."

When Jonah pulled up to the curb in front of the enormous hall, Papa exited and helped Josie out. "Pick us up in three hours, Jonah."

Josie clutched her flute case, and father and daughter hurried inside. Walter Greye must have been watching for her, because he moved to her immediately. "Mrs. Patterson, what a delight to have you here tonight. Welcome, Captain Rayner. I hope you brought a large check to donate."

Papa wasn't the least intimidated by his suggestion. He gave the man a brief nod and moved away.

If Papa had meant to snub the man, Mr. Greye gave no indication he felt it. He turned to Josie. "Let me introduce you to a few of those here. We have a sold-out crowd eager to support my pet cause." He took her arm and guided her into another room where a generous crowd had gathered, mingling, talking, drinking and nibbling on hors d'oeuvres.

By the time Mr. Greye led her toward the stage where he said she'd be performing, her head was spinning with names of people unknown to her. Many of them had accents foreign to her ears, and others spoke in such high-society-vernacular, she was tongue-tied for fear of appearing more ignorant than she felt. Good thing Walter Greye was beside her to fill the silence that persisted after remarks and questions left her speechless.

"You're not nervous?" her new friend asked, taking her hand in both of his as they stood waiting on people to find their table seats.

"No." Josie smiled at him. Regardless of Papa's actions, Walter Greye had been above reproach as far as making sure she was well received. "I'll be fine. I might not be socially adept at speaking but I can wow with the best of them when it comes to music."

"I believe you can." He laughed. "I'll give a short welcome, then introduce you. Enjoy yourself."

"I will."

The people slowly made their way to their tables. Josie, peeking through the curtain, didn't see Papa, but he'd be around somewhere, waiting to hear her and to go home. She was sure as anything he wouldn't be bored. Papa could talk with anyone and feel at home—if he wanted to and it was a subject that interested him.

Walter Greye was giving his speech, and then he turned toward her and held out an arm, and Josie was walking toward him to a polite and a slightly less than enthusiastic applause.

That was all right. She was used to a crowd who didn't know her, and equally as well, to one who cheered for her wildly once they did. She had no doubts—after last Sunday—this group would enjoy her performance too.

She began with Walter Greye's classical choice, wanting to get the hardest out of the way first, then not giving them time to absorb what they'd heard, she moved smoothly into the next one. She'd not known a couple of the songs, but as much as she'd always hated the cliché Emma Jaine had drilled into her head when she was younger that practice made perfect, it was true. In days, she'd mastered the pieces and was quite confident she'd do well tonight.

She put herself into her performance, not naive enough to think tonight was not valuable enough to do her some good professionally. By the time she'd finished, she'd captured not only the guests' attention but their generous approval too. Walter Greye joined her on stage and added his own remarks of appreciation until Josie felt inundated with praise.

Minutes later, Josie slipped off, glad to have a few minutes by herself before looking for her father. She'd been invited to stay for the supper and supposed Papa had a seat for her. She leaned on a wall in a deserted hallway, getting her breath and relaxing.

The faint voices in the distance suddenly became louder, and Josie knew whoever they belonged to were walking toward her. That didn't matter, except they were talking about her and someone called Bhaer. And then, the second voice was louder, and Josie thought she recognized it. Was it—no, couldn't be.

~*~

"She's Bhaer's wife, and you know you've wanted to catch up with him."

Who were they talking about now? The unknown person meant to keep the words private, Josie was sure, but his voice echoed down the hallway, straight to her listening ears. She bit her lip, thinking. Should she cough and approach them, allowing them to know she was in the vicinity—and possibly avoid an unpleasant situation or stay where she was and pretend she'd not heard a word?

Surely Walter Greye would understand. Then again, maybe not.

"How did you find out about her?"

Greye's voice held a hint of annoyance. Why would that be?

A chuckle. "Wills, my favorite guard, clued me in when I questioned..."

Wills? Her Wills? The words faded out, and Josie could have screamed in frustration. Instead she muttered softly and leaned forward.

"—Then my...knows her and insisted the wife is strong-willed, stubborn, and determined, but innocent enough, making her pliable and easily manipulated."

Sounded like her. Josie snickered but caught back the giggle that almost escaped. Was her twin running loose in Cincinnati? Then blank confusion swept over her. Were they talking about her?

Besides who knew her enough to describe her as such? Who would want to? Not family, and surely not the boarding house residents. Would they?

No, they'd mentioned someone named Bhaer.

"Not a particularly great description about Josie Patterson."

Holy Mackerel. So they were talking about her.

"How does she know her?" Dry, with that definite bit of annoyance laced through it, Greye's voice sounded edgy—not as if he was irritated, but more disturbed.

She?

"Worked together, I gather."

Worked together? Whatever was the man talking about? She'd never had a paying job in her life...

"...We could pick her up—" The first person muttered in an even lower tone.

"No." Emphatically spoken, a no-questions-asked decision. Mr. Greye was obviously used to being obeyed.

They sounded near.

Josie's choice was made for her. She opened the nearest door and stepped inside, not closing it completely, one eye peering through the crack. She wanted to laugh at the ridiculous picture she made, but it wasn't really funny.

The two men turned the corner and still talked, still unknowing they had a listener eavesdropping on their private conversation. Would they be upset if they knew?

Josie risked another peek through the crack.

The unknown man—blond and tall—was angry and calling the Bhaer man a traitorous spy. But Walter Greye was as unflappable as usual.

"That's not his name."

"I know it." Unknown man snapped his reply.

"Then why use it?" Walter Greye lifted his glance as the two approached her hiding space.

Josie drew back, the shiver running up her spine, scaring her like few things did.

Why was Walter Greye and the first man talking about her and this Bhaer, and why had her new friend put a decisive kaput to the first man's suggestion?

Obviously, all was not as it seemed with Mr. Walter Greye, and if it involved Jerry—well, then, no wonder she'd felt so strongly about coming tonight. She had to save Jerry. From what, she didn't know yet. But she'd find out if she had to spend every day with Walter Greye.

Buying the farm for her husband was no question.

She took one step backward as the men drew closer, but even in the grave-like darkness, claws of fright scratched at her as the man she thought of as a new friend, scanned the cracked-open door.

Her breath puffed out of her as if she'd held it for minutes instead of seconds. He'd not seen her. How could he? No, it wasn't possible.

Then why had his eyes narrowed that tiny little bit?

~*~

The footsteps behind were measured, and he focused, judging them to determine the man and, hopefully, his intent. He knew the exact instant when they sped up as if to overtake him. On guard, Jerry listened for that soft whisper of wind that indicated the other person was taking a swing at him. Or perhaps a tiny click would be a quick, almost-too-late sign that a gun was about to explode behind him.

Rhoderick?

Jerry was about to whirl, as much as he could whirl

with his bum leg, when the man spoke. "Don't turn around. Need to talk with you."

"Why would you want to talk with me?"

"Maybe you should be asking the question: what would be to your advantage to talk with me?"

Jerry heard the chuckle. "Corner Cafe."

"No. There's a dive over on Second. Be there at eight."

The footsteps receded as if the owner had gone a different direction or turned around. Good. He'd have time to check out this dive before the man arrived and maybe look into a couple ideas he had on finding Rhoderick.

~*~

"I see you found the famous dive."

The voice speaking from behind Jerry was amused and quiet, almost as if the speaker was making a joke. But not quite, because there was a serious thread running through it.

"Glad you picked a first rate meeting place."

A chuckle, then a thin young man with a trim mustache slid into the booth opposite him.

The guard at Marshall's.

He was grinning, the mirth at his private joke, visible and so in-your-face Jerry wanted to bash something.

"I take it you don't know me."

"I'm afraid not," Jerry growled, not at all amused at the man knowing him instead of the other way around.

The man motioned to a waitress for some coffee. "Want some? Best coffee around except for Josie's. No one makes any better than my pal."

Jerry almost came across the booth to grab the man by his shirt collar, but stopped himself at the last minute. "*Your* pal?"

"Sure. She's the best friend I've ever had. I tell you, if you want a good time, spend some time with her. You're a lucky man."

A regular eager-beaver, the man was.

"How do you know her so much?" He tried but couldn't keep the snarl from his voice.

The waitress set down steaming cups of coffee on a stained table cloth that didn't look like it'd been washed in several months.

"I have my ways."

He was laughing at him, and that made Jerry even angrier.

He'd gotten here early, waiting outside for a good twenty minutes, checking out the place. He didn't want to be caught unaware, and at a seedy place like this, anything was possible. When he'd finally walked inside, he'd scoped out the almost-empty room and chosen the darkest corner he could see, in the back. With his back to the wall and his gaze on the door, he figured no one could enter without him seeing them first.

But he hadn't counted on the back door.

~*~

Major Patterson had changed, not just in his personality but his face showed the strain the man must be in. And no wonder. If what the captain had shared with him was truth—the ordeal Patterson had gone through in Germany—then the major was due for some serious relaxation and rest.

Didn't look like he was getting any of that right now. Josie must be going out of her mind with worry, and no one knew as well as he the depth of Josie's love for the man.

Besides working with the Marshall man, his secondary assignment was being the backup for Patterson. For Josie's sake, if for no other reason, he'd do that or die trying.

~*~

"Let's get down to seriousness. Why did you need to talk with me?"

"Captain sent me."

"Why?"

"To let you know you're not alone. You have someone to guard your back."

"But you work for Marshall."

"Yeah."

Why was the man suddenly so tight with the information?

"So where's your loyalty lie?"

"Where do you think?"

"How should I know?"

The man laid his forearms on the tabletop and leaned forward. "We didn't know the identity of the man willing to sell that list of names to Rhoderick, until you discovered it. We've been watching Marshall for several months now, and six months ago, I was able to gain employment there. Saved your bacon that night you snuck into his house, didn't I?"

His grin was infectious, but Jerry didn't feel like laughing.

"I could have ignored you, allowed Marshall and his men to find you."

"That's right, but you didn't. Am I suppose to think that shows your loyalty to the good ole U.S.? Could be you have your own agenda."

"Could be you'd be wrong. You see, I can be accused of a lot of things, but not when it comes to my loyalties. My love for my country falls only slightly behind two of my other loves."

That was interesting. Jerry couldn't resist asking and smiled as he did. "And what would those be?"

The young man gave him a sassy smile. "My God and the woman I love."

Jerry did laugh then. "Are you ever going to tell me your name, or is that a secret too?"

"I could, but then I'd have to kill you." The man stood. "Thanks for meeting me, and you can call me William, if you want. See you around."

Chapter Nineteen

Josie started to step out of the dark room when she heard the steps. Not just steps but hurrying steps as if...as if someone was trying to catch up with someone.

Like her?

Gripping her flute case, she fled.

The footsteps picked up their rhythm, keeping time to her own frantic steps. She turned the corner and halted, listening.

Silence. And then...

The quiet sounds of a stealthy approach.

Josie abandoned any thought of hiding. She ran—or rather limpingly ran, pushing her injured ankle and hoping she'd not damage it again—and no one had ever called her a turtle.

Back toward the dining area, and straight into the back doors of the reception room. Her gaze scrambled over the tables, searching for her father's face, and found him, toward the back, off to the right. She hurried to the other side of the room, and settled into the empty seat, leaning sideways to give his friendly face a swift kiss.

"You wowed them, my dear."

"Thanks, Papa." Josie gasped out the words and nodded at the others at the table giving her big smiles. She picked up her napkin, started to place it on her lap, then let her gaze roam the room once more, for assurance that she was safe.

Emma Jaine's newest tenant, Guy Delaney, stood in the door opposite the room, his gaze seemingly fastened on her. She wanted to avert her gaze, but something in his stare held hers fast.

Another few seconds, then the smallest of smiles crossed his face, and he tilted his head in a mild nod. His gaze flickered to the left, and Josie followed his gaze with her own.

Walter Greye stood in the doorway she'd just passed

through, his gaze flickering around the room.

Josie averted her gaze, not wanting to meet his eyes, that drumbeat in her ears coming straight from her heart.

Was he searching for her?

~*~

Josie's choice of hymns to share with the West Street Community Church Sunday morning was an especially sweet one. It floated softly throughout the sanctuary and had the congregation nodding and smiling. But Josie's heart felt anything but happy or peaceful.

Was Walter Greye here? Would he even show up, or had he had his fill now that he'd gotten her to play for his pet project this past week?

She wanted him here. Oh, how she wanted him here. Once home, two nights ago and safe from the stressful regard of Walter Greye, Josie's nerves had settled down, and anger had kicked into high gear. Now, she not only wanted him here but needed him here to find out why they'd talked about 'picking her up.'

Innocent sounding words, but Josie had heard the words and the tone. There was more to them, and she meant to find out what.

She wouldn't ask, but she'd keep her—and Jerry's—enemy, if indeed he was one, close at hand where she could observe and learn his intentions. Her active imagination might be playing havoc with her brain, but better that than being sorry if Jerry got hurt. He'd gone through too much now.

Forty minutes later, Josie headed toward Claire and Papa when a young bobby soxer stopped her progress.

"Oh, Miss Patterson, your music was just Lulu." She pressed a hand to her chest in an exaggerated gesture. "I couldn't quit crying. How did you learn to play with such passion? Could you teach me?"

Oh, dear, this was uncomfortable. She was definitely no teacher and could barely keep up with her own self. "Thanks, I'm glad you enjoyed it. Sorry, I don't teach anything."

A hand touched her shoulder, and then the crowd pressed in upon her. Josie looked from first one to another, bewildered by the ecstatic praise. When a strong hand gripped her arm, Josie jumped and turned.

Walter Greye faced her, his face sober but not unpleasant. He didn't let go of her arm, but led her away, giving her the opportunity to politely break free of the well-meaning but overwhelming folk bent on talking with her.

"I hope that frantic expression on your lovely face meant you needed rescued." Greye chuckled in a side remark to her even as he nodded and responded to greetings.

"Thanks. I did feel a bit pressured back there although I'm sure they meant well."

"No doubt. That was a touching rendition you offered this morning."

As they exited the church Papa, Claire and Tyrell waited for her at the bottom of the steps. An odd expression crossed Papa's face, but Josie couldn't read it. Anger? Displeasure? Concern? Whatever it'd been, it was gone in a flash.

"Good to see you here today, Greye." Tyrell grasped the other man's hand and shook it.

"I was able to get free and hoped to hear this young lady again." He smiled but somehow it didn't seem quite as warm as the words implied.

"Then join us again today for dinner at the boarding house." Tyrell was enthusiastic in his invitation, but Papa merely nodded.

"I don't want to intrude." His words were directed at Tyrell, but his gaze rested on Josie.

"Of course, you must join us. Why not?" Josie dimpled at him, but couldn't quite meet that intense gaze of his.

"Well, then, thank you. I accept. It will give me a chance to talk over an idea I have with you, Pastor."

"Excellent. Let's walk together. Captain, will you join us? Josie, Claire, you all right by yourselves?"

"Really, Tyrell? We'll be right behind you. Go." Did he think they were weaklings? Her leg still ached, still gave her some trouble if she was on it too much, but that didn't mean she couldn't walk down a street by herself. And she had Claire. Josie grinned, wondering what kind of help Claire would be if they were assaulted. But then, she'd probably lash them thoroughly with that sharp tongue of hers, and they'd flee just to get away from the scolding.

"I wanted to talk with you, Josie." Claire linked arms with her and pulled her along as she walked.

Josie flicked a glance at this sister with whom she'd always felt the most distant. Claire, always the one to err on the polite, correct side of convention, was just shy of being prissy, with enough sass to keep her interesting. As friends or confidants, they were totally incompatible.

So why on earth would this sister want to talk with *her*?

Claire didn't wait on a response. Which was a good thing since Josie didn't know what to say.

"I'm thinking of putting my music studies on hold."

That was unexpected. Claire seldom deviated from her plans.

"I want to do something a little more useful, be of service to my country."

"You want to join the WASPs?" That, Josie could not see.

"I want to use my voice to entertain the troops."

Josie blinked and felt blindsided by Claire's announcement. "Are you serious? The guys can be a bit rambunctious. Besides, they like rowdy tunes."

Her sister gave her glance that would have made anyone but someone with Josie's staunch personality cringe. "I know what men are like, and they can enjoy...I'll show them they can enjoy classier music too. But I don't mind adding a few of the more *fun* type of songs to my repertoire."

"Well, I say go for it. You should do what makes you happy."

"But not what Emma Jaine thinks I should do?"

"You know she's our anchor, but she can't live your life for you. Do what's right for you, Claire. That's the advice I live by."

"I suppose you're right." Claire looked like she might be a little less than sure. Then, as if her mind was made up, she added, "But it's what I'm suppose to do. By the way, who's the new man?"

"Walter Greye? I don't really know him that well. I met

him one day, then he turned up at church and invited me to play at an event he sponsored."

"His name is fake."

"What on earth do you mean?"

"He's not a Walter. Look at him."

"It's a popular name.

"Not for him. He speaks excellent English, but there's something about his accent that gives me the impression he knows another language far better than English."

Josie stared at her sister. Never in her wildest dreams would she have thought Claire so observant. "You don't like him?"

"I didn't say that." She frowned. "I don't know him enough to know how I feel about him. But he's not who he says he is." With that, she let go of Josie's arm and strolled ahead.

Josie let her go, and dawdled the rest of the way to her father's house. She cast a longing glance at her own place as she passed, wishing Jerry was there, standing at a window, waiting on her arrival.

No such luck. Sighing, she hurried to catch up.

~*~

"You know the consequences of backing out."

Josie stopped dead. The low murmuring was clipped and edged with anger. It sounded like...

"I can't do it. They're good people. I want out."

"There is no out—"

"I won't do—"

There was a subdued crack as if someone had slammed into a wall. Josie peeked around the corner of the library. No one had turned on the hallway lights, in spite of those gathered for Sunday dinner, yet it was light enough. Was that Greye? She couldn't see the other man.

Sounded like threats. Who was threatening who?

Josie almost laughed, but the voices sounded too scary.

Another peek, and Greye was walking toward her, one hand casually brushing off his dark gray suit.

Josie backed into the next room and grabbed at a newspaper, pretending to study it, but she needed not bother. The man strolled past the room and stepped inside the dining room.

A smug smile tilted his lips.

~*~

"Would you go for a stroll with me? I have a proposition to make you." Mr. Greye cornered her after Sunday dinner when most of the boarding house residents had gathered in the music room.

Did she want to? An opportunity to see what he was up to for sure, but—Josie hesitated—was it safe? A second later, she scolded herself. *Silly, why wouldn't it be?*

But no need to make it easy for him.

"That's just what I need—a nice walk in the brisk air, but I promised Papa that I would talk with Guy." she tilted her head in the direction of the young man sitting by himself in an armchair close to the window. He stared out it, but once in awhile his attention was drawn to a hoot of laughter or a particular loud voice in the room. He never smiled, and his eyes were sad ones, but he wasn't downright rude.

Had he been following her and Shirley at the concert that night weeks ago? Why had he been at Mr. Greye's affair, and if Mr. Greye had known Guy was coming, why hadn't he suggested Guy for her escort? Something about that night bothered her. Not Guy Delaney himself, but more along the lines of an incident she could not remember.

"Guy? Ach, the boy at the window. I see." Greye smoothed his mustache. "Invite him to go along. Looks as if he needs the fresh air."

"Swell. I'll let you know."

When Josie approached Guy Delaney, he looked up but said nothing.

"I'm Josie, and you're Emma Jaine's newest tenant, I'm assuming."

"I know who you are." The boy nodded. "The second sister—didn't you elope? And the best one of the three, so goes the rumors."

Josie laughed. "Don't believe everything you hear."

"I don't know any of you enough to form a judgment like that." He gave another look out the window, one hand rubbing the back of his head. "But the impression I've got, you all are a pretty swell family. Wish I had the time to get to know you better."

His voice dripped melancholy, and a tinge of pity touched her usual indifferent heart.

"You might wish you didn't."

"I doubt it."

"Mr. Greye wants to take a walk. Would you go with us?"

"Who? Oh, you mean—" For a minute he seemed nonplussed. "The tall man talking with your father? Is he a new tenant?"

"Yes, that's him. He was here last Sunday too. Remember? And, no, I don't think there are any empty rooms here right now." Josie smiled at all the familiar faces.

Bette Williams, who hadn't grown any younger, yet still ran after the illusive dream of becoming an actress. Philo, their modestly successful artist, Tom Atkinson— baching it since his wife had been arrested as an accomplice in espionage, but moving on with his life, and Gertie Hanover, the rich resident gossip and smartest elderly woman in the city. Shirley Largett, librarian, and Guy made up the last members along with the Rayner family and Tyrell. She did miss them all, but not enough to give up her home with Jerry.

Her heart panged with pain.

"I was ill last week. Didn't see him here."

Josie dragged her mental wandering back to the present. "So you want to go with us? I'd like it if you did."

"I don't know." His hands rubbed together as if he was nervous. "Why would he want me to go with both of you? Now if I could get you off to myself for a walk..." His grin was pure and sudden boyish mischief.

Better ignore that last comment.

"Why would he want *me* to go?" Josie tossed the question back at the man and shrugged. "I've only just met him and not at all sure I even like him. It would be nice to have someone from the boarding house along— just in case."

Guy's brows lifted, and he eyed Greye. "I see what you

mean. He does look a little frightening."

"Don't get me wrong. I'm not afraid of him; just not sure I care for him much."

"You're probably not afraid of a lot, are you?"

"Not really. Are you?"

"Depends. I've seen some pretty scary things."

Josie hesitated. She could imagine he had, having been in the military. "So are you coming or not?"

"You twisting my arm?"

"Do I need to?"

"No, and the answer is yes, I'll come. Not sure what kind of conversationalist I'll be, but since you insist..."

"Good." Josie stood. "I'll tell him we're both going. Can you be ready in a half-hour?"

He looked down at his clothes. "I'll grab a coat, and that won't take thirty seconds."

"You're my kind of friend." Josie gave him a crooked grin. He reminded her of the sassiness Wills Mason, their hired help's son, had always tossed at her.

She hoped Wills was all right.

If she'd ever had a brother, she'd have wanted it to be someone like Wills. He'd been her confidant and comrade in mischief the whole time of their growing up. Funny they could be so close in friendship and neither one had given a thought to it becoming more than that. One thing for sure, she hoped God kept him safe. She couldn't endure losing him.

She gave Mr. Greye her's and Guy's answer then headed to check on Emma Jaine. At the doorway, she looked back at Guy. His gaze was fixed on someone across the room, and he was nodding, angrily and almost bullishly. Jerking her head in the direction he stared, hoping to see who he was nonverbally communicating with, she scanned the occupants of the room.

But everyone was chatting with others. No one was returning Guy's glare.

Josie frowned. What on earth?

~*~

It was odd that there was no hint of Rhoderick anywhere. As far as he could tell, he'd not visited at Marshall's again. At least, not any time he'd checked. And it seemed as if Marshall was keeping a low profile.

Had he had a tip he was being watched? Was it this Wills fellow acting virtuous, but as much a traitor as Marshall?

Captain Phil hadn't gotten back with him on the background checks he'd requested. Would it do any good to badger him a little?

No, if the man knew anything to help the situation, he'd have let him know.

So that meant he'd have to dig a little deeper, maybe push some boundaries to get answers. It was past time to end this search.

Who was this young man calling himself William? His face was familiar, as if he'd known him years ago. At one point in their conversation, he'd wanted to give the young whipper-snapper a knuckle sandwich. Who did he think he was dealing with?

But then he did seem awfully young. Fearless and too smart for his own good, but who was he to talk? What he needed was some Josie-time.

How he missed his woman. He wanted nothing more than to forget Rhoderick and be with Josie. He faltered and half-turned. From his side vision, he caught an image some hundred feet back.

Following him?

He walked another dozen or so feet, then as quickly as he could, whirled.

No one was there.

Which didn't mean they'd not been there minutes earlier. Following him.

Or not.

For all he knew, they could still be lurking, hidden, watching him. And laughing at his bewilderment. One thing for sure, even if he got close, even if he could see them, he'd never catch them. Not with his bum leg.

Disgusted with himself and the whole mess, Jerry growled to himself and took off for home. Right now, he couldn't care less about anything but seeing Josie. Regardless of the consequences, he was going home for the evening.

Chapter Twenty

Josie walked between Guy Delaney and Walter Greye. The sun was toying with the horizon, teasing it with violet and orange and yellow, filling her with a lightness of spirit she hadn't felt since Jerry had come home. Well, not counting that Sunday morning at the West Street Community Church.

Guy strolled beside her, saying nothing, and she wondered if he was even listening to their conversation. Greye was talking now and then, pointing out interesting places and things, and Josie answered but as little as she could. She was enjoying the fresh air and sky far too much to talk.

"I talked with your brother-in-law about the church joining in to support my project."

That brought Josie's attention back to the man. "What project?"

He gave her a look. "The project I presented the night you entertained my guests with your flute. I wondered if I could count on your support? I really could use an escort when I attend the various groups to which I've been invited to speak. Your attractive self would give me more credibility with your fellow-citizens."

Her fellow citizens? That sounded odd.

Better ignore that last request. She couldn't imagine Jerry approving such a thing, and if she did agree, her agenda was the reason. "Can you tell me more about the project?"

"Of course." Greye's gray eyes flicked to Guy then back to Josie, studying her. "I'm hoping to start a support group for those who've suffered losses during the war."

"That is impressive. Have you very many supporters yet?"

"A handful. That's why I need your help." He stopped walking, turned to her, and reached for one of her hands, smoothing it. "Josie, you're fast becoming important to me."

Guy half-growled on the other side of her. "You forgetting she's married, *Greye*?"

"I'm forgetting nothing. Stay out of this."

Guy stopped walking. "Sorry. I can't go along with this. Josie..."

"Shut up."

More of a growl then a snarl, it was still shocking to hear the tone from the man who never seemed to raise his voice. Mr. Greye was not happy with Guy. She didn't want them fighting over her.

"Are you two talking about me? Whatever do you mean, Guy?"

Guy stood as stiff as a statue, unspeaking, that same bullish look covering his features as minutes before. He didn't look at Josie, only kept his steel-eyed stare directed at Greye.

Josie touched the boy's arm, afraid that perhaps an old injury was causing his strange mood. "Guy, will you please talk to me? You're making me nervous. Tell me what can you not go along with?"

She must have gotten through to him because his gaze moved to her face. He gave her his usual shy smile. "No need for you to worry about it, Josie. I'm going to make sure nothing happens to you or your family.

"You are?" What was he talking about?

He sketched a swift salute and tossed over his shoulder as he walked away, "I'm through. Got that? Nothing you can do about it."

Was he still talking to her? Kind of sassy, if he was.

"Pay him no mind. I have strong suspicions he's suffering from post-trumatic war injuries. I'm pretty sure I heard his doctor wanted to put him on medications, but he refused."

"Really? Where did you hear this?" Tyrell and Emma Jaine, and definitely Papa, would have heard such a thing. They were intuitive and not easily fooled. Something was bothering Guy and she'd give a lot of moolah to know what.

Josie rested her gaze on Walter Greye.

He stared after the retreating figure of Guy Delaney, but Josie couldn't read the expression playing across his features.

Walter Greye looked down at her and tucked the hand he still held on his arm and covered it with his own. "I'm sorry you had to listen to that. Come, let's walk some more and forget about moody young men."

Feeling as if her hand was contaminated, Josie wanted to jerk it away from his large one, and then give his foot a good stomp. But she didn't. She'd play along, all right. She needed to know what this man was up to.

Important to him, my foot. I just bet I am.

~*~

Jerry paused at the street gate, staring at their house. He'd been so happy to purchase it—with Captain Ossie's help and influence, of course. It'd given him satisfaction to provide Josie with her own private space from the overwhelming one at the boarding house and yet keep her close enough the men could be protection for his wife while he was gone.

The house stood dark. No welcoming lights. So Josie was either not home—he switched his gaze to the brightly lit windows at the Rayner's—or she was out. Again. He scowled at the thought. He wanted her here. Waiting for him.

Of course, he was being selfish. Why should she wait at home when he was avoiding her like the plague? As soon as he admitted the possibility of something else—someone else—being more important to her than him, jealousy like a tornado ripped him. He winced at the thought of her interest waning.

He headed to the door. Could be she was inside moping. He'd check first, then...

Five minutes later, he was out the door again and opening the Rayner house door. The sounds of laughter, music and talking penetrated the halls and drew Jerry back to before his enlistment. Before his and Josie's marriage. Before Germany.

Jerry hesitated at the doorway to the library, and then Emma Jaine saw him and waddled closer. "Jerry, come on in and join us."

"Wondered if Josie was here."

"She was, but I think she and Guy Delaney went for a walk." She checked her locket watch. "They've been gone, maybe forty minutes or so. I don't imagine they'll be gone much longer. Guy doesn't seem well. He'll probably tire quickly. Come in and have something to drink while you wait on Josie to return."

"How are you feeling?" He knew these people. They were family and friends, sort of, but the edge of uncomfortableness kept him from losing himself in the fellowship. His own determination to keep them at a distance probably had something to do with it all too.

"Let me get that drink for you."

"You don't have to do that. I'm capable of getting a drink."

Her smile was a bit shame-faced. "I know, but you know me. Always the hostess. I'll be back in a minute."

Jerry edged toward a corner, hoping to remain invisible. No such luck. Captain Ossie caught sight of him and headed his way.

"Jerry." The man's big, booming voice caused several heads to turn. "Glad you stopped by. How have you been?"

What was there to say to that? "All good. You doing all right?"

The older man nodded at the group gathered. "I have too many guardians watching my health to do overwise."

"I can imagine."

Bette Williams glanced his way, interest flaring in her dark eyes. She was still as flamboyant as she'd ever been. Still a flirt, but he wasn't interested.

"Josie took young Guy for a walk. Do the lad good, I'm thinking."

"Should I be worried?"

"About Josie?" Captain Ossie gave him a look. "You should know. Josie's crazy about you, my boy."

"Still?" Why was he all of a sudden feeling like a lost boy?

"Still? She's never wavered in her devotion to you. You're the best thing in her life."

"With this leg?" He looked down at his injured leg. Why couldn't he swallow the sudden lump in his throat?

What was the matter with him? "Is that fair? To her?"

"Are you saying, you wonder if she should be saddled with a cripple?" The man's lowering eyebrows seemed even more threatening than ever, especially with his abrupt words.

Ouch. That was laying it all out with ungloved hands. "Yeah, that's what I meant. Not sure she signed up to care for a broken man for the rest of her life. Hardly fair."

"Life's not fair, my boy." Captain's Ossie's gruff voice insisted. "I haven't heard her complain. Not once."

He shifted his gaze. The captain didn't need to see what boiled hot inside him. Rubbing a hand across his hot forehead, he groaned. "Everything's a mess, and I..."

No. He couldn't—wouldn't—share his guilty conscience with his father-in-law, of all people.

"Son, I don't know what you went through in Germany, but, remember, I've already mentioned that anytime you want to talk, I'm here. I can keep a confidence, you know."

"I know that, sir. It's just that—"

A commotion at the doorway interrupted his words. Josie burst in with the shadow of a man hovering just outside the doorway.

She shed her coat as she advanced, her gaze skipping across the room, to finally land on him.

He'd never be able to describe the look that radiated on her face. Wild, chestnut-red hair tangled and cheeks red from the spring wind, she lit up, as if seeing him had set her on fire or turned on a light switch inside her. Happiness or joy...or something radiated from her like summer sunbeams.

Why hadn't he noticed how adorably vulnerable she looked when she gazed at him? Because he'd been afraid and hadn't allowed himself to see what his heart had refused to believe.

But her safety. Her life. I can't burden her down with a man like me. She doesn't know—and I can't—won't ever tell about...about Vanda.

But nothing had happened. Not really.

Except you allowed the woman to fall for you knowing you weren't available, the accusing voice screamed in his unwilling ears.

When Josie stopped in front of him, just short of plowing into his chest—as if she'd had a last-minute rein put upon her intentions—teasing, grinning and concerned, but not too much so. "You got home early. Have you eaten? Want some coffee?"

Then she shut up as if biting back her curiosity.

His heart warmed at her attempt to let him come to her. He'd seen her efforts over and over from the first. It would be hard for his rambunctious girl, but when she set her mind, she did it.

"I'd love..." he started to say when Emma Jaine stood up from the piano bench and looked at Tyrell, her face calm and resolute.

"Tyrell, it's time."

No one said a word, and Tyrell seemed rooted to his chair. Then he bounced up. "Emma Jaine, sit down. No, wait. I'll carry you to the car. Someone call Jonah. Captain Ossie, are you coming? Where's your bag, Emma Jaine?"

Jerry felt Josie's hand slip into his as her shoulders shook with laughter at Tyrell's confusion and antics.

Somehow, he didn't mind at all.

~*~

When Jerry led her out of the Rayner house and toward their own home, Josie went. She wanted to go with Emma Jaine, Papa, Claire and Tyrell, but she didn't say a word of protest. Any show of affection from her husband was a good thing, as far as she was concerned, and she wasn't about to rock the boat.

His firm hand was strong and a bit rough as it clasped hers. Josie timed her steps to match his faltering ones. He'd never spoken of his injury—how he'd gotten it or if it pained him—how could it not?—but without a doubt, his manly pride had to be suffering. She wanted to wave a wand and make it go away for him. For herself? She couldn't care less. She'd give up a hundred opportunities for Olympic skating, if it meant the Jerry she used to know would return. But, for now, he was still her Jerry, even though the last few weeks had convinced her he didn't love her.

Now? Tonight didn't matter. He'd held her when she'd

been overwhelmed with excitement at seeing him in her father's home, he'd held her hand as if it was a lifeline and hadn't let go as he'd led her home.

Jerry paused at their gate. He put an arm around her and drew her close. For a moment he didn't speak, but seemed to be studying first the sky, then the street and houses that lined it.

"What are the chances that a married couple would both end up injured, preventing them from pursuing their chosen careers?" His voice was quiet, musing, with a hint of sarcasm.

Of all things he could have said, this was one subject she'd never thought he would breech. She had no answer for such a profound topic that could go either way if she didn't give the answer he was seeking.

Or was it a random comment that didn't need answering?

She'd always loved listening—and chiming in with her youthful comments—when her father, his colleagues and friends had argued everything from politics to war to religion and business. But that had been older men who'd either laughed at her juvenile opinions or cheered her on at her own reckless declarations.

This was Jerry.

"I don't know."

Stay calm.

"You don't suppose God has a—well, maybe a plan, a reason?" She tentatively, cautiously voiced the thought.

"God? What does he have to do with our own stupidity?" He looked at her as if he thought she'd lost her senses.

Oh, dear, what have I started? She wished she'd kept quiet. She shook her head, the frustration biting into her like an angry dog. "I don't know what I'm trying to say, Jerry. Something odd happened when I played my flute at the church a few weeks ago."

"What do you mean?"

"Not sure I can explain. It was almost as if—well, God was speaking to me. Trying to tell me something."

"Are you serious? You?"

He didn't think God would talk with her?

"I don't know if he did, or even if he wanted to. I felt

like beauty and love and sweetness all wrapped up in one package was lifting me above everything else and drawing me, uh, to him. Does that make sense?"

He stared down at the gate, and Josie finally looked down too to see what, if anything, was occupying his thoughts. His fingers gripped a top knob of a post, and even in the semi-light of a spring evening, Josie could see his knuckles whitening.

"Does that mean, you think, you've got religion?"

"How am I suppose to know that? I have no idea what God wants, but I've heard Tyrell enough to know God has a plan for each of us. But if God wanted us injured so we can't pursue the plans we made, what does he want us to do?"

"Have no idea. And why can't you continue to go after your dream of the Olympics? After your ankle heals completely, you can get back into it, surely?"

"You don't know? The doctor said it was damaged too much to ever put the strain and pressure on it that I'd need for my serious ice skating routines. I'm done for."

Jerry's right arm still encircled her shoulder, and now, Josie felt his grip tighten.

~*~

Jerry's heart felt as if it might burst with anger and hurt for Josie's disappointment. She wasn't saying much—not to the extent of the disappointment he knew she had to feel, but it was there. He knew her too well, and because he did, he was ready to raise arms against whoever or whatever had caused it.

Surely not a god who was suppose to love everyone. Not to his Josie.

"Let's go in. I'm needing some of that coffee of yours."

Josie started to turn, but his arm around her prevented it.

At the end of the block, three men were huddled together as if discussing something important.

"Josie, I want you to go immediately into the house and lock the doors. Do you understand?"

"What on earth for?" Her voice was light and bewildered at his sudden demand.

One of them had detached himself and was walking

toward him.

Josie swiveled to locate the object that had captured his attention. "Oh, you mean those men? Isn't that tall one—that one in the gray Homburg—"

"Josie." The frustration at his wife's loitering when he wanted her out of harm's way—if there was harm—was beyond enduring. "Go. Now."

"I won't. If there's danger, I'm not leaving you here to face it alone. I can fight."

Hilarity suddenly demanded release from his tense muscles. He could imagine the man attempting to conquer Josie. Of course, she'd lose the fight, but it'd be a good one.

What was he doing? He didn't have time to dwell on Josie's fighting abilities.

But the man had slowed his rapid advance. Had he decided it was best to leave them alone? Was he reconsidering his possible mischievous plans? Or was he hesitating because of a woman's presence? Maybe Josie being here would be a good thing after all.

"Why that's—Wills! Wonder why he's here again?"

Josie started down the sidewalk, but the other man held up a hand in front of him, awkwardly, as if—as if trying to hide his action from the men behind him still watching?

He motioned frantically, but still with his hand directly in front of his body, for Josie to halt her advance.

It was the man who'd followed him earlier. The man who'd met him in the dive downtown. William.

How did Josie, of all people, know him? Jealousy like a twining vine wrapped itself around his heart.

Josie stepped backward until once again she was beside him, but her face was lit with welcome and warmth for this man whom Jerry couldn't decide was foe or friend.

"Wills, what are you doing here? Why are you acting so strangely?"

"I work for that man back there, Josie. He sent me with a message for your husband."

"But I thought you were in the service. I don't understand." Josie's frown was indication she was ready to get an answer.

"I don't have time to explain, so don't ask."

"But—"

"Josie, I love you, but shut up. I can't talk right now." Wills handed Jerry a folded, sealed paper. "Here. My instructions are to give this to you, and no, I have no idea what's in it. I have to go now. Can't linger. You two take care. I'll be in touch, Jerry."

With that, Wills walked away.

Jerry checked, and sure enough the other two were gone. He wasn't naive enough to think they couldn't be hidden and watching from a hiding place, but why would they? If they'd been bold enough to be seen minutes ago, then why not now? Unless, they thought, 'Mission accomplished' and moved on, trusting this Wills to do what he was ordered.

He was pretty sure that along with Wills, one of the other men had been Marshall. The third could have been Rhoderick, but that would be a definite guess.

"Let's go, Josie."

"Where to?" She resisted his tug for a second.

"Where else? Inside."

Josie clasped his arm and chattered. "Why was Wills acting so oddly? You don't suppose he's gotten mixed up with the wrong people, do you?"

"I have no idea what or who he's involved with." Jerry unlocked their door. "How do you know this Wills anyway?"

Stopping dead in her tracks, she pressed a hand against the door jam. "You don't know him? Jerry, he's my best friend, except for you, of course."

"That still doesn't tell me who he is."

She laughed and pushed ahead into their sitting room, shrugging out of her jacket. "Silly. Our hired help's son, Wills Mason."

It clicked. Young Wills Mason, Josie's partner in crime, the bane of Emma Jaine's life. Their mischief, although basically harmless, had kept Emma Jaine on her toes.

No wonder he hadn't recognized the boy. Wills had grown into a man, broad-shouldered, taller, and more confident. And that mustache had definitely thrown him off. Now the boy-grown-man had a job with a man Jerry despised.

Immediately, worry threaded his thoughts. What to tell Josie? Should he warn her? Clue her into what activities Wills may be involved in?

Or not. Why distress her when, with any kind of luck, she might not have to see the young man for quite some time.

It was time to up the ante a little.

Past time.

Chapter Twenty-one

Wills Mason approached his boss and his boss's friend, trepidation like a stalking cat playing havoc in his mind. Was he up to this game he was playing? Of course, he was. He wasn't afraid, but he needed to keep alert. If his boss got the least hint of what he was doing...

He'd turned the corner and managed to get a quick glimpse back at the Pattersons. They'd obviously gone ahead inside. Good. Jerry would keep Josie safe, but the man—crippled that he was—wouldn't and couldn't be with her twenty-four hours a day and still accomplish what he was assigned to do. That meant he would have to increase his vigilance.

If only he could get into that safe Marshall kept locked. From what he could guess, the man hadn't even shared the combination with his family, let alone his servants and most trusted employees. Which he hoped he was.

Just not valuable enough to share that information.

He was pretty sure that hiding place held documents that could help prove the man behind this recent espionage plan. But that did no good, unless one could crack it. And until that was accomplished this job with Marshall wouldn't be finished.

"Done?" Marshall asked in a low voice, his eyes shaded by the Homburg he wore, tilted at just the right slant. The man might be a senator's son, but he was gangster all the way, and cocky enough he didn't care who knew it.

"Yes, sir."

"His reaction?"

"Mild, but he didn't open it then. Didn't think I should insist—"

"Good thinking."

It was his boss's friend who spoke up, his gaze intense and searching as if drilling into Wills' mind.

Making sure to keep his expression bland, Wills controlled his tone, albeit allowing a trifle of amusement to thread its way in it, when he answered. "Thanks. I got the impression the man was in a hurry to get inside his house."

His boss and friend exchanged a glance that carried a message only the two of them could read.

Wills could make a wild guess though, and he was pretty sure, they thought they had something over on Jerry Patterson. He almost smiled, but froze it. No way would he allow them to guess his real purpose.

A purpose only he and his *real* boss knew.

Chapter Twenty-two

Do you want Josie to know what you did?

Jerry stared down at the simple, but horrifying, words that emphasized a complex statement and sentiment. A threat or a warning? Or maybe a hint of what was coming?

Someone—did he dare think it might be Rhoderick? Or even Marshall?—was trying to scare him into frantic behavior—wild, unthinking actions. But he wasn't about to be fooled by the bait they'd tossed at him.

Not this time.

Josie's staunch stand outside, her calmness in facing unknown intruders, although the immediate threat had turned out to be a past friend, didn't mean that worse danger didn't lurk only a few feet farther away. Whatever the writer of this note had meant to accomplish, scaring him into foolish behavior wouldn't happen. He didn't want to confess to Josie his actions in Germany. Didn't plan to, but if it was to ever be done, he'd choose the time and place.

Josie sat across the room, giving him his privacy. She'd picked up her flute and now played softly, the notes like a soothing balm to his restless spirit. She'd closed her eyes, swaying a little, and the melody was light and sweet, calling him to join her in a slow dance of happiness.

He wanted to. Oh, how much. But he couldn't. Not yet.

And maybe never.

Tonight, after Josie settled for the night, he was going to see if he could contact Wills again. Could he trust him? His parents worked for the Rayners, but that didn't mean William Mason hadn't gone bad. The man had said he'd get hold of him, but he couldn't wait any longer. Surely, he knew something or could help him get inside Marshall's.

Big if.

~*~

An hour later, the phone rang, and after Josie answered it, she whirled to face him, allowing the receiver to settle back into its cradle. "The baby's here. Oh, Jerry, I want to see Emma Jaine and him."

"Him? Is it a boy then?"

"I don't know. *I* think it is. How could a man like Tyrell have anything but a boy for his first child?"

What did that mean? Did she think men whose first child was a daughter less of a man? What if they, perchance, happened, accidentally or however, to have a child, and it was a girl—would Josie think he was not worthy of being on the stand she'd propped Tyrell upon?

His wife was babbling on. "She wouldn't tell me. Wants to surprise me. Can we go to the hospital? Will you go with me? Please?"

He opened his mouth to refuse. He had no business mingling with a family he might soon be leaving.

But the vulnerability in her stopped him. Pled for her way, and Josie, even as willful as she was, never pled for much from him. What could it hurt? They wouldn't have to be there long.

Besides, there was her safety to consider.

"I'll go. How soon can you be ready?"

"I'm ready now."

Jerry walked lazily to her. He pulled her close and ran his fingers through her tangled curls. "You'd better do something with this mop—or else."

"Or else?" She whispered, her voice a breathless, hopeful question.

"Or else we won't be going." He couldn't control the huskiness that shaded his own. Allowing a last chestnut curl to bounce back to her neck, he gave her a gentle shove. "Move."

He was playing with fire, but tonight he didn't care. He didn't have the willpower to resist her. And why should he? She was his. Yes, he'd done some things he wished he hadn't, no, she shouldn't be saddled with an injured man, but tonight, he was very much afraid he could never give her up, whether it was best for her or not. Tonight he didn't care about all that. Tonight he could think of nothing but what he wanted.

Her. His Josie.

Rebellion raised its head and threatened to override any decisions he'd made about fairness to her, doubts about her love for a damaged man.

He clenched his jaw and watched her sway from the room, giving him a last teasing glance before her running footsteps echoed back down the stairs and corridor, pounding into his heart.

Josie. Josie. Josie.

There was only so much a man could endure.

~*~

Josie peeked into the hospital room. Claire and Shirley were oooing and ahing over a blanket wrapped *something*. Tyrell sat in a chair drawn up to the bed, holding Emma Jaine's hand. Papa stood on the other side booming all his comments and probably disturbing the whole floor.

Jerry had dutifully come with her, but once inside the hospital, he'd shied off to make a phone call. Josie had been much too excited to wait, and he'd waved her off, promising to join her soon.

When Shirley placed the bundle in Papa Ossie's arms, Josie laughed out loud at his wry expression, and they all turned to look at her.

Emma Jaine recovered first. "Josie. Come in. Come in. Look who God's blest us with. Tyrell, pull up a chair for Josie. I want her to sit close to me so we can talk, and I can watch her hold my baby—"

Tiptoeing in, scared to death of what she was about to do, nervous tremors rolled through her stomach. This was the bravest thing she'd ever done. She didn't know the first thing about babies except they cried a lot and wanted to eat all the time.

Settled in the chair Tyrell pulled close, Josie eyed askance her approaching father. What was she about to do?

He held out the bundle, and she stared at it.

"Open your arms, Josie. Cradle the baby's head in the crook of your arm and support it's body with the rest of your arm." Emma Jaine coached her with a smile. "She's ready, Papa. Give the baby to her."

Obediently, Josie held out an arm, and ever so gently, tenderly, Papa Ossie placed the bundle in her arms. Feeling as if she might faint, Josie looked down...and fell in love.

The squenched up, tiny red face with the tassel of black hair was the sweetest thing she'd ever seen.

"He—she—it's so tiny."

"Six pounds, five ounces." The pride in Tyrell's voice couldn't have been more evident than if he'd shouted it from a fog horn.

"It's face is kind of wrinkled." Josie stared down at the small creature in her arms.

"That will change."

Was that a smile in her sister's comment?

The baby stirred, yawned, then it's tiny features scrunched up, it's mouth opened and a cry came out.

Panic flooded Josie's body. "What did I do?"

"Rock the baby a bit. Just a little. That will soothe h—it."

Josie moved from side to side, and a miracle happened. The baby quieted and appeared to be sleeping again. "I did it."

"You did, Josie."

"It's beautiful." Josie looked at her sister.

"You're so right. Tyrell, please help her discover whether the bundle she's holding is her nephew or niece, will you?"

"I sure will." Gently, while Josie held the little bundle, he unwrapped the blanket and unpinned the diaper.

Excitement like the lava from a volcano spilled through her. "It's a—

"Don't you want to see this, Josie?"

Josie peeked around her brother-in-law at Emma Jaine who was holding up another wrapped bundle.

Laughter erupted around her.

"What's so funny?" Josie frowned at her hysterical family "What is it?"

Claire walked over to her oldest sister, took the bundle from her and returned to Josie, a big smile on her face. "Hold your other arm out, Josie."

"What for?" Heat rushed through her as the realization

rammed into her mind. "I can't. How can this be? Two babies?" She'd never in her life felt as rattled as she did at this moment, and she tossed Tyrell a pleading glance.

He chuckled but came to her rescue. "Let me help before Josie faints dead away in front of all of us. Look at our second little bundle of joy." With care he proceeded to unwrap the baby's blanket.

Josie stared and tried to take it in. She looked at her father. "Papa, we have two?"

He nodded, but her attention caught the hovering figure of her husband just outside the door, and she called out. "Jerry, come in and see the babies!"

~*~

Her face lit up the room, like one of those spring flowers Harriet Mason kept in her Rayner Boarding house Victory garden. Yellow and filled with sunshine to brighten any dreary day. Daffodils?

Cheeks rosy-red with excitement, mouth wide with a smile, Josie was the epitome of a woman in love. He felt his heart melting.

He'd never have guessed Josie would be holding and oooing over a baby, let alone *two* of them. Laughing uproariously over a joke, plotting a trick on an unsuspecting victim, yes.

But this?

Jerry stood at the door, hesitating, but when Josie called to him yet again, he stepped into the room but kept his distance. He wasn't used to kids, never planned to have any. Not with a father like he had. Who could tell but what he might end up like him. That was a depressing thought.

Still, when the others urged him, and Josie stood and walked toward him—followed by Tyrell with the second one—he met her half-way in the room and looked down at the bundle she was worshipping with love in her eyes.

"This one's a boy, Jerry. Isn't he the cutest version of Tyrell you've ever seen? Look at him wave his little arms."

He stared at his wife, dumbstruck at her adoration.

"And this one. It's a girl." She tilted her head in the direction of Tyrell. "I think her hair has the same tint of red as Emma Jaine's, don't you?"

He squinted at the squirming bundle in Tyrell's arm, but couldn't speak.

"Do you want to hold him?" Josie held out her arm in his direction.

Dumbstruck by Josie's transformation, scared of the proposition she was pushing at him, Jerry backed away, unable to voice any thought to the baby's looks or actions. He was much too obsessed with Josie. With her fascination. With her absorption of such a tiny little thing. Who would have thought that his tomboy, crazy wife would fall so fast?

~*~

Captain Ossie had offered to make sure Josie got home safely later on when Jerry wanted to leave.

"No need for her to go home when you have business to tend to, Son." the older man had walked with him out the door.

"Thanks. Appreciate it." He touched his forehead in a gesture of good-by and walked away, not looking back.

Now to see if he could connect with Wills Mason. If that didn't work, then he would grab a taxi and hope his captain was still up. Either way, he was determined to put an end to this hunt.

When he stepped out of the taxi, he took a quick look around. But only a few lights lit Marshall's house tonight. He could see a couple dogs prowling around the yard but no sign of human guards. He supposed the owners figured the dogs were enough to keep away unwanted intruders. He wasn't up to taking on a couple vicious animals, so snooping on the outside of the fence was all he would attempt. With any luck, Wills, and not someone else, would notice him and come running.

He'd circled the property twice before he got his opportunity. At the far end of the property, the gate was cracked open about three inches. He could have sworn when he'd passed by before that it'd been shut and locked. There was no sign of another human, but he wasn't waiting around to find out.

With senses on high alert, he edged the gate open wider and stepped onto Marshall's property. This corner was tree-shrouded, and Jerry paused, listening and waiting for any inner sense or signal that something was amiss. Only when he was convinced it was safe—not counting the dogs—did he move forward a few steps.

At the edge of the cluttered trees, he paused, using his peripheral vision to detect any movement.

When all seemed clear, he started to move toward a large Azalea bush when a voice demanded from behind him. "Halt. What do you think you're doing?"

Jerry turned, but in the semi-darkness, in the shadowy shrubbery, he couldn't see the man's face. He said nothing, and the other man came closer.

"I said, what are you doing on this property? It's private." He raised a large walking cane and pointed it at Jerry. "Move it. We'll just see if you change your mind about talking after my boys get done with you."

Who was this man? Not a servant. Jerry didn't budge, not that he was assured the man wouldn't try to force him inside, but because he couldn't afford to be caught here on his nemesis's property. On guard, his right hand behind his back fumbling for any kind of heavy branch he could use as a weapon, he waited.

When the man was feet away, he swung the cane. If Jerry hadn't jerked sideways and back, the blow would have knocked him down. He grabbed for the cane and missed, and the man swung again, this time with better aim. The blow caught him on the shoulder, and for a moment, Jerry's arm went numb.

With an angry grunt, Jerry lunged for the man and his stick, and they grappled. Of a sudden, the other man crumpled and slid to the ground, the cane falling from his grasp. Jerry looked up.

Wills Mason stood there. He tossed the heavy stick he'd used into the brush and motioned. "Let's get him tied up and gagged. While I'm doing that, you can tell me why you're on these grounds."

"Come by to see if there was any accessible way to get inside."

"With the dogs? Impossible at night unless they have them fastened, and they only do that when Marshall's throwing functions or dinners here. Good thing they're busy with their supper right now."

"Yeah." Jerry gave a cautious glance around. "Anyhow, wasn't going to enter, but the second time around, I saw this gate open..." he jerked his head in the direction. "...and figured I'd step inside but stay close enough I could get out quickly if the dogs sniffed me out."

"Smart thinking. So what were you planning?"

"Why should I tell you?"

"Cause I'm your best bet, Pal."

"I know Marshall is a traitor and suspect he has more in that safe of his that could benefit our country. If you're as fond of it as you said you were, then I hoped you could help me get to it."

"What makes you think that? Marshall shares the combination with no one in the house—unless it's his girlfriend. He has eyes everywhere in that mansion of his."

"But—"

"I told you I'd get ahold of you. I'm doing all I can to find the combination." Wills' irritated tone showed he was more than a little upset. He looked down at the man lying on the ground. "Do you know who this is?"

"Have no clue."

"Senator Marshall."

"The old fuddy-duddy nearly broke my arm."

"He might put on a staid act while in congress, but he speaks no gobbledy-gook. That mild manner turns mean when he's crossed."

"Figures." Jerry snarled but asked, "When do you think I could get a crack at that safe of Marshall's?"

"I'll tell you what." Wills straightened. "Marshall and his gal will be gone for a long weekend. I don't think he'll need me along. I've got a couple more places I need to search. I know he's too smart to leave it to chance if something happens to him, so he will have written it down somewhere. Until then, don't try to contact me. Too dangerous. But give me a few days, and I'll see what I can work out."

"Sure thing."

Wills tilted his head. "Hear the dogs. They haven't sniffed you out yet, but they're getting closer. Better scram."

"You won't forget?"

"I don't forget my obligations."

Looked like waiting was his only option for now. He turned to leave, but swiveled back and indicated the man lying on the ground, still out. "What about *him*?"

"I'll take care of him. He'll be missed and will no doubt raise questions when he doesn't return to the house. When you leave, shut the gate but leave it unlocked. After I get off work, I'll swing by this corner, and take this one where he can answer for his evil deeds. Hopefully."

Jerry asked no more questions.

Wills' face was grim, and Jerry reckoned the unconscious man wouldn't much care for where he was headed.

~*~

Jerry eased the front door closed as quietly as he could, fastened the lock and went to grab a drink before he slipped off to the room he'd cordoned off for his own use. It was crazy, but he wished Josie was awake. He could do with a conversation that had nothing to do with spies and espionage...or revenge from an enemy.

Captain had made it plain enough that not only the danger to Josie and himself, but the espionage against the good ole U.S. was serious stuff. Made sense that he was so insistent on Jerry finding the spy.

Placing the water glass upset down in the sink, Jerry headed upstairs. He stopped briefly at the doorway to their room, then walked over to her sleeping form and bent to give her his usual good-night kiss. Her skin was warm and soft, and it stirred something in him. He glanced at the other side of the bed—tempted, but turned away before he could act upon the urge.

He just hoped he could go to sleep quickly—and forget—for awhile, all the memories that plagued him.

~*~

Josie stirred, half-awakening, and lifted her head as Jerry's tall form exited their—Josie refused to call it *her*—room yet another night. She wanted to gnash her teeth at his stupidity. After two months at home, and shooting her hopes to high heaven the few times when he'd softened enough that they'd laughed or joked or even flirted heavily—just as they'd done before he left for active duty—she wanted to scream at his resistance at being the man he was before.

Maybe Papa was right, and he'd *never* be that man again. That's what broke her heart. She wanted her Jerry back. The man he'd been, and the man she'd adored.

Josie settled her head back onto her pillow, listening to the muted sounds of him undressing and climbing into the squeaky bed that was in the next room. He was restless again tonight, tossing from one side to another, getting up—probably to take medicine for pain or to make him sleep—and then once again, climbing back into the noisy bed. Another few minutes of the restless moving, and all quieted.

The night surrounded her with blackness, but not any darker than the black in her spirit. How could things go so wrong? Why couldn't something go right in her life? Was she a defect? A person so bad not even God cared about her happiness?

But that wasn't right.

If offering her flute music to Tyrell's congregation, and the experience she'd felt was any sign, then God did care for her. Surely he loved her and wanted her to be happy. Didn't he?

Josie rammed her face into her pillow and whispered a prayer, for the first time in years, perhaps for the first time as a sincere request to someone she'd never paid much attention to and hadn't ever been sure was really real.

"God, I'm pretty sure I believe in you now. I mean, how could I not? I didn't tell Jerry—didn't know *how* to—that I thought you might be talking to me at church that morning, so I know if you were talking to me, you had a reason. I'm hoping it was because you love me and want me to be happy. I know I haven't been a very good person, but I'll try hard to be better. So, if I love you, and if you care about me even a little bit, will you please send Jerry back to me?"

Chapter Twenty-three

The moans were light at first but loud enough to waken Josie from the drowsiness she'd slipped into after her relaxing conversation with the God she was suddenly feeling as a best friend and her only hope.

She propped herself up on one elbow, wondering if Jerry's moans would finally yield to his usual deep sleep or turn into something worse. There was quiet for a few moments, and she'd almost decided to lie down again, when his moans became borderline hysterical.

Josie threw back the covers and ran to his room. Jerry lay flat on his back, his eyes wide open, but she could tell he wasn't seeing anything. She ran to him, soothing him, rubbing his arm and forehead, murmuring softly to him.

When his body finally relaxed, she bit her lip, struggling with what she wanted to do, then mentally throwing up arms of surrender, she crawled in and wrapped her arms tightly around him. She sang softly in spite of her lack of talent in that area.

Drowsily, she loosened her hold on her husband just before sleep closed in.

"Vanda...he's...I can't!"

Her eyelids flew open, and Josie fastened her gaze on her still sleeping husband's form. He was moving again, restlessly, as if troubled, his brow furrowed in a frown.

"Vanda...no! I love..."

Vanda?

Who was Vanda?

~*~

Jerry knew immediately something was wrong the second his eyes popped open. And then it hit him. Someone was in bed with him. Not only in bed, but snuggled up close to him.

He moved an arm, then a leg. When nothing happened, he turned slowly onto his back. A shaggy mess of dark red hair hid the face, and a skinny bare arm hugged the blanket tight against the body.

Josie.

And that brought a smile. He reached out a hand and brushed back the wild curls covering her face. She looked tired.

No matter. He never got tired of looking at her. He scooted closer and gently pulled her to him. She didn't waken, only wiggled a bit, sighed and relaxed.

The sun declared it was at least eight. It was time for him to arise, but he didn't want to. Would it hurt, just once, if he lay in bed far past his usual rising time?

What was she doing in here anyway? Must have been a nightmare, but he couldn't remember Josie ever having such a thing. Too much sleep that had kept her awake till late? No, she'd been sound asleep when he'd gotten home last night.

The thought that she could have been lonesome without him made him happy. But they were playing dangerous games if he meant to keep his promise to himself.

Feeling suddenly pressured, he uncovered and crept out of bed. His mental musings were depressing. Better do something more productive with his day than daydreaming about a wife he had to let go.

Fifty minutes later, he shut the door, and started down their sidewalk. A man unlatched their gate and trod toward him, an envelope clutched in his hand.

"Are you Mr. Patterson? Jerry Patterson?"

"I am."

"Telegram. Sign here."

Jerry scribbled his name then stared down at the envelope. Who on earth would be sending him a telegram? Couldn't be the state department. Captain would have gotten hold of him by another means. And standing here would not help him find out the sender any sooner.

He unfolded the single sheet. His gaze searched for the sender's name.

Robert Patterson. His father.

Heart sinking, Jerry started to crumple the telegram.

But what if there was a reason he'd sent a telegram?

His father would have normally saved on the expense and used the regular mail. So why not save himself the agony of not knowing or wishing he had checked. What if...

Jerry read.

In NYC on business for two weeks. Stop. Swinging by Cincinnati after that. Stop. No need to prepare a room. Stop. Staying at The Crown. Stop. Robert Patterson.

Not even a friendly signature like Father. Or your dad.

Why was his father coming here anyway? He didn't want him, didn't want to see him, and he had no plans of inflicting him on Josie.

~*~

The ringing phone woke Josie. She stretched and ignored it, hoping it would go away. Stretching out an arm, she tentatively searched for her husband, but her hand contacted nothing but a cold sheet. She shook her hair from her eyes and sat up.

No Jerry. So he'd found out her secret in stealing into his bed. Was he angry and was that why he was gone already?

No, he always rose early, no matter how late he'd been out or up.

The ringing had stopped, but minutes later, it began again, and Josie sprang from the bed and ran down the stairs.

"Josie?" Shirley Largett's voice greeted her.

"Yeah, I'm here."

"Did I wake you?"

"It's all right. What did you need?"

"Mr. Greye is hosting a dinner tomorrow evening for all of us and specifically requested you to be there too. Can you go?"

"I guess. Yes, I'll go." Why not? The more she spent time with the man, the more she just might discover what he was up to. Maybe. And if her active imagination didn't get her in trouble by working overtime. Jerry always said she needed to use her creative brain more than she did.

"Good. Do you want me or Claire to come by ahead of time and help you get ready?"

Josie chuckled. "Why not?"

Josie started up the stairs when the phone rang again. Dashing—if you could call it that with favoring her injured ankle—back down, she grabbed at the receiver and spoke into it.

"Josie Patterson?"

"That's me."

"This is Robert Patterson. I'd like to meet with you."

~*~

The next night, Claire showed up at Josie's door, carrying two different outfits and an assortment of hair items. "Tonight we're going to show off that long neck of yours."

"I don't want to show it off."

"But you will. Wait until I'm done with you." Claire crowed over her own abilities. "Look what I found at the local second hand store downtown today. Couldn't resist the color—perfect for your hair. Come on."

Impatiently, Claire led Josie upstairs. "Sit. We'll do your hair first, then you can choose which dress you want to wear."

When Claire at last allowed Josie to swivel on the dresser stool to see what she'd done, Josie stared at her image. Unlike what she'd imagined, she looked far less like a giraffe than a regal woman—something no one had ever described her as.

Claire had tamed and mastered her unruly mass of hair, creating clusters of curls at the top of her head, allowing tendrils of the dark red locks to fall free and touch her neck. Instead of feeling gangly and ugly, the length of her neck emphasized the regal-ness the hairstyle demanded.

Her gaze moved to her awesome sister, but said sister was already lifting one of the two outfits she'd brought with her. "What about this one?"

Josie ended up trying both on. The first one was a light spring green and flowered with a short, mini-cape of a darker green. The second one was a filmy layered look, the rose nylon overlaying the warm rust.

"Which do you like?" Claire raised a brow at Josie.

"The green one. Goes with my hair."

"Nonsense. The rust and rose bring out that lovely

red."

Grinning, Josie allowed her sister to adjust the fall of the skirt.

"Do you have an appropriate cover to wear? It's still chilly in the evening."

"My usuals."

The grimace Claire sent her was anything but pleased, but when her sister pulled off the long, creamy scarf that covered Josie's dresser and wrapped it around her shoulders, she nodded. "Perfect, and just the right touch for this dress. Wear your light heels, and don't get rumpled. We'll be by to pick you up in one hour."

"Thanks. I can't believe you made me look this good."

"I know what I'm doing, Josie. Now remember. Be ready and no lounging or antics. And wear your dark rose hat."

Without a word of good-by her sister whisked herself out the door.

"Applesauce." She tossed the word after Claire's departing back, knowing full well that even if her sister heard, she'd ignore it.

What was she suppose to do for a whole hour? Stand here and twiddle her thumbs? She was afraid to move, afraid Claire's socially proper senses would spot the smallest of wrinkles. Sighing, Josie leaned against the wall and crossed her arms. Being socially presentable wasn't all it was cracked up to be.

~*~

"Papa, do walk Josie inside. She'll be off feeding the ducks in the hotel gardens if you don't latch onto her." Claire held onto Guy Delaney's arm as Tyrell helped Emma Jaine out of their vehicle.

Depend on Claire to make sure she had a young, attractive dinner date even when they all seemed to be busy with serving their country.

"I have two arms available to two of my best girls," Papa barked out a laugh and held out an arm to Shirley, and then the other to Josie. "Come along. Emma Jaine, are you sure you're feeling up to this?"

"Papa, I'm fine. Tyell hasn't allowed me to lift a finger since I've come home. I'm quite bored with home life."

Tyrell slipped an arm around her. "You know they released you early only on condition you stay in bed for the next five days." He smiled at her. "Which, of course, you haven't done."

"I'm fine. I've rested mostly and have been very careful when I am up. I'm sure I won't be allowed to do much tonight and am depending on you to find me a comfortable chair whenever you feel I've talked long enough." She patted his arm.

"Then let's go." Josie tugged on her father's arm.

The hotel was an impressive one, and even during this time of war, seemed to keep up with the pretentiousness of class demanded from the elite. Inside, the hotel manager greeted them and led the way to one of the smaller, more intimate private rooms.

Josie was impressed. Vases and pots of spring flowers filled every available space. Tables were covered with white linen, the place settings awe-inspiring, the small fountain glittering with water spraying from the pitcher the stone lady held.

In spite of her suspicions, Josie's heart fluttered as the tall, gray-clad Walter Greye strode toward them, a smirk on his lips. "Welcome, my friends. Mrs. Walker, how are you doing? And the little ones?"

Josie let go of her father's arm and took two steps back, watching the interaction between these people.

Emma Jaine and Tyrell were at ease, praising the wonders of their twins. Josie couldn't tell if Mr. Greye was bored or interested, but he gave every indication he found the baby information quite riveting.

Papa on the other hand, stood off to the side, he and Shirley murmuring in low tones. Every once in awhile, he would cast a glance at the threesome who continued to chat. Papa wasn't frowning. It was more worry that drew those heavy brows together. But why? Was he concerned about Emma Jaine, thinking perhaps she was up and about too soon?

Or was it Mr. Greye causing that look on Papa's handsome face? He was certainly a protective father when it came to his daughters.

Claire and Guy were circling the room. They paused at a table set up with drinks, and Guy lifted a glass and offered it to Claire. When she smiled and nodded, he picked up another one, and they began their walking again. Had Claire succeeded where no one else had with Guy? He wasn't saying much, nodding, offering a comment now and then. He smiled once at Josie's petite sister, a sad, taut one, but a smile nevertheless.

Focusing on the blond man standing with an elaborately dressed woman, her hair piled and anchored to the top of her head with a diamond clip, Josie did a double take. Wasn't he—she was almost sure that man was the same one who'd walked down the hallway the night she'd played her flute at Mr. Greye's project dinner. The night someone had followed her. She'd never heard his name nor had Mr. Greye introduced them.

And then Josie got the second shock of the evening. The woman tilted her head back, laughing, and slowly turned, her gaze sweeping the room—almost contemptuously, as if she was bored with the guests.

It was Diana. Her ice skating instructor, who'd abandoned her with alacrity and moved on to someone who wasn't a has-been. Which was natural, of course. But given the years spent working together, Josie had felt a little hurt at her abrupt departure. Nervous nausea gripped her stomach at the thought of having to make small talk with her now.

When a maitre de approached and whispered to Mr. Greye, he nodded and the maitre de announced. "Dinner is served. I believe you'll find your places labeled for you."

Josie didn't care where she sat, but hoped it wouldn't be near Diana. In fact, rebellion tickled her senses. She turned to find Mr. Greye to let him know she'd prefer not to be seated near her. But when she did, He was standing behind her and held out an arm.

"Allow me?"

She placed a hand on his arm. Perhaps the situation was resolved without having to cause a scene. She allowed herself a small smile. It'd been quite awhile since she'd created a scene. She kind of missed it.

"Please tell me how is this project of yours doing? Are you hoping you receive enough donations tonight to launch?"

"Why bother your head with business tonight?" He led her straight to the chair at the right of his and settled her into it. When he sat, he smiled at her. "I haven't had a chance to talk with you. I'm glad you came. You are stunning tonight."

"Why wouldn't I want to?" Better ignore the compliment. "I'm finding your efforts in raising money for this project fascinating."

"Let's not talk about the project tonight." His words were impatient as he studied her face, but said nothing while the server offered a ladle of soup. Then he leaned closer and lowered his voice. "Why have I never gotten to meet this husband of yours?"

Senses sharpened at his seemingly-sudden interest in Jerry, Josie searched the man's eyes. Was this a general, polite dinner question, or was he working up to something more private?

No need for him to try. She'd offer no information about Jerry.

"Rumors have it that your husband has been involved with another woman." He whispered and glanced at her. Her face must have given her away. "I'm sorry. I should have been more discreet than to mention it. I thought perhaps with such an open marriage, you would have known."

Of course, he knew she hadn't known. His features were drawn into a contrite expression, but it wasn't sincere, and his intent was as clear as if he'd announced it to everyone in the room. He'd wanted to see her reaction. He'd known she'd be surprised and hurt.

So the question remained. What had been his ulterior motive? To give her reasons to doubt Jerry? To give him an in with her—but for what purpose? With all the beautiful women in the world, why choose her? A random thing? Something else she had no clue about? Or was there a purpose behind his words and deeds?

Giving him a light shrug, she offered, "He's always busy. He works long hours, but is quite agreeable that I enjoy myself when the opportunity comes along. He's very understanding, and I certainly trust him."

That was stretching the truth a trifle. She wasn't at all

sure Jerry was so agreeable with her roaming the city. But her family was here tonight, so what could he say?

"Is that so?" Mr. Greye cocked his head. "I'm quite sure if *I* had a charming and beautiful wife like you, I wouldn't be so agreeable to you enjoying yourself around—"

He let the pause drag out, and Josie's breath caught—caught by his words and the suspense at what they hinted.

"—a man like myself."

Warmth flooded her cheeks, and words vanished at his blatant observation. She had to swallow twice before she could speak. "Whatever do you mean, Mr. Greye?"

Applesauce. What kind of question was that, opening the crack for more opinions from him?

"You want me to spell it out?" His smile dared her to believe his words.

Heavens, no.

"If you were *my* wife, I'd keep you too busy to be fascinated with another man's project."

"I see."

"Do you, Josie Patterson?" His gaze hadn't left her face. "You interest me, and instead of being absorbed with projects and other things in your city, I find myself wondering about you when you're not around. Unlike your sisters—who are indeed worthy of admiration in their own rights—I see a strength—and could I call it, daring?—in you few women have."

"I'm pretty sure Emma Jaine and Claire have much more admirable attributes than I do. I doubt I can compete."

"No, you couldn't. Instead, *you* set the standard, and I love it."

"Mrs. Josie, I've been wondering if you'd play your flute sometime at the house for us. I hear you're quite good." Guy, seated beside her, spoke loudly enough to gain her attention from Walter Greye's sole claim of it.

Josie turned eagerly to him. "I'm not that good, but I'd love to play for you. Perhaps some evening through the week?"

"I'd enjoy that." His eyes smiled warmly at her, shifted

a hair to the side of her, then returned, the smile dimmed. He leaned in close, his lips almost touching her ear as he whispered. "I know where the rumor came from. Never fear, Josie Patterson, Jerry loves you."

Josie drew back to study the man who was a total enigma to her.

Was his antagonistic action for Greye intentional? What happened between the two of them for Guy to have such—dislike?

"Diana, it's good to see you again. How have you been?" Emma Jaine laid down her fork and leaned forward to speak directly to the woman seated beside Tyrell.

"I *am* in great demand. Does not that say a lot? Since my last student failed to discipline herself appropriately, I've accepted two new ones who have exceptional promise. At least I don't have to worry about their bad habits creating accidents that are preventable. Such a relief to work with those who are focused on the goal."

Dead silence greeted the woman's rant.

Fire burned in Josie's body. Rage like she'd never felt before blinded her. Who did her past trainer think she was? Did she actually believe Josie had broken her ankle on purpose? That she'd tossed the stick onto the rink so she would never skate professionally again? The nerve of her.

A hand covered her tensed up fist, and Mr. Greye whispered, "Ignore her. She's not worth your time."

"Diana, really? Must you?" It was the blond man half-heartedly—as if it were a joke—remonstrating with her.

Claire obviously had no intention of ignoring such a slur. "If you were as grandiose as you seem to think you are, then you would have made sure nothing impeded Josie's act. You are the one who failed, Diana, and don't you ever let me hear that you've said another word about my sister, or you *will* regret it." Claire's usual warm eyes blazed with wrath, her tone a snobbish reprimand, her lips a twist of disgust.

Claire turned her head and spoke to Guy on her left, dismissing the other woman with the action.

Josie settled back in her seat, her fist uncurling, her hot blood cooling. She could never have put her past trainer in her place any better. Little Claire, who'd cried many a time at Josie's cruel teasing, coming to her defense. Josie vowed to herself her youngest sister would never hear another teasing comment—unless, of course, it was in a gentle manner and perfectly understood by both of them.

"See what I mean? That's what strength is." Josie picked up a forkful of the fish that had so far lay untouched on her plate. "No one messes with us Rayners."

Take that, Walter Greye.

~*~

Dinner was over. Feeling as if she was about to smother, Josie wondered if she could slip away for a minute. If not, she wasn't sure she could endure the rest of the evening. Mr. Greye had planned some entertainment for the small gathering—a comedy skit, she thought—and she was looking forward to that. But the tension from dealing with his innuendos and listening to Diana's not-so-subtle insult, had drained her. She needed time by herself to regain what control she had.

With a quick glance around to make sure everyone was busy socializing, Josie slipped out the door. If anyone caught her, she was headed to the powder room. Good enough excuse for her.

The farther Josie walked from the small room where Mr. Greye had hosted the dinner, the more relaxed she felt. She hurried around a corner and ran smack into a tall man.

Strong hands grabbed her arms to keep her from tumbling backward, then exclaimed, "Josie Patterson. Where are you going in such a hurry?"

Wills Mason stared down at her, his mouth twisted in a delighted grin.

Josie huffed, but she knew her own grin matched his. "It would be nice if handsome, strong men wouldn't interfere when females are running away from uncomfortable situations."

"Now who would *you* be running away from? Don't tell me my ole tomboy friend is afraid of someone."

"I'm not afraid of anyone." Her response was automatic. "I needed a few minutes away from Mr. Greye and Diana. Why are you here?"

"Don't you remember? I thought Jerry would have mentioned I work for Harry Marshall. Since he and Diana were invited—they're close friends with Greye—I was ordered to come along as a guard."

"I remember you mentioning your work for the man but *her*? Besides, I thought you joined the service, and you never explained *that* to me. I never met Diana's boyfriend, so it was a total shock to see her here. She was quite nasty to me, but Claire put her in her place. What a surprise, but delightful."

"Claire? She's here too?" Will's looked intently at Josie.

"Sure is, all grown up since you left. I'm sure she misses you."

"I doubt it."

"Why would you say that?" Was that a tinge or red on his cheeks? He wasn't *blushing*, was he? Wills?

"We've got a situation."

Ah, he was changing the subject. She knew him too well to think otherwise.

"We? What kind of situation? You know I kind of like confrontations."

"I seem to remember that." Wills lifted his hat and re-settled it on his head. "I let slip to Jerry that I thought you were here tonight, and he went ballistic. Said he didn't want you in the room where Marshall was. Figured I'd better alert you before he came riding in to deliver you from the likes of the man."

"Jerry's *here*?"

"Yes, I, uh, got him a temporary job working in the kitchen, then talked with him minutes before the dinner began. I had a hard time reasoning with him, but told him I'd try to talk to you."

"What am I suppose to do? Doesn't he realize Papa and Tyrell are here, and Guy Delaney too, for that matter? I don't think it would go over well if I disappear with no reason. Of course, I could go back and tell them an emergency came up with my husband."

"Then your whole family would leave to be with you,

there'd be awkward explanations—no, that won't work. Come with me, and I'll take you to Jerry. Maybe together we can talk sense to him."

"Not sure he'll listen to me, but we can give it a try."

Wills led her down several hallways, through a couple swinging doors, and stopped as he opened one of them. "There he is, over at the far table, chopping vegetables and scowling. Let's see what we can do."

"By the way," Josie grabbed Will's arm and kept her face sober, although she knew she couldn't hide the mischief in her eyes. "I do adore that cute mustache you're sporting. I imagine the girls swoon over that."

"It is quite nice, isn't it?" He smirked and smoothed the hair on his upper lip, his own eyes broadcasting quite openly that her teasing challenge couldn't get the best of him.

"Any special gal caught your eye?"

"Wouldn't you like to know?"

"There is, isn't there?" Josie squealed. "Tell me."

"Not on your life. You might be my best friend, but let's not get the cart before the horse."

"She doesn't know?"

He gave her an impatient look. "Let's go talk with your husband."

Chapter Twenty-four

What a muddle. Keeping an eye on Josie was a handful, but to have Jerry here at the same time as Marshall, on top of keeping track of his boss and his movements, was mind boggling.

Jerry's terrible hatred of the man was understandable. But if he'd had a clue of the depth of it, he'd never have agreed to help him get on tonight. Days too late to change the plan now.

His captain had ordered Wills to get a job with Marshall and keep tabs on the other man's activities, reporting on any suspicious behavior. Weeks later, Captain had recalled him to headquarters and given him further orders. "Major Patterson's home from overseas. Normally, he doesn't need someone to watch his back, but he's overcoming some—er—backsets, and I want you to be available, in case he needs help. Keep your job at Marshalls—that's primary."

To say he'd had no time for socializing or even quick visits to his parents and the Rayners would be right. He did well to get in a few hours sleep when he could catch a couple.

Not that he was complaining. Captain had hinted a promotion was in the works if he carried this off well—and he needed that promotion. There was someone very special he wanted to—had to—impress.

So why Jerry despised Marshall he had no clue, and didn't care. No doubt it had to do with Patterson's overseas tour. Whatever. He'd kept his work at Marshall's, and his intuition and senses ready when backing up Patterson. And bringing in Josie, even in a very minor capacity, was a blessing and took a small amount of pressure off him.

Jerry going ballistic over Josie's presence here was another matter. Wills had made a mistake in telling him—and one that shouldn't have happened. Now it was up to him to smooth the guy's feathers, and to keep both out of harm's way. Captain had specifically ordered that there was to be no confrontation between Marshall and Patterson—yet.

Major Patterson looked up as he and Josie threaded their way through the two head chefs and the five or so assistants. His face lit up at the sight of Josie, and then anger replaced it. He tossed down the knife he held and wiped his hands on the huge apron he wore.

Josie picked up her pace, calling to him before she reached her husband. "Jerry, I didn't know—"

"You didn't tell me you were meeting with Marshall tonight."

Even Wills was taken back by the bitter and angry accusation. He almost stepped up to put the major in his place—but held back. It wasn't his right.

His long-time friend paled a little, but her chin lifted.

Good girl. Don't let him bully you.

The man was frightened otherwise he'd never have acted this way. Wills had never once seen Jerry treat Josie with anything but respect before the man had left home for active duty and overseas. Whatever Jerry had gone through, had hurt him, not only physically but deep inside him. He'd bet on that anytime.

As always, Wills sent a silent prayer upward for his pal and her husband.

Chapter Twenty-five

Was Jerry actually accusing her of something wrong? How could he think that? Josie's temper flared a bit. She was already worn out from dealing with the likes of Greye and Diana without having to put up with Jerry's tantrum too.

You're going to have to be stronger than you've ever been in your life.

She wanted to scowl as the memory of her father's advice replayed in her memory.

Her gaze roved over Jerry's face, and a big hand of tenderness squeezed her heart at the distress written on his face, his pinched, still-thin features and the flex of his fingers. He was worried about *her.* She needed to soothe him, not fight with him.

"Jerry, I didn't even know who Marshall was until I heard his name tonight. I've never spoken to him before or been introduced to him. I don't even particularly care for his attitude—seems quite sly to me. Why on earth would I come here to see *him?*"

Her husband studied her face. Searching to see how sincere she was? She had no problem with that. She wouldn't be here if she wasn't snooping for information.

He opened his mouth, but she beat him to it.

"And if I'd known Diana would be here, I'd never entered the door. After the way she dressed me down— underhandedly, mind you—I couldn't care less if I never see her again."

"She insulted you?" Jerry's voice carried a dangerous edge. "Maybe I should—"

"No need. Claire capably took her down several notches."

"Claire?" Jerry's face lost its stressfulness, and he chuckled.

"No less."

"Then if there's no one here you're trying to impress,

why are you dressed so—so outrageously gorgeous?" He growled the question, but Josie saw through that facade, his sudden aroused flirting prevalent in spite of the growl.

"Why else? If I'd known the best looking man in the world would be here..." she allowed her words to trail off, and now, she half-turned and bumped him with her shoulder, gently, hoping he'd take her bait.

"Woman, you're pushing the extremities of danger." He slid out of his apron, and in an instant, he'd wrapped his arms around her, pulling her close.

"Do you think that scares me?" She laughed up into his dear face.

He growled and nuzzled her cheek, the short whiskers on his face tickling. His whisper reached her ear, and she could hear the tremble in it. "I'm afraid for you, my love. Please be careful. You *have* to tell me when and where you're going."

She had to blink back the tears. "I will, my darling. I will."

Most of the time anyway.

~*~

He'd never been so scared—or so angry—in his life as when Wills Mason had blurted out that Josie was here. Tonight. In the same room as Marshall.

It wasn't Mason's fault, and really, now that Josie had explained, he realized she'd had no knowledge of or about the Marshall jerk. As for Marshall knowing about Josie, he wasn't so sure.

He wasn't so sure about anything. Had Marshall gotten control of her someway, or was Rhoderick lurking? Playing a game with Jerry's inability to locate the German man? Was Josie being lured away by those two just to get at him? Were one or both trying to hurt him through her? Something had to give pretty soon or he would confront Marshall in person.

"Who's the man who hosted this dinner tonight?"

"I don't know him very well." Josie touched the big brimmed hat Claire had insisted she needed to wear tonight and wished she could toss it aside and let her hair down. "He came to Cincinnati on business and has been talking with Tyrell about the church supporting his project."

"And this project is?"

"He wants to launch a group of support for those affected by the war."

"Why West Street Community Church specifically? There's plenty of churches around here. Why not one of them?"

"Who knows?" Josie lifted a hand and flipped it up. "I haven't asked, but there could be several supporting him. West Community might be just one in a lot."

"Could be. Does this admirable man have a name?"

"Walter Greye."

"Hmm. Never heard of him." He'd have the captain demand some background checks on the guy. Anyone showing interest in him, Josie or her family was suspect to him. He couldn't be too careful. "You know this guy, Mason?"

"Not really. Marshall has people in and out of his home all the time. This guy's visited several times, but no more than others."

Should she? Josie hovered between sharing the animosity between Greye and Guy Delaney. Whatever her husband was involved in, sounded like he could use some help.

The question was: what was he involved in? Espionage? Another woman? But if she shared her knowledge, perhaps it would coax him to open up a little with her.

"There seems to be some trouble between Walter Greye and Guy Delaney."

Both men turned in unison to stare at her.

"What kind of trouble?" Was that skepticism in Jerry's voice?

"Well, I don't know Guy Delaney that well either. He's a new boarder at the house, but he seems belligerent toward Greye. I have no idea why. He seems bent on contradicting statements Greye offers."

"What kind of statements, Jo?" Wills brows drew together in a frown.

Josie couldn't stop the quick glance she sneaked at Jerry, but when she realized he was staring at her, waiting for an answer, she dropped her gaze. No way would she tattle the *rumor* Greye had spoken. What else then?

She shook her head, fumbling with the annoying curl Claire had left dangling against her neck, stalling for time. "Uh, it's more of subtle disagreement with what Greye says. Like, I won't do it anymore. Stuff like that."

"Right." Jerry nodded soberly, then added dryly. "Doesn't sound too serious."

"No-o-o." Wills' mouth widened in a smile. "But we probably ought to get some background on these two, just for assurance that Josie's not dealing with a couple of spooks."

"Hey, I can handle myself." These two clowns weren't taking her serious. So much for sharing.

"Relax, Josie. We know you've got spunk. Mason, you want me to give Captain a nudge?"

"No, I'll do it."

"Stay on the lookout for my wife, will you? Not sure where my wild, tomboyish Josie has gone. All I see tonight is a glamorous woman that's tempting me with her womanly wiles."

"Will do, Major." Wills snapped a salute and grinned broadly then spoke to Josie. "I'd better get you back to the dinner before your father comes looking for you, Josie."

~*~

It had been on the tip of Josie's tongue to mention to Jerry, Claire's doubt that Walter Greye was the man's real name, of her own questions about his interest in him, and Greye's rumor about an affair, but Josie had hesitated. Why alarm her husband when he already had too many doubts and problems on his mind? It was up to her to get to the root of the problem, if there was one. After that, she could bring Jerry into the picture if needed.

Wills hurried her along, anxious for some reason to get her back to the group. They were nearing the last corner, when Marshall strolled around it, and they almost plowed into him.

"Where have you been, Williams?" The man snapped.

"You're not at your post."

"No, sir. Sorry, sir. Mrs. Patterson had been gone quite a while, and I didn't want her to get lost. I felt you'd want me to make sure one of Mr. Greye's guests was taken care of, seeing he's a good friend of yours."

Why Wills was giving that elaborate explanation was beyond her, but Josie sensed it wasn't a good time to pop up with sassy comments. Let Wills handle the situation the way he thought best. He surely had a good reason.

"Good thinking as usual." The other man was eyeing his employee. "You always have the right answer, don't you?"

Was Marshall being sarcastic?

"I'll see her back the rest of the way. You get back to your post."

"Yes, sir. You take care, Mrs. Patterson."

"Thank you for your help." Josie dimpled at him and allowed her eyes to twinkle with mischief, but Wills kept a serious face.

"Let's get you back, Mrs. Patterson. Our evening entertainment's ready to begin, and Greye's quite concerned at your absence."

Josie wanted to say a lot, but, for once in her lifetime, refrained. When they entered the room, everyone was seated. Marshall dropped her off at a seat beside Greye, who stood then sat when she did.

He nodded at someone and the act began. Mr. Greye leaned close and whispered, "I was getting worried. Where did you go?"

"You needn't have. Too much socializing is not my thing. I needed a few minutes of alone time."

"Next time, tell me, and I'll go with you. That way you won't get lost."

Hadn't the man heard what she said? Alone meant alone, in her book.

Seconds later, Mr. Greye moved, and she felt his arm slip onto the back of her chair. He didn't touch her, but uneasiness washed over her. Good thing the rest of the group sat at tables closer to the front. If she hadn't known it would jeopardize her plans, she'd have risen and moved to the empty seat beside Papa Ossie.

~*~

Jerry felt like he was floundering. Another dead end tonight. He limped away from the restaurant, searching for a taxi, his leg aching like the dickens from being on his feet all evening, body and soul dejected at his failure to find the results he wanted.

Every time he'd tried to get away for a few minutes to check on this gig Mason had reported to him, he'd been hindered by one thing and another. First the chef had complained he was dawdling, then he'd been waylaid by a chatting guy who thought Jerry wanted to hear his sorry life story. And, of course, Josie and Mason interrupting the kitchen work hadn't endeared him to the main chef. He'd rudely and firmly dismissed him, ordering him to not show his face in his working realm again. Ha, as if he wanted to.

What frightened him was the thought he'd lost his edge. The sensitivity that had always kept him one step ahead of the enemy, that had set him apart from his peers, had pushed him to advancement faster than he otherwise would have attained.

When he'd been released from the hospital, the doctors had said they'd done all they could to help him heal. Now—they'd tried to encourage him—he needed to work at resting and recovering his strength. It would be up to him how well his leg regained usability.

Whatever that meant. He wasn't holding his breath.

Raising a hand to signal the lone taxicab that approached slowly, he hoped it would see him now that the street lights had gone out. It wasn't too late to swing by the captain's subterfuge quarters and request a background check on this Greye and the Rayner boarding house newbie. If the man was around his Josie, that automatically set his nerves on edge.

Better be safe than sorry.

He limped toward the cab, but just as he started to open the door, a feminine hand grasped the handle and swung the back door open, almost hitting him with it. He straightened and frowned, but she gave him a scorching glance and ignored him as she settled into the back seat, tossing one end of the fur stole across her shoulder.

Just his luck he'd have a broad steal the only cab in

sight. No doubt they'd all headed to busier streets. Nothing for it but to walk.

Sighing, he watched as it disappeared around the corner.

He hadn't gone fifty feet when a cab zipped around a corner and headed straight for him. He held up a hand, hoping, but not expecting much. The car slid to a stop beside him. He limped toward it, but the cabbie opened his door and exited, and Jerry stopped his advance.

The cab driver strode around the front of the cab, and Jerry watched him come, confused. What was going on?

"Need a ride?"

"Why else would I be signaling you to stop?"

An alarm rang in his brain as a ray of light from a business behind him shone directly on the cabbie's face. Wasn't that the same driver who'd just picked up the woman not five minutes ago? He looked familiar...

Something was wrong.

"Sorry. Changed my mind. I'm walking." He backed away, motioning for it to move on, but before he could turn around, the back door swung open, and a man stepped out. In his hand, he held a gun.

Instead of leaving, the cabbie stepped up close behind him and gave him a shove, his gravelly voice low but serious. "Get in the cab."

Jerry recovered from the shove and swung around, his fists raised.

The man growled. "I wouldn't. The boss wants to talk with you."

"Who's your boss?" He wasn't use to giving in easily to an enemy.

The man with the gun leveled it at Jerry and muttered to the driver. "Just let me kill him now."

"Shut up." The driver snapped at the other man, then to Jerry. "You'll find out soon enough if you don't mind your own business. The boss doesn't like people who meddle in our matters."

He had it. The driver was the big guard from Marshall's who'd stopped him on the stairs.

"I have something for you from the boss."

"What—?"

The guard—Samson—swung a punch at him,

effectively knocking his head sideways.

Jerry lifted a hand and wiped at his mouth, anger like red hot lava pouring through him. If they were planning on killing him, he was going to get in a few good swings first.

Before the thought was completed, Jerry swung, and Samson staggered back, as Jerry's fist connected with the other guy's jaw. He didn't stay back but was on Jerry again, pounding him when he could and taking a few hits himself.

In the midst of the punching, Jerry heard another car door open, and he shifted his feet to see what new problem was developing.

And then, for a second, he was sure a building had fallen on his head. The world went black. He tried to shake his head, clear it, but he was pretty sure he was not accomplishing it. Wobbling, maybe. What had happened?

He couldn't see and his mind whirled in such a dizzying pattern he would never have been able to see clearly if all the street lights were suddenly switched back on.

He didn't pass out completely—not at first. Images faded in and out, blurred and shrunken.

A voice—female?—ordered, no daintiness in her tone. "Give him something to remember. Might keep him from getting killed before his time."

The image of a blond woman wavered in front of his eyes. He saw the men approaching and tried to lift his fists to fight them off, tried to manuever to gain the advantage, but his arms refused to raise, his feet seemed to be shuffling instead of sidestepping smartly.

He felt the blows as the two men slugged at him, hats pulled low over their foreheads, over and over, their beefy fists creating a havoc in his body he'd never felt before. One of them must have had something other than his fists. A tool? Brass knuckles? The gun? He couldn't decide, couldn't move...

He swayed, willing himself to stand, and then as if he was a tree giving into the savage and fatal cut, fell onto the sidewalk, not moving, barely hearing.

He didn't see the next hit, but heard someone walk up to him. A kick in the side, then another crack on the head, and Jerry felt his head explode.

From a distance, the feminine voice said, "Mind your own business, Patterson. Or next time we won't be so easy on you."

Fading footsteps, then the female voice snapped, "Step on it, Samson."

"I didn't know I was getting involved in something like this."

"Shut up and do as you're told or it'll go worse than this for you. Want that?"

The man whined an answer.

And then Jerry knew nothing more.

~*~

Josie bounced out of bed the next morning at an unearthly hour, something she seldom did. But the excitement last night from Jerry's intense flirting had kept her senses flying high. She stayed awake as long as she could, hoping he'd come home early.

Only he hadn't. At least before she'd fallen asleep. So, now, she wanted to be up and halfway presentable, and most of all to have his coffee waiting for him.

And she needed to get in a few hours practice on her flute. Her one-time agreement to play for the church was turning into an every Sunday morning event. And now she'd sort of promised Guy she'd play for him, and what better time than Sunday?

Not that she was complaining.

She ran the brush through her hair, tied a ribbon in it to hold it back, slipped into a blue—Jerry loved blue— blouse and matching polka-dotted skirt, and she was ready for the day.

Touching the door where Jerry had been sleeping since he'd gotten home, as she passed, she smiled and headed to the kitchen. He'd be up soon and that coffee needed to be ready for her man.

Twenty minutes later, she paused outside his bedroom door and pressed her head against the wooden panel. She heard nothing, no signs of him stirring or growling. Maybe he was sleeping in, which would be a shocker.

Was he all right? What if he'd died in the night?

Josie gave the door a shove that bounced it against the wall and rushed into the room. The covers were neatly made, the pillows plumped and straight. Jerry had not slept here last night.

Then...where was he?

She flew down the stairs again, calling, searching in every room until at last she ended back in the kitchen where the smell of the fresh coffee permeated every corner of the room. Josie leaned against a cabinet, thinking.

Had he left early? No. He *never* made his bed.

Then if he hadn't returned home last night, where was he? It'd been several days since he'd stayed away all night, and Josie had hoped he was past that phase.

So where was he? Working? With...someone else? That Vanda he'd called to in his sleep? Or even worse than that horrible thought—was he hurt?

She needed Papa Ossie. Without another thought, Josie tore down the hallway and reached for the door locks when...

The loud rat-a-tat-tat on the front door nearly sent her stumbling backward over her own feet. She started to chuckle at her clumsiness, but the thought that it might be a message from Jerry sent her scrambling to unlock the door. She swung it open, and on the doorstep stood a cabbie, arm slung around a drooping man. Why would this stranger be here at her house? Had there been an accident and he needed help?

But that dark hair, a curl flopping onto a blood-stained forehead, cheeks bruised and cut, one eye swollen... Was that...

Her breath left her body in a loud puff. With a lunge, she was beside Jerry and helping the cabbie guide him into the sitting room. As the man eased him onto the sofa, Josie placed a pillow under his head. She stared down at him, her mind whirling. "What happened to him? Do you know?"

"Have no idea." The cabbie shook his head. "Saw him lying on the sidewalk after another cab took off. Being the sucker that I am for anything hurting, I drove up and checked him out. Realized he was still alive—"

Josie groaned aloud.

"—searched his wallet for a name and address, and brought him here." The man shrugged. "You need to call a doctor. Looks pretty serious to me."

Josie ran for the phone. Time to call Papa. He'd know what to do.

~*~

"Papa, is Jerry going to be all right?"

"Course he is, Josie. He's tough, and Doc Pitman is the best." Her father frowned harder, but his words were soothing.

The man bending over Jerry's bruised body straightened and turned toward Captain Ossie and Josie. "He's pretty beat up, and probably has a mild concussion. He'll be stiff and sore for a week or two, but there's no broken bones."

Josie laid her head against Papa's arm. Could her heart feel anymore bruised and scared?

"He's going to need plenty of fluids and rest." The man's lowering brows hanging over his dark eyes looked like threatening storm clouds. "I can't emphasize that enough, Miss Josie. Your husband looks like death warmed over—forgive the cliche—and needs some serious rest. Are you up to this, young lady?"

Josie started to nod, but Harriet, standing at the top of the sofa, spoke up.

"I want to help, Captain Ossie. Just because Josie's living in a different house, doesn't mean she doesn't need my help. She's going to have her hands full. Her man needs nourishing soup to put strength in him and someone strong enough to see that he rests."

"You're right, Harriet. Do take some time to help." Papa Ossie nodded at Harriet.

"But I want to take care of Jerry." Josie lifted her head and protested.

"You'll have plenty to do, Child. Be glad and accept that Harriet wants to and is making time to give you short breaks." Papa's voice brooked no argument. "You'll need those occasionally."

"I do appreciate it, Harriet. Thank you." She smiled at the woman who'd been like a second mother to her and her sisters. "I don't see how you keep everything so organized."

"Practice, Josie." She cocked her head, a grin on her lips. "When you've cared for a household as long as I have, it's second nature."

"Then it's settled. Good." The doctor slipped on his coat and headed for the hall. "I'll check back in on him late this evening and again in the morning. I'll know more then how he's doing."

Josie handed his Pork Pie hat to him.

"Light food today, Harriet, if he wakens." Giving a nod to all of them, he left.

Harriet reached for her own coat. "I've got just enough chicken broth left from Sunday's meal to make some soup for Jerry and you, Josie. I'll head home to get that done and see you later."

Josie followed the woman who'd cared for the Rayner home for as long as she could remember, out onto the porch.

Spring was nipping old man winter's heels, promising an early spring. Now that the rigors of heavy ice skating practice was a thing of the past for her, she realized suddenly she could barely wait for the warmer weather. She smiled at the errant thought and turned away when a figure caught her attention.

Was that Walter Greye walking down the sidewalk? She studied the man, and the closer he came, the more she realized it indeed was him. Was he coming to see her?

As he approached her gate, he raised a hand in greeting and called out. "How are you this bright morning, Mrs. Josie? Beautiful day."

"It is. What brings you by this early? Are you looking for Papa Ossie?"

Greye unlatched her gate and walked up the sidewalk toward her. "No, not today. Wanted a chat with Pastor Tyrell if he's home. And how is your husband doing?"

"How did you know he was hurt last night?" Josie stared at the man. Was the suspicion boiling inside her evident on her face? She hoped not. And how on earth did he know Jerry was hurt?

"I didn't."

The surprise on the man's face was real and vivid.

"It was a general question. What happened?"

"Jerry was beaten up last night. We won't know how serious the damage until early tomorrow when the doctor swings by again."

"Ach, you must have your hands full caring for him."

"I have plenty of help. My father and others will pitch in to give me breaks."

"Is that so? Well, since I'm here, and you have plenty of help as you put it, would you be interested in joining me for brunch downtown?"

"What about your meeting with Tyrell?"

"That can wait." He grinned. "Especially since I have the opportunity to woo you away from your house."

Josie laughed. He was so openly ridiculous. "I am married, you know."

"How can I forget when you insist on reminding me?" He tilted his hat a shade back on his head. "Nevertheless, I promise to be good if you'll take pity on a lonesome man from out of town."

"I shouldn't."

"Are you sure?"

She didn't want to leave Jerry. But even now, she could see Shirley Largett hurrying across the lawn. Papa was inside too, and Jerry would be in good hands with both of them there to watch over him. In a few hours, Harriet would be back with her soup. When she returned, Josie would plan on spending the rest of the day with him.

Besides, she wanted to find out if Greye was after information about Jerry. What better way than spending time with him?

Not altogether a pleasant thought, but she could do it. For Jerry.

"Give me fifteen minutes. I'll be right back."

He nodded and Josie ran inside.

Twelve minutes later she ran lightly down the stairs again and paused at the sitting room door...and thought perhaps a tsunami had invaded the land and knocked her over.

Walter Greye stood inside talking with Papa Ossie and

Shirley as if he belonged there as much as she did. He was staring down at Jerry while Papa—no doubt explaining what had happened—talked, oblivious of how Josie might view the man.

Wasn't his fault. Hadn't she hidden her suspicions from her father to avoid any lengthy discussions about the dangers of what she was attempting?

Still, she'd left Greye outside. On purpose.

What was that expression playing across the man's face? Amusement? Satisfaction? Delight? Or something...more sinister?

Josie walked slowly toward the threesome. They halted their coversation as she approached, and Papa held out a hand to pull her close.

"I was just telling Greye about Jerry. You go on and one or both of us will watch over him until Harriet gets back, or you return. I told you, you would need hours to relax, and yes, I know you love Jerry and don't want to leave him. Go, Child. We'll see you in a bit."

Josie said nothing, only nodded as Greye took hold of her arm and guided her to the door, Shirley following.

When Greye opened the door and motioned for Josie to go ahead, Shirley said, "Just a minute, Josie. I wanted to talk to you a second. Do you mind, Mr. Greye?"

That was giving him little choice.

The man gave her a nod and stepped outside, pulling the door partially shut.

Shirley leaned close and whispered. "It may mean nothing, but I didn't invite Greye inside. He followed me in even when I tried to deter him from doing so."

"Why would that seem important to you?"

"Normally, it wouldn't, but I almost insisted that we had a sick man in the house and needed quiet and no visitors. He ignored my words and practically pushed me inside."

"Strange." Josie stared at the half-open door. Was it Shirley's imagination or her high sense of propriety that was at work here?

Either way, she needed to remember that she knew little about Walter Greye and should be careful.

"Okay, thanks, Shirley. Not sure how to deal with it,

but I'll be on guard." She gave the librarian a short nod and opened the door wider. At the last minute, she turned to give Shirley a smile, but the woman was hurrying on toward the kitchen. Instead, her father stood at the sitting room doorway. The expression on his face said it all. He was a worried man.

For a second, Josie hesitated, tempted to go speak to her father, but when he lifted a hand and motioned her to go on, she nodded and stepped outside.

Greye straightened and took a quick step backward.

Had he been trying to hear what Shirley said?

Chapter Twenty-six

Only once did a sense of unease move inside her, and that was at Greye's question in the taxi.

"So that was your husband, was it, Josie Patterson?"

"Yes."

"Your father explained that none of you knew what happened. Why do you think someone would do this? I mean, his work surely isn't dangerous? Could he be involved in something—I hate to say this—but illegal?"

Was that a question? Too bad, because she had no idea. Too bad too, because it raked up fears for Jerry Josie did not want to think about. "I think maybe it was rogue thieves."

"Do you really?"

The amusement in his voice hurt.

"Why couldn't it have been?"

"I didn't say it wasn't."

They were silent for a moment.

"He didn't look at all as I re—thought he would."

Re? What had he been about to say? How many words started with those two letters?

Tons.

"No, he doesn't. Jerry's always been strong and brave and a bit daring and cocky, but I liked it."

"I dare say. Must hurt to see him in that—pitiful state now."

What was there to say to that?

Josie couldn't fault Greye for his choice of dining sites. This was no corner cafe, but a small, quiet restaurant with a friendly staff and good substantial food selections. She felt herself relaxing after a steady diet of upclass restaurants that had given her the willies.

Greye was staring at her. Reading her mind?

"You like this place?" And at Josie's nod, he continued. "I thought you might. A friend and I lunched here last week, and I immediately knew you'd enjoy the quiet atmosphere."

"Thanks. The food is good too."

He leaned forward, shoving his cup aside a few inches. "You know what I'd like?"

Josie shook her head. "Have no idea."

"I'd love to have your portrait painted, just as you are now." He sat back as if he'd given a world-shattering news brief. "You are elegant dressed in finery, but I think I like you best as you are now."

"In this? A blouse that's seen better days and a second hand skirt?" Josie plucked at a pleat in her skirt. "You're making fun of me, I'm sure."

"And I'm just as sure I am not."

Josie swallowed, a thread of pleasure at the supposed compliment running through her, yet uneasy at the conflict inside her. The unease nipped at her.

"May I?" Greye leaned forward, one hand in the air as if waiting on her permission.

What was he planning to do? The nervous twitch in her stomach begged for relief. "I suppose..."

He touched her face, skimming over it with his fingertips. "You have beautiful bone structure."

Josie's stomach clenched at his gentle touch. Involuntarily she flinched, but he shushed her, and she felt her eyes closing at the soothingly soft caress. How long since Jerry had..."

No. Josie jerked away, horrified at what she'd almost—almost enjoyed. She started to stand, to run away, but Greye's hand lightly clamped hers and held her still.

"Be quiet, my dear. I won't hurt you. Let me finish."

His gaze drilled into hers. An order to trust? To keep quiet as he'd stated? Or something else, too deep for her to interpret?

"You're tall, but stand well. Your slight weight gives you the ability to handle that, and I suppose your athletic practices has benefited that lean, well-toned body of yours." He let go of her. "All in all, you'd make a delightful model. Will you do it?"

She'd been tempted for a few moments. That deep seated hurt at Jerry's coldness had nearly allowed her to enjoy a stolen moment of appreciation from another man. But not quite. Enough was enough. No matter what emotion she'd buried, she couldn't quite forget that Jerry Patterson was the only man she could or would ever love.

She wanted to shiver, the impression of a snake charming her with his steady gaze sweeping over her in a smothering flood.

~*~

They were leaving when an older man approached them. Greye moved as if to cut him off, but the man nimbly side-stepped him and spoke to Josie.

"Josephine Rayner? Patterson?"

She didn't recognize him, so she hesitatingly answered. "Yes, I'm Josie."

"I'd like to speak with you a moment, if you will." His voice was clipped and not at all diffident as a person's would be if he was unsure of himself.

Josie looked at Greye who returned her look then shrugged. "I need to make a telephone call."

The man watched as Greye walked away, then he spoke. "I'm Robert Patterson."

Robert Patterson? Who...Jerry's *father*? "Mr. Patterson? Does Jerry know you're here? In town?"

"I sent a telegram, if the boy read it."

"And you called me."

"I wonder if we could have lunch together? Or have you already eaten?"

"I have just finished brunch."

"Then is there somewhere we could get a decent cup of coffee?"

Josie grinned, wondering if she should suggest the Rayner house. No, not yet. She needed to see what the man wanted before issuing invitations that would have Jerry angrier than he was.

"My favorite cafe is two blocks over if you don't mind a humble place."

He shrugged. "Fine. As long as the coffee's drinkable."

"Then let me explain to Mr. Greye. I'll be right back."

Mr. Greye was still on the telephone, but placed a hand over it and listened as she explained that she was going with Robert Patterson. She thanked him for the meal, but gave him no time to object. With a wave she was off.

Jerry's father had a chauffeur-driven car waiting, and after he helped her in, he settled into the backseat beside her. Both sat silent until the driver pulled up to the curb in front of the cafe.

The chauffeur promptly stepped out of the car and opened Patterson's door. Once Patterson had exited, the chaffeur hurried to the passenger side and swung open Josie's door, but it wasn't him who helped her out. Robert Patterson held out a hand, and Josie took it as she stepped out as graciously as she could.

Motioning to his driver to move on, he growled out a time for the chauffeur to return, then abruptly headed for the diner door.

Josie watched the man, a bit of wry amusement on her lips, as she read and understood Jerry's antagonism against his father. Seemed he was every bit the bully her husband had insisted he was. Hmmm. No need for him to try that stuff with her. She could give as well as take.

But Rome wasn't conquered in a day. She hurried to catch up.

They settled at a back booth and gave their orders to the hovering waitress.

Robert Patterson studied her face. "So-o-o, you're the reason Jerry refused my offer."

She'd really hoped they would have a decent conversation. That she'd be the intercessor between father and son to bring them together again. Ha. Didn't look like that was going to happen.

"Tell me about yourself."

Was that an order? Josie didn't like orders.

"You want to hear about *me*? I would have thought you'd want an update on Jerry."

He flapped a hand at her words. "We'll get to that. I want to hear about you first, find out what sort of woman my son married, without so much as a by-you-leave. Are you what he needs?"

The glare he fixed on her as he leaned forward was anything but friendly. One hand wrapped around the cup the waitress had set down. The other flat on the table top as if in preparation to rise.

Josie felt the temper inside herself flaring. No one, not even Jerry or her family ever spoke to her in that tone, let alone with derogatory words such as he'd just spewed.

Shoving aside her cup, Josie placed her hands on the table top and half-stood, leaning toward him. "Am I what he *needs*?"

She saw his mouth open as if to shoot back more sarcastic words at her, but she wasn't about to give him a chance. Not until she could scorch him with her own.

"What does he need? Who's to say? Not you, Mr. Patterson, even though you're his father. His friends? Me? I wouldn't attempt it. The only one who can know for a certainty what Jerry needs is himself, and well, I suppose God. But certainly not you or me."

She drew in a deep breath and ignored his stare, determined to stand up for Jerry, to put this man in his place.

"What sort of woman am I?" Josie tossed her head and half-snorted. "What do you think by now? I'm no lily-white, soft spoken, afraid-of-her-shadow person. I'm strong, athletic and stubborn. I've drunk hard liquor and said a few words I shouldn't have."

Josie stopped, her chest heaving with the emotion that felt like a dam breaking. How much more could she take? Hadn't she already endured more than any normal woman had? She wanted to glare angrily back at the man who'd done so much emotional damage to her husband, but she couldn't. She wasn't at all sure she could make any sense from what she knew would be a wobbly voice the next time she opened her mouth. She swallowed.

"But what I do know and believe with all my heart is that I love and adore Jerry Patterson. Father Patterson, I can't speak for your son. But I know I'll never meet another man like him. I'll never love another man like him. If I die tomorrow, I'll not go out wishing I'd met ten other men. I've met the only man *I'll* ever need."

Josie plopped to her seat and laid her head on her crossed arms. How could she spout off like some deranged maniac attacking a helpless person?

She surreptitiously wiped her damp eyes, scrambling to devise a ploy to get away from Jerry's father who probably was hoping he'd never come in contact with her again. Still he didn't exactly seem the fearful type. She lifted her head, straightened her back and peeked at the man sitting across from her.

Was that a hint of a smile on his face?

Josie wanted to flop back in her seat again and gape, but she didn't. Instead she sent him a lopsided grin. "Sorry. I get a little carried away when the subject of Jerry comes up..."

"You've got plenty of spunk, I'll agree." And then he laughed. "I think you and I'll get along just fine, Josie Rayner Patterson."

~*~

It was dark in the room with only a dim light in the corner. Jerry moved his head and the pain that shot through it had him gasping for breath. Seconds later, as the pain eased, he reopened his eyes. A stocky figure of a woman sat in a wingback chair, her head laid back against it. He squinted, but already knew it wasn't Josie. Josie would never have been called stocky.

Who was it then?

Jerry turned his head slowly and stared up at the ceiling. Why was he lying here on the sofa with *someone* sitting in the arm chair close by as if—as if he was sick or hurt?

He shot another glance at the figure lightly snoring. Who was she? And more important, why was he lying here?

He remembered...

The thought had him shooting straight up from his pillow, but the agony blasting through his head sent him collapsing back onto said pillow. He groaned, but tried to ignore the pain as one thought played like one of those tinny-sounding calliopes in his head.

He remembered nothing.

What had happened.

Where he was.

Who he was.

Nothing except the image of a red-haired woman named Josie, but who *was* she?

~*~

The man who sat across from her looked like a

dejected outcast. Those were real tears in his eyes. His head was shaking back and forth. And, from Jerry's occasional mentions of his father, she'd had no idea her relating of his condition would affect Robert Patterson so much.

"Doesn't sound like my Jerry."

"I assure you it's true." If her tone was a bit dry, then so be it. "Whatever happened to Jerry overseas, it was bad, and more than his injury, although that might have something to do with it. I have no clear idea of what."

"What can I do to help?" Robert Patterson reached across the tabletop and laid a hand on top of her's. "I'm positive Jerry won't be happy to see me."

Clamping her mouth closed, Josie swallowed back the automatic retort that begged to be said. Why would Jerry welcome the overbearing, demanding father Robert had always been to him?

She leaned forward. "Sir, if you truly want to help, I'll welcome it. But I'd like to suggest you do it from afar. I think it would be better to break it to him that you've changed your mind and are willing to work at getting along, if he is, gradually."

"Not pleased at waiting, but I'll agree to that."

"Vague as it is, here's my plan." Josie whispered, and her father-in-law leaned closer to catch her words. "Come around tonight..."

~*~

Josie stepped out of Robert Patterson's automobile and cast a glance around. For now, it would be better if no one saw with whom she'd been for the last two hours. It was late and time to see how Jerry was doing. And begin getting a hint of the atmosphere after she put out the feelers for a reconciliation between Jerry and Robert Patterson.

She watched as the luxurious limousine pulled away from the curb, then made a complete circle, looking for she knew not what in the spring evening coolness. Sighing, she headed inside to check on her husband. She'd been gone way too long. She hadn't meant to be. Jerry would be wondering where she was. Why she was gone and not at home taking care of him.

Josie slipped inside and shut the door as quietly as she could. Pausing, she listened but no sound came from the sitting room. Was he asleep still?

Peeking inside, she saw a blanket-covered figure lying on the sofa. Across from the sofa, sat Harriet, knitting needles gently clicking, giving the evening a cozy and warm sense. Josie smiled, loving the scene and that her best friend's mother was here, in Josie's own home, leaving a touch of motherly warmth.

"I'm home." Josie whispered the words as she entered, casting a quick glance at Jerry.

"You have a good time?"

"Yes, stayed longer than I planned, but ran into someone that, uh, was important I talk with."

"Shirley and I alternated through the afternoon. Jerry woke for just a bit but has been sleeping mostly." Harriet gathered her knitting supplies. "If you'll be okay, I'll head over to the house and make sure supper's ready to go. I'll send over something for you and some soup for Jerry." She slipped into her spring jacket. "You make sure to let one of us know if you need anything, you hear, my dear?"

Josie walked with the woman to the back door.

Harriet gathered Josie in a smothering hug. "You're like a child of mine, Josie Patterson. You call me if you need me."

"I will. Thanks, Harriet." She waved and smiled as the woman hurried across the lawn and headed to the back door of the Rayner house. She was probably anxious to make sure those she'd left in charge had carried out her orders.

Jerry lay in the same position as when she'd left him earlier. She stood for a moment staring down at him, her heart melting at the sight of his helplessness. What had happened to him? Did it have something to do with his work?

Would he be okay if she ran upstairs to change? It would only take five minutes. Surely...

He was still sleeping, but it must have been a restless sleep because he was tossing and turning, muttering incoherently. Josie touched his forehead but it was cool. Kneeling beside the sofa, she ran her fingers over his cheekbones, then up over his temples and across his forehead, smoothing back his hair. She wanted to croon to him, but she didn't want to startle him.

She chuckled, remembering Jerry's pretense of agony whenever she croaked out a song—holding his ears and twisting his facial expression into one of misery. What fun they'd had the two weeks before he'd left for his military duty.

What had happened to that man?

Her heart crept up her throat, threatening to choke her, threatening to allow her tears the release they demanded. She wanted all this to stop.

Josie scrubbed at her eyes then studied the room. Standing, she moved around the room to light a soft lamp and then refilled the small pitcher of water Harriet had left on the end table for Jerry.

Her deserted flute case left lying on the cushion of a wing back chair caught her attention, and she moseyed over to it. She stared down at it, then glanced back at Jerry. His muttering had stopped, but his body still jerked and twitched. Maybe playing softly for him would ease the tension.

It surely couldn't hurt.

Snapping the locks open, she lifted her flute, gave it a lick-and-a-promise wipe down, then took a seat on the opposite love seat from him. Pausing to reflect on what song to play, she lifted the flute to her lips and blew softly into it, and the tune of "*I Love You for Sentimental Reasons*" filled the air.

There was no immediate reaction from her husband, but gradually the twitching stopped. Josie played on, losing herself to the music, feeling the tune embed itself in her being and relaxing the tense muscles in her own body.

Chapter Twenty-seven

As if he'd been on a long journey and just returned home, Jerry felt the warmth and contentment before he opened his eyes. He could feel heat—fireplace heat and dim lightness even from behind his closed lids. There was soft music playing. He didn't recognize the tune, but it was soothing and restful.

When Jerry finally stirred enough to glance around the room, the image from somewhere deep in his consciousness had come to life and sat across him, highlighted from the blue flowered loveseat, playing softly on a flute. Josie.

The one thing he remembered.

He allowed his eyes to study what he could see from around the room, but nothing looked familiar. Only this Josie. But who she was and why he remembered her and nothing else—he had no clue.

She had her eyes closed and swayed a little with her music as if she was totally absorbed by it. If his image of her was any clue, her eyes were a vivid brown, and they must laugh a lot because his image did. At him, he was sure. A smile tugged at his lips at the sight of the curly dark red hair that topped her slender head, in spite of the blue ribbon that he supposed had been put there to help discipline the straying strands. Didn't help, but he didn't mind. He kind of liked her wild look.

He wanted to sit up, to question the woman across from him, but the pain that shot through his head at the slight movement convinced him to lie still.

At least for now.

~*~

Doc Pitman walked into the room. Harriet must have already filled him in earlier on whatever may have happened this afternoon with Jerry, because he snapped his questions at Josie.

Josie laid her flute aside and stood. "No, he hasn't

wakened, but he was really restless. Moaning a little and twitching. He settled down when I played for him."

"Anyone would want to lie still with that beautiful music you make, Josie Patterson," Dr. Pittman growled, but the growl was muted coming through the big grin on his mouth. "We surely have been enjoying that on Sunday mornings."

"What about Jerry?"

The doctor bent over Jerry's prone figure and checked his eyes, his temperature and pulse. When he straightened, he nodded. "Everything looks good. I think once he gets some rest and some of Harriet's good food—no offense, Josie—down him, he'll spring back to himself fairly quickly."

"None taken, Doctor Pittman." Josie was so relieved she wanted to give him a hug.

When the doctor headed to the door, Josie slipped upstairs. It was time to change into more comfortable clothes for the evening. She meant to stay right here with him for the rest of the day. She'd done enough running around earlier. When Jerry woke, she wanted to be here for him.

When she ran back down the stairs twenty minutes later, refreshed from a quick bath and a change of clothes, her heart bounced at the sound of light laughter coming from the library.

Peeking into the sitting room to make sure Jerry was okay, Josie waved at Harriet, now returned from caring for the Rayner House people, who motioned for her to go on. She went, straight to where she knew some, if not all, of the Rayner House people would be gathered. Gathered to keep her company tonight, to keep her spirits up, to show their support. She was grateful, but a tiny bit of distress edged out a complete happiness at their presence. She'd wanted to spend the evening with Jerry.

"Josie, I hope you don't mind we're here." Emma Jaine saw her first.

What was there to say? She adored her family. Just not quite as much as Jerry.

"We brought a basket filled with picnic food." Claire, holding on to Guy Delaney's arm, threw at her. "And

Emma Jaine wants me to sing. She thought it might be soothing for Jerry."

Josie settled on the floor beside the huge chair where her father sat. She felt the moment he laid his huge, kind hand on her shoulder and reached up to touch it.

She'd never appreciated his strong will and strength while growing up; only chaffed under the unreasonable restraints she'd thought them to be. Now—now she couldn't imagine a world without Papa Ossie in it.

"Are you sure, Josie, we won't disturb Jerry?" Shirley's concerned voice broke into her thoughts.

Shaking her head, Josie asked her own question. "Why aren't you all having dinner at home?"

"Several of our residents were dining out tonight, so the rest of us decided you needed some company. Besides, we wanted to see you. It's been awhile since you've been over." Papa patted her hand.

"You didn't have to. I know how much you love the gatherings at home."

"Nonsense. I wanted to come. It was practically my idea." For her father, his roar of contradiction was a mild one.

Minutes later, Tyrell asked the blessing, and everyone filled their plates with chicken legs, potato salad and Harriet's famous baked beans.

Josie placed a few items on her plate, then watched as her family talked and laughed in subdued tones. She realized she'd missed them and all the fun evenings of games and music at the Rayner House. Emma Jaine had had a swell idea when she'd opened the boarding house.

Guy stood alone, the first time since he and Claire had entered her house, Josie would venture to guess, so she walked over to him.

"How's it going, Guy? Is Claire keeping you sufficiently entertained?"

"Yeah, she's quite a charmer, isn't she? And I don't mean that badly. She's lovely and sweet mixed with a lot of determination to be her own person." Guy's face grew redder the longer he talked.

Josie laughed. "You've described her perfectly. She's all that and more."

Claire *had* grown up. She'd been giving subtle hints of

it, but as usual, Josie had paid little attention till now. In fact, before the last few weeks, she'd ignored her and tried to stay out of her path as much as possible. She glanced at her younger sister.

Claire stood near the piano, her plate of half-eaten food, abandoned on a side table while she leafed through sheet music. Was that sadness on her face?

Josie studied her more. No, couldn't be. Not Claire.

Claire lifted her gaze then and nodded at Emma Jaine, who hurried to Josie and Jerry's second hand piano. Claire and Emma Jaine hovered over the music a moment, then Emma Jaine stroked the first notes, and Claire sang.

The words of "I'll Never Smile Again" floated around the room and tore at Josie's heart. The nightmare she'd lived in since the day Jerry had boarded that train to leave for military duty, had suddenly become a live thing in the room, leering and smirking as if it knew things would never be the same.

Josie sank her teeth into the meat of her chicken leg instead of screaming in defiance at the imaginary creature taunting her. When a big hand rested on her shoulder, she turned. Papa stood slightly behind her.

"Want to take a stroll around your yard? Would that help?"

How did he know? Josie didn't care. She didn't need to ask how he knew. Papa had sensed her mood and, in his unique way, had responded. A nippy breath of spring air was what she needed.

She nodded at him, set her uneaten plate down and went for a jacket.

Papa Ossie met her at the back door and grinned. "Shall we make our getaway before the others notice?"

Nervous laughter exploded from her very being. Trust Papa to give a hilarious twist to a simple action.

"Old man winter is doing his best to hang on. But Spring will prevail as always. We can always count on that."

It was warming up. Sadness tugged at Josie's heart, yet she couldn't long entirely for her favorite season. The winter in her heart had hung on too long for her to feel much favor for it.

The branches of the one willow tree in their backyard drooped with enticing gracefulness even though the leaves had yet to appear. The old wrought-iron bench sat close to the trunk inviting her to sit and enjoy a few minutes of solitude. She'd loved sitting here after they'd first bought the house. She and Jerry had held hands, close together, laughing and talking about both serious and foolish things.

Foolishness, like going to Washington to meet President Roosevelt.

And serious stuff like their dreams for the future and their pledges that neither would ever love another, and...

But there was Papa, and he hadn't finished walking around their yard—for her benefit. For some reason the thought that Papa had singled her for a walk gave her a moment of peace from the hurt that brewed inside her since Jerry's return.

They were approaching the front of the house again when a man appeared at the corner of the property. It was just dark enough that Josie couldn't at first recognize him, then the streetlight shone on what could have been a handsome face had it not been for the severity lines etched into it, and Josie knew him.

Robert Patterson.

"Papa, this is Jerry's father, Robert Patterson. Mr. Patterson, my father, Ossie Rayner. You're early."

The man batted an impatient hand at her remark. "I know. Couldn't wait any longer. Can I see my son?"

"Of course. But we have company, and I thought you wanted to remain anonymous for the time being."

"I do." He frowned, agitation riding across his stern features like a bucking steed.

"When did you arrive in town? If you'd let us know we could have arranged a place—" Papa started.

Another sweep of the hand. "No need. I have a nice suite downtown. Besides, I'm sure Jerry wouldn't want me anywhere around."

"I thought we were going to forget the negative past—"

Again the man interrupted. "I know. That's true. It's hard to focus on the possibility that things could change for the better when my son has—when we've been enemies for so long."

"Well, if you do your part, I'm sure Jerry will respond." But was she? Jerry had changed, and not for the better. Right now she wasn't sure of anything to do with him.

"Well, since you're here, why not come in and meet the family?" Papa Ossie offered.

Josie could see her father-in-law's impatience and hurried to rein it in. "It would be a good start."

"Very well."

It was abrupt, but at least consent.

"Josie, you go ahead and alert Harriet and Emma Jaine that Jerry's father's here. He and I will talk for a few minutes while you prepare them."

What was Papa up to? She stared at him but couldn't read any undercurrent objectives.

Hurrying inside, she shed her jacket, tossing it toward the hallway clothes tree, then peeked in on Jerry. He was sitting up, a tray on his lap, and half-heartedly spooning the thick soup into his mouth. Harriet bustled about the room, murmuring to him now and then.

"Jerry?" She stepped closer, hoping his spirits would be better.

Instead, he frowned. "Who are you? I know your name is Josie. I've seen you but can't figure out who you are. Can someone tell me why and what I'm doing here?"

As if she'd suddenly been locked in a freezer room, Josie halted. She stared first at her husband then at Harriet, who'd turned and gaped at the man as if in unbelief. The woman's voice grew graver as she flicked a glance at Josie. "Child, I think we've got trouble," she whispered.

As if she didn't already have enough. She bit her lip then hurried to kneel beside her husband. "Jerry, I'm your wife. We're married. You were attacked on the street and hurt. That's why you can't remember."

Confusion flicked across his face. "We're married? That must be why you seem familiar. Do I know her?" His head tilted in Harriet's direction.

"Yes, Dear. She lives at my father's house and offered to come over to help me care for you. She's a real jewel."

A bit of a smile tipped his lips. "I can see that. She's a

regular hound dog when it comes to eating, isn't she?"

Josie laughed. "You've got that right. How do you feel?"

He lifted a hand and touched his head. "Better, I think. At least the headache has eased. I'm ready to get up."

"No." Josie held out a hand to stop him. "Not yet. You have to wait till the doctor okays you to get up."

"I don't know how I would have responded—I can't remember—but I feel like digging my heels in and doing it anyway."

"Please wait. He'll be back in the morning. We'll see what he says then."

He leaned back against the cushions. "Well, since it's you asking, and you say you're my wife—is she really?" He tossed a questioning look at Harriet.

The Rayner housekeeper nodded, grinning.

"Seems what you're saying's true, and I can't say I object. Come closer and kiss me. Maybe it will awaken me from this fog."

Heart pounding with sudden—what was it? Fear? Excitement? Would he hate her and blame her for taking advantage of his forgetfulness once memory returned?

No matter. She wasn't allowing this opportunity to pass.

Leaning close, she pressed her lips against his. Fire shot through her, feeding the hunger of him that she'd missed so much. Forgetting Harriet and the people in the next room laughing softly and enjoying Claire's talented voice, Josie prolonged the kiss, not wanting it to ever stop.

She could feel the second he drew back, and she hastened to do her own drawing back, reluctantly giving him the space she'd grown use to since his return. Heat blossomed in her cheeks—but she waited for his response.

His gaze was on her face, his hand still in her hair, but he pulled it back even while studying her. "Doll, that was some kiss. No wonder I couldn't forget you."

Josie laughed up at him and rose to her feet. "I don't think you remember *everything*."

"Are you taunting me, woman?" He made as if to

throw back his covers, but Harriet's gentle but firm touch stopped the move.

He growled, but his lips were spread in a teasing grin. "I'm in the bed rest joint for now, but you better watch out."

She wrinkled her nose before exiting the room. "I'm not afraid of you or anything."

He laughed then, and Josie loved the sound.

"I'm sure you're not." He tossed at her back then murmured to Harriet. "I do love a spunky woman."

Josie hesitated, waiting to hear more.

"Now where did that come from, Harriet? I have no idea what I like and what I don't like."

Ah, he remembered the name of the mainstay of the Rayner house. That surely was a good sign if she'd needed more than his response to her kiss.

"Josie could be a nag. We might hate each other, for all I know." His voice was sulky and low. "Am I a good person, Harriet?"

The woman had not only raised her son, Wills, the man Josie called her best friend—except for Jerry, of course—but had mothered her and her sisters for most of their lives. Josie gazed at her with suddenly new vision. She suspected her own newfound wisdom in understanding the people in her life came from the heartbreak of Jerry's coldness. In the same way she'd come to realize how much her father loved her, the Rayner housekeeper's value was suddenly clear. Harriet had not only shared her motherly heart with the motherless girls but loved them and understood their whims and stubborn streaks, guiding them in the way she thought God and Papa would want them to go. What a woman. Here was another person Josie had never appreciated fully.

But Josie had never been big on showing affection for anyone but herself. With a wince she continued her watch of the two across the room.

Harriet crossed her arms, the expression on her face melting Josie's heart as the Rayner housekeeper looked down at Jerry. "No, Jerry Patterson, you're not a bad person. Maybe a sinner—that I wouldn't know. Only you—and God—know that. And as far as you and Josie—I've seen few couples more in love than you and Josie are."

"Really?"

The woman nodded. "Crazy about each other."

Jerry stared at the blanket covering his legs. "I sort of thought that. Have I hurt her? I saw something in her eyes before she kissed me. Made me think—I don't know, like maybe I'd said something to her."

Harriet lifted her gaze to Josie, standing at the doorway, and Josie—through tears threatening to overflow—saw the question in her eyes. The woman had no idea how to answer Josie's husband. Only someone wise and godly and good—and Harriet was that, and more—would know how much Jerry had hurt his wife.

Chapter Twenty-eight

Josie whispered to Emma Jaine about Robert Patterson even as her heart ached from the tenderness she'd heard in Jerry's voice. It'd been a long, long time since the last time.

If what she and Harriet suspected was true, Jerry had amnesia. Was this another struggle her man would have to endure? Where was God? Why didn't he make these things stop?

She had no more time to ruminate on the idea. Papa's booming voice preceded him into the room, and he was followed by two men. Josie did a double take when she spied the second man. Walter Greye. She'd not expected to see him for several days. Why had he turned up tonight, of all nights when Robert Patterson and Jerry were to meet again? Not that Jerry would know his father.

Greye's eyes flicked to Josie, a dangerous gleam lurking in the depths. One hand held his Homburg, but he lifted the other to touch his forehead as a greeting.

Josie wanted to sneer at him. That wouldn't work. Jerry was at stake here and until she knew why Greye was so interested in her husband, she'd play along, regardless of the cost to her.

Papa introduced Robert Patterson to the group, and her father-in-law surprised her with affable words and politeness. So the man did know how to behave around others. Probably only when it benefited his cause and he wanted to. Otherwise, woe to those not in his favor.

Greye had planted himself close to Guy Delaney, and they seemed to be having quite a chat. At least neither looked disturbed, so it must be a peaceful one. Unlike the one on the walk where Greye and Guy had argued.

Might be a good time to check on Jerry again.

Josie hesitated, feeling something—was it in the atmosphere? Was there an argument heating up in a corner of the room? Was Papa insisting on his way?

Scanning the room, all looked calm. Yet...

Her gaze fixed on Guy. He stood with his back to a front window, his features drawn and tense, his gaze fixed on the retreating back of Greye as he walked toward Tyrell across the room.

A movement from somewhere close caught her peripheral vision, and Josie turned to stare. A wobbly figure stood in the doorway, clutching the jam, the wild look in his eyes scaring her. Jerry.

"You. What are you doing here?" Jerry's arm lifted, and he pointed.

Running to him, she slid an arm around his shoulders. "You shouldn't be up. Where's Harriet?"

He didn't have a chance to answer.

The shattering sound of glass striking the floor...and the distant, but still loud crack of a gunshot seemed to fill the room. Guy swayed, bewilderment then resignation crossing his face. His eyes went blank, and he tumbled to the floor.

At first no one moved. As Josie turned to go to Guy, she nodded at Harriet to take Jerry. Captain Ossie beat her to the young man lying on the floor, calling on someone, anyone to call the doctor.

Guy's chest was a blood stained, red mess. Kneeling, Josie laid the cloth someone handed her on top of Guy's chest and pressed. "Papa?"

Her father shook his head. "He's not going to make it, Child."

What was happening? Head spinning and chest heaving, Josie heard her father's words but didn't want to believe them.

"Steady, Josie. Concentrate on Guy. He needs you."

Josie blinked and felt weak fingers gripping her blouse sleeve. She dropped her gaze to Guy's white face.

"Mrs. Jo—"

Josie clasped the cold fingers and bent over the man on the floor. "Yes, Guy?"

"Be c—aref...you—" Gasping, blood spilling from his mouth, he spit out the words. "He's bad."

"Who, Guy?"

His gaze drifted beyond her then refocused on her. "Him."

"Tell me. I'll do whatever I can for you."

If Josie hadn't known the young man was too weak to do so, she could have sworn a tiny smile crossed his lips.

"You...the best. You're in...danger."

Guy's eyes closed, his head drooped sideways, and the grip from the hand Josie held loosened.

Josie's gaze shot to her father's.

"He's gone, Josie."

"Papa, are you sure? He's too young."

Papa Ossie nodded. For a moment daughter and father were quiet, then Josie's father stood, pulling Josie up with him. He slung an arm around her as he led her away.

In the hall, Papa faced Josie. "Do you understand what Guy was saying?"

"No, not really. He was so weak his voice kept fading."

"Tell me his exact words."

"'Mrs. Jo.' There was a break as if he was willing himself to go on. Then: 'Be k.' A fade out, then 'karf?' 'You,' and another fade out."

"Hmmm."

"His last words were 'you.' Fade out. 'the best.' Fade out. 'You're in.' Fade out. 'Danger.'"

Papa Ossie stroked his goatee, his gaze on the distant kitchen doorway. "What if..."

"What, Papa?"

"Josie, what if Guy was trying to tell you something?"

"Like what?"

"'Mrs. Josie, be careful. You're the best. You're in danger."

It made sense. And giving his strange moods of antagonism, it might just mean something important.

"What's running through that head, Josie?"

Papa's sharp intuition had sensed her thoughts.

"His gaze drifted past me, Papa, as if he was trying to tell me someone in the room was the danger to me. But that's crazy."

Her father's eyes grew wary. "Maybe not."

She wished she'd chanced a look over her shoulder but hadn't wanted to look away from him, afraid she'd miss anything he said. He was such a likeable boy.

"What?"

"Nothing much, but Guy—the few times I've been around him—has seemed, at times, antagonistic."

"To *you?*"

"No. Never." Should she mention Greye? Yes? No? Her gaze met Papa's, and she knew he suspected she wasn't telling all. Oh, well. "But Guy had a special dislike of Walter Greye. He disagreed with most everything he said, at least when I was with both of them."

"Is that right?" That far-away look eased back into Papa's eyes. "Tell me about them."

"The first time was when Guy, Greye and I took a walk. Remember?"

Papa nodded.

"Guy told Greye he wouldn't do it anymore. That he would make sure we would be all right, and..."

"Josie? This could be important."

Josie's sigh was one of resignation. "He objected strongly with Greye's flirting with..."

"With you?"

The way Papa said those two words sent chills through Josie's already cold body. Her teeth wanted to chatter but she clamped her lips together. Papa didn't need to see how upset she was.

"Greye has been flirting with you? I'm surprised you allowed it."

Was that a rebuke?

"Papa..." How to explain this? "It was nothing to me, I assure you. But it's a long story..."

"Then before the authorities get here, you and I need to have a talk."

"But Jerry?"

"I'll take care of it. Give me two minutes. Go to my office, please."

"I feel I need to go to Jerry. Papa, please give me a half hour with him, then we can talk."

Her father stared at her then nodded.

Whatever was going through her father's head she'd better think of some plausible explanations. Her father would see through any fabrications she could make up.

~*~

Josie settled Jerry back on the sofa while Harriet fussed and fretted over Jerry so much Josie sent her to the kitchen to warm up some milk and toast bread for Jerry.

She knelt beside the sofa and took his hand in both hers. Smoothing it, she admired his firm grip even in the weakened state he was in. She wished she knew how to make him well again. Whole and happy, like he'd been before.

"Can you tell me what upset you?"

His eyes were closed, almost as if he was asleep, but she knew he wasn't. They slid open—mere slits—and looked at her. The horror flickering in them daunted her.

"Someone came in here and stared down at me."

"Who was it?" Why would that be so frightening? She frowned. "Did you recognize him? Did he speak?"

He shook his head slowly. "I don't know his name, but I know I know him. And I could sense the hatred even though he didn't speak. We must be terrible enemies."

His father. "How? How do you know him, Jerry? Where from?"

"I have no idea." His head shook back and forward. "But the animosity illuminated his whole being."

"Why would you be such enemies?" Josie studied her own hands wondering again what Jerry had gone through overseas. The feeling of someone watching her spread through her, and she glanced up.

"You don't believe me." It was a statement and not a question. Jerry's eyes held a disturbing emotion for just a moment, and then they shuttered as if closing a door to keep her from peering within. Was that emotion anxiety—perhaps he feared her response? Or was it something deeper? Did he really know who the man was, or at the least, where he'd met him, why they would be enemies, and declined to let her know, for whatever reason?

"Can you describe him to me?"

"Tall, debonair, dark hair and eyes that radiate a trace of meanness." He shifted as if uncomfortable. "He's trouble, Josie."

That didn't sound like Robert Patterson. He was tall

and dark, but the eyes? Jerry's father had plenty of self-absorption in his eyes, but meanness? "I'm not worried—"

"But I am. I saw it in his eyes, Josie, and I know he means to hurt you." Jerry clutched at her hand.

"But you said he was staring at you. Why hurt me?"

"Not sure, unless he thinks it would destroy me."

"That's crazy. How could it destroy you to hurt me?" Josie laughed but Jerry didn't.

"I think I must have loved you a lot before." His voice grew husky. "If that's the case, I suspect I would be devastated at losing you."

Was that her heart beating in her throat? Did he mean he still loved her or was his show of affection from the past? Josie wanted to hurl herself at this unknown man who'd invaded their lives just to see Jerry's reaction.

"Jerry—"

"Josie." Papa stood behind her. "Are you two okay?"

Josie leaned back to stare up at her father. "Yes, Papa. We're fine."

"The Detective from the police will want to speak to you, but I told him you were caring for your husband. I can't put him off for long."

"Fine, but give us a few more minutes."

Her father nodded. "Then I'll tell him to talk with you after he finishes with some of the others."

"This is your father?" Jerry's dark brows puckered. Confusion rolled across his face as he gazed at Josie. "That word makes me uneasy."

"What word, *Father*?" Was he uneasy about *her* father? Was Jerry losing his mind?

"Yeah."

The wariness within him made *Josie* uneasy. "Papa Ossie loves you, Jerry. He'd never hurt you—or me—for the world."

Skepticism reigned supreme in those brooding eyes of his.

"So you say." He settled back against his cushion, dismissing Josie's departing father. "What did your father mean about the police wanting to talk with you?"

"Guy Delaney died a few minutes ago, and the police will be here shortly. He'll want to question anyone in the room."

"Guy Delaney?" He casually pulled up the blanket covering his legs

Josie stared at her husband. Had that been a touch of *sharpness* in his voice? As if he'd recognized the name? And why had his gaze dropped to the blanket so conveniently? Was Jerry Patterson getting his memory back?

Chapter Twenty-nine

Josie gently laid Jerry's hand on his stomach and rose to her feet when Detective Nelson sauntered into the room. She wanted to grimace with impatience, but instead, settled into the nearby wing chair and motioned for the police detective to take the matching one.

"How you doing, Miss Josie?"

She'd never known the man well, but her father did and had always said he was a good and just servant of the law. She hoped so. Someone needed to find out who had killed Guy.

"How well did you know Guy Delaney?"

"Not very. I'd only gotten to know him lately. Took a stroll with him and Walter Greye one night." She shrugged. "That's about it except seeing him with family on the occasional visits I make."

"What's his occupation?"

Her mind went blank. "I have no idea. Never gave it a thought. Emma Jaine's pretty good with the boarding house thing. She'll know."

"I see."

"Wait. I think he must have been in the service."

He wrote in a notebook, but was frowning whether from thinking up another question or disagreeing with something she'd said, didn't matter to her. She had more important things to think about.

"So run the events of the evening by me, Miss Josie. You have a pretty keen mind, I'm told."

"By who?"

"Whom, you mean?" The detective grinned at her.

"If you say so."

"Your father, if you must know."

Her father had said that about her? Hmmm. Maybe he did like her. She was just as sure she'd never made it easy for him to do so.

"The events?" Detective Nelson's no-nonsense way was

234

almost over-powering.

"Right. Harriet and I have been attending to Jerry, taking turns, you know. I ran upstairs to freshen up for the evening, and by the time I'd returned, everyone showed up with a picnic supper. We were mingling, eating and Claire sang for us. Jerry's father showed up, and at the last minute, Walter Greye stopped by."

"Who is this Walter Greye?"

His snapped question must mean something, but she had no answers for him. What was she going to do? Tell him she suspected the man of plotting to hurt Jerry? That he'd invited and paid her to play for a fund raising group? That she hated the man's smirk and flirty ways with her? Or that she'd do whatever to make him go away?

She didn't think so.

"I don't know him well either. We met at the end of winter. He was lost and looking for Tyrell's church to talk with him about that new project he wanted to begin. I've been playing my flute, going as a partner to different functions and dinners with him. That sort of thing."

The detective lowered his head and peered at her sternly. "And your husband approves?"

She couldn't resist. "He doesn't know."

He only stared at her until she burst out laughing.

"He's been gone, Detective, and now laid up. Mr Greye and my relationship is an entirely plutonic one."

"What's plutonic, Josie? Why are you using that big word?"

Detective Nelson shifted in his seat to stare at her husband, and Josie, after that quick searching glance at the detective, adjusted her own seat to study her husband.

He'd awakened and now fixed his gaze on her. It didn't waver, didn't shift to the man opposite her, but continued to question her?

"I do know a few bigger words, Jerry, my love."

"More than you let on, I'm thinking."

His dry tone sent her into a full laugh. Then she sobered. How would he know that with his amnesia? Her sharp glance roved over his face, searching for the truth, and caught the teasing corners of his mouth as it quirked.

"You know?"

"That would be telling."

He wasn't going to tell her if or what he remembered, but she didn't care. This Jerry was well worth waiting for when he was ready.

"Mr. Patterson, can you tell me what you remember about this evening?"

Jerry chuckled. "Afraid I don't have much to say. I was stuck in here."

"Heard you made a brief entrance into the parlor."

"Very brief. Startled me when someone I didn't recognize stopped in the library where I was. Opened my eyes, and there he was staring down at me."

"You don't know him?"

"Seemed familiar, but couldn't place him."

"Then why did you ask, 'What are you doing here?'"

~*~

Robert Patterson sat at her kitchen table when Josie entered. Glad to be done with Detective Nelson, she almost felt relieved to be talking with Jerry's father again.

"I figured we'd better talk now with all the excitement here. Is this the normal atmosphere for your household?"

"Hardly. Jerry and I live very private lives."

He didn't believe her, but she didn't care.

"Then let's get with it. What can I do to help?

"Since I've got a—a project that's taking most of my time..." he didn't need to know what that project was or that it involved Mr. Greye, a fact she was sure he'd disapprove of. "...I'd like to ask you to help me keep an eye on Jerry. The work he's doing is dangerous, and I can't do both projects at the same time."

"Why on earth does he need watching?"

"I don't know all the details but was asked to watch out for strangers following him. Keep him safe. Don't interfere with his business or approach him in any way. Can I trust you to do that?"

"He's into something illegal, I fear."

"That's not for you to suppose. I need your guarantee you won't bother him. He has very important duties. If you can't do this..." She wasn't about to share the news that she knew nothing about his work. She suspected a lot but whether that was imagination or truth was yet to be seen.

"Don't be crass. I'll do it. When do I start?"

~*~

Jerry watched as his wife switched off all the lights except a dim one in the corner. He'd had a time convincing her to go on to bed; that he'd be fine and wasn't planning on going anywhere.

Truth was, he'd almost let the cat out of the bag.

Josie had an intelligence in her that most people didn't see. All his memory hadn't returned, but information about Josie just sort of popped out of his brain at weird times. And he could feel his memory ready to release if, he figured, he could relax enough to allow it. He adjusted his pillow and folded his arms across his chest as he stared at the bit of moonlight peeking through a crack in the curtains.

He knew he loved her—felt it in his bones.

Laughing at himself for expressing such sentimental stuff, he shook his head—gently.

And he was wild about that crazy hair of hers. Fitted her somehow. He couldn't remember but was sure she was a lot of fun and up for anything he would suggest. She was a humdinger of a flutist. That music she made kind of ripped his heart out of his chest. He'd never tell her but...when she played that thing there wouldn't be anything she'd ask for that he wouldn't move the earth to get for her.

He felt the smile coming from way down deep inside himself at his next thought. Those eyes of hers— cinnamon had always been his favorite spice even as a kid, and for hers to have that color—he'd loved her eyes flashing with fun and mischief and probably some secrets too.

What kind of secrets would she have anyway? Another man?

No. That's another thing her eyes revealed. Her love for him.

That motherly woman—Harriet?—who'd been hovering

over him and insisting he eat had told him he'd been in the military—something important and secret, and that, no, he hadn't gotten this loss of memory from that. Josie had said he'd been attacked, but Harriet'd refused to give him details. He wished he could snap his fingers and all would be as before.

But maybe he wouldn't like the past. What if he'd been a scoundrel, mean to Josie...

Crazy thinking. Josie's eyes said different, and he'd rather believe them than his own suppositions.

He pulled the coverlet up a bit higher. The heat from the fireplace felt good. Made him drowsy. He yawned and grimaced. As if he'd done a lot of hard work today. Head still pounded but not as bad as earlier on. His body felt as if he'd been run through one of those washer wringers his mom use to have. He hadn't looked in a mirror yet...

The sleepy orb that circled through his brain in kaleidoscopic circles drew him deeper into sleep...

The creak woke him.

He didn't move his head, only his half-open eyes, but the figure of someone climbing through the front window kept his gaze fastened on the intruder.

He let the person edge closer. Not that he planned on suffering through another attack. The other time there'd been too many of them—how did he remember that? But here, in his own home, one intruder? He almost scoffed aloud, but caught back the verbal sound.

His muscles tensed.

The intruder's arm lifted...

Jerry prepared to launch himself at the person, and then the person shifted, and the moonlight revealed...

A gun.

Jerry threw himself forward. Too late. The gun blast nearly deafened him, and he drew back a fraction.

But the person didn't hesitate. There was a soft mutter, and he ran—not toward the window, but to the hallway, and back toward the kitchen. Locks clicked, a door slammed open, and Jerry, staring after the retreating figure, saw him disappear outdoors.

The pounding on the front door collided with the running footsteps of his wife clambering down the stairs.

Josie hurled herself at him. "Jerry, are you all right?

Was that a gunshot?"

Wrapping his arms around her, he dragged his wife along beside him as he headed for the door. "I'm fine, and yes, it was a gunshot."

She started to speak again, but he nodded at the door. "We'd better see who's trying to pound down our door."

Clicking the locks, he opened the door a crack, and a bellow of outrage greeted him.

"Let me in. What's going on?"

"Papa Ossie." Josie grabbed his arm. "What are you doing here? Did you hear the gunshot from your room?"

Her father ignored her question, motioned for them to follow, and marched into the sitting room. He didn't stop but headed toward the open window. With a grunt, he shut and locked it, then whirled to glare at them. "Why is this window unlocked for an intruder to enter at whatever time he deigns?"

"You know very well, Papa, we didn't leave the window unlocked. I would never do that. You drilled it into our heads too many times to keep doors and windows locked."

Mild spring shower clouds gathered in Josie's eyes. Jerry wanted to chuckle, but he didn't. Now that the excitement was over, his wounds were making themselves known. If he didn't sit...he staggered a bit as he headed for the sofa that'd been transformed into his temporary bed. Josie followed and spread the coverlet across his lap.

"Papa?" Josie glanced at her father again as she stood.

"I was strolling around outside, Josie."

If he was any judge of people, Josie's father had something besides strolling around in the dark on his mind. The feeling of unease was beginning to return. Why had Ossie Rayner been outside their home anyway? Looked kinda suspicious.

The older man's brows drew together as his gaze drilled in on Jerry. "Why would someone be breaking into your home, my son?"

My son? Jerry winced. "The question, sir, I think, should be: why was someone shooting at me?"

For the first time, Ossie Rayner looked a bit shame-faced. "I'm afraid the shooting came from me."

"But—I saw a gun in the intruder's hand."

"Only one gun shot, right?"

That shrewd expression meant what? He knew something Jerry didn't? "One."

"Came from my gun." The man reached behind him and drew out a gun. "By the time I got to the window, he was ready to attack you, so I shot. That was what you heard."

Josie gasped, but Jerry suddenly grinned. "I hope you weren't shooting at me?"

"Of course not. But when I saw that man sneaking into your house, I knew he wasn't up to any good. Figured I'd give him a good scare."

"You certainly gave me one, Papa!" Josie laid her head on his shoulder then lifted it to stare between him and her husband. "But why would someone want to break into our house, and worse, why would they want to shoot Jerry?"

Why indeed? Jerry had no answer. Not yet. But he would.

~*~

She and Papa had gotten Jerry settled for the night again, but instead of leaving, her father motioned for her to follow him and headed to the kitchen.

"You have any coffee left from this morning?

"Sorry, Papa, I don't. Will water do?"

He nodded and she set a full glass in front of him. She had a feeling that the meeting with him she'd skipped out of earlier was in plain sight and happening now. He hadn't forgotten he wanted answers from her.

"Now, Josie, tell me everything you know about this Greye fellow."

"What do you want me to say? Didn't you ask Tyrell to have his cousin, Ben, check at the FBI on—well, certain people?"

That was close. Too bad she'd forgotten it'd been *Jerry* he'd wanted checked on. Josie corner-eyed her father to see his reaction. It didn't reassure her one little bit.

"Have you been eavesdropping, Daughter?"

"Could I help it I overheard you and Tyrell talking?"

His lowered brows and steady, piercing eyes assured

her he was not to be fooled by her prevarication. "My request to Tyrell was not about trust, but worry for your husband, Josie."

She should have known. Giving a masterful sigh of resignation, she answered his previous question. "I don't know all that much about him. The only reason I began wondering about him were the questions he asked about Jerry. Why would he be so interested in him?"

"Why indeed?"

"Then once in awhile he'd say words that made no sense to me."

"Like?"

"Foreign words."

"Hmmm. And was he flirting too much? Is there cause for concern, Josie?"

Applesauce. Papa wouldn't understand her trying to find out answers about the man, even if it meant pushing boundaries she ordinarily wouldn't.

"Not on my part, Papa. You know I love Jerry more than my life. I might weasel around trying to get answers and clues on what's going on, but I would never betray my husband's trust."

She stared him straight in the eyes. That much was true.

"I'll leave it at that then. You're smart, my girl. Sometimes I think too much so. Just be careful. I don't trust him and neither does Shirley. Be careful. Very careful.

She nodded, but didn't speak. She'd already figured out how dangerous Walter Greye could be.

~*~

The strong, aromatic scent of coffee tickled Josie's stomach as she descended the stairs the next morning, and she stopped on the third step from the bottom, drawing in deep breaths. Harriet must be here already, unless Jerry was up. She hoped not. He needed more rest to heal quicker, but then she wanted him well and whole again. Pray God it would happen soon.

Seconds later, she peeked around the corner of the kitchen door. Jerry, still looking peaked and unsteady, stood at the stove whisking something in a bowl.

"Waiting till I get all the work done?"

God had answered her prayer. Her old Jerry was back.

"Whatever you're making—it smells divine. Can I have some of that coffee, or are you going to keep it to yourself?" Josie stepped inside and headed for the coffee kettle.

"See that you only pour a half cup. The rest is mine."

His teasing in that growl had her heart spinning with lightness. She whirled closer and bumped him, but not too hard. He was far to weak to be too rough with him.

"I hope you like scrambled eggs, woman, cause that's what you're getting."

"Can we have sausage with those eggs?"

Josie whirled and gaped at the suave looking man leaning casually against the door jam. But she knew him instantly and flew across the room to give him a hug. "Wills, what are you doing here? Can you eat breakfast with us? Have you been to see your parents yet?"

Wills laughed and danced a jig across the room with Josie, his laugh echoing around the room. When he finally stopped, both of them breathless, he answered, "Come to talk with your husband. Yes, I can eat breakfast, and no, I haven't seen my parents. Any more questions?"

"Why—?"

"I was just kidding, Josie. I only have a couple hours and really need to talk with Jerry." Her friend's gaze settled on Josie's husband.

"And not me? You want me to leave?" What was so urgent that Wills suddenly had to speak with her husband? No one had talked with him for days, other than she and Jerry.

"Up to you." Wills questioned Jerry with his eyes. "But first, fill me in on what happened last night."

"How did you know about it?"

Wills grinned. "I have my ways."

By the time both husband and wife had retold the story, Wills had eaten two plates of Jerry's scrambled eggs. "Not half bad. Quite an evening, sounds like."

"Is that all you have to say after Jerry was nearly killed last night? Why weren't you here guard—"

Wills said nothing for a minute, but his eyes flashed a

warning to Josie. "I had duties elsewhere. Now I need to talk with Jerry."

"Why not—"

"Not now, Josie. I don't have much time."

Nice to be left out of the know. Josie wanted to sniff, but decided otherwise. There was more than one way to figure out what was so secret.

"Do I know this guy, Josie?"

"Yes, he's Harriet's son and a friend."

Jerry studied the other man. "You do know my memory's not up to par?"

"Yes. Captain filled me in on the details of your recent, uh, injuries."

"And Captain is...?"

"Quit talking goggledygook."

"Seriously, I've got nothing on this 'captain.'"

"Never mind that. We still need to talk."

"Right." Jerry settled back in his chair then looked at Josie. "Do you mind?"

For a moment, Josie wanted to dig her heels in and force them to include her. Instead, she shook her head and left the room. That didn't mean she'd leave the vicinity. Out of sight of the two men, only a few steps down the hallway, Josie lingered, listening.

"Wasn't sure how much you'd told Josie."

"Nothing. She knows nothing, and I want to keep her out of this. Got that?"

Jerry's words would have angered her, but the panicked tone told her he was worried.

But about what? What on earth were these two into?

And where was Jerry's amnesia?

"Good. Glad to hear it. Josie's smart but too outspoken to be trusted with..."

The words trailed off in a mumble.

I am not. Almost, Josie spoke aloud but held back the words, if not the thought, before they could be spouted. She cast her best injured glare back toward the kitchen.

"Captain wants to brief you. I can't take you there, and I assume you don't remember where his set up is?"

"'Fraid not."

"Here."

There was a couple seconds of silence, and Josie assumed he would be handing over an address.

Wills' voice lowered, and Josie stepped nearer the doorway.

"I have the combination to the safe."

A pause and murmur from Jerry.

"Your nemesis. If we can crack that—"

What was Wills dragging her husband into? Cracking a safe? Were they going to rob someone? Not Wills, the brother she'd never had. Not Jerry. The only man who could break her heart.

Scrapping of chairs being pushed backward. Quiet noises, then a soft door shutting as if they were sneaking out.

Without telling her where? They didn't want her to know.

It took less than five seconds for Josie to make up her mind. Grabbing her older jacket hanging on a hook, she slammed out the door and ran to the front of the house. In the distance, two men walked steadily, although slowly, toward the corner.

When they turned the corner, Josie ran after them.

Enough was enough. She was a big girl, perfectly able to care for herself. This time, Jerry couldn't shut her out. She'd find out what these two were doing...or her name wasn't Josephine Patterson.

~*~

The gray-coated man paused at the opposite corner from where Josie was headed, brows lifted, hat shading his face. It was too warm for his coat, but he'd had no time to order another lighter one. He'd have to get that done tomorrow if he wanted to stay on top of fashion in a big city like this one. He had no plans to move on yet. Not till he finished his main business. Regardless of his boss's orders, this was priority. After that he'd complete the job he'd been trained to do. And gladly.

Right now, it seemed feasible to follow this woman who'd captured his interest. What or who had sent her down the street in such a hurry?

No time like the present, and since he'd planned to stop by her home and lure her away for another couple hours, this might just work out even better. A *chance* meeting downtown would be the perfect ploy to invite her to lunch again.

He picked up his pace.

~*~

Josie wasn't about to lose Jerry and Wills, so instead of the street car the two boarded, she hailed the first cab she saw and gave the driver directions to follow the car. He gave her a look in the mirror as if he wondered if she was either crazy or a Mata Hari.

Whatever he thought, she couldn't care less. Nothing was as important right now as finding out what these two were up to.

After several minutes had passed, and the car continued its weaving along the streets, Josie sat forward. "You have any idea where that cab's headed?"

"No, Ma'am." A quick glance in the mirror at her and a shake of the head was the only response as the driver spun around a corner.

"Take it easy. I don't want them to spot us."

He nodded and tapped the brakes.

Fortunately, the street car in front of them slowed and stopped. Wills stepped off, but there was no sign of Jerry.

What to do? Follow Wills or wait and see where Jerry was headed?

The answer was made for her when the street car moved and the cab followed suit. Twisting her neck, Josie watched as Wills headed down the street back the way they'd just come, walking quickly and with purpose. Wherever her old friend was going, he was in a hurry.

Four blocks later, the street car slowed, and this time Jerry stepped off. He paused staring down at a paper in his hands, glanced up and looked around, then walked off, the limp, if nothing else had, giving him away.

Josie tapped the cab driver on the shoulder, handed him a bill, and flung open the door. Her pulse was racing when the cab took off. Now was the time for some subterfuge. Could she escape Jerry's detection of being followed? Josie chuckled. Of course, she could. Wills and she had played that game many times escaping from Emma Jaine and Harriet's sharp eyes when they were being sought for certain chores.

Jerry walked one more block and paused before a dark, drabby green building. He disappeared around the corner, into a narrow alley, and Josie wondered if she'd lost him, when, turning the corner herself, she didn't see him. She hurried down the alley, avoiding the debris left lying on the street. Halfway down, in the same green building, was a side door, and Josie hesitated, studying it. Moving cautiously, she edged closer and touched the door knob.

Should she?

She firmed her lips. Now was no time to falter. She twisted the knob but it was locked. Before she could let loose, something clicked, and the door opened slowly. There was nothing to see. The darkness inside gave her no indication what awaited her if she advanced.

When no one appeared, Josie grinned.

She stepped inside but hadn't moved five feet when a gruff voice demanded, "Halt. Who are you?"

Two sets of hands gripped her arms.

Chapter Thirty

The man with the gray felt hat stood quietly before the green building. He hadn't been quick enough departing his cab to see where Josie Patterson had gone, but surely not this place. Still, her spontaneous, adventurous spirit might push her to explore, or worse. Was this a clandestine meeting? He was too close to the victory-revenge he craved to mess up now.

Walter Greye edged up to the alley-way door and twisted the knob, but it was locked. So either Josie Patterson had had a key or she wasn't anywhere near this building.

Stay or leave?

Was it really that important to find out what she was up to? She hadn't given him any indication she was involved in her husband's shenanigans. But then his sister hadn't been involved in politics either...

He turned away but hadn't gone ten steps when the door behind him slammed open and low voices echoed down the alley. He'd never moved so fast in his life.

Even with all the debris left on the narrow alley pavement, there was seriously nowhere to hide. He should have thought of that. But he'd had no legitimate reason to believe that the woman had gone into *this* building.

It was too early to show his hand. He had a big score to settle. The right time and place was predominate in his plan.

Chapter Thirty-one

"Halt! Who are you?"

Strong hands gripped her arms, and Josie jerked, trying to get away. "Stop it. What are you doing? What is this place?"

"You have any idea who she is?"

"No clue. Best thing, take her to the captain."

They were talking over her head as if she couldn't hear or speak, or maybe they thought her too dumb to answer.

"Captain who?" Josie tossed in the question with no hopes of getting an answer.

Sure enough, the first soldier—and Josie figured he had to be American, giving his uniform—nodded at his companion, but ignored her question.

"Come with me, ma'am."

Ma'am? How old did he think she was? Given the demand and the still tight grip on her arms, what else was she to do?

They finally let go of her arms, and the first one motioned for her to follow.

Well, she might at least learn what was going on.

The soldier knocked on a door, and when a grumble from inside was heard, he cracked open the door, gripped her arm again and marched her into a dimly lit room. "Captain, I found this woman lurking around outside, who then entered without permission, Sir!"

"Josie. What are you doing here?"

Jerry? Josie's gaze swept the room searching for the voice and the man behind it. Was that him standing beside that desk that'd seen better days? She shouldn't be surprised.

"Jerry? What are *you* doing here? What is this place?"

"The better question would be: what are *you* doing here?" The man detached himself from his position and walked toward her.

His tone was grim, but as he came closer, Josie could see the teasing twinkle in his eyes.

"I was following you and Wills." She tugged at the front of his jacket.

"What? You followed us?" He guffawed. "Why on earth—"

"You chased me out of the kitchen—my kitchen, remember? Did you think I'd let that go? I had a right to know what was going on, what was so important. I wasn't included in what sounded like a..."

What was she doing? It was one thing to tell Jerry, but she didn't know these other men. They could be the worst crooks in the city. For all she knew they could be the ones dragging her husband into their bad business scheme.

But what about the uniforms? Were they soldiers gone bad? Or worse?

"Why are you here, Jerry?" She whispered the words. "Have they forced you into something—"

"No. You've got it wrong—"

"When you're done talking with your wife, I'd like to finish our conversation."

"Yes, Sir. What should I do with her?" Jerry gave a nod at her.

The captain scowled. "How could you let her follow you?"

"You don't know my wife, Sir."

"I see I've missed quite a few things in the dossier I have."

He had a dossier on *her*?

"Major, have Sergeant Troyer escort your wife to the outer room. We'll deal with her afterwards."

"I want to stay with Jerry."

She might as well have not objected. No one paid her the least mind, including her husband, and the Sargent who lightly grasped her elbow, ignored her rapid-fire questions. Once they'd exited the room, he placed a chair in the middle of the room and motioned for her to sit. She would have objected, on general principles, but why push his buttons? Jerry should have...

Never mind. She'd content herself with plotting all the

questions she'd pound at him when he came to get her.

~*~

"I've got the information you wanted." Captain Phil stood at a small, smudged window that looked out onto a dismal street. "Not much."

"Anything's better than nothing."

"Maybe. We did an extensive search on both Guy Delaney and Walter Greye. Delaney was born in the U.S., had a short stint at a local college, and was in several militant groups. He never advanced much and was never arrested, but the little things he was involved in sent an alarm antenna up. He's been on our watch list. You say, he seemed to have a change of heart?"

"That's what my wife thinks."

"Probably a good thing he's gone. You can't always put your trust in those kind. Hard to say what sets them off."

"Could be. What about this Greye? I've never met him, but Josie seems to find him pleasant enough."

"Nothing."

"Nothing?"

"None of our sources had anything on a Greye. Mystery man all the way around. Are you thinking he's in disguise?"

"Who knows? I never seem to be in the right place at the right time to meet this person. So *you've* got nothing about him?"

"I don't."

"You don't suppose it could be Rhoderick?"

Captain Phil lifted his gaze to Jerry's and studied him a long moment. "God help you if it is, Patterson. Sounds as if he's way too friendly with your wife."

~*~

"Who were those men?" Josie slipped her arm in Jerry's, shamefully glad that he hadn't gotten all his memory back yet. What if he never? She tapped down the surge of happiness that sprang from knowing that if he didn't, he might never go back to the sullen man he'd been since his return.

Was it worth it, knowing he'd forever lose part of his memory? Did she really want him like this, not knowing why he'd been so bitter?

No, she wanted him whole and well. The man he used

to be. She didn't want to go through life wondering why he'd changed. If he remembered he didn't love her anymore, then so be it.

She bit down hard on her lip. Ouch. She didn't want that, but the peace flooding her inner being encouraged her. She was strong. She could handle it.

Glancing at him, wondering at his silence, Josie realized he was watching her, a hint of a smile hovering at the corners of his mouth.

"What are you thinking about? Those expressions flitting across your face tell me there's some serious thoughts going on. Weren't thinking of leaving me, were you? I'm pretty sure I'll be heartbroken."

Josie's throat went dry, and for one moment, she couldn't swallow. This man.

"I'm thinking about you and how stupid I've been."

"You?" Jerry laughed.

"Yes, me. I thought I knew you completely, but I'm seeing there's a lot about you I still don't know."

"You don't have to sound so serious about it. I'm perfectly boring…"

"Don't patronize me."

"Did I treat you badly—before? I can't imagine patronizing you."

"No, you didn't. I…"

Should she tell him what had been nibbling at her senses? That a persistent feeling his amnesia was lessening? And then what, if he denied it? Insist she was right?

You're going to have to be strong to get through the next few months.

Her father's words from weeks ago rang in her mind like a discordant bell.

Chapter Thirty-two

"**A**s you know, I'll be gone all weekend."

"Yes, Sir. Do you need me to accompany you?"

Marshall glanced at Wills, a hand lifting to smooth his mustache. His gaze flicked away but returned to settle on him, and it seemed to deepen.

"How long have you been with me, Mason?"

"A year and half, Sir."

"A short time compared to some of the others. You've proven yourself over and over that you're loyal." The blond man turned to stare out the window for several seconds. When he finally swiveled his chair back toward Wills, he nodded. "It's time to step you up a notch. In a few days, things will change around here. I've got some important business to take care of this weekend. In the meantime, I want you to do some observing of the men around me. Let me know who needs terminated in my employ. I've got a few issues with some of my men. Failure to carry through on orders, sloppy obedience. I reward generously but expect total obedience."

There was a pregnant pause.

"You can do what I'm asking?"

Wills straightened even more. This was it. What he'd been working toward. What he and the captain had hoped for. Too late to gain the safety box code. He'd already found it, but what else could he learn with this sudden well-earned trust Marshall evidently had for him?

Time would tell, but the question remained: how much time did he have once Marshall realized the box had been broken into?

Chapter Thirty-three

The gray coated man dialed the number at the public telephone booth, his gaze fastened on the couple walking arm in arm down the street.

"What were you doing at the Patterson house last night?" He could hear the cold rage in his tone, but right now he didn't care. If this fool thought he could take matters in his own hands, he was gambling with his life.

"What makes you think it was me?"

"I'm not a fool, so don't underestimate me."

"You want him dead. I thought—she thought—"

"Don't presume to do my thinking. Stay away from him. I'll take care of that job when it's time."

"If you'd quit mooning over the broad—"

Rage burned inside him like a simmering log ready to explode into a raging forest fire. But he dampened it and drew in deep breaths. It was time to get rid of Marshall. Past time. And that girlfriend of his who thought she knew all and ruled the man as if she was Queen of Sheba...

"Meet me at the river bridge at eleven tonight."

"I can't—"

"Do it." Gray-coated man almost hung up the receiver, but he caught the other man's beginning words and snarled under his breath. "What?"

"If you'd listen once in awhile. I'm leaving the house right now. Gone all weekend and won't be back till Monday morning."

"Now? Of all times? You are one piece of worthless..." His words trailed off as he realized he'd lost sight of the Patterson couple.

Never mind. There was no way to get to Josie Patterson now. He had much bigger things to arrange before the final meeting with Marshall.

Chapter Thirty-four

His memory was returning.

Yet he could sense something in his brain was holding part of it hidden when it came to this beautiful woman walking by his side. Why would that be? He could see she obviously adored him even with that wary look in her eyes at unexpected times. And everyone assured him they were madly in love, so it had to be true, yes?

It was a puzzle considering he remembered Captain—not everything, but once he saw him again many details flooded his mind.

"I believe you're close, Patterson, to finding the man we're looking for. Not only your country, but your wife will benefit by capturing this traitor. Do you understand me? You must increase your search. Be vigilant. Trust no one."

Even his wife? The words had almost spilled from between his lips, but he clamped his jaws together. He still had no real clue of what had happened before...with he and Josie. Sure sounded like Captain warned him not to trust her.

Rebellion rose like an angry lion. Fingers tightening on his wife's shoulder, he pulled her closer to him. She was tall, almost, but not quite, as he, and Jerry liked that. Tall, confident women who weren't afraid to show their fears and worries when needed. That was his Josie—or at least, he was pretty sure she was.

Her head tilted sideways and upward a bit. "Are you going to tell me what you were doing with those men? Were they military men?"

"Why do you want to know?" He tossed the question back at her.

Her response was quickly forthcoming and believable. "Because I overheard you and Wills talking and was afraid you were in trouble. I wanted to protect you."

He should be protecting her by...

Where had that come from?

"Why?"

"You need to ask?" Her eyes questioned him even more intently than her words?

"Yes."

She stayed within his arm, but her minuscule withdrawal was noticeable. Then she whirled to face him, halting their walk.

"You're getting your memory back, aren't you?"

"Yes, some."

"Do you remember *us*?"

"Some. Not as much as I want, and that troubles me. Every one assures me we were madly in love, and yet this is the last thing I can remember clearly?"

Josie's eyes lowered. She was trying to hide the wariness again.

"Doctor says there's a memory that your brain is refusing to acknowledge."

He lifted his brows as she gazed at him again. "I'm to believe I'm so weak I refuse to remember something from my past?"

"Not weak. Perhaps...it's hurtful? Or painful?"

"Or bad? Wicked? A betrayal? Was I a traitor?" He wanted to smash his fist into something as the thought of what all he had been and couldn't remember swarmed over him again.

"Of course not. You could never be that."

Josie's assurance eased the pressure building inside him.

"I think maybe...it could have been—what I mean is..."

"Just spit it out, Josie. I won't bite."

"One night you seemed to be having a nightmare, and kept mumbling a name over and over."

"Yours?" He smiled at her.

"No-o-o. Vanda. That's the name you were saying. Was it someone who hurt you?"

In an instant, his mind whirled with conflicting scenes. Images of a ballroom and laughter. Strange military attire. Cigar smoke. Loud gunshots. Pain. And sadness.

Jerry's body shook with emotion, and he could do nothing to stop it as the circling image whirled slower and focused in on a fuzzy portrait of a face. A woman's face, and not Josie, his wife.

The skin was smooth, and hair, beautiful and fashionably wavy. Dimples appeared and disappeared as the smiling lips laughed at him. But the kaleidoscope refused to focus on the eyes. It was—it was...

A curse slipped from between his lips, and instantly, the vision disappeared. Jerry was left to stare at the greening trees and yards, the houses of the city and speeding buses and cars that hurried to their unknown destinys.

A hand touched his arm.

Josie's eyes were wide and questioning, but before she could toss all them at him, he flung off her arm. "Don't! I should never have married you."

And before he could see the tears and hurt he knew would fill her eyes, he walked off, noticing irrelevantly that the pain in his leg was not nearly as bad as it'd been two months ago.

It would have been great news had it not been for that devastating remark he'd just tossed at the only woman he'd ever love.

Was the woman in his vision the Vanda his wife had mentioned? Why did her name send a snake of unease up his spine?

~*~

So much for being strong and steady for Jerry.

What on earth had possessed her to spout out that name? Now she'd undone all the good he seemed to be making.

He meant it. Saying that awful declaration to her— twice, in a matter of a few weeks? How could he not?

Jerry was walking better. Following along behind him—well, that gave her a chance to examine his halting steps. The limp was decreasing. His shoulders were hunched as if carrying a heavy burden. From that statement he'd made, of course. Was that really how he felt? Her heart ached with the finality in his words, and worse, his tone.

Her head shook backward and forth of its own. How could that be when minutes before he'd hugged her close to his side as if he'd never let go?

Maybe Papa was right that Jerry would never be the man he was before.

Maybe Wills was right that Jerry was on a serious mission. He'd asked her to be on the alert for any strange people hanging around, and there'd been no one...

What about Walter Greye? And he did show a definite interest in Jerry. He'd been nothing but kind to her, even with his pushiness in trying to touch her and his constant questions. He knew she was married and seemed to know a lot about her—and, well, Jerry, too, but what did she know about him?

Claire's words replayed in her mind. *That's not his real name.*

Then who was the real Walter Greye?

~*~

Should she catch up with Jerry? She picked up her pace and felt the touch on her arm. She almost jerked her arm free from the firm grasp, but when she turned, Walter Greye smiled at her.

"Mr. Greye, you startled me."

"I perceive your mind is a million miles away."

"Not quite that far." She couldn't help returning his smile.

"Then, why the pensive mood?"

Josie flicked a gaze at the figure in the distance, still moving as if trying to get away from a snarling dog.

"Ach, I see. A poignant moment of disagreement, yes?"

"I think I spoke too quickly and hurt him." The words had no more been spoken then she regretted it. Airing their problems had never been a habit with either of them.

"You think perhaps a space of time would ease the problem?"

Josie shrugged but the anxiousness inside her nibbled at her being.

"May I entice you to come with me? I have a pleasant surprise that may possibly take your mind off this matter."

"A surprise? For me?"

"Just for you."

"Sounds intriguing, but I really need to get home."

Josie tugged against the grip he still held on her.

Greye let go of her and stroked the mustache he sported as he turned to stare at the retreating figure. "Looks like he could use some time alone. Come go with me. You won't be sorry, and it'll take your mind off a disagreeable husband."

She'd been wavering, but his last words set her on edge. "What if I don't want my mind off a disagreeable husband?"

"Then I'm sorry to have disturbed you." He gave her a slight nod and turned to leave.

Had she lost her opportunity to find a still-hidden nugget of information about him? And what was she suppose to do with it if she did? Share it with Wills, of course.

"Wait. I'll go."

"Are you sure?" His back still faced her as he asked the question.

"Yes." What else to say now that she'd agreed?

He turned, a smile on his lips, and placed her hand on his arm. "Good. Then let's go."

Josie looked back at her husband to see if he was watching.

To see if he cared enough to check on her.

But he was gone.

Obviously not.

~*~

Captain had ordered him back to follow Jerry and Josie. After sharing with his captain the new in-the-works promotion Marshall had offered him, he'd given him directions to use any spare time he had keeping an eye on Patterson's back. It was the captain's impression things were beginning to move, and he wanted Wills there as a backup if Patterson needed it.

Right now, Wills wondered why the man had insisted on the extra eyes. Strolling, arm in arm, laughing and seeming to have a fun time, no one would have guessed the problems the two were battling. But when Jerry pulled away from Josie and the man stalked off, leaving his best friend to stare after her husband, Wills' heart pounded with heartache for Josie.

He wanted to clout the fellow over the head and would

have, too, if he hadn't known a little of the agony his best friend's husband had gone through overseas. It was bad enough to suffer the danger of being a spy in a different country, the stress on a body and mind and the agony of being far from your country and family, but to be seriously injured?

When the Greye fellow approached Josie, Wills hesitated. Patterson was his main charge, not Josie. But his instincts and heart wanted to make sure she was all right. She was tough, but not used to the real world of espionage and danger. Still, if the captain got word of what he'd call a 'weak' decision, he'd be in for an uncomfortable chewing out.

Reluctant decision made, Wills skipped through several properties and came out a block ahead of Jerry. He leaned against a dull gray building and waited.

Jerry turned the corner and trudged toward him, yet uneasiness lit Will's insides. Something was wrong but he couldn't put his finger on what.

Patterson had been touted as one of the best spies of the country so if anything was wrong, he'd sense it too. Wouldn't he?

But distracted as he was on top of his injuries from his last job, *and* the beating he'd taken a couple weeks ago, it was amazing the man was doing as well as he was.

Unfortunately, that just pointed to the fact that he'd be even less aware.

Patterson was walking slowly toward him, and as he drew closer, Wills could see the strain on his face caused by—what?

Their argument. He loved Josie so how could he not be upset about hurting his wife?

Had Jerry been the one to utter quick and hurtful words at Josie or had his outspoken friend allowed her mouth to speak of things that hurt Jerry? Which? But did it matter?

Wills sighed wishing he could wave a wand and make it all better for his friends. That wouldn't work, but prayer would.

And what of Josie marching off with a man *he* scarcely

knew? Every time he turned around, he was bumping—
well, not literally, but he saw the man, and most times it
was with Josie...or with Marshall.

Was the man carrying a torch for Josie?

That was a cock-eyed idea. Josie was as loyal as they
came.

Unless something, or someone, had given her reason
to change.

Jerry?

This Walter Greye?

Whatever was going on, Josie was in danger. Now. It
was up to him to save her, whether from herself or some
outside influence.

As Patterson drew nearer, he blurted out. "Do you
know where Josie's headed?"

The man's features shifted into cautious distrust.
"Home, I suppose."

Was the man dense?

"Last time I saw her she was headed off with a very
elegant, very pleasant gentleman."

"Who?" The question exploded from between Jerry's
frown.

"Walter Greye. Who else has been hanging around
Josie like she's the lost jewel of a crown prince?"

"Is he trying to hurt her?"

"More like he's trying to win her affection." Wills
tossed back a look at the haggard man. "She's your wife.
You should know."

That was as close as he'd ever come to putting the
man in his place.

"You think she's in danger?"

Despite Jerry's recent antagonistic ways with Josie,
the panic and distress in her husband's voice assured
Wills that his love was as strong as it'd ever been.

"I have no idea, but I mean to find out. Coming?"

Jerry didn't answer, but his one hundred eighty
degree turn and stepped-up pace was answer enough.

Chapter Thirty-five

"**S**he's not here, but then I didn't expect her to be." Wills propped his hands on his hips and studied the street.

"Meaning?"

"She's with Greye."

"What do you know about him?"

"Nothing. He's not on my duty list to keep track of, so I've paid him little mind. Seems he's an affable enough guy and has a reasonable, admirable mission in plan."

Jerry didn't like Josie hanging around other men, especially if what Mason said was true. He didn't want to worry about someone far more agreeble than himself stealing his wife's affections. He might not be worthy of her, but that didn't mean he was reconciled to giving her away to someone else.

"I've already checked with the Captain. Asked him awhile back to do some background checking on this Greye and Guy Delaney. But his men had found next to nothing on Greye and nothing too incriminating on Delaney. Josie won't be off skating with that injured ankle of hers."

"We're probably worried over nothing. Josie's smart. She won't be fooled for long if Greye is trying to put something over her. Besides, it's not the first time she's spent time with him. He could be legit."

Jerry rubbed his forehead, hoping the thumping in it would go away. "Are we still on for tonight?"

"Sure. They'll only be a skeleton crew and looks like I'll be in charge this weekend. I'll let what staff is there have an early evening. Don't show up till around midnight. Got that?"

"I'll be there. If anything changes, or you hear from Josie, leave a message at that coffee dive we met in." Jerry didn't give him time to answer, but trotted away, glad to feel less pain even though his leg still ached from the constant activity he put it through.

"Wait."

"What?"

"If I were you, I'd go have a talk with Captain Ossie."

"Whatever for?"

"He may have the answers you need. He's been doing some questioning himself."

"How—"

"He and our captain are old buddies from way back. Served together..."

"Never suspected the old man had it in him." Jerry chuckled.

"I've known him a long time—all my life, and always figured there was more to the man than we knew."

"I suspected the same of Walker last year, the way he kept asking questions. But he seems to be over all that and settled into marital and pastoral life."

"Right. While you go to see Captain Ossie, I'll take a stroll around looking for Josie. If I find her, and if she seems fine, I won't bother you. Otherwise, you'll hear from me."

Jerry nodded and began walking away, tossing back his agreement. "Sounds good. Hopefully, I won't be hearing from you."

Wills' chuckle was a surge of strength and lightening to Jerry's spirit. For whatever reason, the sun seemed to take on a new brilliance and the breeze blew a bit cooler.

"And don't forget to tie those mutts up. Don't want my good leg chewed off."

This time Jerry's own chuckle reassured him that, as bad as things had seemed for the last few months, maybe there were hopeful days ahead. If he could laugh...then all hope was not lost.

Perhaps Captain Ossie would have the answers he needed to bring an end to what had been thus far, a fruitless search. He'd never gotten close to Josie's father, although Tyrell, and now Wills, it seemed, had. If Josie's father could give him some workable clues, he'd make sure to appreciate him more.

Even if that meant spending more time with the Rayners.

~*~

What was Walter Greye up to?

It had been an interesting and pleasant afternoon, given she loved the outdoors. Greye had been amenable to walking in the park and generally keeping to outdoor afternoon past times. When he finally led her toward a well-lit restaurant, Josie pulled back.

"I'm not dressed for here, and I'm quite sure I look a mess."

"On the contrary, you are adorable."

"Besides, it's time I go home. I have—uh—things to do."

"Your husband calls?"

He was mocking her, but why should she care?

She didn't.

The only reason she'd agreed to this outlandish wasted afternoon was to pump him for information—gently, but persistently. Unfortunately, he either was the most dense man in the world or utterly ignorant when it came to sharing what he knew—which would mean he knew and planned nothing against Jerry.

Either way, she was fed up with subterfuge—and him—and wanted nothing more than her own quiet home—and Jerry. Whether he'd be there or not, was another story.

"Aren't you even mildly interested in my surprise proposition?"

The surprise he'd promised. She'd spent all this time trying to get information. Would a few more minutes hurt?

Yes, but she'd do it anyway. She wanted to puff out a heavy sigh and give him the most cross frown she could. Instead, she tossed him a light smile and nodded, not trusting herself to speak without a begrudging tone in her voice.

Mr. Greye stared at the ground for a second, then moved to face her. "Josie. Sweet Josie. Do you realize what you've done to my heart?"

What on earth?

"You've stolen my heart—me, who has had plenty of women in my life. I could have picked any I wanted. But I never did—not until I met you. From the first, you captured my attention, then my attraction by your attitude and your independence."

"Please—" Josie lifted a hand to ward off his words.

"I can give you anything you want. Riches and jewels. I can set you up to entertain with your flute, and you will be famous. I only have to say the word and set in motion the action."

Riches? Fame? Hadn't that been what she'd craved with her skating, and now it all seemed so superfluous compared to her life with Jerry. To have him back—hurting and injured didn't matter. She could get through that. *They* could get through all that with their love intact and stronger than ever. She more sure of it than ever.

Mr. Greye was still talking, and Josie looked at him with new eyes. She'd known he found her interesting. But the interest he'd shown in her husband was more disturbing. She'd been prepared and determined to do what she had to, to find out why. Right now though, her patience had grown thin and weariness at the constant interaction with him flayed her body and soul.

"Mr. Greye. I want you to know I appreciate the opportunities you've given me to play for your acquainances, friends and patrons. But if you're asking me to go away with you—I can't do that. You see, no matter what disagreements or problems my husband and I have and share, I love him. There will never be another man for me. Only him."

"Are you sure, Josie?" The man's gray eyes studied her face, searched her eyes as if to find the smallest of cracks to penetrate with his persuasive way. "We could have a wonderful life. Anything your heart desires."

Except for Jerry. "I have no doubts this is the path for me."

He turned away from her then and seemed to be studying the street ahead of them for a minute. Josie was quiet, giving him a moment to regain his thoughts. Hopefully, not more attempts at persuading her to agree.

"So be it." He cast a glance at her, but it wasn't the friendly look he'd given her so many times before. "If I can't have you, then..."

His words trailed off.

What was he saying?

"I've had a busy week and need a few quiet evenings at home."

"Are you sure it will be quiet?" The sinister tone sent shivers up her spine.

"What do you mean by that?"

"Is your husband a quiet man?"

Sudden, unexpected tears pricked her eye lids. No, Jerry wasn't a quiet man around her. He was loud with his teasing and loud with laughter. They'd played tricks on each other, delighted when they succeeded. They'd raced outdoors, out of sight of nosy eyes, and laughed and tried to outdo each other with their games and jokes. Hands clasped, they'd strolled around their yard, meditating and quiet as they faced Jerry's upcoming departure for service. Long crazy tales of the adventures they longed for their future were strung together, as they lay side by side, on the floor in front of the fireplace.

Josie blinked. Greye was staring at her with an odd expression.

"Are you crying, my dear?"

"No, I am not. I have to go home. Now." With sudden and carefree unconcern, she fled, leaving him, she supposed, gaping at her wild action.

But Josie didn't care. Whether Jerry was home or not, his presence would be there. And she wanted to breathe in that atmosphere.

Chapter Thirty-six

Captain Ossie's gruff voice answered Jerry's knock on the study door, and Jerry stepped into the room.

Josie's father sat at his monstrosity of a desk but looked up when Jerry entered. The smile he sent Jerry was warm and welcoming. He laid down his pen and stood. "Jerry, my boy. Good to see you. Is Josie lost again?"

"I think not." Jerry grinned, then sobered. "According to Wills, she's with that Greye man."

Captain Ossie's features settled into a disagreeable mask. "Hmmm. I wish she wouldn't give him the time of the day."

"Why not, Sir?" Jerry sat in one of the big overstuffed chairs in front of the desk. "That's one reason I stopped by. I talked with Wills Mason this afternoon, and he said I needed to talk with you."

"Why would he say that?"

The cautiousness in the older man's tone clued Jerry in that he was being careful.

"He knows I'm looking for a man."

"I see. I've been hoping you'd share this with me. What is this man's name?" Captain Ossie's eyes glowed with interest.

"Rhoderick. Winfield Rhoderick."

"Ah, Captain Phil mentioned the name. We go way back, in case you don't know."

Jerry nodded, but he was too interested in finding his enemy to listen to ramblings about the past. "I lodged at his estate, and it's where I stole vital information from a traitor."

"Not Rhoderick?"

"No, he was to receive the information, but I got my hands on it before he could."

"And the traitor?"

Jerry studied the other man. He'd been on strict

orders to keep quiet about his mission, but would Wills send him to Captain Ossie if he hadn't thought the man could provide beneficial information? Sometimes it took a little give to gain a lot. He figured this might be one of those times.

"Harry Marshall."

"Senator Marshall's son." The older man sat back in his chair, satisfaction written all over his features. "I've known for a long time the Senator had his hands in a few deals not exactly on the up and up, but didn't realize the son was as bad."

"He's the one who gave me this." Jerry pointed at his injured leg.

"Maybe someday you can share the details, but we don't have time right now. I'm sure you're after any information I might have gathered, seeing as you've talked with Wills."

"Yes, Sir. Anything you can give me to locate this Rhoderick—if he's in the country, might prove helpful."

"Don't know a lot, and frankly, not sure it will be useful to you. I've put out a lot of feelers. I had a feeling you might need a little help, and wanted to be prepared if you asked. Of course, I have my own reasons for asking questions. I do have my sources, you know. Some are not exactly as the military would use, but useful enough for my purposes."

"Understood."

"Here's what I know so far. Whether you can use it or not is another story." The man paused as if to catch his breath. "Walter Greye is a mystery man. It was like squeezing a lemon to get information, but once it started, tidbits kept pouring in. Rumor on the back streets say the man slipped into the U.S. illegally. He's been seen talking to some questionable characters—foreigners that speak German as well as some high class officials in the government. Now mind you, all this may be conjecture or it might be worthwhile."

"What gets me is the no-knowledge thing, even from the military. If he was legit, then you'd think someone in there would know something." Jerry ran a hand over his injured leg.

"It troubles me that he's influencing Josie. I don't like him hanging around her. Have been suspicious of him from the beginning. Seemed way too smooth, and though it doesn't show much, a bit too secretive to suit me."

"I can't understand why he alludes me." A vague image of someone hovering over him days ago as he lay on the sofa after the cab attack flashed in his mind. Could it have been him? Jerry didn't fear much, but if it was Rhoderick, if he was in the states, here in Cincinnati, then he feared him. He was after one thing, and one thing only. Him. Jerry. And the bitter man would use any and all means to destroy him. Including Jerry's most prized treasure—Josie.

"What troubles me are the inquiries the man has made. Seems when he first arrived he was asking a lot of questions about a man named Bhaer." The old man's eyes grew sharp with intuition. "You wouldn't know such a person, would you?"

~*~

Jerry stood outside Marshall's place at five minutes past midnight. All the lights were off except a dim one coming, no doubt, from a foyer on the first floor. On the second floor, only one room was lit up. Wills, waiting on him, Jerry figured.

Unlatching the gate, Jerry slipped into the yard, listening for any unusual sound. He sensed, rather than heard, the presence of another person, but before he could whip around, Wills spoke.

"Decided to wait on you outside. Didn't want a knock on the door. Some sleepless worker might get it into his head to answer it. Never hurts to be alert for nosy people."

"You almost got decked."

"Yeah, I guessed. Figured I'd better speak before I ended up on the ground." Wills motioned. "Come on. Let's get this over with."

"I assume you didn't locate Josie?"

"Nope. Would have kept to our plans if I had."

"Neither did I. I only hope she's safe. None of this is worthwhile if something—" Jerry's voice broke, and, for a second, he couldn't go on. "—has happened to her."

Wills was quiet as they headed to the house, but

before they stepped up to the stairs that led to the Marshall's study, he laid a hand on Jerry's shoulder. "I pray to God, I'll always have that same passion for the woman I love. Pal, do whatever it takes to keep that."

As if he'd been turned to stone, Jerry couldn't move. For the first time in his life, an emotion swept over and through him that had him trembling from head to toe. He gripped the rail to keep from falling. Memories tumbled through his mind.

His and Josie's laughter.

The two weeks together after their elopement where every night was a scene in paradise, every day was pure heaven.

Josie's serious face as she talked about her experience during church.

The sweet music flowing from her flute. The lost-in-the-moment, unguarded look on her face.

The days they'd sat under their willow tree talking and dreaming big dreams and silly plans.

He'd lied to Josie when he'd thrown the words into her face earlier. *I wished I'd never married you.*

Because he knew now, had always known, that he couldn't let her go. That he loved her and regardless of his uselessness, of his deeds in Germany, he'd have to make it up to her someway.

He *would* die without her in his life.

"Are you coming?"

Wills whisper broke the spell, and Jerry shivered from the cold that seemed to blow from an arctic wind. Step by step, he climbed the stairs, holding on for fear his spagetti legs would tumble him back to the ground.

"Is something wrong?"

He said nothing, only shook his head and pointed to the door. How could he talk when his body and mind had just returned from the dead?

Both men slipped into the room, and Wills pulled out a small flash light and wasted no time in moving to the big picture of Marshall's father hanging on the wall. Carefully, he lifted it down and propped it against a chair. Then, glancing at Jerry, he dialed the code for the safe.

Once again Wills glanced at Jerry, but at his nod, Wills pulled open the door. There was money in the safe—a lot of it, but Wills ignored that, and searched through the papers, until he stopped, scanned the paper he held, then passed it to Jerry, brows lifted.

Jerry glanced through the paper, his heart sinking at what he was reading, but when he once again lifted his head, he returned Wills' nod. This was it. The paper that many had already died for, the one that his captain wanted at all costs. The list of potential areas in the U.S. that would be most effective bomb targets. And at the very bottom, ten names of men and women who were assigned to pull off the havoc.

As Wills turned to shut the safe, a creak in the hall penetrated the door. Both men froze. Had someone heard them and come to see who was roaming the house? Could it have been a rat? No, the creak was way too loud for a smaller creature.

Wills made a move toward the door, but Jerry raised a hand to stop him and shook his head. If anyone was out there, and perchance they had a key, then Wills, at the least, would be caught, and at worse, possibly lose his position and advantage here. With a cautious move, Wills flicked off his flash light, and followed Jerry toward the back door.

Jerry hesitated, his hand on Wills' arm, waiting, listening. His breath slowed as his senses kicked into high gear. If someone inserted a key in that door lock, they'd have only seconds to exit the door—and the outer door was locked too.

Chances on both of them getting out with no detection was slim.

They had no time to ponder their move.

Motioning to Wills to go ahead, he tilted his head at the interior door and pointed to himself. But Wills vigorously shook his head and made the same motions to himself and Jerry. Then returning Wills' grin, he paused a second, eased open the door, and, with Wills following, scampered quietly down the outdoor stairs.

It was only when they reached the back gate, that they paused.

"I'm going back in and make sure all things are as

they should be. With you gone, and me in charge of Marshall's place, I have a reasonable explanation to be moving about this time of the night." Wills gazed at the big house from where they'd sneaked. "You'll get this to the captain?"

"First thing in the morning."

"Be careful out there. Whoever you're looking for, the captain says he's a very dangerous man."

"You've got it. You do the same. Marshall's nothing to sneeze at."

"Got that. You heading home? I'm sure Josie's home by now, but let me know through the cafe if you need me."

With the tension of the moments before Jerry had almost—but not quite—forgotten his worry over his wife. Now, it flooded back like a tidal wave. It was time to head for home.

Chapter Thirty-seven

It was early when the knock came on the Patterson door. Jerry jumped from his bed and ran downstairs, hoping the continual banging would stop before it wakened Josie.

Flinging open the door, he barely escaped being knocked in the face by the upraised fist ready to pound again.

"Wills, why are you here at this hour?"

"We need you pronto. Go get dressed and be quick about it. No time to waste."

"What on earth—?"

"Go." The young man waved a hand and headed to the kitchen. "I'll grab a spot of coffee if you don't mind."

"Help yourself." The grudging remark came off as sarcasm, but Jerry didn't care. What was so important, the man had to wake him at the crack of dawn?

Climbing the stairs, he heard Josie's off-key singing coming from the bathroom, and his heart lightened. She was up and ready to tackle the day, by the sounds of it. Finding her home and in her bed last night had been like shedding a cumbersome load he'd carried on his shoulder.

He was down the stairs and headed to the kitchen in fourteen minutes. Wills was pacing back and forward, and by the way he carried on, you would have thought Jerry'd taken two hours.

"Fill me in."

"Marshall arrived home last night, and he's on the rampage."

"At you?"

Wills chuckled, but Jerry sensed the underlying dryness of it.

"Believe it or not, no. He hasn't given me a name, but swears he's getting even. This morning."

"This morning?"

Wills pulled out a pocket watch and glanced at it. "We have exactly forty-five minutes to get there."

There was no time to loiter.

Outdoors and two blocks later, Jerry raised a hand and flagged a cab.

"He didn't want you with him?"

"Nope. No one."

"What kind of "even" is he thinking, you reckon?"

Wills didn't answer only gave Jerry a grave look.

It took them forty minutes to get to the park. Wills tossed a bill over the seat, and they exited the cab. Jerry knew he couldn't keep up with Wills if he ran full tilt toward his destination, but the young man must have kept his pace in check. Jerry had no trouble.

"What's the plan? You going to stop him from doing something rash? Not that I care..."

"We'll see what happens."

"Is that—there's Marshall." Jerry stopped running and edged behind the nearest shrubbery. "Where's the other guy?"

"Have no idea. We'll have to get closer, but if we don't want to be exposed, we'll need to be careful. I doubt Marshall would be thrilled to see me."

"So what's the purpose of this spying? And why do you need me?"

"I have my reasons. Let's move. I'll go left, you right."

"Got it. Just remember, don't interfere unless necessary, right?"

Wills nodded and moved, and Jerry turned his attention on getting to the best spot possible to view what was about to transpire.

There was an abundance of shrubbery and trees, but too many bare spots to be certain a sudden move wouldn't attract attention especially this early in the morning. Easing into a position was a must.

Marshall leaned against a tree, smoking. The morning sun rays turned his blond hair into spun gold. He was, Jerry supposed, striking in his appearance, at least to certain women. Jerry didn't like his cocky attitude he used on those he thought lower than himself, and he particularly didn't care for his sardonic tone and the slyness peeking through his irises.

But then, maybe he had a bone to pick with him after the shot in the leg Marshall had given him.

And maybe Marshall hadn't fared so well with that last meeting in Germany. Looked to him like—Jerry squinted, wanting to be sure—and he chuckled silently. Marshall's nose was a bit out of line, as if it'd been broken at some place and time.

The time when Jerry was making his escape from Marshall's room and had slammed his elbow into the man's nose? He reckoned that could be just the suitable pay back for the senator's son.

Jerry had a frontal visual of Marshall, less than fifteen feet away, but slightly to the left of him, so the vague expression of alertness registered with him almost as soon as it did on the man's face. Someone had arrived.

In slow motion, Jerry adjusted his stance and spied the other man approaching. The shock that raged through him weakened his body until he slouched against the oak tree trunk. Sweat beaded his forehead.

But as instantly as the hot emotional lava flowed over and through him, it vanished, and the dead calmness straightened his spine.

Winfried Rhoderick walked briskly toward Marshall, and he was just as he remembered him. Tall and statuesque, the impatience that always brooded beneath the surface of his personality, showed today.

He stopped ten paces away from the other man and pulled the cigar from his mouth. Extending it away from him he studied the smoke swirling into the air, then flicked a glance back to the other.

"So you decided to come home did you? Nice trip?" Rhoderick's contempt was as thick as the molasses Jerry's grandparents used to serve as a daily supplement to their meals.

"I wouldn't go otherwise."

The smirk on Marshall's face infuriated Jerry. He couldn't imagine how it made his arch enemy Rhoderick feel.

"Glad to see you could make it on *my* terms." Marshall blew a puff of the smoke from his own cigar toward Rhoderick, then tossed it onto the ground. One foot ground it.

Was the man crazy? Had he never seen Rhoderick's anger? Obviously not. Or else he thought he had the upper hand.

But why would he think that? Why would Marshall even need the *upper* hand? Was there more afoot than he realized?

"Mr. Greye..."

The higher pitched voice reached Jerry's ears, and if hearts could quit beating for a matter of seconds and still live to tell the tale, then his did at that moment.

Josie Patterson walked into the setting, hesitating.

"Ach, Josie, I'm glad you could make it." Rhoderick stretched out an arm, and Josie walked to him, although she stopped short of him touching her.

"Why do you need me here?"

"You didn't tell her your plans?" Marshall's mocking voice was clear. No one could mistake his meaning. He'd known ahead of time what Rhoderick was planning—whatever that was.

"What's he talking about?"

Josie was clearly puzzled, but the longer Jerry watched the more he was convinced something more serious than a verbal confrontation was at stake here. And that meant Josie was in danger.

Why had she come running when he beckoned? There seemed no clear explanation except one. She was attracted to the man.

"Never mind, Josie. I want you to see what a fat head this guy is. Did you know he's your former skating instructor's mellow man? Did you know he shot your husband?"

No! Jerry nearly staggered into the clearing hoping he could stop the words from reaching Josie's ears.

Too late. Her face blanched. One hand lifted outward as if to stop the words. She stared at Marshall even as she addressed her words to Rhoderick.

"He tried to kill my husband?"

"Yes, he did."

"Tell her why you're here, Rhoderick. Excuse me, Mr. Greye."

While Rhoderick stood as still as a frozen statue, Josie suddenly whirled to face Rhoderick "Is he talking about you? Is Rhoderick your name? I thought—"

"Not now, Josie. Pay no mind to this mad man's ramblings."

If Jerry hadn't known better, he would have thought Rhoderick was a little on edge.

"Why do you think he came here? For that sham charity he's constantly talking about?" Marshall laughed. "There is no charity to benefit those who've suffered from the war. He entered the states for one reason only: to get revenge on the death of his sister. The one your husband wooed."

"My husband wooed her? I don't believe it." Josie still stared at Rhoderick. "And who is this sister?"

"Tell her, Rhoderick."

"I've had enough." Rhoderick reached inside his jacket.

"I wouldn't, if I were you. Did you think I'd come empty handed? Did you think I'd trust you? Hardly." Marshall held a gun pointed at Rhoderick. "Her name was Vanda Rhoderick, Josie Patterson. And he certainly did woo her. To her death."

And for the second time in so many minutes, Jerry watched the face of the love of his life pale.

This had gone too far. If he could sneak around—

The loud explosion of a gun blast split the morning air.

Josie fell to the ground, and the awful, black future glared into Jerry's face.

Chapter Thirty-eight

The minute it took Jerry to reach his fallen wife seemed an eternity. He'd never been so frightened in his life. Not when his dad had switched his legs till they were bleeding. Not when he'd escaped for his life in Germany. And not even the thought of giving up Josie.

But now, the thought of her dead, without a chance to take back those awful words he'd thrown at her, to tell her he'd never let her go, that he loved her more than anything...

God, don't let my Josie die. I'll do anything.

Jerry bent over Josie's figure on the ground. Was she dead? He could see no blood, but she lay so still, her warm, golden skin now a pale ghostly white.

"Josie, are you all right?"

Her lashes flickered, then opened, shut and opened again. She gazed at him a moment, then turned her head. Her eyes closed again and the longest sigh Jerry had ever heard escaped between her lips.

She was upset but that was all right. He'd take that any day rather than her death. His heart still hammered like a drummer who couldn't quit drumming.

She moved as if to get up, and Jerry stretched out a hand to lift her up. Instead she placed both hands on the ground and stood, wavering. Ignoring him, she brushed at her skirt, then looked around. Moving around Jerry, she headed toward Wills bending over Rhoderick.

"Is—is he dead, Wills?"

Wills looked up, glanced at him, and Jerry shrugged. With that, Wills' gaze moved back to Josie. "Yes, he is, Josie. Are you all right?"

"Of course, but I would like to go home. Would you—?"

"Give me five minutes. Come, let's sit you down on this bench."

When Wills approached him minutes later, his words were truly contrite. "Sorry, old chap. I didn't realize what would transpire here today, or I'd never have asked you to come."

"Doesn't matter. Josie will never forgive me now. I saw that."

"I take it Rhoderick was the man you were looking for? And Vanda?"

"His sister." Jerry rubbed a shaking hand over his face. "I used her to get close to the family. She helped me escape and bought the farm for it."

"Too bad."

"The sad thing, she was a good cookie. Betrayed her brother to save me. It haunts me."

"I understand, but don't let it get you down. You did your job. In war, there are innocent casualties. Sad, but true."

Josie sat quietly, her gaze on the ground, her whole body slumped and dejected. It took all of Jerry's will power to stay where he was. All he wanted was to gather her in his arms and make her listen.

"Best thing to do, Pal, is to give her a few hours to think things over. I know she loves you, and when she's sorted things out, she'll come around. Let me take her home. I'll talk with her."

Jerry nodded, wanting to vigorously oppose the idea.

"Here come the authorities, and pretty sure the captain and recruits are right behind them. You go ahead and get things sorted here. Tomorrow will be soon enough to talk with your wife."

"I don't like it, but guess you're right."

"I know I am. By the way, you didn't see where Marshall headed, did you?"

"He's not here?" Only then did Jerry realize that the man hadn't stuck around to answer any questions. "Well, can you believe that? I was so taken up with the thought Josie was shot, I paid no attention to anyone else."

"Captain will have our hides."

The words were serious, but the laughter in them belied the fact.

Jerry didn't feel like laughing as he watched Josie walk away, arm-in-arm with Wills.

Away from him.

Chapter Thirty-nine

Three days later, Jerry woke early with a sense that something was different. Turning over, his gaze roamed over the room, but there was nothing out of place or different. The other side of the bed was wrinkle free, so Josie hadn't sneaked into the room as before.

But then, why would she after those harsh words he'd spat at her days ago?

I should never have married you.

His heart might insist they were a lie, but she didn't know that. Captain Phil had kept him so busy running from one clue to another that he'd had no time to make amends with his wife.

If she'd listen.

After the information she'd learned about Rhoderick—and him—she might never speak to him again. Might want him to go.

The warm morning spring sun shone through his window when he parted the curtains. A light, cool but not cold, breeze drifted through the screen. A sign that it was going to be a nice day? With all his heart he hoped so.

The sound of soft music filled the air as Jerry readied for the day. Then not able to refrain from checking it out, he headed downstairs and peeked through the window as he poured a cup of already-made coffee.

Josie sat across the lawn, under their lone willow tree, seated on the old, but refurnished and rustic bench. Flute at her mouth, the music floated straight toward him, and the melancholy sweetness had him blinking more than once at the emotions awakening inside his body.

Picking up his cup, he stepped outside and headed to her. She couldn't have heard him because there was no interruption in the music. He watched her for a long moment, then eased onto the bench where she sat. Her eye lids flickered but she didn't open them. Instead she settled into *"You'd Be So Nice to Come Home To,"* and Jerry felt his heart constrict.

He wasn't a singer—not much by any measure, but he whispered it anyway, and when she gave no indication she could hear him, let alone listen, he sang louder and allowed all the emotions he'd been hiding, show.

It was only when he started on the second verse, not about to give up, that she faltered, her eye lids flew open...

...and he saw the tears. Like someone had sprinkled sparkles in those cinnamon orbs. Like someone had splashed fresh raindrops in her eyes.

She didn't speak but studied him, and he allowed her to see what had always been in his heart.

"Jerry?" It was barely a whisper.

"Yes, my love?"

"Are you—are you *back*?"

He knew what she meant. Back to his original self. Back to the person he'd been before pity and anger and self-loathing had taken ahold of him. Back before he'd lost his self-confidence.

"Better."

"Better?" She laid her flute on the bench beside her.

"Better. Now I know I can't give you up. Now I know I've never loved anyone else and never will. I can't live without you in my life. Can you forgive me for everything?"

She seemed to be pondering his words.

"Josie, I don't deserve you..." He was coaxing and didn't care. He, who had always been so tough.

"You don't."

"When I thought I'd lost you—when Marshall shot— that you'd die, I wanted to die too." Should he tell all? Of course. "I was so scared that I—I prayed."

"You prayed?"

"Yes, I did. I've never done that before in my life, but I promised God I'd do anything if he'd let you not die."

"He listened. I didn't."

"He did. You didn't." Jerry couldn't have stopped the grin on his face if he'd tried.

"That's something."

"Do you want all the details of my—my time in Germany?"

She sat silent for a long moment. "I don't, at least not right now. Someday, soon?"

His heart eased its ache a bit as he heard the 'someday' and 'soon' words from her. Maybe, just maybe, someday—soon she'd be able to forgive him.

"We can do that, and I promise..." He touched her chin and lifted her face upward. "...I promise I'll never keep secrets from you again. Good or bad."

She nodded, tears sliding slowly down her cheeks.

"I'm so sorry, Josie. How can I make it up to you?" This time it was Jerry whispering even though he wanted to shout it so the whole town could hear. He brushed away her tears with soft strokes.

She tilted her head, still studying him. "Well, for starters, you could kiss me."

That he could do. He pulled her close and allowed his lips to touch hers.

"Now isn't this a cozy scene?"

Chapter Forty

"**D**id you think I'd forget about you? Forget you made a fool out of me with Rhoderick in Germany?" Harry Marshall leaned against a fence post, not more than ten feet from where Josie and Jerry Patterson sat. Though dapper and quite up-to-date in his Zoot suit, the simpering smile on his face did nothing but detract from his blond good looks.

"What are you doing here?"

"Come to get a certain paper you stole."

"What makes you think I have it?" Josie was closest to the man. Was she in danger? What did he have in mind?

"Too late. The authorities have it."

"That's too bad because that means I have no more use of you."

"They know about you. You'll not get away."

"We'll see. My father is a senator, you know." Marshall chuckled and snapped his fingers. "Oh, that's right You're nobody important. You wouldn't know."

"You haven't seen him? Your father is in a lot of trouble and spending time with the authorities. It won't be long till they have the proof they need to put him in the joint for a long, long time. What I do know is, you're crazy to stick around after what happened yesterday. Do I hear sirens?"

"Think you're funny, don't you? *I* didn't shoot Rhoderick."

"I saw you—"

And then, from the corner of his eye, he caught a glimpse of an old man. A white haired man who was big and strong, a bit overbearing and loud, but, right now, a wonderful sight.

Captain Ossie was stealthily making his way toward them.

He'd almost reached them, when Marshall must have sensed another presence. He started to turn, but too late.

Captain Ossie pounced, knocking the man to the ground. "Jerry, get the rope from my pocket."

Jerry stood, but Josie beat him to it. Running toward her father, she pulled her scarf from around her neck. "Papa, are you all right? Here, use this."

"What did you think you were doing?" Josie demanded once Marshall was bound. She stood tall and stiff, directing her question to the senator's son as Papa Ossie jerked him to his feet.

Jerry grabbed the man's gun from his waist and tossed it over by the bench. "Thanks, Sir."

"Good thing I was keeping an eye out for any trouble."

"Why would you do that?"

"After yesterday? Besides, Wills clued me in there might be more trouble."

"What a nice party." The hissing voice came from behind them, and father, daughter and son-in-law whirled.

Diana? Josie's ice skating instructor, and in her hand was the gun Jerry had tossed away from Marshall.

"Thank goodness you're here. Get this thing off me." Marshall held out his bound hands.

"Why were you dilly-dallying? Ach, I knew I couldn't trust you to do this right just like you failed to get it right three days ago. You talk too much and not enough action. Du Bist Ein Dummkopf!"

German? Marshall's woman was German?

"I needed to goad him a bit before the deed." Marshall's voice took on a placating tone. "But *I* coaxed Rhoderick to come, for you, didn't I?"

"You wouldn't be thinking of his money and estate, would you, my darling? Just because I'm Rhoderick's only living cousin and relative, doesn't mean I plan to share with you. Your placid self makes me sick."

No wonder the endearment didn't ring true. She was playing him big time.

The question was, how could he get his wife away from this mess? Diana might be a woman, but she was alert and smart. She'd know they'd be looking for a way to gain the advantage.

"But I've done everything you wanted. I brought him to

you."

"Where I could shoot him?" The dry tone didn't bode well for Marshall. "Why am I cleaning up your messes? You have failed on every task I've asked of you. I'm better off on my own."

Marshall started to speak, but she cut him off.

"No. Be quiet. My patience is gone. I am done with you." Before anyone could react, Diana pointed the gun at Marshall and shot him in the chest.

A look of surprise—or was it hurt?—spread across the senator's son's face faster than the blood staining his white shirt. He looked down, tried to lift a hand, then tumbled to the ground.

Shock registered on Josie's face as she stared white-faced at the woman.

No expression crossed Diana's face as she shifted the gun toward Jerry. "I think now I must get rid of you, the troublesome Bhaer—Patterson man who will not stop his snooping."

Without a word, Josie stepped in front of him.

"Ha. Do you think that will save him? I shall be glad to shoot you both."

"Josie, get out of here." Jerry shoved Josie away. "Listen, Diana, let her and Captain Ossie go, they are of no use to you and have done nothing."

"Do you think your words will save her? What happens when I shoot you dead and the old man? Who will save her then?" Diana's lips were taut with sarcasm.

"You'll not get away with this, you crazy woman." Captain Ossie's bellow wasn't quite as impressive outdoors.

"We shall see. I have no more time to waste. I have a ship to catch." She raised the gun again, this time at Jerry.

"No. Don't please. I beg you." Josie stepped up beside Jerry. "Why are you doing this?"

"Why else?" Amusement threaded her voice. "To save my—how do you coarse Americans say it? To save my hide."

Desperation edged Jerry's voice. "Let her go. She's done nothing to you."

"Hmm. Is that so?" The woman lightly tapped the gun

barrel against her lips. "You two amuse me, but I think not. She goes first."

He saw the gun lifting again...

Like a banshee from the darkest corner, a figure leaped at Josie, and the gun exploded. Two figures tumbled to the ground. Captain Ossie sprang for the former skating trainer, and Jerry looked down, afraid of what he'd see.

Josie peeked from under the man on top of her. "I'm okay. Get your father off me."

Robert Patterson moved and half raised up. "Some help here, Son."

Jerry reached for the outstretched hand, and it was only then he spotted the blood on his father's arm. "You're hit. Dad, are you okay?"

"I'm fine. Took my breath for a minute or two there. Help me stand. You'd better check your girl here." Robert Patterson nodded at Josie. "She's a spunky thing. Hope I didn't mash her too much."

When all three were standing once again, they stared at Papa Ossie.

Diana had crashed to the ground, screeching and floundering when Papa Ossie had tackled her and wrestled the gun from her. With a twist—or two—of the rope he jerked from his pocket, he encircled it around her hands, then for good measure, wrapped another piece around her ankles. Only then did he stand and kick away the gun.

He turned, grinning.

"You're bleeding. Are you shot?" Josie turned to Jerry's father.

"It's nothing. A bare scratch. I've suffered worse than this from paper cuts."

"Well, I think we timed all this just right, don't you, Robert?"

"What do you mean, Papa?"

"We had it planned out. When we saw this Marshall guy lurking around, we decided I'd come in first, while Robert called the police."

"Pretty good team, if I say so myself." Robert Patterson crowed his enthusiasm.

"You both could have been killed." Josie scolded while she dabbed at his arm. "But I love you for it. From now on, you're Papa Patterson to me. Or do you prefer Papa Robert or Papa Robbie?"

When the man sputtered, Josie threw her arms around him, careful of his wound, and hugged him. "Thank you for saving Jerry. Thank you for saving us all."

From over Josie's shoulder, his father gazed at Jerry. "Are you all right, Son?"

The man *had* saved their lives, and particularly, Josie's. He must be really changed like he claimed, but it was hard to grasp. The man who'd been so overbearing, so indifferent to his family, demanding the best from them all... He wasn't sure if he could forgive him and let bygones be bygones.

But...maybe, someday.

"Why are you here?"

"Because I'm determined to show you I've changed. I can't undo the past, and I'll probably always be opinionated and overbearing, but I can make sure the future is a good one for all of us. Whether you like it or not, I'm in your life to stay. Will you give me a chance?"

He wanted it to be true. Hoped it was. But whatever the future brought, he and Josie would see it through. They'd take it one step at a time.

With a nod at his father, he took Josie's hand and led her away.

Chapter Forty-one

Josie and Jerry sat on the floor in front of their sitting room fireplace—without the fire—discarded plates on the end tables across the room. She laid her head on his shoulder, his arm wrapped around her, and snuggled closer.

"Promise me we'll always love each other, no matter what."

"Even if we disagree?"

Josie waved away his question and snickered. "We won't do that if you agree to everything I say."

His arm tightened around her. "You do know I love you more than I can express?"

"I'm pretty sure you're going to have to tell me every day for the rest of my life. By then, when I die, I'll probably realize you do."

He leaned close and kissed her again. "Remember the times we sat and made crazy plans of what we wanted to do with our lives?"

"You're so much fun, Jerry Patterson. I thought I'd die without you."

"I'm not going anywhere, my love. Now, enough sobering thoughts. Tell me, what's the craziest thing you think we should do next?"

She drew back a fraction and eyed her husband. The tenseness in his face was gone. He even looked more filled out, not that her cooking had done the trick, but Harriet's sure had.

So should she tell him what she'd been thinking about for awhile now? Should she? It *was* very crazy.

She leaned toward him and pressed her lips against his ear and whispered. "Can we make a..."

One Year Later

The baby's cry stopped Jerry in his tracks.

Josie's family and his father laughed, and Jerry whispered. "It's here?"

"That, my son, is the sound of a newborn baby making his entrance into the world known to all." Captain Ossie slapped Jerry on the shoulder.

The bedroom door swung open, and Emma Jaine stepped out, shutting the door squarely in Jerry's face as he tried to edge into the room.

"The doctor needs a few minutes. Give him and Harriet time to get things ready for you, Jerry."

"Josie?"

She stared at him silently, then grinned. "She's fine as she always is."

Jerry sank onto a chair, and stuffed his shaking hands into his pockets.

"What is it?"

"It's a boy, isn't it?"

"No way, I say a girl."

"Twins like Peter and Jaine Marie."

Emma Jaine raised her hands at the barrage of questions. "I will not tell you. Josie has the honors..."

The door swung open, and Harriet stepped out, her arms crossed and a stern expression on her chubby face. "You can go in now, but only for ten minutes. It was a hard delivery, but Josie's a trooper as always. Remember, ten minutes."

The whole group jumped to their feet, headed to the door, but Papa got there first, holding up a hand. "Wait. Jerry gets the first five minutes, then the rest of us will go in. Agreed?"

When they all nodded and settled back into their seats, Jerry shoved open the door, and his gaze fastened on his wife, her hair more tasseled than usual, her face a little pale, but the smile on her lips a happy one. She was the most beautiful woman in the world. He tiptoed to the bed.

She was sitting up, a blanket-wrapped bundle in her arms, her eyes twinkling in mischief. "I have something for you, my sweetest."

She unfolded the blanket and looked up at him.

His gaze rested on the tiny human. Without reasoning out his action, he held out his arms, and Josie placed it in his arms.

"Here, sit beside me so we can both see."

"Are you sure you're happy?"

"How could I not be when Fina has the best daddy in the world?"

"So you decided, did you?"

"That's what you wanted, wasn't it? If it was a boy we'd name him after you. A girl, named after me."

"You're sure you're not disappointed?"

Josie frowned at him then leaned on his shoulder. "Can you look at this tiny love-bug and be disappointed? I'm thrilled and so-o-o happy."

"Can you see their faces when they see our baby?"

"Yes, and before they knock demanding to enter, I want you to kiss me and tell me you love me. Again."

"That's a demand I can live with." Jerry pulled Josie close with his free arm. His kiss was long and utterly satisfying, if her sigh of contentment was anything to go on.

"Thank you, Sweetheart, for our baby." She'd given him the best gift ever. He wanted so much to live up to his duties and be the man he should be.

Whatever his father had failed to do in the past—whoever his parent had refused to be—that was him. Jerry had come to terms and was determined to be his own person. He refused to accept the fear that he'd fail. Mistakes? Of course. But he could and would accept the challenge—whatever the obstacles before him.

For one long moment, Josie's eyes wooed him, assuring him that her love was as steady—and stronger than ever.

"I plan to not only be the best husband and daddy the world's ever seen, but somehow, get God on my side too, I think that would be a good idea. How's that for crazy plans?"

"I love them, and I really think He's already on your side."

"Do you think so?"

Josie's curls bobbed in agreement. "Oh, yeah. If he can be on my side, then I'm sure he's rooting for you too."

The knock on the door was quiet but insistent.

Rising and replacing the bundle in Josie's arms, he went to open the door, but turned back. "What's the baby's second name, Josie?"

"You remember when you told me that your mother died way too soon and how much she meant to you when your father didn't care about you?"

"How could I forget?"

"You won't ever have to. Josephine Elana, after me...and your mother, Jerry, my sweetest."

Jerry said not a word. He didn't have to. His heart was bursting with happiness and love, and Josie would know.

Carole Brown

Sing Until You Die

Did her promises mean anything
when she couldn't even keep one?

The Spies of World War II

Chapter One

1944

Wills Mason stared at the stage. Or more specifically, the woman on the stage. Her voice was like the sweetest singing bird in the world, bringing tears to even the most hardened soul. And those who shied from showing such emotion, casually and furtively swiped at those traitor drops of moisture. Her voice rose to powerful, heart-stopping heights that boosted the most depressed individuals to levels of enthusiasm they'd never have dreamed they could achieve. The depths her voice sank to, crooned words of love, encouragement and hope to the most depressed.

Wills' own heart responded to that voice, the voice that belonged to the woman he'd loved all his life. Her blond hair with its touches of red gold shone like a crown on her shapely head. The white gardenia adorning her shoulder placed her in a different category than many of the singers who entertained the troops. She was confident and radiating love to the soldiers making each one of the men staring up at her feel she was their personal encourager. But more than that, in many a man there, memories of mothers praying and wives longing for their husband's returns, lingered as precious images in their minds.

The men adored her, and rightfully so. Not because of a romantic love, but because her voice evoked emotions some of them had not felt in a long, long time. Many of these men would go to sleep tonight dreaming, remembering the songbird who'd boosted their spirits as they prepared to leave on their tour of war

He hadn't seen her for over a year of the two years he'd been serving as a spy. She was still as small as he remembered her, but instead of remaining a young girl she'd bloomed into a woman.

1

The WAC who stepped up beside him didn't say a word until Wills glanced at her.

"He's ready for you, Sir."

Wills didn't speak, but turned again to stare at Claire Anne Rayner. He might never see her again, given what he was about to be asked to do next. His heart said "*stay,*" but his mind insisted he do his duty as he'd been trained.

"Lead the way, Owens."

The young woman, barely out of her teens, led the way, and Wills followed, not looking back at the woman who despised him and who would never forgive him for their past.

Chapter Two

The lights were bright, but not so much Claire Anne Rayner couldn't see the upturned faces of the men seated below the stage. Most times she avoided looking directly at them. She didn't want to see the expressions written across their faces. Too heartbreaking. Too emotional. It was better to focus on singing topnotch to give them the hope—and a bit of laughter and fun—they desperately needed before heading out to their war destinations.

She loved to sing. It'd been her passion forever—well, except for a brief period when she was rebelling a bit over her oldest sister's domineering ways. But Emma Jaine had been right, and Claire was glad she'd buckled down to do the study she'd longed for with the most prestigious voice teacher in the state.

She'd put all that on hold after a couple years of study. Singing for the service-men meant she was doing something good—giving a part of herself to help in this war that raged across the seas. Proving to her family and others she could do something beneficial. Maybe they wouldn't consider her so spoiled after this.

They loved her. Very much so. She missed them when she was away. All of them. From Papa Rayner to her sisters, Emma Jaine, her husband Tyrell Walker, and their adorable twins—Peter and Jaine Marie, to Josie, Jerry Patterson and their beautiful daughter, Josephine Elana. And could she forget Harriet and Jonah—their forever house-help?

Her gaze swept over the large group of soldiers and landed on the man and woman leaving the room. She could only see the back of them. Was that...Wills Mason, Harriet and Jonah's son? That straight back. That honey brown hair.

Turn around, you.

Of course, the man didn't turn around.

And why should she care anyway? She really, really didn't like him.

Chapter Three

"**S**he's an emotional singer. The men love her." The man spoke in a low voice to his companion, his feet shifting constantly as he waited on the desired approval he craved from his boss.

"Never mind that. All we care about is that the guy gets the message. That he knows the date and place."

"Yeah."

"Yeah?"

The snapped word, the sarcasm and anger coming from between the lips of the man's superior, caused the man to cringe. He hurried to correct his response. "You're right as always."

"You don't have to tell me something I already know."

The scorn in the voice didn't ease the man's concern any.

His superior went on talking as if not seeing—but probably gloating over his weakness. "I don't care how it happens, but it must be done. I want this more than I can express. You'd better be sure you don't mess it up for me, or I'll see that you disappear. No one will ever find your body."

With a cursory gleeful glance at the paleness of the man, his superior continued, "You keep your eyes peeled and report to me any sign of rebellion on her part. Are you listening?"

"I am." A vigorous nod of the head.

"She is not to get a hint that she's aiding us. Do you know what will happen if she starts sniffing around?

"I think I do."

"She'll not only get hurt, but you, being my right hand man, will suffer severely."

"You've made it very clear."

"I want to emphasize once again that this means more to me than anything. I will not hesitate taking down anyone who stands in my way. I will get what I want."

The man nodded. "I understand. I won't fail you."
"Good. You do the job, and I'll make sure you're recompensed right along with me."
A lofty look and a smirk at the man was not much reassurance that his superior one could be trusted.
But the man decided he'd better take what he could get. Anything was better than an unknown grave.

Other Books by Carole Brown

Denton and Alex Davies Mysteries:
Hog Insane
Bat Crazy

Spies of World War II
With Music In Their Hearts
A Flute in the Willows
Sing Until You Die

The Appleton WV Mysteries
Sabotaged Christmas
Knight in Shining Apron
Undiscovered Treasures
Toby's Troubles

Troubles in the West
Caleb's Destiny

Women's Fiction:
The Redemption of **Caralynne** *Haymen*

Misc
West Virginia Scrapbook
Christmas Angels **(WW II short story in the Anthology From the Lake to the River)**

Award winning author Carole Brown loves to weave suspense and tough topics into her books, along with a touch of romance and whimsy.

She is always on the lookout for outstanding titles and catchy ideas.

Carole and Dan, her pastor husband, reside in SE Ohio and have ministered and counseled across the country. Together, they enjoy their grandsons, traveling, gardening, good food, the simple life, and did she mention their grandsons?

Carole loves to connect with her readers. You can find her at her blog:
Sunnebnkwrtr.blogspot.com/
And facebook:
www.facebook.com/CaroleBrown.author

If you enjoyed reading this book, let others know... and bless Carole Brown with an honest review.

www.ingramcontent.com/pod-product-compliance
Lightning Source LLC
Chambersburg PA
CBHW032157190626
46814CB00005BA/2002